Diaries Of A Fashionista

SOPHIA LAROCCA

authorHOUSE®

AuthorHouse™
1663 Liberty Drive
Bloomington, IN 47403
www.authorhouse.com
Phone: 833-262-8899

Published by AuthorHouse   07/23/2021

ISBN: 978-1-6655-3294-5 (sc)
ISBN: 978-1-6655-3293-8 (hc)
ISBN: 978-1-6655-3295-2 (e)

Library of Congress Control Number: 2021915073

Print information available on the last page.

Any people depicted in stock imagery provided by Getty Images are models, and such images are being used for illustrative purposes only. Certain stock imagery © Getty Images.

This book is printed on acid-free paper.

To my friends in creative writing 2B
And the wonderful Mrs. Blasi
For if it wasn't for you, this book would have-
-quite literally-- not been created

CHAPTER ONE

September

Overkill

There are certain rules you have to follow when you are a journalist. Not any journalist though, a journalist for the acclaimed *DuVull* magazine.

I'm not saying that being a financial journalist or a normal news journalist is easy. Oh no, I would never be able to inform you about money or politics. No way in hell.

But what I can inform you about is fashion. All the ins and outs of it. I can tell you why people wear what they wear, and what you should wear on your first date judging by what you are doing.

Bar date- fancy sparkly cocktail dress.

Coffee Date- denim romper.

Bowling Date- cute blue jeans with a bodysuit. (*No* dresses. Please god, no dresses. I made that mistake once… never mind that though!)

You see, I look at the world like it's a *DuVull* fashion column.

I could completely analyze any person I see on the street by the outfit they're wearing. I could honestly even tell you what they do for a living probably! Although, looks could be deceitful sometimes.

I don't *judge* people by what they wear, never! But In order to prepare myself for writing fashion columns and articles, I *love* to analyze and describe people's outfits. I love to do it for myself as well!

Like today I'm sporting my *Balmain* black pencil skirt with detailed gold buttons going down a straight line in the front. It's a bit above the knees and high waisted.

Then I'm wearing my long sleeved, silk, white, *Valentino* blouse. I have it tucked into my pencil skirt and the blouse has a knotted tie neck in the front. It's so cute, and quite professional if I do say so myself.

I've paired it with my new *Guess* pink fur coat. It's so fluffy and big! I have it draped over my shoulders. You *always* wear your coats draped over your shoulders. Never on. Unless it's chilly, but mostly it's for the look.

Then last but never least, my white, kneehigh socks. It goes well with the whole vibe of the outfit!

My shoes are *Loeffler Randall* pearl colored, opened toe heels. It has an ankle strap and a big white bow in the front.

See! Isn't it fun!

But as I was saying, there are certain rules you have to follow if you want to be a *DuVull and Co* journalist.

Rule number one- If you feel passionate about something and you want to write about it, you better have the wits, means, and knowledge to do so.

Rule number two- Ms. DuVull is *always* right. Even when she's not, she is. Bite your tongue and nod. If you're stubborn and non-compliant you might as well just get out now.

Rule number three- *Always*, and I mean always be on your toes at all times. You never know what's going to happen here.

Rule number four- Keep your articles to yourself. If you are discussing it with a close work friend, that's fine. But NEVER give info about your article to someone who writes in the same genre.

The fashion and magazine industry are two of the most cut-throat industries out there and I'm right in the middle of both of them.

"Hey Pops," I'm snapped back to reality when I hear Jeannie call my name from her desk directly in front of mine. "what do you think attracts women to bad boys so much?" I look up from my daily horoscope and shrug.

"I dunno?"

Jeannie does this thing where she waits till the last minute to write her articles. She says it 'helps her artistic abilities.' It would just give me a panic attack and massive migraine.

Jeannie is one of the top romance Journalists here at *DuVull and Co.* She's actually one of the only ones. That is afterall what *DuVull* is. A love, fashion and lifestyle magazine. We're mostly known for our fashion columns though.

Jeannie's truly a whiz at romance. She'll ask for my opinions sometimes. She'll say, 'I don't get what you see in men. They're such work.'

"I really need your help on this one. I could see the appeal in them, I just don't have the expirence... fortunately." She looks at me with a knowing glare.

Jeannie has been a great friend since I started working here four years ago. Nothing gets past Jeannie. When I mean nothing, I mean *nothing*. Her ability to read people like a book has always amazed me. She practically knows everything about me and more including what she is currently refering too.

I roll my eyes at her knowing glare and sigh, now looking out at the huge modern buildings of Manhattan right next to us. They look so close it is as if you could almost touch them through the shiny, glass windows of the tenth floor of the office.

Three months ago I broke up with my boyfriend Liam. (Well, ex-boyfriend now.)

When I met him my freshman year of highschool I didn't know what to make of him. He always hung out with my friends. (I was friends with mostly guys. The cattiness of girls always got on my nerves. Well look at me now!)

Anyway, Liam always seemed to be angry at the world, but he was sweet to me and strikingly handsome. These feelings for him just manifested and Liam kept building his way into my heart. One day in P.E I asked him out and we were together ever since.

Years went by and I realized he *was* angry at the world. When I moved into my apartment in Brooklyn he didn't come, but we remained together.

You see, I always looked at Liam as if he were a backyard project. It was beautiful, it just needed to be fixed.

Finally, seven months ago when Liam came to visit we went out for dinner and got into this absolutely explosive fight.

'You know why you have hardly any friends? Why no one invites you anywhere? You wonder? It's because you're a priss! No one wants to be around a priss, Poppy. No one!' He screamed in my face.

That night is still so blurry. I just remember telling him It was over and leaving the restaurant.

I'll paint you a picture; I walked home twelve blocks because Liam had the car. I had to take off my heels because my feet were in so much pain and It was pouring rain.

When I finally got back to my apartment I just passed out on my bed. I woke up to worried messages from my best friend Tiff and numerous from my parents. Before I knew it, everyone in my family knew. (And probably everyone on their block as well.)

I think that's the day I realized never to date a backyard project, because it's not your duty to fix anyone. You could bring them some tools! Maybe a hammer and a chainsaw, but you can't do the whole construction project yourself.

Jeannie knows that Liam was the bad boy type, getting into fights and such. She's met him a couple of times. She never really liked him. I thought she was crazy.

'His vibes are off.' She used to tell me. Jeannie and her 'vibes' were right. As usual.

I guess that goes to show you, you should always listen to your friends.

"I suppose women fall for bad boys because it's a chase. A lot of women like that chase. They find it... exhilarating." I shrug like I'm totally going off a whim here. Really, I am!

"Sounds accurate." Jeannie starts typing on her computer. "Especially innocent and naive women." She says, her eyebrows raised.

"I am not!" I hiss. "Liam tainted me."

"Poppy, do you remember two months ago when me and Riley hooked you up with that hot surgeon and he went in for a kiss at the end of the date and you punched him in the throat?"

"You can never be too careful with people! I was shocked, honestly."

"Pops," begins Jeannie. "the poor man was rushed to the hospital. You knocked the wind out of him."

"I said I was sorry and sent him one of those cute fruit bouquets!" I retort. "Stop preaching to the choir and type it. Why are you even writing about things you don't know the first thing about anyway..." then all of a sudden I hear my phone buzz beside me and I quickly pick it up.

'CRAZYS COMING. BETTER HAVE THAT COFFEE READY. SHE'S IN A MOOD.'

I drop my phone, grab one of the two coffee's on my desk, and give Jeannie a look as if to say 'It's here.'

I watch as everyone around the office scrambles around comically, fixing themselves up and cleaning up their desks as I run towards the big glass doors of Ms. DuVull's office.

As I stand there--coffee in hand--I hear Ms. DuVull's voice echo through the office and everyone gets into position.

"No, just tell Poppy to cancel my lunch with Natalie. She's such a bitch, I'm really not in the mood to hear her nag. Oh, and tell Poppy to pick up my new pants from--ah--Poppy, there you are." I immediately put a big smile on my face as I perk up a bit and hand Ms. DuVull her coffee.

"Hey, hey, hey, Poppyseed." She greets as she swiftly grabs her coffee out of my hands and we walk into her office.

"Morning, Ms. DuVull. How was your drive here?"

Jane DuVull; founder and CEO of *DuVull and Co* magazine and certified boss lady.

Jane is in charge of everything around here. She's also the editor in chief as well as the person who started the magazine. She always said that she rather do everything right herself then have multiple people do a job for her, half assed. And I don't know how, but she does it.

I started working as Jane's assistant when I started my first year of college at FIT around six years ago.

I was Jane's assistant for three years until finally she gave me a job as an actual fashion journalist.

I know things about Jane that no one should know about another human being. I had to hear every result of every Gynecologist appointment in the last four years. I once had to go on a date for her because she was 'too busy' to. (God, that was awkward.)

She popped her arm out of its socket at her aerobics class, and I was in charge of popping it back in for her.

Oh, she also insisted I be in the room while she got a consultation for her boob job just so, 'if she forgot anything, I would be right there to tell the doctor.'

For better or for worse though, Jane is my boss and I truly care for her.

How could you not care for someone you spent six years of your life helping in every single way possible. How could you not care for a person who looks at you like their backbone? She'll never admit it, but she cares about me too.

I started out as her assistant when I was nineteen, so she kind of watched me grow up.

Jane plops down on her black leather rolly chair behind her marble desk and takes off her huge designer sunglasses.

She vastly starts typing on her computer and rolls her eyes, huffing at whatever she is looking at it.

Jane is 46, she doesn't look a day over 35, I swear.

"Oh, my morning was just peachy." She begins. "You know Riley…" she begins to mimic him. "'I have to drive safely, Ms. DuVull, they're crazy here in Manhattan. Do you *want* me to drive us into a stop sign?' Screw you, Riley. Just get me to work before all my patience wears off." I'm pretty sure Jane's patience wears off the minute she wakes up.

She looks up from her computer.

"Anyway, I'm going to need you to pick up the pants I ordered from *Burberry*. Lizzy will be at the front desk with them if she knows what's good for her. I also need you to cancel my lunch appointment with Natalie."

"Ms. DuVull, you've already canceled with her three times this month."

"She creates problems, Poppy. That's all she knows. Sleep, eat, eat, eat, eat again, take photos for magazines and start problems. I don't need that right now. It's not good for my aura, you know."

"Well ok…" I sigh.

Now, here's the thing, Jane has fired the last ten assistants I hired and got for her.

'But no one gets my coffee order right but you, Poppy.' she would cry. It's actually quite easy, go to *Starbucks*, get a venti vanilla iced coffee, only three shots of Vanilla, freshly brewed, light on Ice with a straw. 'I'm not a baby and I do not give a shit about the environment, I am *not* drinking out of one of those plastic sippy cups.' She'll say.

Oh, and a pink cake pop on Thursdays. ONLY Thursdays. Therefore, now I'm doing two jobs. Journalist and assistant. Nobody said the job was easy.

'Why would you put up with that?' someone might ask.

Well, believe it or not, I love my job. I love Jane and I love writing and I love fashion. (Not to mention, I get paid double then any other journalist here since I'm doing two jobs. The money is absolutely fab!)

"I'll run and get your pants from *Burberry* and I will cancel lunch with Natalie, and when she asks when we would like to reschedule I will respond with, 'Ms. DuVull is a very busy woman, and we will get back to you when her schedule clears up.' Which in reality means, 'We won't be calling you back. Ever?'"

Jane doesn't even look up from her computer but instead clicks her tongue and gives me a thumbs up. I click my tongue back as I walk out of her office and back towards my desk.

I see Jeannie and Riley chatting and Riley has pushed up a chair in between me and Jeannie's desks like he always does. They really are some sight to see, both of them.

She has long, black hair that shines wherever the light hits it and the most prominent cheekbones I have ever seen. She has sharp and prominent features everywhere actually.

A sharp noise, round grey eyes, and huge pink lips that have a tiny diamond piercing right above them.

I'm actually the only person who knows that black is not her natural hair color, even though it really seems like it. (She spilled that secret one night when we were both working really late in the office about four years ago.)

It was just us left in the office and we were hyped up on pizza and caffeine. We absolutely spilled our guts to each other that night with secrets and embarrassing stories.

I think that's the night I realized that she was going to be one of my best friends.

Jeannie sure is the rebel of the group though. She also has multiple tattoos. The one that always sticks out to me though is the chain and lock around her calf and up to her high thigh.

Riley is the absolute opposite, but just as stunning looking.

He has bleached light blue hair and big round, puppy dog-looking brown eyes. He has very soft features and zero tattoos on his pale body.

He is actually quite short and scrawny too. He looks like a Ken doll, or a statue of a Greek God with blue hair.

Riley is Jane's full time driver. So, until Jane has to go somewhere he usually just hangs here with me and Jeannie. Trust me, the job is harder than it sounds. He is also a really close friend of mine.

"Hell no." I hear Riley. "You don't want a bad boy."

"Well, you don't want a Bible study, mama's boy, goody two-shoes either." Retorts Jeannie.

"The perfect middle ground," I say sitting down at my desk, settling them. "you don't want a goody two-shoes, but you don't want a criminal kleptomaniac either."

"See," retorts Riley. "that's what I'm saying."

"Says the man who has the most goody two-shoes, mama's boy of a boyfriend ever." Scoffs Jeannie.

"Don't you dare question my Arlo's relationship with his mother." Arlo is Riley's long time boyfriend. We love Arlo.

I hastily grab the stack of pink sticky notes on my desk that has multiple important peoples numbers on it and dial in Natalie's.

After a couple of awkward minutes of telling Natalie Ms. DuVull can't make it to their lunch for the third time, I grab my purse and get ready to head to *Burberry.*

"What are you doing tonight?" I ask the two.

"I'm going to the club." Begins Jeannie. "The cool new one on eighty-second street. It's gonna be fun, you should come." She says singsongly.

"Can't." Begins Riley. "Arlo and I are going to dinner tonight. Some place he said had great steak. He's lucky we could afford our grocery's let alone go to a five star steak house." He scrolls through his phone, shaking his head.

"Pop's, what about you? You really need to get out, you know." Jeannie lifts an eyebrow at me.

"Thanks, but I don't think I can." I shrug. "I wanted to visit my parents." I perk up. "And pick up a new blouse I saw in the window of *Express,* but that's about it."

"Say hi to your mom and dad for Arlo and I" Riley says.

"Yeah, give them my love," Jeannie begins. "but Pops, I'm worried about you. You just don't go out. I mean you go out and buy a new *Chanel* purse at *Saks* or stress shop at *Bloomingdales,* but you don't go out and explore the nightlife like someone your age should! Since everything happened with Liam you just shut yourself down. You threw yourself into your work. Next time I'm not taking no for an answer. Me, you, and Riley and Arlo are going out next Friday. No exceptions."

"Sounds good." Nods Riley. "But don't judge. *Express* is a great place to spend a Friday night." He debunks.

"Well, you never know..." begins Jeannie. "maybe something interesting will happen." I just roll my eyes and huff. She's right I guess. Maybe there's a sale at *Burberry!*

CHAPTER TWO

Pleasing the storm (AKA family)

I walk up to my parent's row townhouse in Staten Island. They all look the same as each other just with different decor in the front, which I always found cute. They're the same layout, but all have a different personality.

I make sure to tread lightly as I take out my old key and walk in.

I look at all the familiar relics and furniture that hasn't moved since I was twelve. I make sure to quietly close and lock the door behind me and just as I do, I start to hear bickering come from the sunroom.

There they are.

As I start to make my way towards the sunroom, their conversation gets more coherent.

"Geoff," I hear my mom. "we live in a different generation. These kids are just getting more disrespectful by the mound. You can't just go around house to house asking if kids want to mow your lawn for forty dollars. They are going to think you are a pedafile."

"This is absolutely horrendous. You can't go around asking teenagers to come and mow your lawn for twenty minutes for forty dollars!"

"This is the generation, Geoff."

"That's ridiculous, Molly"

"I know, Geoff." My dad is on a ladder hanging up Christmas lights by the screen door. It's september...and we don't celebrate Christmas.

My mom is watching him do so, a cup of tea in hands. My sister Diamante and her boyfriend Carlo are sitting on the other couch.

Diamante is typing something on her phone at the speed of light and Carlo is just sitting next to her, arm around the old black leather couch, looking like a deer in headlights. As always.

I'm standing in the doorway of the sunroom and no one seems to notice.

"Hey guys." I interrupt quickly before my dad goes off on even more of a tangum.

Everyone turns to look at me as if I said some terribly controversial statement.

"Hi dear!" My mom smiles, jumping off the couch and giving me a huge hug. "How was the train ride here?"

"Oh, it was fine." I assure her. "Hi, Dia," I say bubbly. "hi, Carlo."

"Hi." Diamante chews on the gum in her mouth and doesn't even bother looking up from her phone. Carlo just gives a timid wave.

Sometimes I feel bad for Carlo. There's not even room for you to talk when you're around my sister, let alone dating her.

Diamante is three years older than me, so 27. She was always the popular one in school, the trend setter. The one who wore short-shorts and crop tops.

I was the one who wore blue jeans and cute striped sweaters and big glasses. The girl who wrote poetry and read in the corner of the room.

A lot has changed since then. My sister moved in with her long time boyfriend, and I got contacts.

Everytime I see her beautiful bleach blonde hair and skinny, tall figure, a part of my self-esteem diminishes just a little. There's not a lot to begin with though.

She has a round plump face and so do I. But she has more color on her than I do. She always has a gorgeous tan, and I have somewhat paler skin with little rosy cheeks. We look alike, but she *does* look a tad bit older than me. (Just saying.)

She has round blue, doll-like eyes, and I have the same. I also have naturally bigger lips than her. (Not anymore. She got them done.)

We both used to have a bit of a hook nose. Mine was always tinier and more cute. (Not anymore, she got a nose job.) Now she has her perfect little curved up nose and her huge plump lips. My parents were *pissed*. Can you blame them? She came home from college with a new face!

I have no clue who she had to sleep with to buy her a whole new face at just nineteen, but she did it!

Diamante is a lawyer now. Mom and dad say she's so good at it because she could argue that the sky is green when it's blue. She could convince you that it's green too. (Or she would just make you give up trying to convince otherwise.)

She's a great lawyer and is certainly working her way up.

"Hey Pops." My dad says from the ladder. I don't dare ask why he's hanging up Christmas lights on the 18th of September.

One thing you need to realize about my dad is to never question him. He'll one; Get offended. Or two; Go into a whole spiel about why he is doing what he is doing. And no one wants to hear that!

My parents are truly a beautiful couple. My mom with her tall, thin stature and blunt, brown bob. My dad with his handsome features and black hair with only a sprinkle of gray at the top. I'm definitely a mix of both of them, but was not blessed with their tall Jeans. Somehow I ended up being 5'1.

"Hey dad, how are you--"

"Do you think it's in suspicious nature to go around asking the teenagers in the neighborhood to mow our lawn for forty dollars?" I look towards mom and watch her mouth 'do not answer that' then she quickly changes the subject.

"Here, come with me to the kitchen. Let's make you some coffee." I go into the next room, connected by a sliding door which leads into the tiny kitchen I used to help my mom cook in. I watch as she takes out my favorite red mug. I always happen to leave here. Maybe I always leave it here so I always remember to come back.

"How was your day?" She asks as she puts my mug under the coffee machine.

"Oh you know," I begin. "the usual."

"And what's the usual again? Working yourself to death because you are stuck working two jobs?"

"It's not that big of a deal. I get my articles done nice and early in the month, so the rest of the month is dedicated to being Ms. DuVull's assistant."

"Poppy Paxton, I don't know how you don't just speak up for yourself. You have me and your father as parents for crying out loud. I mean, look at your sister! She's out protesting something different every other weekend practically. She's trying to save the Turtles now or something." Mom waves it off.

Let's just say, I grew up in a family that was always protesting and fighting for something. I'm pretty sure her first words were 'Save the Polar Bears.'

My family are hippies at heart, that's for sure.

"Mom, there is absolutely nothing to fight for. I love my job! Plus, I get paid double since I do two jobs. It's all good." My mom gives me a worried stare but then quickly shrugs it off.

"Well ok. As long as you're ok with it, dear." She then perks up as she hands me my coffee. "You are coming for dinner though on the 26th, right? It's the start of Rosh Hashanah." My family is Jewish (if you couldn't already tell by their loud nature and the fact we don't celebrate Christmas.)

"I wouldn't miss it." I say as I sip my coffee, racking my brain for ways to get out of an uber awkward family dinner. Maybe I'll fake a sprained ankle? Nah, I can't walk on crutches. Say I have a cold? No, I'm horrible at faking coughs. Oh screw it, I have nothing better to do! How bad could it be?

CHAPTER THREE
Band Boy

I get off the crowded bus but not without a struggle. The transit was crazy of course. Friday Night.

Speaking of Friday night, so much for one. Jeannie was right. I do have to get out more often.

I stayed longer than I thought I would at my parents house. Diamante went into this whole rant on how we should have a vegan Rosh Hashanah and literally wouldn't let me leave.

I didn't even get to pick up the blouse I wanted from *Express!* Oh well. I'll get it tomorrow.

The cool nighttime Brooklyn air hits my face as I start to walk towards my apartment building. I listen to the clacking of my own heels against the concrete as I walk towards the many light brown brick buildings clumped together.

Friday nights in Brooklyn. There is truly nothing like them. There are lights shining through every apartment window and some kind of music is blasting through half of them. Mostly non stop rap music.

All the windows are slightly cracked open to let the cool breeze in and I watch as thin drapes attached to them dance to the beat of the wind.

I hear the jubilant laughter of children just as four boys pass by me, playing Basketball.

I look off to the side and see their mothers chatting about on the bench in front of the building. I give them a kind smile and they give me friendly waves as I walk up to the dirty and fogged up glass doors of the apartment building. It must have been broken at least fourteen times in the matter of two years with all it's cracks and such.

I live on Avenue W. in Brooklyn. It's nice. It's obviously not Tribeca, but it's home.

I open the door with the old rusted handle wrapped in decaying duct tape. I wipe my hands on my skirt as if it will get the germs off.

I enter the building and hear loud echoes and music through the metal doors. It makes the whole building vibrate, but I'm quite used to it by now.

The building looks dangerous and dirty, and sometimes I wish it didn't smell of weed and rotting fish, but we all can't live on the upper east side. (Unfortunately.)

But I also can't stress enough how much I love it here. Even if I could, I'm not sure I would change anything about this building. It has personality!

Growing up my parents always preached street smarts to me and my sister. It's honestly quite simple. Don't look in the eyes of someone that seems sketchy, do not walk about with your valuables out, and keep your head held high.

There are many more but I just can't focus on them right now because I am absolutely fuming as I hop into the filthy elevator with it's horrifying flickering lights.

You know, I can't stand my sister sometimes. She was mentioning this 'Vegan Rosh Hashanah' idea looking dead at me.

I was eating a burger.

She wants us all to eat plants or something for dinner! Well you know what? Diamante could watch me eat my big, fat, juicy, rare hamburger and watch as the blood runs down my hands too! I rather enjoy my burger in peace, thank you! We're here for a good time, not a long time!

Oh, and my Dad has the nerve to *agree* with her! He said it was a great Idea. Who asked him? Certainly not me!

My Mom almost had a heart attack though. She almost fell off the couch. God, I wish you were there to see it.

'You will eat whatever I make for dinner! We're *not* eating plants for our holiday. This is an asinine conversation we are having right now!' She said and stormed into the kitchen.

I had to go follow her to calm her down. I actually thought she might have had a stroke. That reminds me, Liam once got into an argument with a person on the train because they said they were vegetarian. He was under the impression that if you don't eat meat, you'll just wither away…what a moron.

As I get off the elevator and make a sharp turn towards my apartment, I hear a loud and unfamiliar Brooklyn accent boom through the hallways.

"I told you the damn couch wouldn't fit through the door. Dallon, get over here and help me, will ya?" I reach my apartment and see the man with the accent standing at the door across from mine, a huge couch sticking out of the door as he shouts on his phone.

"Get over here right now." He says threateningly as he shoves the phone violently in his back pocket.

I watch as he desperately tries to push the couch through the door with all his body weight and might.

Huh. I didn't know anyone was moving in.

I observe the situation and scrunch up my nose, as I fix my pink fur coat draped over my shoulders and dust off my outfit a bit.

"Hello…" I say in a quiet tone and give a feeble wave. The man turns around out of breath and his eyebrows raised.

"Hi neighbor." He says as a smile spreads across his face.

He has the deepest dimples I've ever seen and a wide smile to boot. He's relatively tall it seems, maybe 5'12. He has shaggy dirty blonde hair that lies in front of his face in messy--now a bit sweaty--locks.

He has ripped blue jeans rolled up to a little above his ankles showing his white socks with black writing on it. He has a long sleeved green and black striped sweater shirt with tiny rips throughout. Very grungy.

He rests one arm over the half stuck out couch and one on his hip.

"I like your door." He motions to my very decorative apartment door. It has cute, long different colored beads draping over it. Very 70's. I decorated when I first moved in. The door just looked so dull.

"Oh thanks!" I give a triumphant smile. "I'm Patricia. Patricia Paxton, but you can call me Poppy. Everyone does." I gladly put my hand out.

"Atticus Mckeen. You can call me… Atticus." He says with a chuckle.

He happily takes my hand and shakes it.

He has huge hands compared to mine and his fingers are scattered with bulky silver rings along with black painted fingernails. I could tell he's not using all his strength to shake my tiny hand. He's being gentle, being careful and cordial. Which Is a good sign for a new neighbor.

"Do you need any help?" I motion towards the couch stuck halfway in the door. "I could try to help you push it in. Although it's probably useless, we could try?"

"Nah," Atticus shakes his head. "I've got a couple of my buddies coming over to help me. They should be here any minute."

We stand there in awkward silence for a couple of moments then Atticus speaks again.

"So, you come here often?" He quirks up a brow and I give a tiny laugh at his attempt at small talk.

"Yep, everyday..." welp he's not playing with a full deck of cards. Good to know.

He laughs and his breath reeks of cigarettes and mint. He has a nice laugh though. Sort of annoying but nice I suppose. His accent peaks through it.

"Are you from around here? I mean obviously you're moving in," I motion towards the door. "but are you from Brooklyn?"

"Yeah." He nods looking up at the ceiling and squinting. "Seventy-ninth street. My whole life. No other place I want to be in the world. Brooklyn's where it's at." He looks back down at me with a closed mouth grin.

"Staten Island," I point to myself. "been here for four years. I love it!"

"Yeah, I finally got my own place. I've had a roommate for the past five years of my life. Not fun. Especially when you have a band."

And like that, loud sirens go off in my head. A band? Are you kidding me? I hate my life.

This might not be a big deal to *you* but I'm the one that has to live across from it! We have thin walls here!

"What kind of band?" I dare ask.

"Oh, we're like punk rock and pop punk." Oh shit. It could be worse though! It could be country.

Although I'm pretty sure if he played country around here, he'd get crucified.

"Well," I bet he could see the forced smile on my face. "I hope all goes well. If you need anything, just let me know. Do you want a bottle of water?"

"Not now, but who knows what the night will bring. We could be out here all night."

"Well, I'm not going anywhere." I nod. "So don't hesitate to ask."

"Oh, so I could wake you up at 1:30 in the morning and ask for a bottle of water?" A sly smirk lands over his features. His dimples are popping out in their full form now.

Oh, so I'm dealing with a Smartass. Great!

Before I know it I'm opening my door, going into my kitchen, grabbing a bottle of water out of the fridge, then walking back to Atticus and handing him the ice cold bottle.

"Here you go." My forced smile is now just a straight line, and Atticus's cocky smile is now just a shocked stare, his bushy eyebrows raised.

He quickly recovers with that strange, cocky smile and he gives a slight chuckle.

He takes the bottle out of my hands and from the force where he grabs the bottle, it somehow pulls me to stumble even closer--almost onto--him.

I knit my eyebrows and give him a glare. I back up and dust myself off.

"Thanks." Is all he says. "Oh, and Patricia," he stops me just as I'm about to walk back into my apartment. I feel chills run up and down my spine. The last person that called me Patricia was Liam. He never called me Poppy. And he was in the same position Atticus is in. His back was slightly turned to me, and he was doing what he does best; Leaving.

"As I said, I do have a band. So if we get too loud just come and tell me. We are, afterall, neighbors now. Ya know, just a friendly reminder." He has this overly confident smirk on his face.

I fight the urge to take that water bottle out of his hands and knock him upside the head with it. I just give him the kindest smile I could manage and a tired nod.

"Goodnight and... good luck." I motion to the couch.

"Thanks. Night, Blondie." His voice is one of somewhat annoyances, and perhaps, curiosity.

I close and lock the three locks on my door behind me. What a strange man.

Well, fantastic, that strange man is my new neighbor.

I attempt to take off my heels but I need to unclasp the ankle straps, so I hop towards my couch and do just that.

I give out a deep huff as I toss my shoes to the side, cringing when I hear them meet with my hard floor.

I practically spent three month's salary on them and I would usually walk them into my closet with all my other shoes, but with all due respect to all my designer shoes, I'm exhausted.

I live in a two bedroom and one bathroom apartment. My kitchen and my dining room are all in the same room and my living room bleeds into both of them. I love my apartment though, don't get me wrong.

As I reach my kitchen I'm faced with a picture of me and Liam, sitting on my granite counter. Haunting me.

I can't take it down though. I just can't. What if we get back together!

I don't know... maybe it sounds silly, but I just don't think I'm ready to part ways with it.

We looked so happy. It's when we went to the movies. I don't even remember what we went to see. Something he wanted to see I'm sure.

He's bending down to my height, his face is squished against my long blonde strands and we're both laughing.

I look at the picture fondly but then my smile fades.

Yeah, he *looked* happy.

He loved putting on shows. Or maybe he was actually happy at that exact moment. I don't know. I never knew where his head was. Did I ever? He seemed to have it lost somewhere along the road of our relationship. Maybe he never had it.

Upon observing the picture, I decide it's just more of a reason to pour myself a glass of wine and break off a piece of chocolate I had in my refrigerator.

I plop down on my couch once again and turn on the TV. I mindlessly flip through the channels until I find some wedding show on *TLC*.

I hear rucces from outside my apartment.

"Well, did it fit in the elevator?" An annoyed male voice asks.

'Of course it didn't, dingous. I used the stairs." Atticus's accent rips through my ears.

"How the hell did you get it up the stairs?"

"You're both idiots." Another annoyed male voice huffs.

I make the sound on my TV extra loud so I don't have to hear the banter of the boys outside.

I fight the urge to help them and just keep my eyes on the beautiful model like women trying on wedding dresses.

You know, when I get married I want a big, flowy, princess ball gown with sparkles everywhere. But also regal, and somewhat form fitting. Oh, and lace. So victorian.

I dig into my chocolate and sip my wine. What. A. Day.

CHAPTER FOUR
The Oh Wise One

"*The one with the long* sleeves." I say into my phone walking down the crowded and rambunctious streets of Manhattan, bumping shoulders with the crowds of people as I do so.

I've walked down these streets so many times, I don't even have to look where I am going. It's like I have eyes on the top of my newly touched up blonde head or something!

"Are you sure?" Asks Jane on video call with me, currently slumped down on a chair in the dressing room of *Gucci*.

"Positive. It's Fall. It's going to start getting chilly."

"Alright…" she mutters unsurely.

She holds up the long-sleeved, red *Gucci* shirt. It has an embroidered heart with white wings. It's cute.

"It's perfect, Ms. DuVull. You're going to be happy that it's long-sleeved, trust me. So fab."

"I suppose." She sighs. "Ok, I'm going to pay for it. Maybe get a bag. Who knows, C'est la vie, Poppyseed."

"Bye Ms. DuVull. Have a good day."

"I'll try." I hang up as I enter *Starbucks.* God, that women really can't make a decision without me, can she?

I feel so chic as I walk into the overly crowded, tiny cafe.

I'm wearing my *Milly* high waisted, form fitting, pink mini skirt. It's tweed and so in right now!

I'm also wearing my *Alice and Olivia* cream colored top with these big balloon style type sleeves. The Balloon style sleeve is *so* in right now as well.

I've paired everything with my *Alexander McQueen* jeweled, leather clutch. It's *so* pretty with it's green and yellow rhinestones.

I walk up to the barista and order my usual when I'm *not* working. A grande vanilla iced coffee with room for milk and extra ice. I'm a basic bitch when it comes to that stuff. Unlike Ms. DuVull who needs to make a simple order the most complicated thing in the world.

I usually just get two of her orders during the week. One for me and one for her, just in case something happens to hers.

I say a polite thank you when they call my name and put milk in my coffee.

I then go sit at the tiny, round wooden table in the corner by the huge window in the front of the cafe.

The *Starbucks* is relatively small and oddly shaped but it just makes it more modern and fancy. I alway feel so important walking into here! Like some kind of business lady who has her life together in a *Bottega Veneta* suit.

Before my dad retired, he worked down here in Manhattan as an electrician. When I would go in to work with him, we would always go to this exact *Starbucks*. My Dad loves *Starbucks*. It's like an unhealthy obsession, I swear.

After coffee he would always take me to some kind of high end department store so I could look in awe at all the things I used to only dream about having.

I remember looking at all the smart, wealthy women going around the store with their personal shoppers. Trying on shoes and swiping their credit cards without cringing in fear of the dreadful beeping decline sound.

I sip my coffee and read the new issue of *DuVull* I had tucked under my arm the whole time I walked here.

Of *course* I bought it! What kind of journalist would I be if I didn't buy it literally every time I see one? I usually go to Jeannie's romance article before I go to mine. I'm always thoroughly entertained while reading Jeannie's articles. She's the most entertaining person I know. It's also very informative!

I would go up to the counter to get Tiff's cloud macchiato for her, but I don't even know how to order that.

She gets it with extra caramel or mocha…oh I don't know! She's complicated too!

But long story short, me and Tiff meet here all the time. It kind of turned into our meeting spot over the years.

Tiff is my absolute best friend on this entire planet. I have known her since diapers. We grew up together. We did *everything* together. We still do. Her parents are family friends as well along with her little sister Lottie.

Lottie is eighteen and currently in college down in Florida. Let's just say, she's the polar opposite of Tiff. Much like Diamante is the polar opposite of me.

"Hey." My model of a best friend walks in.

"Hi!" I get up and embrace her in a huge hug. Tiff's hugs have always been the best.

She's wearing plain blue jeans, and a striped red and white, fuzzy sweater. Tiff has never been into fashion as much as I am. She was always into sports. Number one female softball player in Staten Island.

Now she's a second grade teacher and coaches her very own softball team. She still plays in a league as well. It's crazy how she balances it all. I could never.

"I'm going up to order my drink," she begins. "and then we have a lot to talk about, my friend." She gives me a smile and sideways glare.

"Can't wait." I murmur.

Whenever Tiff says we have something to talk about, It's usually always about me. She's a problem solver, she likes to get to the root of things.

I, for one, rather let those problems build up until they eventually have no choice but to go away.

As Tiff talks to the barista, she gives him the most wide and kind smile. Tiff is secretly a model, I swear.

She has long brown, almost black, hair and deep, clear skin. She has huge brown eyes and the widest, most bright smile you will ever see.

Most of the time I can't find a physical flaw on her.

Growing up next to Tiff and my sister I was always a bit self-conscious. I still am, but Tiff never seems to realize her inner and outer beauty. You see, Tiff has this amazing ability to see the good in every situation. To be an extremely strong person, and not stay down for too long because she remembers better stuff to do, bigger stuff to take on.

Sometimes I wish I could be Tiff.

"So," she sits down across from me with her cloud macchiato and two toasted bagels, one with cream cheese and one with butter. She passes the bagel with butter to me and takes the latest issue of *Duvull* out of her bag. "what is this about?"

"What is what about?" I munch on my bagel.

"Oh don't even *ask* me that, missy. You know what I'm talking about." She turns to Jeannie's article and points to it indignantly. "'Why do women find bad boys so attractive?' First of all, ew, second of all, this is the textbook definition of Liam! Did you help Jeannie with this article?"

"Of course I did."

"Of course you did!"

"You're making this a bigger deal than it needs to be, Tiffany." I retort, mouthful of bagel. "Jeannie needed my help with an article so I helped her. Did you get the new *Ulta* catalog?"

"What? No... I don't get the *Ulta* catalogs..."

"I sent it to you in the post. I saw a Lipstick you might like."

"Poppy, stop distracting me! I thought we said we weren't going to be discussing Liam anymore. That you needed to get over him?"

"I *am* getting over him!" I yell and get the attention of an older man sitting next to us. I glare at him. What? Him and his best friend never had an argument in the middle of *Starbucks* about an ex boyfriend?

"Oh ok," Tiff crosses her legs. "then why is that picture of you two still on your kitchen counter?"

"I look good in that picture."

"You're looking for trouble, Poppy Paxton." Tiff begins to eat her bagel and sips her drink.

"How so?" I ask shrill.

All of a sudden Tiff starts to burst out into giggles. She puts her hand over her mouth and I can't help but fall into giggles as well.

"What?" I manage to ask defensively.

"Your face...you're making that face..." her face is scrunching up in laughter. "you're so angry and defensive right now."

"I'm you!" I practically shout. "You're the most defensive person I know. Where do you think I get it from?"

We just sit in our chairs for a good minute laughing, my head down on the table and Tiff's hand still over her mouth. We finally calm down after multiple people come in and give us dirty looks.

"How's mom and dad?" Tiff asks. Tiff and her sister were raised to think of my parents as their aunt and uncle. Same with me and her parents.

We would play dress up, and our moms would help us host mini tea parties between the five of us. Our dads would even help sometimes.

Tiff and I still dress up and have tea parties, but it's just more adult now. (By that I mean we'll go to the mall and try on clothes in all the high end stores, then Tiff will yell at me when I buy over-priced jeans, then we'll just come here.)

"They're fine. You know them..." I begin. "same old same old. Always bantering about something."

"Hey, as long as they're bantering things are ok."

"Is that healthy?"

"For them."

I think for a moment and look up.

"Me and Liam always bantered."

"Not in a healthy way." Tiff states vastly.

"There is no *healthy* way to banter."

"Sure there is." Tiff shrugs her shoulders. "You watch your parents do it everyday."

"Yeah I suppose..." I begin. "but they're from a different generation."

"Well," Tiff thinks for a moment. I can tell she's deep in thought as she rests her sharply defined chin in her hand. "fighting and banter or bickering are two very different things." She takes a sip of her coffee. "Don't get me wrong, couples fight but it shouldn't be every second of every day. As human beings we disagree on things, therefore, playful banter and sometimes even arguments."

I can't help but stare at Tiff like she has two heads. I still get surprised sometimes at Tiff's knowledge having to do with life. Our parents always told us that with my wisdom and Tiff's knowledge, we'd make fantastic adults in society. Well... look at Tiff and look at me!

I could hardly manage to put my heels on in the morning.

I think Tiff does this adulting thing much better than I do. She was practically moving out at ten years old.

"You and Liam fought," she begins after a couple of seconds of silence. "and for no apparent reason. He would just pick fights with you because he was bored and that's all he ever knew."

I wish I could tell Tiff she was wrong, but I can't. I sip my coffee and look down, not bothering to say a word.

"Well, enough of that." She turns the magazine to my article. "Very fine job. I loved it."

"Did you?" I perk up.

"Of course! You're a genius." I wrote an article on the latest fall styles and what you should pair it with. It is pretty good, I must say. "You're right. I've been looking around and the checkerboard pattern *is* very in." Whenever Tiff gives me a compliment I feel as if I'm seven years old and my mother is telling me what a fine job I did on a test

"I know!" I squeal. "Isn't it fab!"

"I suppose." Tiff shrugs. She's more into saving than spending on fashion. She's more of a *Kohl's* type of girl, I'm more of a *Bloomingdales* type of girl. Then she gets mad at me because I'll spend $200 on a skirt. $200 for a skirt at *Bloomingdales* is generous!

She's very modest, Tiff. She's more Wall Street while I'm more Fifth Avenue, Ya know?

"I don't know. I guess I like more of a cozy kind of look. Like some nice red plaid, and a pair of blue jeans." She shrugs.

"Red plaid is for Winter. It's Fall. Leather is *so* in." I state.

"Wow, you would think I would know this by now. My best friend is, afterall, the fashionista of the century." She says sarcastically.

"You're just jealous you don't have my adorable sense of style." I say fixing the sleeves on my shirt.

"Yes, extremely. How much was that now?"

"Shut up." I scowl. "How's work?"

"Good. Kids will be kids." She shrugs. Tiff hates talking about herself. "They're all so cute. It's early though. They'll eventually show their true colors. I can't wait to be a mother one day."

"You're going to be the most fab mother." I say.

"Yeah well first I need to find the right guy." Tiff sighs.

Tiff's not that romantic. I sure hope that her future husband is the lovey dovey one. She loves romance, she just doesn't quite know how to react to it.

Once a guy tried to kiss her on the first date and she didn't want to hurt his feelings, so she decided to tell him she had some infectious disease that could be spread through mouth to mouth contact. She then continued to run out of the restaurant. But I punched someone in the throat on the first date, so I can't say anything.

"You will find the right guy. I'm on the lookout." Oh, and trust me I am. Since we were fourteen.

"Well ok then. I suppose I have nothing to worry about." She laughs.

"You suppose right! You're destined to find someone. You're perfect."

"Ok Pops."

"I'm serious, Tiff!"

"I know, I know." There is a silence then Tiff asks, "Anything new?"

"No." I deflate a bit.

"No?"

"Well a new guy moved in across from me?"

"Well that's nice." Tiff's head pops up.

"Not really. He's kind of a jerk." I scrunch up my nose.

"Oh please, have you even said hi to the poor man."

"Yes." I say, shrill. "I offered to help him with moving in and everything! Oh, and get this, I asked him if he wanted a bottle of water and he said no. So I told him if he needed anything just to let me know. You know, being polite. *Then* he has the nerve to say some smartass comments. Something like..." I begin to mimic Atticus's (or at least I think that what his name was) deep Brooklyn drawl. "'Oh, so I could wake you up at 3A.M in the morning and ask you for a bottle of water?' So, I went into my apartment, got a bottle of water and handed it to him. He had this sly, condescending smirk on his face. Argh." I take a swig of my coffee to calm me down.

"Are you done?" Tiff asks with a chuckle. "Ok, that does sound somewhat miserable, but in reality, what effect is he going to have on you?"

"He has a *band*."

"Ok…"

"A *pop punk* band."

"Pops…" Tiff pinches the bridge of her nose.

"Thin walls, Tiff, thin walls!"

"Well, maybe the band is good."

"At least It's not county."

"That's what I was thinking!"

I walk back towards my apartment building door, texting Jeannie. 'WE SHOULD GO THERE! IT WILL BE SO FUN! WHAT DO YOU THINK?????' Reads my phone.

'I DON'T KNOW! HOW WOULD I KNOW????? YOU GO OUT MORE THAN ME AND RILEY COMBINED.' I answer back.

Jeannie's really trying to get me out of the house. She wants to go to some new high end bar restaurant in Tribeca called *The Lounge*.

Supposedly it's one of those restaurants where all the Manhattan IT girls and social climbers go. Where you network, have fancy cocktails and watch all the classy socialites drink Brandy and eat tiny steaks.

I'm shocked Jeannie wants to go. She's usually more into the club scene. Me and Riley are the ones that like those high end restaurants. Although, the only things we could really afford there is a rum and coke.

So me, Riley, Arlo, and Jeannie always end up at *Houlihans* and stay there till one in the morning, just chatting and gossiping about work and life.

Me and Arlo are usually the designated drivers even though I hate driving. I don't even have a car. We use his.

One time Jeannie got so drunk that she passed out on the table and it took me, Riley and Arlo to carry her.

She's extremely tall but very skinny. Her weight wasn't the problem, it was the fact that she was dragging her legs on the concrete, refusing to walk, singing *Madonna's* "Like a Virgin" at the top of her lungs.

Therefore It took two gay guys and a 130lb 5 foot girl to drag Jeannie about ten feet to the car. Oh, and don't even get me started on once we entered the car, how she so graciously continued with *Elton John's* "Tiny Dancer." It was a long night.

JEANNIE- 'YOU SOUND SO EXCITED, POPPY.' Even though we are texting I can still hear her sarcastic tone.

ME- 'WE'LL ASK RILEY ON MONDAY." I respond back and then all of a sudden look up and shriek.

I see a body lying unconscious on the floor and give an even more shocked gasp. It's Atticus. Oh my god! Is he ok? Is he hurt? Am I the victim of a crime scene?

I look around cautiously like they do on *Law and Order.*

When I woke up this morning the couch was still in the doorway, but Atticus was nowhere to be found. Now the couch isn't in the doorway, and he's passed out in front of my apartment!

To my relief though, I watch as his body goes up and down as he breathes.

I give a big sigh. God, that was terrifying!

"Hello..." I kick him very gently on his side but he doesn't wake up. "Atticus?" I kick him gently once again.

He's snoring softly. It's weird to see this stranger I don't even know peacefully sleeping. I like him better sleeping, honestly.

"Atticus!" I shout and kick him a little harder.

"What?" He wakes up in a frenzy, hands up and taken out of a deep slumber. His eyes are wide as he realizes who I am and pushes his hair back a bit, still on the floor. "Hey... Poppy, right?" He points to me, still not exactly all woken up yet.

"Yes, yes, hi. Why are you asleep in front of my door?" I ask somewhat rigidly.

"Well," he looks between our two doors. "I'm more in front of *my* door than yours."

"It doesn't matter!" I retort. "I can't get through to *my* door."

"Walk over me."

"You're *asleep* in the middle of the hallways."

"So?"

"'So?' So, you're sleeping in the middle of the hallway! I thought you were dead!"

"Dead? Well that's a little extreme, don't you think Patricia." And there it is. That shit eating grin. For some reason it makes my stomach turn.

"Don't you ever call me Patricia. Ever." I manage to say quite sternly, crossing my arms. Yes, that's right, Poppy. Be Firm!

"Ok, ok, ok, I'm sorry..."

"Thank you."

"Patricia."

"You jerk!" I erupt. "You haven't even been moved in for a week and you managed to annoy me more than the three neighbors that have lived here before you combined"

"Thank you?"

"It's not a compliment, trust me. Are you crazy? You must be..."

"Why do you hate me so much? What have I done to you?" He almost shouts and I pause for a moment.

"Are you high?"

"On life!" He retorts, cockily.

I think for a moment and remember what my dad always tells me. 'Keep your friends close, and your enemies closer.' Although I don't think Atticus is an enemy. Yet.

Plus, I suppose I am overreacting a bit. Maybe he's not so bad! I guess if we're going to be neighbors I have to give him some chances. Even if he is a bit of a dumbass.

"You know what," I shake my head. "I'm sorry." Atticus's head pops up in surprise. "Really. I'm sorry. I shouldn't have been so rude to you... or assumed you were participating in recreational drug use." Atticus just stares at me in shock then gets up off the floor. See!

"Yeah..." He begins, dusting off his jeans. "I'm sorry too. I shouldn't have told my friends you were probably horbering dead bodies in your apartment."

"What?"

"What?"

"Are you kidding me!"

"They knew I was kidding!"

I just huff and roll my eyes.

"Well, whatever. The past is in the past I suppose." I didn't even notice Atticus is in the same clothes from last night. He must have been so tired he just passed out after he pushed the couch in.

"For sure." Atticus lifts his brows in shock and offers a charming smile.

"Well, I'm going to go…" I awkwardly motion towards my door.

"Ok, Blondie." He smirks. "Have a nice night." Then there's that nickname. Wait until I tell him I'm not naturally this blonde!

CHAPTER FIVE

Monday Morning Air
And Leaps Of Faith

I take a good wif of the Monday morning air as I start to walk towards *DuVull and Co.* There is nothing compared to walking to work on a breezy September morning in Manhattan.

The air smells of construction and pine nuts. If you know Manhattan you'll understand. I love that smell. I don't understand how people hate it so much. It smells like… well, it smells like construction and pine nuts, but it also smells of Manhattan and all the possibilities it has to offer.

I sashay through the huge glass doors of the modern, glass skyscraper that my boss runs and owns part of.

"Morning Jerry." I say to the security guard walking past me. Jerry has been working here for years. He tips his hat at me.

"Morning, Poppy. New outfit?"

"You know it." I give him a happy smile, holding both me and Jane's coffee.

I'm in my new *Victoria Beckham* high-waist plaid wool pants that are half pink and half orange. (I got such a bargain on this one!) Accompanying it, an old white bodysuit. It's cute though. The pants are really the star of the show.

I also have a matching head scarf that goes perfectly with the pants. It lays around the top of my head as my long blonde hair cascades down past each of my shoulders with properly specifically placed curls at the bottom.

I get out of the elevator and pass all the different rooms *DuVull and Co* have to offer. You could look through each and everyone of them with their big glass, see through walls and doors. So chic, so modern.

I wave at everyone in photography as I pass all the hung up, framed issues *DuVull* has. From the first issue to the latest.

Finally I reach the main room where Jane's office and all the journalists are. Everyone is frantically getting their articles together for the latest issue. I give myself a triumphant pat on my shoulder, knowing I finished mine.

I get to my desk, dropping my bag on it and look towards Jeannie. She's typing something on her phone, eating her croissant.

`Her legs sprawled on her desk and some rock song is blasting from her computer. At least it's not terrible.

"Hey girly," I say, opening up my computer. "how was your weekend?"

"It was ok. I went on a date with that chick you and Riley found me on *Tinder*. Major fail."

"Why? What happened?" I ask, appalled.

"Turns out we had nothing in common." She shrugs. "Whatever. Off to the next." Jeannie's always so carefree about relationships. I'm always much more serious. How could you not be? There is a chance you could be spending the rest of your life with this person. What if they hate your family, or even worse, your sense of style!

"Oh Jeannie, I'm so sorry." I say wiping off the condensation on Jane's iced coffee. She hates condensation on her iced coffee. I do too. Obvi.

"It's ok." Jeannie shrugs once again. "You know, she wasn't even that cute anyway." I give Jeannie a sympathetic smile, stand up, and pick up Jane's coffee.

"Ok, I'm off."

"Good luck. Remember, if she starts yelling at you, just throw that iced coffee on her. She'll melt right away." I snort to myself, reaching Jane's office.

"Oh thank god, I need caffeine." Jane rips the coffee out of my hands and takes a long sip before slumping back down into her desk.

"Good morning." I say politely.

"Is it?"

"I would like to think so."

"Good job on the article, Poppyseed. Quite impressive." Jane says going through the latest magazine issue that's getting sent out soon.

"Thank you, Ms. DuVull." A bright and proud smile spreads across my face.

"Don't get a big head on me though. I'll have to hit you over it with a glass vase, or whatever the nearest object is that will do the most damage."

"Duly noted." I nod pinching my lips together.

"Ok, great, good. Now get out of my sight. I have a lot of work to do." And with that, I quickly turn around without another word and walk out of the office back into the Lion's den.

I spot Jeannie and Riley now having a conversation at our desks.

I hop back into my chair and turn back to my computer.

Riley looks at me, his chin resting in the palm of his hand and his blue hair in front of it. He's in a cute pestaled sweater with flowers all over it and skinny jeans.

"How was *your* weekend? I'm tired of listening to this debbie downer." He motions towards Jeannie.

"It was ok." I laugh. "A new guy moved in across from me. So that was...eventful." I watch as Jeannie's head immediately pops up and she throws her phone down on her desk. Riley doesn't move, but his already huge brown eyes widen to the size of a volleyball.

"Oh, what's his name?" Riley attempts to ask carefree.

"Atticus." I state, reviewing my daily Horoscope. I look up to see Riley's face scrunched up in disgust and I can't help but giggle.

"Well *that's* a sexy name." Jeannie points out.

"If you say so." Riley huffs. "Is ummm... Is *he* by any chance sexy?"

Him and Jeannie are looking at me expectantly and I scowl at them.

"No." I say shortly.

"What does he look like?" Riley prys.

"Like he is a goth wannabe member of *Fall Out Boy* who smokes a lot of weed and shops at *DollsKill.*"

"Oh, If I was straight..." Jeannie hums and clutches her heart. "that would be *my* type of guy." I scrunch up my nose and shake my head.

"Is he nice?" Asks Riley.

"He's kind of an ass." I respond

"Poppy," I hear a cool voice ask from in front of me, Riley and Jeannie. "It is Poppy, right?" I look up to see a petite body standing in front of me in black and red *Prada* heels.

"Yes it is!" I say.

Isla Hattie. She transferred here from *Cosmopolitan* about a month ago. She's a very talented fashion journalist.

Her long platinum blonde hair is pushed to the side, cascading down to almost her stomach.

She's very short, as short as me, but skinnier. She has big gold hoops and pale skin that goes perfectly with the crimson color on her big plump lips. You could tell that blonde is not her natural hair color because her deep bushy eyebrows don't match, but somehow she makes it work.

She has huge green eyes and cheekbones that can probably give you a paper cut if you touched them. But yet, she still manages to come off as having soft features.

She's wearing a long-sleeved, lacy black shirt, with a colour that goes up to about the middle of her neck. She has a belt over the shirt, around the middle of her stomach that looks to be solid gold and she has shiny leather pants. She's always in black. Basically only black. Everything black.

"Well done on the article." Isla says. "Quite interesting."

"Thanks." I smile proudly. "Your article was lovely." She wrote about the correlation between what you wear and your different moods. *Genius.*

She gives a nod and a tight closed mouthed smile.

She looks down at Jeannie and Riley and gives them the same smile but she sure doesn't look like she wants to be.

It sooner turns into that type of smile where she is barely even smiling anymore, rather just pursing her lips together.

I watch as both Riley and Jeannie give her an intimidating glare.

"Well," she turns to me again. "I must be going. I have a lot of work to do. I just wanted to congratulate you on the success of the article and what not…" she looks around then back at me. "well, ciao." She waves slyly and walks away. I've never seen Isla Hattie smile before.

"Cow." Jeannie retorts as Isla's out of reach.

"Bitch." Riley agrees. They both look towards me expecting me to call her any derogatory name in the book.

"Totally?" I ask more than say and all three of us burst out into a fit of giggles.

"So," Jeannie begins. "Friday..."

"Oh yes," Riley perks up excitedly. "you know Arlo, he already made reservations for eight. He was all worried we wouldn't get in."

"Poppy..." Jeannie starts. "what about you? Are you excited?"

"Very, actually." I nod. And I actually am.

"Well good. I'm glad. It's about damn time."

CHAPTER SIX
Brooklyn Friday nights

As Friday night rolls around I find myself brushing on the last of my mascara and setting my face with powder. I look in the mirror and I have to say, I'm quite impressed.

I'm sporting this *Likely* mini dress I just bought. It seems quite 90's inspired with a straight neck and spaghetti straps. It's a straight silhouette and is absolutely dazzling with hot pink sequins.

It is *so* fab. It shows a lot more cleavage on me then it did on the mannequin, but we're going to a restaurant, not a church. (Not to mention, the mannequins in New York city shops hardly have chests as it is.)

I also have a pair of white *Christian Louboutin* plain white heels.

It's about six o'clock. Riley, Arlo, and Jeannie are wandering around my apartment, doing their own things to get themselves ready for tonight. I linger a bit around my room. I honestly can't wait to go to *The Lounge* but I'm a bit worried. Am I dressed fancy enough? Am I dressed *too* fancy? Oh screw it! I open my bedroom door and am faced with Jeannie and Riley bustling about in my living room.

"Hey Pops, can you zip me up?" Jeannie Asks, turning around.

"Sure!"

Jeannie's in a tiny, tight black cocktail dress. I would've let her borrow something, but in all honesty, it probably wouldn't fit her. I'm... well... I'm a bit more chubbier than she is and way shorter.

"Suck it in." Riley says, standing next to where Arlo is on the couch. He can never stay in one place for too long. He has one of my pink scrunchies in his short blue hair. God knows why. Jeannie just scowls at him.

Arlo's just sitting on the couch on his phone shaking his head at Riley, a soft chuckle coming out of his mouth.

"You're good." I say zipping Jeannie up.

All of a sudden Riley turns around wearing a pair of my black, almond shaped sunglasses giving his best pouty and we all burst into a fit of giggles.

"Guys, take a picture. I'm Jane's newest model."

"Let's go, we have reservations." Arlo rips the scrunchie out of Riley's hair.

Riley's in his normal skinny jeans and a cute little button up hawwian shirt.

Arlo's wearing a black denim jacket, black jeans and his short chestnut colored hair is now full at the top and swept to the side with the new haircut he got.

They're so different from each other. You would never think they would be together, but after all, you would never think the four of us would be friends. We're so different from each other yet it's what makes us such good friends. If we were in Highschool together all of us would be in completely different clicks. Well, I'm glad we were not in highschool together because I love them.

There will always be clicks though. We're a click. The days of clicks will never be over. Especially in New York.

"Let's go!" I say grabbing my purse in a rush excitedly.

"Hey," I feel a hand grip my arm. "what's the stress about?" Arlo turns to me, tilting his head.

His round hazel eyes are pouring into mine, concerned.

I sometimes swear that Arlo and I are long lost siblings. We're so much alike. He really is like a brother to me.

He's a worrywort just like me. Him and Riley have been together for as long as I've known Riley. I'm as close to Arlo as I am to Riley. He just gets me.

I hear a loud rustling in the hallway as I begin to answer.

"Nothing!" I retort.

"Yo, will you just stop? Calm down. We'll be fine." A voice practically shouts from the hallway. I automatically roll my eyes at the annoying slur.

"No we won't! You're 'winging it' technique never works!" Another voice shouts.

"Oh my god, what are they def?" Jeannie says fixing her hair. No, Atticus is unfortunately just extremely loud. She turns up the speaker connected to her iphone on my kitchen counter playing, "Rio" by *Duran Duran*.

"Pfftt, Yeah...vibe check much?" Riley says, pulling a face.

"Riley, stop. You literally hold no right whatsoever to say 'vibe check.'" Jeannie says, and Riley frowns.

Arlo turns his attention back to me. He just gives a glare and a lift of his dark, bushy brown eyebrow.

"I... I just want to go before I change my mind." I find myself saying. I need not say much when Arlo frowns a bit before nodding his head and turning around.

I'm excited to get out but if I stay in my apartment I might just change my mind. I haven't really gone out with my friends to a club or fancy dinner since me and Liam broke up.

I tried so hard to get out but I just couldn't. People deal with breakups differently. Some people dye their hair crazy colors, some people stress eat, and some people drink a lot. I just stayed at home and went to work. I didn't go out, I didn't do anything. I shopped, that's about it.

I went out here and there, but I haven't been out to a fancy club restaurant in Manhattan with everyone since before I had my breakup. This used to be our favorite thing to do. I haven't really *lived* since Liam left. I have definitely bettered myself since him though. At least I would like to think so.

"Come on, let's go." Arlo says to Jeannie and Riley.

"Hold on." Jeannie says unplugging her phone, rushing around the apartment frantically.

"We'll be fine. Come on, get a move on. We have work to do." Atticus's loud voice in the hallway slowly starts to fade away.

"Who the hell was that?" Jeannie motions towards the hall.

"Atticus." I shrug, but they all look at me expecting more. "The asshole neighbor?"

"Ohhhhh..." Jeannie and Riley both nod.

"Well, Jesus, do you have earplugs?" Arlo laughs.

"Nope. He sounds like my family," I give a fake shutter. "loud like them."

"And you're any different?" Riley scoffs and I scowl at him.

"Well I'm dying to see this dude's face." Jeannie admits.

"Me too." Riley says in agreement.

"No you're not." I shake my head.

"Oh, please, how bad looking could he be?" Jeannie grabs her coat and purse.

"I *never* said he was bad looking…"

"Ooohhh, is that our issue with him?" Riley cuts me off, eyes widening.

"Nope. Not my type." I answer simply. "Now can we please go!" I beg.

"Yep. Come on, gang." Arlo says motioning us out the door. It's like trying to round up a group of kindergarteners.

"Gang? What are we fourteen years old in eighth freaking grade?" Jeannie sneers.

Arlo looks up at the ceiling and throws his hands in the air as if to say, 'what else, Jeannie?'

We all walk out into the brisk September air and I wave to the little boys and girls who are always outside playing on the weekends.

They all give me a kind smile and a couple oh 'heys.' Their moms are super sweet. A bunch of yenta's though. I can't say much though, so is my mom.

We all hop into Arlo's old red convertible. Me and Jeannie in the back and Riley and Arlo in the front.

As Arlo turns on the radio and Jeannie and Riley both start singing along, I look out the window as we pass by my huge brown brick apartment building. The whole area is surrounded by them, and they all look the same.

As we go through Brooklyn and enter the highway the sun begins to set and the sky turns into almost a peachy orange color.

Before I know it, we enter on the Gowanus and it's pitch black outside but there are lights everywhere surrounding Brooklyn as we leave it. It's going to be a long night, I just know it.

CHAPTER SEVEN

Green Guitar Go!

The Lounge is in the very middle of Tribeca. Of course the Friday night traffic was horrendous, but luckily (not without struggle and fight between Arlo and Jeannie about the proximity of the restaurant,) we reached the park and ride.

My favorite way to view Manhattan has always been in a car sitting in traffic. You're close enough to take in every detail, yet far enough to see the whole thing. You're not exactly in the action yet you are, ya know?

Very rarely do all of us go into Manhattan together after our week of work is over. Even back before my whole fiasco with Liam. I usually go to *Saks* or *Barneys* sometimes, or to meet Tiff at our favorite *Starbucks.* But me, Arlo, Jeannie, and Riley never go into Manhattan on the weekends. Maybe we should start.

We all live in Brooklyn, so we usually just go out there.

Plus, Riley always says he doesn't go into Manhattan for pleasure, it's bad enough he needs to drive through the Manhattan traffic everyday. He doesn't care for Manhattan very much. He did come from Florida, afterall. Very different.

He's still not the biggest fan of city life, but Arlo adores it, and Riley adores Arlo. So I suppose it's all ok.

As we walk towards *The Lounge,* there are big golden lights that say it's name on the cool looking industrial-like building.

The nightlife in Tribeca is amazing. It's just filled to the brim with lively young people. They have something for everyone here. Soho and Tribeca are the two most artsy places in Manhattan. Along with The Village as well.

There are spray painted murals all over and old fashioned brick buildings. Tribeca never grows up. Tribeca is that one friend that stays twenty-five forever.

All four of us pass by different and diverse groups of friends giggling and walking hand and hand, chatting and gossiping about random things I can't really make out.

"Do you know what happened between Sarah and Billie?" One girl says.

"Oh, do tell." The friend remarks as they pass by. I almost want to hop in. What *happened* between Benji and Billie? I suppose one we'll never know.

We walk down these steep, brick stairs and look at the big, wooden black doors. It has a printed out version of the menu taped precisely straight on the door and people in suits and dresses smoking cigarettes stand off to the side.

Arlo swings open the doors and we walk into the overly crowded restaurant. It's beautiful. I haven't been to a place like this in so long. I missed the fab Manhattan nightlife vibes dreadfully.

We all squeeze through the fancy Manhattan highflyers, smoking, drinking, and just chatting up. It almost looks like a scene out of the *Great Gatsby*. Very 1920's but of course with modern flair.

I cough at the amount of smoke that's in the air entering my lungs and cringe at the loud guitar playing alternative club music, it's practically shaking the building.

We finally reach the host's counter and Arlo steps in front of us. I hear him talk but it's all muffled over the loud noise of the restaurant. I twist my fingers a bit and look down at my pumps. They sure are cute...

"Are you ok?" Jeannie asks, her hand on my shoulder and a concerned look on her face. "Do you want to go outside? I'm going to have a smoke anyway."

"Never better." I reassure her. "Why don't you stay here? You won't have to go through that awful crowd again." I've been trying to get Jeannie to stop smoking since I met her. I'll most likely die trying.

"I suppose." She shrugs.

"This is too much for me." Riley shakes his head. "Look at all these people..." He leans in closer towards me and Jeannie. "absolute snobs."

"I would jump off a bridge to be as successful as those 'absolute snobs.'" I answer honestly through the hubbub of the restaurant.

"Oh please! Half of these people are just here because they slept their way to the top…"

"Sssshhh!" Jeannie hushes Riley. "Stop it! They're all over." She points to them like they're maggots. Me and Riley just giggle.

"Ok, come on." Arlo motions us deeper into the restaurant and feels as if it goes on forever. We slip into the cool red and gold booths and I grasp the huge silver menu in my hand. I *love* eating out. It's so Lux. I also deserve to treat myself. I wonder what I should get…

My eyes wander across the huge menu assorted with all different types of foods, from Italian, to sushi, burgers and fries…*Ohhhhhh* burgers! Maybe I'll get those cute little fried mushrooms too!

The waiter walks over to us and asks us what we would like to drink.

"What are we getting to drink? Poppy, you choose. What do you think? You have a good palate." Jeannie says, staring up at me.

"Oh ok." I say. "Just your most expensive red wine will do." I shrug. How expensive is wine, like, really?

"Our most expensive would be four hundred dollars, ma'am." States the waiter, lifting an eyebrow at me. Oh crap. For wine? Has the economy lost their mind! Who's manufacturing this wine, I want to talk to them!

I hear Riley let out a gasp from across from me. I finally let out a deep sigh and look at the waiter, already not quite feeling this place just yet. Four hundred dollars for wine? I blame social climbers and fancy wine testing suburban moms in the south.

I'll happily spend four hundred on a blouse, but a wine? No thank you. At least the blouse will last me!

"Just give us your cheapest bottle of wine at this point." Riley states throwing his hands up in surrender.

"That would probably be around twenty dollars, sir."

"Perfect."

"I'll just take a coke, thanks." Says Arlo politely.

I watch as everyone around us sits at the bar and tables conversing and networking. They're all relatively young.

The Manhattan IT girls just walk around with their champagne or cocktails, holding it loosely in their hands. No worries. If they drop their twenty dollar drinks, they can surely get a new one multiple times, no qualms about it. With their pretty faces they'd probably get it for free. They're tall, and skinny, and their heels are all at least six inch *Pradas*.

Each and every one of them have work done somewhere and you can tell.

They're lips are bigger than the normal size and aren't proportional to their long, young faces that get injected with botox at least every two months.

They are all in short cocktail dresses and are either talking to one another or a fancy young guy in a suit with a bourbon in his hands. The men are holding their expensive tiny glasses of bourbon loosely too. It kind of represents their grip on life; Loose

They don't need a tight grip on life. They have enough money to solve global warming *and* get that expensive dinner jacket at *Dolce and Gabbana* their wife they're cheating on thought looked nice on them.

Manhattan IT girls don't have to worry about money either. They don't have to worry about anything. They're highflyers. They have great jobs, great apartments, and great boyfriends they cheat on with an even richer man who owns a boat. Everything is easy for them. Everything is just delightful in their world. Everything's just peachy.

To be a Manhattan IT girl is the dream. I would still be me though.

Of course if me and Liam ever got together again I would *never* cheat on him. I would still work really hard, but being a Manhattan IT girl just makes sense to me.

I want to walk around fancy restaurants holding a cocktail loosely. I want to shop at *Gucci* without worrying if I can afford the newest belt. I want to be able to be my own boss. If I'm not going to be a Manhattan IT girl, then who am I going to be? I work so hard, it has to happen eventually right? Will I ever get there?

I get hot just thinking about it, so I fan myself with the napkin that was resting on my lap.

Our wine came about an hour ago and I've had three glasses, just looking aimlessly around the restaurant. I ordered a burger, and I don't know what else to do.

I'm a lightweight too. I do have to say, I'm feeling a bit light headed. The music in this restaurant is so freaking loud. It matches the setting of the restaurant though. A monotone guitar riff and drum solo with some guy singing some alternative pop-punk song. It matches the vibe of the restaurant I guess.

The singer has a deep drawl, but not too deep, just deep enough. I hear it through the mindless chatter and laughter that fills the table. I'm not even listening anymore. I'm just... kind of dizzy.

"I'm going to go get another drink. Does anyone want anything?" Jeannie asks.

"I'll go with you!" Riley perks up. "Pops, wanna come?"

"Nah." I shake my head. "I'll stick here." I don't quite feel like getting up yet. I watch as Jeannie and Riley get their drinks and socialize with other people. I could be doing that too. Social climbing. I don't know why I'm not.

"Poppy?" Asks Arlo across from me. "Are you ok?" He squints his eyes and purses his lips together, concerned. When it comes to me, Arlo seems concerned often. I'm *offended.*

"Pfft totally." I pour myself my fourth glass of wine, and fill it to the brim.

"Thank you, thanks a lot. We're *The Deadbeats.* Look us up on *Spotify* if you liked us... hopefully you did." The male singer says on the stage and gives a raspy chuckle at the end.

Ha, *Spotify.* Lame. I can't quite see his face through the crowd by the stage so I stop trying. I don't really care.

"You had enough of this, my friend." Arlo slides the wine bottle towards him but I don't really care at the moment. In the spur of the moment I rest both my hands on both sides of my cheeks and look towards Arlo.

"Arlo, what's your *worst* fear?" I ask skeptically.

"That you're either going to pass out or throw up on me in a couple of seconds."

"Interesting."

"I'm glad it's interesting."

"Why hasn't our food come yet?"

"Maybe the chef is making yours special."

"You think?" I don't catch on to the sarcasm at first. After a couple of seconds I keep going. "Arlo?" I ask.

"Yes, Poppy?" He asks with a sigh.

"I want to network like everyone else." I exclaim.

"Then why aren't you?" He mimics me, putting both hands on both sides of his cheeks as well.

"Who would want to talk to me?"

"Well, a lot of people! I'm talking to you, aren't I?" Arlo spreads his arms smiling kindly.

"Yes, but you're Arlo, and Arlo has to talk to me."

"I don't have to do anything but pay taxes and die." Arlo states and I roll my eyes. He reminds me of my dad sometimes when he says stuff like that.

"You know what I mean. I want to *be* like them. I just don't know how to get there. What do I do, Oh wise one?"

"Well," Arlo pulls a face. "why don't you look around the restaurant for a friendly face. I'll keep a close eye on you. I'll get you out of any awkward situation. Scouts honor."

I think for a moment.

"We need a safe word."

"Ok..." Arlo looks around the room and I follow his eyes. Both of our eyes land on a shiny neon green guitar sticking out five booths away from us.

"How about guitar?" Arlo says.

"Guitar." I repete. "Got it." I cautiously get up with bated breath and begin to walk around the restaurant.

Friendly face? None of these people look friendly. Or maybe my eyesight is just a little fuzzy. It's probably my eyesight. There are still friendly people in the world, right?

As I look around the room I get pushed and shoved by people passing me but I still remain looking posh and brush off my dress every time someone does. Don't they know this is *designer*.

My eyes scan the room for a friendly face once again. Then I see it. It's a friendly face but also a face I know. I know someone at *The Lounge!* Look at me! I'm *networking*.

The only somewhat bad part is it's Atticus Mckeen. The worst part is, he's the one with that green guitar.

I turn to see Arlo encouraging me with a thumbs up. I give him one back, take a deep breath, and walk over to the table.

As I reach the table I see Atticus and two other boys laughing and sharing an appetizer platter.

One of the boys has the sharpest looking cheekbones I have ever seen and round blue eyes with jet black hair and a colorful sleeve of tattoos.

The other boy looks short and skinny with curly black shaggy hair, and big light brown eyes. He has a tiny silver nose ring and a slim face.

"Hello…" I begin walking over to their table but they don't seem to hear me.

Should I just go back? They just look like they're laughing and having a good time. I should just go back…

I look at Arlo but he urges me to continue.

"Hey Atticus." I say friendly, getting louder and now closer to the table. All three boys look up from their conversations silently and perplexed. Oh god…

"Hey…" Atticus says. He looks extremely confused, almost not believing what's in front of him. Well, it's just me. Duh.

He then turns to his friends.

"Umm…Dallon, Finnick, this is Poppy. Poppy, this is Dallon," Atticus points to the tattooed boy. "and Finnick." Then to the curly haired one

Dallon just gives me a nod and Finnick gives me an enthusiastic wave.

"Hello…" I give a feeble wave back.

I look back towards my table and see Arlo watching the ordeal, and Jeannie and Riley back with new drinks watching intently, both fighting to get a better look and shouting something at each other.

Riley now tries to climb on top of Jeannie to see better and Arlo gets him off her back.

"So, I better be on my way—"

"How did you like the show?" Atticus asks. Show? What show…

Then suddenly a waiter bumps into me and I drunkenly stumble onto the table.

I finally make direct eye contact with Atticus, and for the first time capture the stunningness of his eyes.

They're kind of round yet have a nice shape to them, and light brown. Like a butterscotch color but just a bit darker. They're actually quite beautiful. I also notice what he's wearing.

He's in a long sleeved, skin tight black shirt with a black blazer over it. He has black slacks and a shiny, leather black belt.

He has a big silver cross around his neck and a matching dangly earring.

He also has this weird thing attached to his pants. It's like a chain, but the loops of the chain are very tiny, and at the very top towards his belt is a big silver circle attached to the chain. Strange but intriguing. I'm not sure if I quite like it, but who am I to say!

Atticus gently touches my arm and guides me to sit across from him and next to Finnick. My vision is a little blurry and I put my head in my hands and shake my head a bit.

"What show?" I ask.

"The bands show. Our show."

"Your show?" I squint and ask stupidly.

"Yes..." Atticus laughs and touches my hand, pushing it away from my face so he could see it. "Poppy, how much did you have to drink?"

"Just a little." I perk up. "That was *you* guys up there! Wow, that's cool, I thought you were some lame little cover band. I didn't know you were on *Itunes*."

"*Spotify*."

"Oh, *Spotify!* How very hipster of you." I snort at my own joke. I look next to me and see Finnick nodding with a slight frown on his face.

"How are you?" Atticus asks smoothly.

"Drunk."

"I'm aware," He chuckles. "Is there anything I could get you to help?"

"A vanilla swirl iced coffee from *Dunkin* with a tad bit of milk would be nice." I answer confidently. Atticus laughs and his mouth twists into a wide smile that highlights his intensely deep dimples.

"I'm pretty sure they don't have iced coffee here, but, I can see what I can do…"

"Never mind that." I wave my hand. "How are *you?*" I rest my chin on my palm.

"Just dandy." Atticus rests his chin on his palm mimicking me.

"Ha." I giggle. "Dandy."

Atticus just burst out into laughter with me and shakes his head as if in utter disbelief.

"To think, Poppy Paxton at a place where *The Deadbeats* perform. I would think you'd gravitate towards more of a… structured place. Although, I don't know you very well. Yet." He squints his eyes as if trying to figure me out and gives me a little smirk.

"Oh, I do like structure. You need structure. My friends dragged me here." I shrug. "Also, I'm not quite sure if you want to get to know me." I begin to answer his comment, thinking. "Sometimes people see me as a bit too much." I babble.

"Yeah, well, that makes the both of us." Atticus leans back in the booth. "I'm glad your friends dragged you here though." I watch as Dallon and Finnick look up at each other, a confused look on Finnick's face and a grin on Dallon's.

"I am too." I say matter of factly. "Cause then I wouldn't have gotten to see you, and listen to you perform and prove me wrong about your band." For a second I can tell Atticus doesn't quite know what to say. He just sits across from me, somewhat speechless and a bit confused.

"I like your guitar." I sigh carelessly. "It's so pretty."

"Thanks…"

"Poppy," I hear a voice from behind me not even a moment later. Atticus looks up, so I turn around and I ses Arlo standing behind me. "Ummm… Jeannie and Riley want you. Sorry to take her from you."

"Oh, ok!" I perk up and slide out of the booth, almost falling as I do so. It's ok though, Atticus and Arlo catch me. "Thanks." I turn to Atticus. "Oh, and thanks for talking to me. You have a *divine* voice." I say kindly.

For a moment I catch a genuine kind smile from Atticus, but before he can say anything I'm dragged away with Arlo.

"Why'd you do that?" I ask Arlo as we walk towards the table.

"You said the code word!" Arlo retorts. Damn, I did.

"I was just trying to make conversation!" I retort back.

"Well, enough of the conversation." Arlo helps me through the booth next to Jeannie. They both look at me expectantly.

"Who's *that?*" Jeannie asks.

"God, I hope you got his number." Riley sighs.

"Of course I didn't get his number, silly," I begin as our food finally comes. "It was just Atticus."

And at that moment, Jeannie spits her cocktail back into her glass in shock and Riley practically chokes on his linguini.

"I honestly don't know why you guys are making such a big deal. He's nothing to write home about."

CHAPTER EIGHT

Iced Coffees and (one) Really Annoying family

I wake up the next morning with a blistering headache. There is a sharp pain in my right eye and I have aches and pains everywhere. The only thing soothing the headache is the cold, white, fluffy pillow underneath me.

The beaming blue light beside me reads 10:02 and the golden Saturday morning sun is shining through my window. Through them I hear the commotion of the city beneath me.

The sudden ding of my phone on the dresser beside me has never been so loud. I groan as I get up slowly from my bed, holding my hand on the side of my head as my feet hit the pink rug beneath me.

I walk straight into the bathroom, squinting when I turn on it's annoyingly bright light. I give a jolt of fright when I reach the mirror and see my own reflection.

My blonde hair is in every which way and I have huge black circles under my eyes, a mix of black eyeliner and the result of four hours of sleep.

I have one of Arlo's sweaters on along with black biker shorts. I muster up the energy to brush my teeth and attempt to rip the knots out of my hair. I then take a hot shower in hopes that it will make my headache at least a bit more tolerable but it doesn't.

I get out of the shower with a towel wrapped around me and walk back into my room to rip my phone out of it's charger for any hints of what happened last night.

I remember going to *The Lounge,* but after that, it's completely blank. I curse myself off in my head for drinking so much. I'm surely never drinking again.

I have one text from Jeannie and my mom and one from Arlo. I open Jeannie's first.

'MORNING, SUNSHINE. HOW YA FEELING???'

'HORRENDOUS.' I answer back. 'WHAT THE HELL HAPPENED AFTER WE GOT TO *THE LOUNGE????*' Not a second later I get a full paragraph back from Jeannie and all the memories of last night came flooding back to me like a bad dream.

JEANNIE- 'WELL THEN I SUPPOSE I HAVE TO TELL YOU HOW INCREDIBLY DRUNK YOU WERE. AFTER YOU SAW THAT HOT HIPSTER NEIGHBOR OF YOURS, WE ALL GOT OUR FOOD. WHEN WE FINISHED EATING WE LEFT. WHEN WE STARTED DRIVING HOME YOU SAID YOU WERE GOING TO THROW UP. THANK GOD WE WERE BACK IN BROOKLYN BY THAT TIME. WE HAD TO STOP AT *TARGET* AND YOU THREW UP IN THE BATHROOM.'

ME- 'THE ONE ON GATEWAY????' I ask frantically. Please, God no... not the one on Gateway...

JEANNIE- 'YEAH, MAN. I'M SORRY...' No! That's the only *Target* I go to! They have that cute little *Pizza Hut* cafe and the girls there know my *Starbucks* order by heart! I feel as if I might cry. "ME AND RILEY HAD TO HOLD YOUR HAIR BACK AND ARLO GAVE YOU ONE OF HIS SWEATSHIRTS. THEN WE ALL JUST HELPED YOU BACK INTO YOUR APARTMENT. I GOT OFF WHAT I COULD OF YOUR MAKE UP FOR YOU AND YOU WERE OUT LIKE A LIGHT, DUDE. ARE YOU OK THOUGH?' I pace frantically through my apartment.

ME- 'NO! I MADE AN ABSOLUTE FOOL OUT OF MYSELF!'

JEANNIE- 'IT WASN'T THAT BAD, POPS!'

ME- 'TELL THAT TO ATTICUS AND THOSE POOR SOULS AT *TARGET*!' I rush to my closet and start to rummage through my clothes.

'I KNOW... STAY CALM THOUGH, WILL YOU? I DON'T NEED YOU HAVING A CONNIPTION.' I sigh at the text.

'I'LL TRY NOT TOO.' I respond and open the text from Arlo.

'HEY. HOW ARE YOU FEELING?'

'I'M FINE. THANKS FOR THE SWEATER. I'LL GO TO THE DRY CLEANERS AND CLEAN IT, I PROMISE!'

'DON'T WORRY ABOUT IT.' I now go to my mom's text.

'HEY, SWEETHEART. HAPPY ROSH HASHANAH!! ARE YOU STILL GOING SHOPPING WITH ME FOR THE FOOD THIS MORNING??? IF SO, I'M GOING ABOUT 12. I'LL PICK YOU UP AND WE CAN GO TOGETHER.'

Holy... crap. Holy crap! I completely forgot today was Rosh Hashanah. How could I forget! It was marked on the calendar. It's a holiday, how could I forget it!

Part of me wants to desperately tell my mom I can't go shopping with her, fake a cough over the phone, and go back to sleep until dinner tonight. I won't do that though.

I don't get a lot of time alone with my mom and when I do I want to take advantage of it. Diamante never spends time with mom, she never has time.

I've always been closer to my mom and dad than my sister has. Am I a bad person if I get mad that she's not really jealous of that?

My parents always treated me differently. They were more strict on me and I don't know why. Maybe because I was younger, I don't know. I try not to think about it much.

'SURE THING!' I answer my mom with a tone that surely doesn't match my mood. 'CAN'T WAIT! SEE YOU AT 12!' Great. And with that I throw my phone on my bed and pick out my clothes.

I look at myself in the full body mirror as I curl the ends of my hair, half my body in the bathroom and half my body in my bedroom.

I'm wearing my *Rotate Birger Christensen* off-the-shoulder, light blue mini dress completely made out of feathers. It has feathery, big long sleeves and falls mid thigh.

I've paired the dress with my *Sophia Webster* heels. They're silver and opened toe with an ankle strap. And in true *Sophia Webster* fashion, it has big butterfly wings sticking out on the back of the heel as if the shoe is ready to fly away.

The wings are pink and yellow and the design on the wing bleeds onto the sides of the shoe turning into a mint blue color that matches my dress.

I ran out of contacts, so I'm wearing my round, clear glasses that are a bit too big for my face.

Is this grand enough? Is this too grand? Am I overdoing it? Surely not!

It suddenly dawns on me that I have to walk into the supermarket like this. What if the feathers on my dress get stuck in something! Well... too late now.

As always, my sister will of course look absolutely stunning without having to do anything, while I'm in the bathroom strategically curling the ends of my hair while also suppressing a hangover while also looking like an exotic bird. Great.

It reminds me of when we were younger and how every holiday my sister would come out of her room with something skimpy on and her favorite *Mac* lipstick.

One year, I must have been seventeen, I was in my room doing my makeup for *hours* and it honestly looked beautiful. It was for a Passover. We were going to my Grandparents on my dad's side.

Diamante walked out in her skimpy little black dress and heels and no makeup. Just that stupid, overly lined, red *Mac* lipstick. My heart dropped and so did my confidence.

I found that I overdid it and ran into the bathroom and wiped all my makeup off. My mom screamed at me. She thought it was stupid that I took two hours doing my makeup just to wipe it off. I told her I probably wasn't even going to wear it anyway. My dad kind of caught on though. He just felt bad for me.

I shake my head out of that memory and the pain from my already existing headache takes it away. Well you know what, I like my outfit and that's all that matters! And I love my fashion sense as extreme as it is.

As I look away from the mirror I walk out of my room and pass my kitchen, now even more agitated than I already was before.

I glance at the counter and I roll my eyes in frustration when they land on the picture of me and Liam. I slam the frame downwards on the marble, not feeling like looking at Liam's face at this moment.

It's like he's ridiculing me, and I'll have enough people ridiculing me today.

The minute I unlock the door to my apartment I look down to see a *Dunkin Donuts* cup right under me with a yellow sticky note on it.

I look at the wet sticky note and see a little message in black marker. It's pretty neat handwriting as well.

"A vanilla swirl iced coffee from Dunkin with 'a tad bit' of milk as requested. You probably need it. I thought I should get you one, I was going anyway. I caught your friends coming out of your apartment last night and they told me what happened. Hope you're feeling better. If it's any constellation, I'm glad I ran into you. It was fun talking to you (even though you were kind of hammered.) I'm glad you liked the band (Or at least tolerated it.) Enjoy your coffee, Blondie. -Atticus."

All the memories of me talking to Atticus and his friends run through my mind. I cringe at how drunk I was but smile uncontrollably at the kind gesture.

Oh my god, did Jeannie, Riley, and Arlo really have to tell my neighbor everything that happened last night! Great, he's going to remember me as the drunk girl who threw up in *Target*.

I walk towards his door to thank him for his kind gesture when I see a yellow piece of construction paper taped to the door in the same handwriting. It has the words *'DO NOT DISTURB. EITHER OUT OR PRACTICING!!!!!!!'* Then in tinier writing at the bottom it states. *'IF I'M OUT, PLEASE DON'T ROB ME. I PROMISE I HAVE NOTHING VALUABLE, I'M KINDA POOR. THANKS!'* I snort at the bold words in all different colors. It looks like he took an unnecessary long time on this. It's cute.

I quickly run back into my apartment, grab one of my pink note cards, and run back out.

I abandon my coffee back on the floor for only a second and lean the card against the wall by Atticus's door. I begin to write a note back with the green sparkly gel pen that was in my bag.

"Thank you so much for my coffee, it was much needed and quite sweet of you. It was nice running into you as well. I'm extremely sorry about my behavior, it was obviously not an accurate representation of who I am. It was nice talking

to you and your friends and from what I've heard, you and your band did a fab job last night! You have a divine voice. -Poppy"

And with a tiny heart, I slip the note card under his door, picked up my coffee and headed out the door.

"You won't believe what David told your father! He said he and Shelly are getting a divorce! Can you believe it?"

"David and Shelly from next door?" I gasp.

"Yes," begins my mom throwing a tray of pre-made cookies in the cart. "what a sad time. Shelly found some man in England on some british dating website. They have been dating for a year all behind David's back! She said she's moving to England to start a life with him. Some 90 day program, just like the *TLC* show."

"That's a shame." I sigh. It really is. I've known David and Shelly since grade school. I went with their son Cameron. Everyone thought they were this little perfect family. I suppose not.

"Yes, well that's life, dear." My mom shakes her head. She takes a box of frozen appetizers and places them in the cart. She's going to most likely claim that she made them all herself and that it took five hours to get them perfect.

We'll all be forced to go with it or she will surely flip the table upside down.

I take a long sip of the coffee Atticus had so generously left at my doorstep that now has a napkin wrapped around the sides. It's soothing my headache just enough to be able to deal with the complete yenta my mom is. (Honestly, where do you think I get it from?)

I watch as she looks at me from the corner of her eye as we walk through the frozen food section.

"You know, if you went to get coffee before we went out, you could have asked if I wanted one." I roll my eyes at her unnecessary comment.

"I didn't." I retort. "My neighbor got it for me."

"Oh." Her head pops up in surprise. "How kind. Who would that be?"

"Some new guy Atticus." I shrug. "Kind of him, right?"

"Very…" mom pulls a face, nodding. "Is he cute…or…." I roll my eyes and groan at the same question I feel everyone has been asking me. Whenever you mention a new person that is of the male species to your family and friends, they seem to lose their minds. It's quite annoying.

"No." I say in frustration. "He looks like a wannabe rock star who smokes a lot. He is for sure one of the *dumbest,* most clumsy people I have ever met, and I've only known him for three weeks. But…" I sigh, suddenly feeling bad for being so rude towards Atticus to my mother.

He's not terrible, he bought me a coffee. He was also quite kind to me yesterday at *The Lounge.*

"he's very kind though, and he's funny. Sometimes. When he's not being cocky." I add.

"He sounds better than Liam." She says under her breath. My mom never liked Liam. Well, let's get real, she *hated* Liam. I'm not going to sugarcoat it.

Do you know the saying "familiarity breeds contempt"? Well, that was the situation. I would tell my mom everything. I still tell my mom about everything, but I think she knew Liam a bit too well. It's weird though because from the moment my mom met him she knew she didn't like him.

'I hate him. I hate him from his stupid hair down to those ugly basketball shorts. He doesn't even play basketball! Doesn't he own anything else?' She used to say.

My mom's a very brutal person when it comes to Liam. My mom is brutal when it comes to a lot of things actually.

"He's not better… he's different." I nod. "And there is no competition! I'm not interested in Atticus. He is not competing with Liam. We can't compare them, it doesn't make sense!"

"Oh please," my mom stops me. "you can compare Liam to anyone. You can compare Liam to a junkie and the junkie would surely win."

"Not true!" I squeal. "You will never understand the way I feel about Liam. I loved him so much. I still love him. You're so harsh sometimes." I mutter but cringe at how much of a love struck teenager I sound like.

"I'm harsh because I care." My mom states calmly. "Liam stopped caring about you a long time ago and you know that, darling! It's life…"

"No, he didn't!" Now I'm on the verge of tears in the middle of the frozen foods section. She could be so caring yet so cold sometimes. Just like Liam. Maybe that's why they didn't get along after all.

"I'm working on getting over Liam, I really am. I can finally breathe without his hands around my neck, I refuse to be interested in anyone else. Especially a guy like *Atticus*. I'm positive he's no better than Liam. And I'm not even interested in him, but no one cares, do they?"

Am I really getting over Liam though?

After I finish, mom turns around to look at me and puts her hands on her hips.

"Poppy, stop being so dramatic. It's a holiday. I'm not fighting with you, darling." And like that, I know the conversation is over. I just nod my head, not in the mood to fight either. I don't have the energy.

I sit in the tiny dining room in my parents house. They have had the same table since I was born and nothing has moved since then. Not the table that's too big for the room, not the china cabinet filled with relics behind the table, and not the little glass table off to the side with an old stereo on it and pictures.

Nothing ever moves in this house, not even the old vintage typewriter in the living room or the piano in the very corner of it as well. I used to love playing with both when I was little.

My dad sits at the head of the table as always and I sit next to him. Diamante and Carlo sit across from me. My mom earlier on had told me they have been having issues.

When they walked in they were in the middle of a pretty bad argument. Diamante is the most possessive, most jealous person I know. Carlo can't even look in another woman's direction without getting screamed at. He can't even make eye contact with another woman. It's bad.

Let's not even talk about the time he politely said thank you to the waitress at *Applebee's*.

Diamante sits up straight in her chair and is arguing with my dad about politics. That's they're favorite thing to do. Carlo just sits, his tall body slumped in the chair as he looks down at the god awful gold placemats mom bought at *HomeGoods* last week. Poor Carlo.

"Hey, I thought the party started without me. I got nervous." I hear a loud voice say as the front door opens and closes.

A smile suddenly becomes plastered on my face now just like when I was little. My Aunt Eva comes into view and I run up and hug her.

Her arm is in a sling, but she looks divine in her blue jeans and white dress shirt.

My Aunt Eva is my mom's older sister by three years. She looks just like my mom but they have complete opposite personalities.

I have always been extremely close to my Aunt Eva, she's my Godmother. I just adore her. But let me tell you, no one has a crazier life than her.

No, like, literally, she has the craziest life ever.

She was a teacher, then she owned a restaurant at one point but the FDA closed it down. Now she works at some restaurant as a waitress.

My dad still thinks she sells drugs and that's where her money comes from but my dad's crazy too.

Regardless of what anyone says about my Aunt Eva though, she would give you the shirt off her back. She truly is kind and the most hardworking person I know.

"Geoff, how's my favorite brother in law." She pats my dad on the shoulder as we both sit down.

"I'm living the dream, Eva." My dad sighs. She drives my dad nuts. She always did.

"Diamante, Christian, how are ya?" Her deep Brooklyn accent shines through when she says that.

"Carlo." Diamante answers for him, with a tight smile.

"Ah, yes, sorry Carlo." Aunt Eva says and Carlo nods his head with a tiny laugh. Diamante and Aunt Eva never really clicked. They just have nothing in common. We all have those certain relatives we are close to and Aunt Eva was mine, and I am Aunt Eva's. It's just the way the cookie crumbles.

"Aunt Eva," I begin. "what happened to your arm? Why is it in a sling?"

"Oh," she looks down as if realizing just now it was there. "some eighty year old lady rammed into my car on the highway." Everyone gasps.

"Are you ok?" My dad asks.

"Yeah," she shrugs it off. "I am pretty sure she was sent by the government to spy on me. Don't laugh, I'm a smart person. Maybe they want to experiment on my brain or something." Aunt Eva states seriously.

"I don't think that's plausible..." Diamante begins but Aunt Eva cuts her off.

"Yes it is, shut your hypothetical mouth for one minute and listen." Diamante sits back in her seat defeated and I give a little smile.

"Ok..." begins mom, walking into the dinning room. "dinner is served." She puts the roast with carrots and potatoes in the middle of the table after she hugs my Aunt Eva, plopping down next to me so I'm between them.

After a while of hearing my dad and Diamante go back to fighting about politics and listening to Aunt Eva talk about what her physic told her last week, I began to pick at my carrots and push my potatoes around the plate in boredom.

The dining room sounds like a noisy highschool cafeteria and there are only six people at the table.

I watch as Carlo murmurs something under his breath and wonder if he's actually going insane. Oh my god, he probably is. I wouldn't blame him.

"That's it." He finally says and everyone looks up at him in awe. Carlo hardly ever talks. He's been with my sister since I was nineteen and I'm pretty sure he overall has said ten words to me.

Diamante likes to say he's shy. It's more than that, let me tell you. He dramatically throws his head in his hands and shakes it. "I... I just can't."

Oh my god I knew it. I *knew* this was coming. Carlo is having a breakdown, he's going to break up with Diamante. On a holiday! What do we do? Mom must have been right about them fighting.

Carlo stands up, still shaking his head. Everyone looks up in confusion and shock.

My dad continues to chew on his food, not particularly caring about anything but my mom's roast.

"Oh shit." murmurs Aunt Eva, leaning in towards me. "Your sister is going to blow up the whole of Staten Island if this bastard cuts it off with her."

"Diamante, I'm sorry…" Oh my god my poor sister. My poor, poor, ignorant sister.

This was going to happen one way or another, though.

Diamante just looks up at him in annoyance as if he dares interrupt her vegan plate of just carrots and two tiny, cut potatoes.

My heart begins to pound fast and I feel a panic coming on. Does he really have to do this? Now? My mom grips onto the table as if not to pounce on Carlo.

"I just have to do this…" and all of a sudden I watch as Carlo gets down on one knee and takes a black velvet box out of his pocket. Wait… what!

My dad practically starts choking on his roast and my mom stands up, throwing her two hands over her mouth. I just sit there, gobsmacked.

Aunt Eva sits next to me, snorts, and takes a huge swig of her wine.

Diamante stands up and begins to cry. Not an annoying cry, but a little sniffle.

"Diamante Dilan Paxton, will you do me the great honor of being my wife?" Now my dad's coughing has increased and my mom is bouncing up and down in excitement. Aunt Eva just raises her glass at both of them and sighs.

My face gets hot and I feel embarrassed. I thought they were having issues. A person can't get married if they're having issues from the get go. They just can't!

I feel tears prickle at the corner of my eyes, and I don't know why. Well, actually, I know exactly why. I should be happy for Diamante and I am, I swear! It's just… If there is someone who can deal with Diamante, there surely must be someone out there who can deal with *me*. I just look down at those god awful gold placemats and sniffle. Stupid, ugly placmates.

"Yes, of course!" My sister sniffles and they engulf each other in a huge hug. Everyone stands and claps and I put a bright, fake smile on my face and clap with the rest. I mask my tears for tears of joy.

Of course I'm happy for my sister, I just… I don't know.

My mom practically shoves me out of the way and embraces both of them.

"Oh I'm so happy!" Is all she can muster through tears. My dad stands up, still in shock. He hasn't even congratulated them yet but he walks over to me and gives a trying smile.

Dad takes his big hand and moves my glasses on to the top of my head, wiping the tears from my face as if I'm five years old once again. He gives me a knowing nod as he polks the little beauty mark a bit under my eye with a caring smile. My dad could always speak a thousand words without saying anything.

I give him a tired sigh as he walks over to shake Carlo's hand.

Diamante shows off the new shiny diamond on her ring finger. It looks like litteral twigs wrapped around her finger with one diamond hiding in the middle.

You know, people say diamonds are the rarest of all the stones. The most beautiful. Well, they're not. I wrote an article about it a couple of months ago actually.

Diamonds hold very little value. The only reason people hold value in them is because it's what the traditional engagement ring has on it. When I get married, I don't want a diamond. I don't know what I want, but I know I don't want a diamond.

I feel a hand on my upper back and realize it's Aunt Eva pulling me into her shoulder that's not wrapped in a sling. I gladly oblige.

"They'll be divorced within a week…"

"Don't say that." I giggle.

"Don't be so down, kiddo…" she begins. "you got your whole life to live. Go live it. Look at me, I was married twice! Nothing good came out of it. Test drive the car before you buy it, you know what I'm saying?" And like that I throw my head in Aunt Eva's shoulder laughing through sniffles. She always knows how to make me laugh. I want to be like Aunt Eva. (Minus all the craziness.)

CHAPTER NINE
Guitar Boy

On Monday I sit at my desk and tell Jeannie and Riley about my sister and Carlo as we patiently await a team meeting for the newest issue coming out for October. (Well technically it's the November issue, but it comes out at the end of October. Like most magazines, so you're prepared for next month's trends.)

Jeannie just looks at me with only a look that I could describe as 'The Jeannie.'

Her eyes are wide and she goes from being slumped in her chair to sitting straight up and one of her bushy brows is lifted high. You'll know the look.

Riley is just sitting there, a disapproving glare on his face and his cheek in the palm of his hand.

"So *why* is this an issue?" He asks.

"Why is this an issue?" Jeannie retorts back at him. "I don't know, have you *met* Poppy's sister?"

"Unfortunately."

"Then you know why! It's just…" Jeannie thinks for a moment. "It seems like your typical recipe for disaster. I don't know, man. I don't wanna be in love." She shrugs.

"Why?" I ask appalled

"Too much work."

Riley just rolls his eyes at Jeannie's response. I just shrug. Riley then turns his attention back to me.

"What I mean *is*, why is there an issue? Are they having relationship problems?"

"According to my mom." I state.

"Pops, I love your mom. She's a sweetheart, but she's also the same woman that got sage to 'cleanse' the house because she thought she saw a ghost, and it turned out to just be your dad replacing their white bed sheets." Jeannie says unsure. Riley nods in agreement.

"Ok, boomer." Riley mutters.

"Riley, how many times have I told you this, your not cool nor young enough to say, 'ok boomer.'"

"I suppose she might not have seen things clearly..." I think for a moment then ask what I've been meaning too. "Is there something wrong with me?" It's so brash, it's so sudden. So... serious, but I have to know. It comes out wrong but Jeannie and Riley seem to know exactly what I'm referring to. "Is there a reason why no one wants to be with me? Was Liam right? Am I that prissy? Am I that hard to impress?"

Jeannie purses her lips together and frowns and Riley pinches the bridge of his nose between his thumb and pointer finger.

"Well..." he begins when Jeannie punches him in the gut.

"Of course there is nothing wrong with you!" She practically cries. "All you wanted was for Liam to be a good man. That's *not* you wanting to be impressed, that's you wanting the best for the man you loved."

"He wasn't the right one." Riley says suddenly. "If he was, he wouldn't have called you prissy, and he wouldn't pick fights with you, and he would *never* get tired of trying to impress you. There's a man out there right now who's your soulmate. All you have to do now is find him."

"I don't *want* to find him!" I retort. "I don't want to find anyone." I don't want to be the girl constantly looking for love, looking for a connection. I hate that girl. That girl is not me, it never was! I found Liam, he's the one I have a connection with!"

"How many times do we have to tell you, Liam was your jerky Highschool sweetheart, and you're not in Highschool anymore. You're a strong, independent woman." Jeannie nods, matter of factly.

"Period." Riley agrees.

Jeannie's right, she's absolutely right. But I could have swore Liam was the one.

"I don't want to go out looking for anyone else..." I mumble under my breath.

"You won't have to find anyone." Jeannie assures. "He'll come to you." I give out a huge sigh.

I don't *want* anyone to come to me. I *want* Liam to come back.

"Who knows..." Jeannie clicks her tongue. "he might be right in front of your face and you don't even realize it."

As we enter the conference room, me and Jeannie sit next to each other around the long glass table in cool, black leather rolly chairs.

Riley went to pick some stuff up for Jane. He never sits in on meetings. He hates all the people here anyway. Riley hates everyone in general. I think the only people he likes on this earth are Arlo, me, Jeannie and--on occasion--Jane.

Me and Jeannie butter our bagel and sip our coffees. Team meetings are amazing. Free food!

I take out my pink notebook and my mechanical pencil to write some notes.

As me and Jeannie discuss what we might write about, I spot Isla Hattie walk through the huge glass doors and purse her lips together as if judging each and everyone of us in this room, and she probably is.

As always, she looks like she's on her way to a funeral. She's in black leggings, a black shirt and a beautiful bedazzled black leather jacket with silver rhinestones all over it. Her red lips pop on her pale skin and her golden hair cascading down her back.

Jeannie scoffs when Isla walks in. No one quite knows how to talk to her. She's intimidating for absolutely no reason. She is no higher up than any of us are. It makes you wonder if all that confidence is masking insecurities. It probably is. It always does.

"Ok people, get settled in. We have work to do and a November issue to discuss." Jane sashays in the room in true Jane DuVull style. "Give me fall, give me the start of the holiday season, give me freshly made turkey from Grandma's Oven vibes. Ya know what I mean?"

She's in the new sweater I told her to get. I told her she would want the sweater version.

I look towards Isla and she still looks lost, her head still held high though. Against my better judgment the little voice in my head tells me to invite her to come sit with me and Jeannie. She always sits by herself, and if I was Isla (and sometimes I wish I was,) I would want someone to invite me to come and sit with them.

"Isla," I give a friendly wave and smile, pointing to the empty seat next to me. No one wants to be a loner. "over here." I whisper.

Jeannie vastly turns to me wide-eyed and with a warning glare. I glare back at her and give a face as if to say, 'stay calm. How bitchy can she actually be?'

Isla looks at us then around the room almost confused. I can't tell if she's embarrassed or shocked that we invited her over.

She walks over to us, heels clicking the marble floor as she does so. She sits down on the chair and puts her notes and pencil next to mine. Her red lips curve into a short, closed mouth smile towards me as she turns her attention to the front of the room.

Jeannie looks at me and rolls her eyes.

"Be nice." I hiss under my breath to Jeannie as Jane speaks again.

"Ok kitty cats," she claps her hands and throws her long black hair behind her ear. "let's get to brainstorming, shall we? Let's make this fast, I got a facial at one." Jeannie raises her finger in the air, which causes everyone to turn to her.

"So, I'm thinking me and Poppy could coordinate together on our articles. I could do the romance and psyche behind a person with a pop punk or scene style and personality. Poppy?"

"Totally. I could just overall talk about the style in general!" I shrug and look at Jeannie who has an ecstatic smile on her face. She's been wanting to do this for a while. She loves all that punk stuff. I don't quite understand it, but I think it's a fab idea!

I watch as Jane screws up her face and thinks for a moment. All of a sudden she starts to nod.

"It's different...I like it. We could be bringing a whole different group of people in as an audience....ok." She perks up. "Deal. I'll make it due for the January issue. I actually *really* like this idea. Shockingly. I trust this and I don't trust often. Don't screw this up. I suggest you start working on these articles now. I expect six whole pages from both of you with *facts,* data and opinions. I don't want a rushed shit show ladies, the January issue is *huge.* I expect something grand. Make it happen. I want at least a thousand words for each of you. At *least* which, if you know me, means more than a thousand words." And like that me and Jeannie look at eachother like the wind has been knocked out of us.

Jane DuVull loved Jeannie's idea. I haven't seen her that excited about an article since *DuVull* skyped with *Justin Timberlake* for love advice.

"Oh my god." Jeannie mouths as Jane talks to everyone else about articles they have to cram in this month's issue. I squeal excitedly and slap her arm. "That was easier than I thought."

Jeannie sits in her chair in amazement and denial for a couple of seconds then snaps out of it and starts writing stuff down that Jane is saying about a stronger writing technique.

"Isla," Jane begins and Isla's head pops up. "we obviously won't have Poppy writing an article for the November or December issue, so you're going to have to come out of the wood works and come up with something amazing. Wow me."

"Of course, Ms. DuVull." Isla scribbles something down in her notebook.

"Great, amazing. This November issue will probably come out on the 27th if things go off without a hitch."

For the next hour we all just listen to Jane talk about our competitors and the importance of having the best articles in the fashion industry, and how at this time of the year--starting with October--is no joke. How we have to get our act together big time.

When she dismisses all of us, me and Jeannie scramble for our things and I watch as Isla does the same.

"You're going to write something amazing, I'm sure of it." I say to her kindly. "You always do." She looks at me in confusion for a moment as she grabs her notebook off the table and holds it with a loose grip.

"Thanks..." she says apprehensively, but then shakes her head and looks up at me. "thank you for letting me sit with you. That was... uhh...very kind of you." Her nose is stuck in the air.

"Oh." She catches me off guard. "You're welcome. Maybe we can hang out sometime. Me, Jeannie, and Riley go out a lot on the weekends--" Jeannie kicks me under the table but I ignore it. "maybe one time you could come. Here," I scribble my number on a piece of paper in my notebook, rip it out, and give it to her.

Isla takes it and looks up at me with wide eyes. She looks a tad bit confused. Why? I just gave her my number.

"Thanks." She says for the seventeenth time.

"Of course!" I say happily. "Happy writing. See you later!" I wave and walk out with Jeannie.

"Giving that cow your number is the stupidest thing you've ever done. And I've been around when you've done some stupid shit." Jeannie mutters as we walk back to our desks.

"Oh please. What's the worst thing that could come out of being kind to her?"

After a long day of planning a dream board about our January article with Jeannie, I walk into my apartment building and wipe my hand on my blue fur coat after touching the handle to the door.

I secure my *Coach* purse between the crook of my arm and fix my hair in it's low ponytail.

My eyes meet Atticus who is standing by the elevator waiting for it. He's in blue, ripped jeans and a tie dye mint blue, yellow, and purple hoodie that's up. It causes his hair to fall in front of his face more than it usually does.

"It's out of order." I hop aside his tall figure and pull a face. "If you're going to be living here I suppose you have to learn the sad truth that the elevator is broken at a constant rate, and when it *is* fixed there's always a new, weird stain inside of it. Like someones been murdered or something." I scrunch up my nose. "You'll get used to it though."

"Pretty dope." Atticus purses his lips together and nods.

He turns around, looking at the stairway and sighs. Not a moment later, he turns back to the elevator and shoves his hands in his pockets.

I'd like to think I could read people pretty well and Atticus seems quite emotionless right now. You could cut the tension between us with a ginsu knife and you could smell the awkwardness in the air.

I don't know Atticus very well, but I know he's *not* an emotionless person. At least I don't think so. He seems to have a pretty good personality. I can't stand emotionless people. They bug me.

Liam could be very emotionless and cold at times but I suppose those two go hand and hand. As I said, I don't know Atticus very well, but he seems far from cold.

"Oh by the way," I begin. "thanks for my coffee. I hope you got my note. How much was it? I'll pay you back." I say embarrassed at the thought of that night.

"Nope. Don't even think about it." He shakes his head. "I was heading that way anyway."

"Well that was very sweet of you." I say walking towards the stairway, Atticus in tow. "So..." I try to make small talk. "where do you work?"

"A record shop. I make a lot of my money through gigs though."

"Oh. That's nice." I shrug nonchalantly, not knowing how quite to act.

I hate when people ask me what I do for a living, I think it's kind of awkward. You never know what their reactions are going to be.

I was actually interested for once though. He really does love music, doesn't he?

"Yeah I guess." He shrugs and plays with his hair, knocking his hoodie back in the process. Atticus has amazing hair. It's dirty blonde and shaggy. It always seems to be in his face and pretty messy. In a good way though.

He looks me up and down, shrugging again.

"What? Guitarists aren't good enough for you?" He scoffs.

Whoah, whoah, whoah, wait what? Did I miss something?

What does he mean? I didn't say anything to him referring to that. I would never judge anyone's job!

"No, I didn't—"

"Nah, it's cool. I see how it is." He just continues to shrug for the hundredth time.

"No, I swear. I would never judge anyone's job! That's really not how it is!"

"It's fine. Whatever."

What is he even talking about? He's actually getting on my nerves now. I have been nothing but kind to him!

"Don't put words in my mouth. Everyone constantly does that to me 'Oh, Poppy feels this way, let's all jump down her throat!'" I take a jab at my family, especially my sister and Liam. "You have *no* right, do you understand? No right to jump down my throat. I wasn't even rude to you, I said nothing!" I shout and my voice booms through the stairway.

His attitude reminded me of Liam's for a second and I feel my invisible big, brick wall go up.

"I said nothing about your career. Just because you're having a bad day does *not* mean you get to take it out on me, Atticus. I apologize if you thought I had an attitude, but with all do respect, *you're* the one with the attitude."

We finally reach the top of the stairs and to our apartments. Atticus is just looking at me in confusion and somewhat awe.

His bushy eyebrows are knitted together and his mouth his taut.

It only lasts a couple of seconds though because all the sudden he gains this cocky, sly smile. It's as if the devil himself is standing behind him and pulling at both sides of his mouth like a puppet.

He finally opens his mouth and leans forward a bit.

"Are you done? That was kinda dramatic, don't you think, Blondie?" I take a step back but am stopped by my own door, the colorful beads hanging from it digging into my lower back.

My blood is boiling and it takes everything inside of me not to slap that smug smile off his face.

"No, I don't think it was very dramatic." I hold my head up high and scowl at him. "I think I was being... rational."

"Oh, rational..." he repeats and nods his head.

"Yes, rational." I stutter a bit. "Plus, you're being a jerk, so my speech was... needed, I suppose."

"Oh, you mean your tantrum?"

"Tantrum?" I quip.

"Yeah, tantrum." Atticus folds his arms, looking down at me.

"That's a little extreme don't you think, guitar boy." I snap back.

"Touche." He smirks.

"Well," I begin, looking up at him confidently. "I should be getting into my apartment. I'm a very busy woman, you know."

"Oh, I'm sure." Atticus nods, seeming to be pondering over something.

All of a sudden I see his friends and bandmates Dallon and Finnick enter the hallways, all their band gear in their hands. I remember them from the night at *The Lounge*. (Shockingly.)

"Hey, Poppy." Says Finnick politely holding practically his whole drum set. He's holding his leg up to try to stabilize the set but it's seconds from falling.

"Oh, hi Finnick! Wait, let me help you." I rush over to him and grab some of the equipment out of his hands.

Atticus rolls his eyes and unlocks his apartment door.

"Thanks." Finnick shoots me a kind smile. He has a red shirt and colorful cargo pants on with his unruly black, curly hair. Dallon is already inside, setting up his guitar.

I drop the drum set on the floor carefully in the beginning parts of Atticus's apartment, barely even entering it.

"Thank you again, Poppy." Finnick smiles and says a bit out of breath. He's so scrawny. In a cute way though! He's maybe the same size as Riley but just a little bit taller.

"Of course." I give him a feeble smile, trying to make up for my behavior from the other night. I'm cringing just thinking about it!

"How are you feeling?" He asks. "Atticus told us you weren't... yourself." Finnick tries to find a nicer word for drunk, and I really do appreciate that.

"I'm fine." I give a gracious smile. "So I'm guessing you guys are practicing?" I ask as we walk back into the hallway.

"Yeah, always practicing. Atticus would sing himself to death if he could. He insists we do the same. Truth is, he'll never be attached to anything but that guitar. But, who knows!" He chuckles and slaps his hands to his sides. "Maybe, just maybe *he's* capable of loving another girl. Besides his guitar he named Ashley, of course."

I can't help but giggle.

"No but seriously," Finnick chuckles. "he's a good guy."

"How good is good?" I quirk up a brow.

"A rebellious, flamboyant, hipster with two left feet and a dangerous smile. As good as it gets."

If I didn't know better, I would think Finnick is trying to set me up with Atticus.

"Oh yeah? And what would you call that?"

"Umm..." Finnick squints and taps his chin with his pointer finger. "a westerner. He's a westerner. You know, someone who lives a life with no rules, rebellious, independent."

"Really?" I think for a moment. "I'd call him more of a... loner."
Speaking of the devil, Atticus begins to walk towards us in the hallway.

"Finn, come on!" Atticus starts to jump up and down excitedly, his guitar wrapped around him. It's white and has little sketches and writing all over it in what looks like black marker. "We need to start practicing!" He looks between me and Finnick, his whole mood changing from an excited child-like giddiness, to somewhat confused and defensive.

He steps in between both of us with one swift motion and seems to suddenly be agitated with Finnick, nostrils beginning to flare and his jaw clenched.

Well someone's having an off day.

"Finnick, why don't you go inside and set up your drums." It's more of a statement than a question.

Atticus has this tight, fake smile on his face. I cross my arms at his sudden aggression and abruptly turn to Finnick.

"Don't let him tell you what to do. He's being an ass." I tell him seriously.

Finnick just gives me the warmest smile I've seen all day.

"Don't worry, I know. He's just..." Finnick thinks for a moment, giving Atticus a smirk. Atticus has somewhat of a panicked yet warning look on his face. "he's just Atticus." Finnick uses his words smartly and gives me another one of his warm smiles. "Have a good night. Thanks again for all your help."

"Anytime." I wave at him and just like that, me and Atticus are alone in the hall once again.

"Busy women, huh?" He turns to me, mimicking my crossed arms and cold stare. "What does this busy woman do for a living? You know, since you were *so* invested in what I do."

"I'm a journalist." I state matter of factly. "A fashion Journalist, for *DuVull and Co.* You know, the fashion magazine. Are you too cool for that?"

"I like fashion." He pulls a face and nods, debunkinking my question.

"I'm so happy you approve of my job." I state sarcastically.

"I could tell."

"Am I that transparent?"

"A little."

"Great." I purse my lips together. "So I'm the one that threw the tantrum? Ok, then what was that little stunt you pulled with Finnick?"

"We all have our moments." He answers, his voice getting a bit higher. The mood between us suddenly changed.

Maybe he was just having a bad day, we all do. Or maybe the Atticus I just saw wasn't really him. It was a mere illusion to try and look cool in front of his friends and overly quirky, opinionated neighbor. Although, Atticus doesn't seem like the type to shy away from being himself. He seems relatively comfortable with himself actually. I don't know. I'm not sure. I'm intrigued to find out though, I gotta say.

"If I didn't know better I would think Finnick was trying to set us up with all he was telling me." I giggle.

"What was he telling you?" Atticus once again becomes serious and suddenly I wish I hadn't said anything.

"Oh...oh nothing really. Just that you're ummm..." I clear my throat. "a pretty cool guy I suppose."

"Yeah, well I'm glad he thinks that but he knows I'm not really into the dating game." He chuckles.

"You have a girlfriend?"

"Nope," He shakes his head. "I've just never been... I don't know." he gives me a closed mouth smile. "I'm just not good at it. Plus, I'm positive I'm not your type either." For some apparent reason that hurts and it wasn't even a diss at my expense. He was just stating a fact.

"Well, I gotta go. I'm a--"

"Busy women?

"Yeah." I laugh and look down at the plain, dirty, yellow floors that echo everytime I walk on them.

"Well, I'll let you get back to your writing and..." Atticus motions with his hands. "all your fashion thingys."

"Yes. And I'll let you get back to your guitar playing and... singing thingy." I want it to come out as a joking tone but it really comes out as a quiet tone.

"Ok. Well night, Blondie. I'll see you around I'm sure." He gives me a playful salute and dances back towards his door to the beat of Dallon's muffled guitar on the other side.

Finnick was right, he really does have two left feet. He's quite a laugh, that's for sure.

"Goodnight, Atticus." I smile, still looking down at the floor as if distracted by my heels.

He whistles a tune and slams the metal door behind him with a loud bang. Not on purpose though, the doors always slam in this building.

Of course the sound runs through the hallway. I take a deep breath and sigh, the smile Atticus put on my face still there. He sure is strange.

CHAPTER TEN
November

Writings and weddings are one and the same, both a long and hard process

"Yes, I know mom." I hold my phone between the crook of my neck and my shoulder.

"No Poppy, you don't know because it sounds like you're shrugging me off!" There she goes again.

Mom is always in a perpetual state of frustration and panic. It never ends for her, I swear. Now you know where I get my crippling anxiety from.

"I'm not shrugging you off," I retort looking through the bargain books at the *Barnes and Noble* on 5th. I love it here. Sometimes I just come here to think. I tend to think better in crowded places, crazy, I know. "I'm just... thinking."

"Well, we need to start helping plan Dia's wedding."

"Mom, she's been engaged for two months."

"And?" She quips. "We don't even know where she's *having* the wedding. I swear, if it's not at temple..."

"She'll probably want to get married by a lake or in the woods. Somewhere majestic. She told me last week." I rat her out.

"No, it won't happen! Does she even want a Huppa?" Mom cries.

"No."

"What! She will respect tradition, I don't care what her little vegan people say... or... or Carlo! God, she needs to have *some* respect. Why can't she have a traditional wedding?"

"Why don't you ask her yourself?"

"Oh, don't be ridiculous, dear. I don't feel like listening to her scream at me over the phone about starting new traditions and that crap. Last week I talked to her and she told me that she wanted to do handfasting. You know, where they tie the bride and groom's hands together. That's an Irish tradition! That's just... cultural appropriation! We don't have an Irish bone in our bodies." She scoffs.

"Mom..."

"She wants to follow everyone else's traditions but our own. I won't let it happen, I won't!"

I look over the bookshelves and see Tiff giving me a glare of sorts. I roll my eyes and shake my head.

"Ok, well--"

"I'm serious, Poppy." Cuts off mom. "Your sister needs serious help planning her wedding. She's going to regret it in a couple of years when her, Carlo and their children are looking through their wedding album and there is not one tradition to be found. No Huppa, no rings, no cake. She wants cakepops! Can you believe that?"

"I know, it's terrible." I can't help but say. "She can at least have a little cake to cut with Carlo."

"That's what I said!" I look at Tiff who's giving me a look as if to say, 'You just *had* to give your opinion.'

"Ok, I have to go now. Tiff is missing me." I smile at Tiff who in return pulls a face and raises her macchiato towards me.

"Oh alright, dear. Tell Tiff I love her. She should help us plan too! Tiffany's a wonderful planner." It's true.

Tiff has planned every party I've ever thrown since we were fifteen.

"Ok, I'm sure she will. I love you, bye!" I quickly hang up the phone before she can say anything else. I give a huge sigh and continue looking through the books on the shelves, moving to the romance section. I cringe at almost every cover I see.

"Diamante's having an issue planning her wedding. Why am I not surprised?" Tiff states, picking up one of the tacky romance novels.

"I don't know if it's so much of an issue as it's just my mom giving her a run for her money."

"So basically your mom is just being your mom." Tiff pulls a face.

"Basically. By the way, she says hi and that she loves you."

"Give her and your dad my love. Also your sister. Even though sometimes I don't quite want to."

"I feel that." I look down at the iced coffee in my hands and an instant smile comes over my face. Almost like magic.

Everytime I drink iced coffee I can't help thinking of Atticus, which is actually quite often. Well, It's actually everyday.

It's been two months since that fiasco happened. Can you believe it? Time really does fly by. Not much has happened since then, I have to tell you.

Jeannie and I have been doing mini articles here and there for the magazine. Just fillers really, but we've been working day and night, planning our article. It's already November first!

I've seen Atticus here and there. Just around the building that is. He's doing good I suppose. He's...well, as Finnick said, he's Atticus.

I still find myself smiling down at the coffee in my hand like an idiot. It's the small things people do, you know?

"Ok, what are you smiling about? You're starting to scare me." Tiff looks up from her book and I look up from my coffee.

"What... oh, yeah." I giggle a bit. "Just...errr... these book covers!" I pick up some random book with a shirtless cowboy on it. "So tacky. Kind of gross too." I shudder.

"Ok sure." Tiff purses her lips together and picks up a novel.

"What? You don't believe me?" I retort.

"No, It's just that wherever we get a cup of coffee together, you look down at it and smile as if it were down on its knees offering you a diamond ring." She shrugs.

"Not true!"

"So true!"

"Ok, well maybe I just appreciate coffee!"

"No one appreciates coffee that much." She throws the novel back on it's shelf and when a bunch of other novels come tumbling down next to it, she hurriedly bends down and picks them up. "Is the reason you're smiling down at that coffee like an idiot have something to do with Guitar Boy?"

"It's Atticus." I correct.

"Ahaha." Tiff gives a sarcastic laugh like a ten year old school girl who just tricked her best friend into saying something silly.

"No. Don't do that." I shake my head and roll my eyes.

"Ok whatever," Tiff shrugs. "then I don't want to see you staring at your coffee like it's your date to the prom anymore." She looks at me expectantly and I just change the subject.

"How's work?"

"Same old, same old." She scrunches up her nose. "Kids of all ages around November start to get rowdy. It's the holiday season. You could only imagine how second graders get."

"I could." I nod my head.

I'm the most rowdy person I know during the holidays beside my mom. I could only imagine teaching a class of second graders during the holiday season(or just in general.) God, Tiff is such a saint.

We are near the magazine section and I head straight for the fashion shelf. I quickly snatch the newest issue of *DuVull* as does Tiff. I also get *Cosmo* and *Brides*.

I know, I know, supporting the competitors. I could never give up *Cosmo* and *Brides* though. Ever. What about when I get married in the future? Where will I get the latest wedding dresses and trends? *Brides,* duh.

As for *Cosmo,* what kind of fashion guru are you if you don't get *Cosmo?* You're not. Plus, they have a more accurate horoscope section than *DuVull*.(You didn't hear that from me though.)

I sit on the bench close by, as does Tiff, and we happily line up all three magazines getting ready to read them. Tiff reads *DuVull* as I read *Cosmo*.

"Pops, look at this article," Tiff pops up. I glance at the article that reads, *'How moving in with your best friend could possibly end your bond.'*

I heard little talks and discussions here and there in the office about this article. I believe Ginger Lovet wrote it. She's part of the tiny lifestyle team we have. I don't care for her that much. Typical Ginger, glass is always half empty. How does she know moving in with your best friend can't *strengthen* your bond, hmmm?

"Do you think that's true?"

"I think it's rubbish." I quip. "If your friendship is strong, it's just bound to get stronger if you live together. Everyone knows that."

"Do you think so?" Tiff lifts an eyebrow.

"Oh, for sure."

"Popss," she begins again and I look back up from my magazine. "would you ever move back in with me? I've been finding I'm awfully lonely in the house by myself." As soon as Tiff says that I feel a little pang in my heart for her.

I lived with Tiff for about two months as I was finishing school at *FIT.* I already had my down deposit on my apartment but it wasn't quite ready yet and I needed to get out of my parents house.

Tiff went to *Bank Street* College so ideally we were going to the same place every day which was Manhattan. It just made sense.

We split rent checks and had pizza on Fridays and shared clothes. (Or at least Tiff took my clothes. She's way skinnier and taller than me. But I borrowed her shoes!) It was just so grand! Tiff lived and still lives in Staten Island, right by my parents and hers.

She lives in this beautiful townhouse on Hyland with stairs, and white pillars, and it's always clean and cozy.

Tiff wouldn't have it any other way.

I could imagine where she would get lonely though. It's quite large for one person.

"Tiff," I begin apologetically. "I wish I could, but I can't drop everything and move in with you. It's just not reality." Me giving Tiff a reality talk is a complete one-eighty for us. She usually has to give me these talks. Tiff has always been the rational one.

Part of me wishes I could help Tiff, but if it were up to me, I would never move back to Staten Island. I moved for a reason.

I like being distant from my childhood. I never fawned over the idea of living in one place forever as some people do. I would gladly live in Brooklyn forever, but in Staten Island where a lot of people have known you since you were tiny? Yeah, not quite my thing.

Everytime I go to the deli around my parents house, the owner Mike still asks me about Liam.

I don't have the heart to tell him we're not together anymore. Mike's fragile.

Everytime I go out to the New Dorp Diner with my parents, our favorite waitress Kelly still asks me how Diamante and Freddie are doing. Do you know who Freddie is? No, you don't because Diamante and Freddie haven't been together since she was in twelfth grade.

Everytime we tell Kelly that Diamante has been with Carlo now for quite some time, she always seems to forget.

Kelly also still asks about Liam. I couldn't bring myself to tell Kelly either. I still can't.

You know, when I broke up with Liam I thought all of Staten Island knew. I guess I forgot how big Staten Island was.

It's funny, Staten Island is so small until you realize Mike from the deli and Kelly from the diner doesn't know you broke it off with your boyfriend of eight years.

I miss him. I miss him a lot.

Days like these I miss him the most. Rainy Saturdays in Manhattan that is. The wind is cold and harsh, but Liam was colder and harsher. I often have to tell myself that.

It would be nice though for him to smile at me like he used to, to laugh like he used too. I think I miss his smile the most. When he wasn't brooding he had such a fab smile. I could swear it could light up a room. Maybe it was just me though.

I also miss how he protected me. No one in the world ever protected me the way he did.

Sometimes I wonder if he thinks about me as much as I think about him on these rainy Saturdays. Probably not. He probably has a new girlfriend right now. And I'm here, I'll always be here waiting for him like a fool.

"I suppose." Tiff nods, bringing my attention back to her. "I'm sorry, that was sudden. The apartment thing."

"No!" I quickly wrap my arms around her. "Tiff, I'm only a phone call away, you know that. I'll always be around!"

"I know." Tiff nods. "No need to worry about me, I'll be fine. Do you hear me, Poppy? I'm fine." She knows I'll worry about her. I have too! It's what best friends do!

"Yes, I hear you loud and clear." I dramatically say in her face as she swats my arm and pushes my face away with her hand. I just giggle into it.

"So, are you looking through this issue of *Brides* to help Diamante?"

"No." I vastly shake my head and we both laugh. "She's not going to want my help. You know that. I'm not 'one with the earth' as she is."

"Carlo's not 'one with the earth.'" Tiff retorts.

"Therefore I still don't know how they're going to work out. She could be so cruel, so judgmental, you know."

"She's judgemental because she compensates. She knows what she has and what she doesn't. You've always been so jealous of her, but have you ever considered she might be jealous of you?"

"Yeah right." I murmur, practically drooling over a vintage white dress with lace sleeves and a beaded bodice I found in the magazine.

"Ok..." Tiff begins. "you just watch."

I sit at home pondering over what Tiff was saying a couple of hours ago.

Is Diamante jealous of me? It can't be! It's a silly idea, really. She's a lawyer and she's engaged and she's pretty and skinny and little miss perfect.

Diamante has the ability to be a Manhattan IT girl, but she never takes the opportunity. She'd rather protest for some new unnecessary law instead of social climbing and making a name for herself. To teach their own I guess, but still!

She has everything I don't. She has the ability to be everything I want to be and she still doesn't take it. Is she not grateful for the position she is in!

She once told me the reason she puts things off is because she has no motivation. No, she's just lazy. I'd give my soul to be in Diamante's position. Not her job, but her status.

My whole life she's gotten everything I wanted yet tossed it away and now it's starting to irk me like it's never irked me before. I'm happy for her, I love my sister. It's just so damn hard to love someone who's such a raging bitch to you.

All of a sudden I hear my phone ring and I immediately pick it up. I balance it on the coffee mug sitting on the tiny glass table in front of my couch.

"So," I begin to Jeannie before she can say anything. "we both need to start writing our articles because we both need to be on the exact same page. It's a collaboration you know, your normal Jeannie Harrison method of waiting till the last minute isn't going to cut it..."

"Pops, will you chill?" Jeannie looks up from her sketchbook she is doodling in as we FaceTime. Jeannie's a great artist. "We've been working so hard on planning our articles, now we just need to start writing it and send it to Jane." She shrugs like it's so easy.

"Do you know how much Jane expects from us? These articles need to be spotless Jeannie. They need to coordinate perfectly."

"You're just stressing about this because one; you stress about everything, and two; you want the promotion." She quirks up her brow.

"What's wrong with that?" Ok, I haven't been *exactly* very transparent.

There is a rumor that Jane is going to be promoting someone to fashion editor and I want it desperately. Yes, editor for the fashion portion of the magazine. You heard me right. Isn't that crazy! I suppose it's not *exactly* a rumor though because...well because Jane told me she was promoting someone to fashion editor.

I asked her who, and she said she didn't know. This could be my time to prove to her I deserve this position, I deserve to be at *DuVull*. That this is where I belong!

Jane just couldn't take the pressure of being editor of lifestyle, romance and fashion while also running the company. I'm just shocked she's letting go of the fashion editor status. We're one of the number one fashion magazines. It's what we're known for!

I want to be fashion editor so badly! All the fashion articles would be going through me first. How exciting is that! And I mean, let's get realistic, Jane can't keep holding *all of DuVull and Co* on her back forever! Being it's founder and editor and chief is tough enough. I really couldn't imagine it!

She does need help, and who better to help her then someone as close to her as me! It's like this opportunity is practically being handed to me on a silver platter. My brain is screaming at me just to go for it, and that's exactly what I'm gonna do.

I'd be responsible for deciding what goes on the pages of the fashion portion of *DuVull*. From photo shoots, to top trends, to styling for shoots, and networking. I'd be in charge of it all.

I need this promotion, I just *need* it.

"There is nothing wrong with that, you just need to calm down a bit. Now, who are you interviewing for your article? Are you going to get in touch with some famous punk singer cause if so, I want to be there for that phone call." Jeannie says, continuing to sketch.

"I actually talked to Jane about that. She said that was more *Keerange,* and *Alternative Press's* lane. She said she wants me to interview actual people."

"You can interview me!" Pops up Jeannie. "That would feed more into the collaboration feel of it all."

"Oh my god Jeanie, that could be so fab--" at that moment I hear the sound of a guitar and the banging of drums to the beat of a somewhat coordinated song. Then hear a tamberne go along with it. The whole thing is so loud, it starts to almost shake the apartment building.

Jeannie looks at me squinting her eyes and tilting her head to the side.

"That's from your end right?" She refers to the sound. I could see my face from the little tiny corner of the phone and I sigh in frustration. I look as pissed off as I feel. My tongue is polking the side of my cheek and my eyes are squinted.

"Yeah don't worry, you're not going crazy." I finally state.

I hear Atticus start to sing. It's so loud, I feel as if he could be next to me.

His voice is literally embedded into my mind now. Not only his normal, dopy yet somewhat intimidating raspy drawl, but the voice he sings in. It's very unique and deep.

"So," I try to ignore it all. "what does love possibly have to do with pop punk? What are you planning to do?"

"Love has everything to do with punk," Jeannie begins as I try to drown out the noise from outside.

"People who sing pop punk, or alternative or rock music know love the best."

"How so?" I tilt my head.

"The people writing and producing the music have no issue putting their feelings out there. They aren't shy about how they feel, they don't try to mask anything..." she shrugs. "some people who write your typical pop music just mask their feelings for a catchy beat. That's why you don't hear a lot of punk on the radio anymore, like in the 90's and early 2000's. All mainstream listeners care about is a catchy beat. Punk singers write and sing with passion, with meaning."

"That's bold of you to assume."

"You can't tell me it's not true though." Jeannie smirks.

I take time to think for a moment back to all the music I used to listen to when I was a teen. Pop Punk and such. Now that I think about it, everyone was really open about their feelings. It was very different. Quite cool actually.

Just as I go to answer Jeannie, the beat drops in the song they're playing across the way and my phone comes crashing down on to the table due to the vibrations. I vastly pick up my phone, frustrated.

"Are you ok?" Jeannie begins. "Is that your next door neighbor and his band? Holy shit, they're playing loudly..."

"Can I call you back?" I ask shortly. Before she can answer I hang up and throw my phone on the couch, storming towards my door.

I can't believe I'm walking out of my apartment like this.

I'm in a light pink nightgown with spaghetti straps and white lace trim around the deep neckline.

The nightgown falls *way* above my knees and I have a messy bun on top of my head. I spray on some *Dior* perfume before I go out the door. (I have to have *some* dignity.)

I make sure to check if anyone is hanging out in the hallway and when I see no one isn't, I sprint across the way.

I indignantly bang on the door with the palm of my hand, being careful not to break a nail.

When no one answers, I rip off the colorful 'Do Not Disturb' sign Atticus always has on his door and start to kick the door, slamming my hand on it at the same time. I feel the song just gets louder and louder. How is no one else complaining?

"Atticus," I scream. "open the door!" The song gives off somewhat of a freeing feeling. It's definitely pop punk, but not heavy.

It has one of those beats where everything is cohesive and it all goes together. It sounds like one of those songs that make you want to live forever. Maybe I would like it if it wasn't so damn loud and interrupting me and Jeannie trying to get work done.

"Atti—" As I hit the door for about the seven-hundrereth time, it finally swings open, causing me to fall forward a bit. I catch myself as the music comes to an abrupt halt. (Thank God.)

Atticus stands in front of me with his long sleeved black shirt, blue jeans, and black beanie. He has a lot of silver chains around his neck and one silver earring dangling from his right ear.

He is looking down at me and his doe brown eyes are wide with a slight "Innocent" smirk on his face as if he has no clue why I'm standing in front of his apartment.

He looks me up and down and quirks up an eyebrow, his smirk becoming even more prominent in a cocky sort of way.

I cross my arms in front of my chest self consciously but still manage to hold my head up high. Damn! I should have gotten a robe, why didn't I get a robe...

"Can you *please* play a little quieter? I'm trying to work." I almost plead.

Atticus looks at me, squinting his eyes and tilting his head.

I could tell he wants to make a comment about what I'm wearing so badly, it's eating him alive. The question is, is it good or bad what he's thinking? What is he thinking? Why do I care? Out of all the people in the world, why do I care what *Atticus* thinks about how I look in my little nightgown? Seriously.

"Oh... sure." He nods his head and looks at Dallon and Finnick behind him who are watching intently. Well that was easier than I thought!

"Thank you." I sigh in relief.

"What are you working on?" Asks Finnick. "Something important I bet." He smiles and it warms my heart. He's so adorable. Atticus is lucky he has him, but I can't help but try to cover myself out of embarrassment feeling quite exposed.

"Oh It's some collaboration article I'm doing with my friend. It's going to be huge. Well, hopefully." I smile, looking past Atticus.

"That's right, Atticus said you were a journalist." Dallon states and nods. Ah, so the mute *can* talk.

"What kind of journalist?" Asks Finnick.

"She's a fashion journalist." Atticus answers for me shortly. I glare at him then smile kindly at the boys.

"I'm a fashion journalist." I answer now for myself. "At *DuVull and Co.*"

"Yeah that's wonderful," nods Atticus hastily. "I'll walk you out…" he grabs both my shoulders and tries to turn me back towards my door.

"Atticus, aren't you going to offer her a drink?" Dallon asks.

"Yeah. Come on, where's your manners?" Finnick looks at Atticus wide-eyed.

"Where's your head?"

"In the clouds." I answer for him as he did for me. Atticus looks at me with mock offence.

"My head is very down to earth, thank you very much." He scoffs and Finnick gives an exasperated laugh, doing the ba-dum-tss sound on his drums. I can't help but snort.

Atticus gives a little chuckle at my snort, so I stop laughing and swat him on his arm, prompting him to stick his tongue out at me.

"Nice pajamas." Atticus smirks arrogantly. I just scowl and cross my arms across my chest even tighter.

"Nice beanie. Do you ever take those silver chains off or are they glued to your body?"

"I want to live life with heavy emo vibes." He retorts and I roll my eyes.

"Oh please," I hear Finnick in the background. "Poppy, why don't you come in for a little while. Atticus, are you really going to let her stand in the hallway and not invite her in? She's out here in a nightgown. Don't be an ass. Invite her in, give her a blanket and make a coffee."

"Would you like to come in?" He asks with a sarcastic smile but I'm too focused on the invisible lightbulb that went off on the top of my head to make a snarky comment.

"N-no, I… um… I have work to do." I answer and swallow thickly.

How have I been so blind? I've been racking my brain for weeks on how I can interview a normal person who is into pop punk. Someone who embodies that type of…well, that type of vibe.

Who embodies that punk vibe more than Atticus! No one! The answer is no one! I can study his band. It's perfect, it's absolutely fab! It's genius!

How could I not have realised it sooner!

All of a sudden I feel a huge pit in my stomach. I don't know why. It's probably because the idea is so good, or I'm just nervous that

Atticus might say no to my idea. Which, he probably won't because he is extremely vain and being in one of the most prestigious fashion and lifestyle magazines would do him and his band wonders. It's a win win really!

"You good?" A sudden worried expression forms on Atticus's face. "You just got like, really pale. Why don't you come sit..." why did he get worried all of the sudden? His facial expression just went from joking and annoying to worried and paranoid. As if he did something wrong.

"I'm fine." I assure. I try to mask the nervous shake in my voice but he could probably tell I'm deep in thought. "I gotta go." Is all I say as I sprint back into my apartment.

I could tell his eyes are on me the whole time, an amused smile on his face as I hurriedly open my door, give him a kind smile, and lock the two locks behind me hastily.

I hop on the couch and video chat Jeannie once again. When her face pops up on the screen I don't even give her a moment to speak.

"I got it! I have the most fab idea!"

CHAPTER ELEVEN
A blooming Lilly

"So, your genius idea that you just *had* to have a little meeting for is to reel in your hot, emo neighbor to help you with your article?" Riley ponders and sits slumped on one of Jane's comfy, white, leather couches in her office.

"It's smart," Jeannie retorts. "he's obviously not the brightest, but if he's smart business wise, he'll snatch this opportunity up. It promotes him and his music."

"I didn't say it wasn't smart," Riley lifts one of his bushy brows. "I'm no journalist, but *how* are we going to reel him in? That's my issue"

I rack my brain wondering how I might pitch this idea to Atticus. It makes me quite nervous actually. What should I do? What should I say?

Jane sits in her rolly chair behind her desk and I could tell she's pondering over this idea as well. She has her reading glasses on and her long, black hair is in the world's most professional looking ponytail.

"Well," begins Riley with a tad bit of laughter. "there's always one thing that works…"

"No Riley. I'm not a prostitute." I finish before he can say anything else.

"It would work!" He retorts.

"At times." Jane chimes in.

"No, the both of you! I'm not doing…that."

"Yeah, no…" begins Jeannie. "Poppy's not seducing Atticus. Isn't prostatution illegal?"

"Is it really?" Squints Riley.

"Only if you get caught." Shrugs Jane.

"Ok…" I interrupt once again. "Ms. DuVull, what do you think?" I turn to her.

"About prostitution?"

"No! My idea about Atticus!" I cry.

"Oh, I think it's wonderful. Can you pull it off though? You see, I know you can pull this article off... but do *you* believe you can?"

"I don't know..."

"Now, there's your problem, Poppyseed. Have some self confidence, why don't you?" Jane throws her hands up in the air and Jeannie nods in agreement.

I feel I hear that from everyone. Tiff, Jane, my parents, everyone. It's not like self confidence grows on trees, if it did, I would've picked some!

"I--I think I'll be ok." I manage.

"You think?" Jane inquires.

"I know." I sigh. I don't *know* but that's besides the point!

Jane screws up her face and nods her head, deep in thought.

"You're smart, you're persuasive, you're beautiful. You know what you're doing. You have been in this game for a while now, how many articles have you written? You know the drill, Poppy. You get the truth and nothing but the truth. If this neighbor of yours is going to give us the truth about pop punk fashion and culture and make me money while doing it, you better reel him in. He'll say yes if he has at least half a brain."

"He'll say yes." States Jeannie crossing her arms sitting next to Riley who is rubbing his temples. "Once again, why would he pass up the opportunity to promote himself in one of the biggest magazines in the world--"

"Ms. DuVull, I apologize for interrupting but they need you down in photography." Isla walks in and states huffing and puffing.

She's in a huge, black fur coat almost as big as her. Her hair is on both sides of her with a gold headband and matching gold pants. Her boots are up to her knees and they are leather with silver spikes all over them.

"Who asked?" Jane sighs.

"I don't know," Isla replies annoyed. "I don't pay attention to photography. That's not my job. Whoever it was said they called Poppy, but," she shoots me a glare. "she didn't answer her phone." Oh, crap! The phone! We really need to invest in walkie talkies or something...

"Poppy has more important business to discuss right now." Chimes in Jeannie.

"Yes," agrees Jane. "we are in the middle of a very important conversation, but photography calls." Jane gets up and strides towards the door but not long after, turns her attention back towards me, Jeannie, and Riley.

"We will finish this discussion later." And like that, she's off. It's just me, Jeannie, Riley, and Isla left in the room now.

Isla's arms are crossed and she's glaring at all three of us. I make contact with her round, green eyes and there is this little flicker in them. They grow soft for a moment, she grows soft, but it doesn't last a while because she quite literally shakes her head and snaps back to the position she was in before.

"Aren't you Jane's assistant as well as a journalist?" She hisses.

"Y--Yes. I'm sorry, I didn't mean to cause you any trouble. We were just talking about my--"

"Ah yes, your article. I'm well aware." Proclaims Isla. I'm almost stunned. I'm speechless. I don't know what to say to her.

"Ok now that we have all of this sorted out, why don't you get back to work?" Riley sasses.

She squints her eyes at him and gives an exasperated sigh, like a five year old whose mother wouldn't buy her the toy she wanted. Why is she being such a *bitch?*

"Don't you have a yoga class to drive Jane to?" Isla snaps at Riley.

"Don't you have a mideocar article to write?" Snaps Riley right back.

"I wouldn't mess with me." Isla warns.

"Or what?" Jeannie laughs. I just stay quiet, looking between them frantically.

"Or you won't like what will happen next."

"Which is?" Riley laughs. Isla is just scowling.

"Why are you being so mean?" Is all I ask. It is all I could manage to get out. I don't understand why she's picking a fight with us. "We didn't do anything to you."

I see a flicker in Isla's eyes just like what happened before. As if she's just been inflicted with pain, her whole demeanor changes and her eyes grow soft.

"Don't be so naive, Poppy." Is all she says, saddened and avoiding looking me in the eyes. "It won't get you anywhere." And like that, she struts out of the room.

Riley turns to me and Jeannie with a stunned look on his face.

"What the living hell was that about?" He scoffs.

"Princess was just upset she became the errand girl for Jane. God forbid she helps anyone but herself." Jeannie rolls her eyes.

"Do you think we'll get in trouble? Do you think she'll report us? We were so nice, I don't understand--" I begin panicking.

"She's not reporting anyone because she knows no one will be on her side. Honestly, you really think Jane will take her side over yours?" Jeannie interrupts, rubbing my shoulder soothingly.

"Maybe."

"No. You're Jane's right hand woman. You can't even escape being her assistant, you really think she's going to fire you?"

"But..." I sigh. "but we were so nice." Riley and Jeannie both raise an eyebrow and smirk. "I was so nice." I correct.

"This is what happens when you give people the benefit of the doubt, Poppy." Riley begins. "somehow they'll come up with a way to disappoint you."

"Shut up!" Jeannie pushes him where he sits and turns to me. "Just be careful, that's all. She's just jealous cause you got the promotion in the bag and she has no chance." She wraps her arms around me and holds me to her tall frame. Jeannie's hugs are just the best.

"I suppose." I sigh.

I sashay happily down the street towards the transit. In my hand I'm holding two shiny, new *Saks Fifth Avenue* bags. In it, a new pair of Bastian leather white combat boots by *Micheal Kors*. Perfect for the chilly winter months! In the other bag is the cute little beauty basket I got for spending, well, well spending... you know what, it's not important how much I spent!

What matters is I got nice, sturdy, fashionable boots to last me the winter. And next winter, and the one after that. Who knows, it might last me the rest of my life! I internally pat myself on the back for my investment.

I'm feeling *so* chic today!

I'm wearing a straight denim skirt with a cotton white shirt tucked into it. With it I paired a light blue, short fur coat. The coat and denim skirt are two different shades of blue, but they flow so cohesively, so perfectly. It's just so fab!

I'm also in my *Alexander Wang* white beret placed on top of my straightened long hair. Headpieces are very important you know.

As I hop on the transit, I move my bags so a family could sit next to me. It's a mother, father, and a little girl no more than six.

The little girl with the long, thin, blonde locks plops herself down on the cold seat next to me. She's in a cute little red dress, with long sleeves, stockings and black little combat boots.

The mother is in a sweater almost identical to the little girl's dress and the father is in a suit and tie. Red as well.

The little girl has glasses that wrap around her face and under her hair. I look down at her and realize she's staring at me in awe.

Her parents are fighting about something. I try to grasp some of the conversation. 'She has nowhere else to go...' 'But, Lilly must be our priority...' 'She is, but we need to help out some family... She will only be moving in with us for a little while...'

"I like your dress." I say to the little girl. "Very festive."

"Thanks," she says in a very low voice. Her parents get louder.

"Where did you get it from?"

"I dunno." She shrugs. "*The Gap.*"

"I like *The Gap!*" I gasp. "They have nice jeans." The little girl's face scrunches up against her glasses and she starts to giggle. Her parents just get louder and louder.

I ponder over something else to quickly ask her. I would want someone to talk to me if I was on a bus and my parents were loudly arguing. Especially if I was young and tiny. I wouldn't want to hear it.

"What's in your bag?" She asks, pointing at my shiny, new *Sak's* bag.

"Oh," I say, happily taking out the boots and showing her them in their shiny, black box. "They're combat boots. For the Winter." She looks at them, and I could practically see her bright blue eyes twinkle.

"Like mine." She says happily.

"Just like yours." I respond with a smile and nod. I put them away and back into their bag. "What's your name?"

"Lilly." She responds with a matter of factly nod. "What's yours?"

"Poppy."

"That's a pretty name." She says and looks down at her legs, swinging back and forth.

"Yours is prettier." I say sweetly.

"You think?" Lilly asks.

"I know." I responded.

"I can't take it anymore!" The mother screams "She is my niece, she is moving in and that's final!" She looks manic, and like she hasn't slept in days.

"Where are you from?" I turn the little girl's attention to me once again.

"Jersey." She says with a nod.

"Oh, Jersey's so pretty." I begin. "So much water. Do you live by the water?" She nods her head, a big smile on her face.

"We went to see a Broadway show. Now we are going to see my Grandma in Brooklyn." The way she says Brooklyn is too cute.

"Oh how lovely!" I clap my hands. "You know, I live in Brooklyn."

"You do?"

"I do!"

"You're pretty." She sighs out suddenly. And like that, I pause.

"You're prettier." I say in a gentle voice.

"You think?"

"I know." And like that the bus stops, and I'm in Brooklyn. "This is my stop." I say happily and get up.

"The next stop is ours." Says Lilly. Her parents stopped fighting and now they are just staring at the both of us, strangely.

I desperately want to hug Lilly and tell her it's all going to be ok, and that whatever is going on in her family, she still will be top priority. Even if it might not be true, sometimes someone needs a little reassurance. Or hope.

I wish to tell her the world will keep turning, and she will come out on top, like an angel in the myths of all this drama within her family. But I can't, because I don't know this girl like that. I don't know her at all. But I feel as if I do. Is that crazy?

The best I can do is look down at her and throw her a reassuring wink. So I do.

Lilly's mom looks at me, tears in her eyes, and a quivering smile on her face. I give her the same kind smile. Lilly's Father just stood off to the side, loathing.

"Well... have a lovely day." I say and offer one last smile. I get off the bus and exhale a deep breath.

As I start to enter one of the rougher areas of Brooklyn, I hold more of a grip on my bags. Force of habit, I suppose. Just being cautious.

No one looks at me, and I don't look at anybody. Everyone in Brooklyn picks their battles carefully. You smile at someone in the street if you feel like it. If someone looks suspicious, you keep your head up and don't make eye-contact. Street smarts. As I said before, something I learned very young from my parents.

My parents are very nice people until you make their horns come out. Once you do that, those horns don't go back in. I suppose that's how I am. Do I want to be like that though, that's the question.

I wish I could smile and wave and make everyone happy, and keep everyone in my life. But I can't. No matter how hard I try I will never please everyone. I can't please my mom and dad without disappointing Ms. DuVull, I can't get along with my sister, and I just can't make Liam love me.

No matter my efforts, no matter my kindness, no matter all the love I managed to pull from the deep depths of my heart to give him, it was just not enough. It never is. For anyone.

Everyone just leaves. I mean, I can't make them stay if they don't want to, but sometimes I feel as if I have a virus no one wants to be around. Very few people stay in your life and it's hard to grasp sometimes. I'm thankful for who I have though of course.

Everyone deserves someone to look at them as if they're a new pair of *Louis Vuitton* pumps. As human beings we all want to be the reason someone says 'Ah, you make me feel good. You actually make me feel great. You make me feel absolutely fab! I love you, that's why I deal with your quirks. You are the reason I do the things I do. It is because of you.'

I don't think anyone's ever seen me like that. Not even Liam. And to be quite honest, I don't know if I want a person to look at me like that yet. Too much pressure! As I said, you can't please everyone. I'm already trying to please too many people as it is.

Oh, who am I kidding! Of course I want someone to feel that way about me!

"Sir, you are going to have to move." I snap out of my daze and see some sort of construction going on in front of me. It looks like they are trying to knock down some store.

"Pry my hot, dead body from it then." I hear a raspy, male voice say. Oh… oh no. I know that voice anywhere. *Shit.*

Without even thinking, I walk around the construction site and see Atticus standing in front of the building.

God, what has he gotten himself into this time?

CHAPTER TWELVE
Protests and Pizza

Atticus has a black and white, long sleeved, striped shirt and a black, short sleeved vest on. It looks like a bullet proof vest with a bunch of pockets. Is that a new trend?

He has one silver chain that's down to his stomach that's a cross, one that lays in the middle of his chest that's a lock, and a couple of chains all in one necklace forming somewhat of a choker. Of course paired with skinny black jeans.

He locks eyes with me from behind the construction guys and gives me a manic, pleading look.

"Excuse me sir," I begin and the construction men turn their attention to me. "what are you doing?"

"We are trying to knock down this building, but this asshole won't let us." One of them bark.

"It's in my constitutional rights to fight tooth and nail." Atticus retorts.

"It is in your constitutional rights to shut the hell up."

"Ok," I begin completely and utterly confused. "I'm sorry Atticus, my hands are tied. I don't know if you have a history with this place, but they're taking it down. Let's go back home. I'll make you a hot cup of coffee or something." And just as those words come out of my mouth, I realize how they sound and I cringe.

The construction workers turn to me skeptically.

"We live in the same apartment building." I quickly state. They need to mind their own business!

"Sure..." one of the construction workers hum.

This reminds me too much of when my parents and sister used to drag me to protests. They still try to.

"Atty, my boy, please go. They will call the cops if you don't." My eyes meet with a stressed out, older man with sprinkled grey hair and olive toned skin. It is then I realize this building must be his. What even is this place? I look up to see a big sign that says, *Brooklyn Record.*

I've passed this place so many times, not even knowing what it was.

"No," Atticus starts to shout. "screw these construction guys and screw Brooklyn! They're not shutting you down, Mr. Davis. I won't let them!"

I see it in his eyes, he's getting upset as he holds onto the older man's arm. I've never seen Atticus like this before.

"Excuse me," I push through the construction workers and reach Atticus and the man he calls Mr. Davis. "Atticus--"

"Poppy, please..." he turns to me, a sudden desperate look on his face. "you need to help me."

"Atticus," I give a stressed laugh. "these men are doing their job. This is illegal! You'll go to jail!"

"Not like it's something that's never happened before, am I right?" He gives a little laugh and goes to highfive Mr. Davis. Mr. Davis just shakes his head disapprovingly and Atticus brings his attention back to me, putting his hand down.

"Oh by the way, Poppy, Mr. Davis. Mr. Davis, Poppy." I give a kind smile to the older man and he gives one back. "This is not how I would have chosen to introduce you two, but--"

"You truly are a piece of work Atticus Mckeen," I begin to walk away. "It was very nice meeting you, Mr. Davis, but I'm sorry I can't stay. I hope Finnick or Dallon bail you out..." Just then I feel Atticus grip my hand.

I turn to look at him with annoyance until I see a face Atticus has never worn before, genuine desperation, genuine worry.

"Poppy, please. I'm begging you to help me. And I don't beg people. *Ever.*"

I give a long sigh and look into the older man's eyes.

He seems to be staying out of it until he says, "Atty is very persuasive. He's a charmer." I can't help but give a stressed chuckle and nod my head.

"I'll never bother you ever again."

`"That's not true."

"I will try to play with the band a little more quietly. You won't even hear us."

"Uh, that's false."

"Please…" not only does Atticus's eyes melt a part of my heart right now but also something occurs to me. If I do this for him, do you think he would help me with my article?

I sigh in surrender.

"Ok, but--"

"We prevail!" Atticus shouts as he picks me up from behind.

"Atticus!" I scream. "Put me down!"

"Oh, you have got to be kidding me." One of the construction workers sighs. "Listen, move and no one gets hurt."

"Please sir, I'll get them away, just give me a couple of moments." Mr. Davis stutters.

"I'm not leaving." Atticus says surly.

"You will go to jail." Says the construction worker.

"I'm supposed to be scared?" He starts to mock and puts me down. "'Oh, oh… jail! I'm horrified.'" He says sarcastically, with the confidence of a man who's been to jail before.

"You should be!" I shout.

"Atticus, please…" Mr. Davis begs.

"Tearing down buildings, eviction notices, it's just… it's just cultural hold back." Atticus retorts. I lean in towards his ear.

"Do you know what that means?"

"Not a clue."

"Ok," I turn towards the group of construction men who are absolutely seething now. "what I think Atticus is trying to say is, maybe we could work something out…"

"It's no use, hon." Mr. Davis touches my hand. "They are evicting me. Shutting me down. I have no choice. I never have a say in anything anymore." And when Mr. Davis says that, something inside of me boils.

The Paxton inside me finally reaches the surface. He doesn't want to leave but he has too. They are using his age and frailness against him. How could they?

"Who are you working for?" I ask the men.

"Uh, a construction company." Another one answers shortly.

"I wouldn't recommend being a smartass, sir. I asked who you work for?" I get a kick of confidence. Learned this trick from my parents. Always set your dominance in a protest.

"Is she kidding me?" One of them murmurs. "Who are you?"

"She's Poppy-freaking-Paxton." Atticus retorts, stepping in front of me. "Journalist, fashion expert, certified badass."

"Move out of the way." Says the man.

"No." Atticus looks him in the eye stubbornly.

"Move, asshole!"

"No, asshole!" One guy gets into the big bulldozer in front of the building and I watch as Atticus gets down on the rough concrete sidewalk. He lays there. Just lay there. Me and Mr. Davis just look at him in awe.

"You wanna knock down the building? You'll knock it down with me underneath!" All the men give a collective tired sigh and so do I.

"Atticus, please get up. I will be fine." Mr. Davis sighs, obviously tired.

All of a sudden a bright yellow taxi rolls up to the curb.

"Go." Atticus says to Mr. Davis. "I called it for you."

"Not without you and Poppy." He says. I grab Mr. Davis by the hand and smile.

"Mr. Davis, I don't know what's going to happen, but you must leave. Let Atticus do this for you. I won't let him do anything *too* stupid." Mr. Davis looks at me, the worried expression on his face fading.

"He's lucky to have you. I didn't know Atty had such a great girlfriend. He doesn't tell me anything. He's been so good lately too. It's you. I'm certain." And with a kiss on the hand he hops into the taxi and it leaves, but not without a lot of hesitation.

'Girlfriend?' I want to shout. Oh god, is that what he thinks? Who else thinks that? I suddenly feel Atticus's hands begin to pull me down on the concrete with him.

"No, this is an Alice *and Olivia* skirt!" I cry.

"Who's *Alice and Olivia?*" Asks Atticus and I give a shocked gasp. "Just get down, Patricia!" He says and pulls me down onto the concrete against my better judgment.

And then here we are. Just laying on the street. I almost want to cry. I might just do that.

Why am I doing this! Do you know how many feet are on this exact spot every single day? How many germs are in this one area? And I have to lay my *Sak's* bags down too? *Alice and Olivia* are quaking.

"Oh, what am I doing?" I whisper quietly to myself, not realizing I'm speaking it out loud.

"Standing up against the unjust and unfair rules Brooklyn has forced upon us." Atticus says matter of factly.

"You sound like my parents."

"Your parents must be really dope then."

"Not really." I finally turn to look at Atticus only to realize he's looking at me already.

He has a look of confidence on his face, but I could tell very well it's a mask. He's terrified. But I bet Atticus is just like Liam. Like any man. Terrified, absolutely terrified to admit they are scared of something.

He gives a tiny eyebrow raise and smiles as he looks up at the light blue sky with clouds that almost look like it's just mere scenery for a movie.

"So," he begins. "what about some *Uno's* after this. Are you hungry? I'm hungry. I could go for some pizza right about now. Oh, or one of those appetizer platters."

I just give a laugh, that turns into a couple of snorts and put my hands over my face to block the sun, but also because I'm laughing and I don't want the workers over there to think we're crazy. Oh who am I kidding, they already probably thought we were crazy the minute we started to lay on our backs on the concrete with a bunch of big men driving big machines above us. Maybe we are.

Atticus turns to me but then continues to laugh harder as I throw my hands over my face.

He's doing this certain smile when he looks up. The smile where you know it's genuine.

His dimples are up to his ears and his eyes are all squinted and we both just look up at the sky and laugh. It wasn't that much of a funny joke, and I'm pretty sure he was serious, but we just laugh.

I hear the stopping of the machines above us and take a sigh of relief.

"We did it!" Atticus laughs in awe. "We actually did it." He quickly gets up and puts out his hand to help me up.

I dust off my skirt as Atticus picks up and dusts off the studded beret that fell off my head onto the concrete while I was laying down. He also picks up my *Sak's* bags and I cling it to my chest like it was my lost child.

I give Atticus a polite thank you and put the beret back on my head.

"Yes, two kids. Maybe about... about twenty-something? I don't know! Just come here as soon as you can." I hear one worker say. Oh... oh no. Oh no.

I look towards Atticus and see the defeated look on his face. He looks as if he might cry.

His blonde hair in front of his face, messy and disheveled like he just ran a marathon. I can't help the little pang I feel in my heart for him. He looks like a lost puppy staring at the workers. He's breathing heavily and his eyebrows are furrowed together.

"Atticus..." I begin to panic. The workers give me and Atticus smirk smiles and shrugs. The best I could do is scowl at them. "I think we should leave. They called the cops now. I really don't want to be chased down by the Brooklyn police department. Or any police department for that matter." I give a stressed chuckle. Wow, that's something I thought I would never say.

"No... no! They can't..." Atticus shoos. "Mr. Davis is a good man. He's done nothing but better Brooklyn. This is Brooklyn's last record shop. Please..." And the minute Atticus says that, something clicks in my brain that didn't click before.

This is where Atticus works. This is his job. I remember him telling me he worked at a record shop. He just lost his job. God, I'm such an *idiot*.

"Sorry, we're just here to do our job." Says the one construction worker that's been speaking for the rest. I start to hear the loud sirens of a cop car.

"Atticus, please." I grab his hand desperately. "We got to go." I turn to the workers.

"We'll leave, we'll leave, ok! We're going! Atticus come on!" I watch as Atticus looks up at the building one last time and nods his head, no words coming out of his mouth.

I take off my heels. I definitely can't run in those pumps. Atticus grabs them and puts them in his one hand as he grabs my free one with his.

As we hear the sirens inch closer, Atticus yanks my arm so we could run down the blocks even faster. I don't even care if I'm not wearing any shoes, I just care about getting away from these cops.

People don't even pass us a glance. Cop cars, and people running from them is a normal Monday afternoon in Brooklyn. Especially the part of Brooklyn we're in.

As the sirens become out of reach and can't be heard anymore, Atticus pulls the both of us into an alley where we could take a breath.

We're about two blocks away from the apartment building and it's like I could finally manage to relax. I lean on the brick wall of one of the buildings we're in between, and Atticus leans on the one across from me.

We're so close, our chests are practically touching and I could feel his breath against my skin.

We both just stand there quietly for a moment trying to catch our breaths. We had to have run at least eight blocks.

"So..." he begins. "are you still down for pizza?"

CHAPTER THIRTEEN
Pizza and Propositions

I stir the sugar in the steaming hot coffee I just made. It warms up my hands and in return, warms up my whole body.

I look up and see Atticus sitting on my couch and studying my every move, walking over to where he sits and handing him his coffee. Then I put the one I made for myself on the coffee table in front of us.

I sit on the spot next to him as he sips on the light coffee with lots of cream I just made for him. He looked like he needed a coffee, and I gladly offered to make him one. He just seems so… distraught. Seeing him like this brings a pang to my chest. I feel so horrible for him.

He has my little blanket wrapped around him that my great grandmother sewed together for me. He looked a bit chilly and, honestly, what's more comforting than a knitted blanket!

"Thank you." He rasps out.

"You're welcome." I nod my head and sip my coffee as well, the hot steam hitting my face immediately.

"I ordered pizza." I pipe up.

"I heard. Where'd you order it from?"

"*Pronto's.*"

"Not *Uno's?*"

I just chuckle and shake my head. There is a beat of silence then Atticus turns to me, a look of curiosity in his light brown eyes as they squint.

"Poppy?" He begins carefully then shakes his head. "Never mind."

"No," I look back at him and sigh. "you can't do that. I hate when people do that. Just say what you were going to say."

"You take life very seriously, don't you." He says more as a statement than a question. It takes me by surprise.

"What I have to take seriously." I answer honestly. "I definitely don't take *everything* seriously."

"What are you talking about, you have your whole life mapped out for you in a binder."

"I did." I mutter, looking away, not in the mood for this conversation.

"Sometimes people don't have to have their whole life mapped out in front of them. Sometimes you have to just live in the moment and know your next move. It's a strategy. Like a board game or something." He says.

I never thought of it that way, nor was I brought up to think of life that way. I suppose he has a point though.

Atticus gets up and starts to walk towards the kitchen counter.

"Who's this?"

"Who's who?" I get up from my spot on the couch and walk to where he stands. He's holding the picture of me and Liam in his hands.

"My ex." I say bluntly, sipping my coffee.

He tilts his head and just stares at it. After all these months of knowing Atticus, telling him about Liam never crossed my mind. He never asked and honestly wasn't planning on telling him? It's kind of irrelevant to him, isn't it?

"Why do you still have a picture of him?"

"Because I want to." I retort a bit shrill. I have every right to be! Who does he think he is, walking into my apartment and asking all these questions? Well he has a right of course, but it's making me feel some type of way.

"Why'd you break up?" He still has the picture in his hands.

"We broke up because he didn't know how to handle his emotions." I say quickly and rip the framed photograph out of Atticus's hands, setting it back down on the counter. The little poloroid, stupid thing it is. I haven't paid attention to that picture in a while.

I don't know who that girl is in that picture, I really don't. Isn't it funny how much we could change in such a short amount of time.

"When things got weird or rough, he would just shut me out, or leave, or… I don't know. It's none of your business!" I shout, flustered.

"Damn," begins Atticus. "I'm sorry."

"'Damn. All you can say is 'Damn'? Wow, your favorite record store, or whatever it is, got bulldozed today as I tried to help you save it and we ran from the cops. Damn. You just lost your job. Damn. Show some emotion, why don't you?" I snap.

Atticus slaps his hands on the sides of his legs and scoffs.

"What do you want me to say?" He asks, voice rising to a squeak.

"Don't say anything!" I yell back. "I let you into my house, I give you a blanket, I make you coffee, and *then* you think you have the *right* to question me about my ex boyfriend?"

"Well, with all due respect Poppy, I was under the impression that we were *friends* and friends ask each other things."

"Oh ok," I begin. "so tell me Atticus, you once told me committed relationships are hard for you and you refuse to be in one. Why is that?" I use my fist as a fake microphone and put it up to his lips.

He takes my wrist, as if it was an actual mic stand, leaning in trying to compress a laugh as I'm dead serious. His lips graze against my knuckles and it makes me shutter, chills consuming me.

"My parents have been divorced since I was six months old, my mom left me and my dad before I could even speak. Never met her... that's about it."

"I'm sorry." I say, my stern exterior slowly fading.

"It's fine. Doesn't bother me all that much." He pauses then begins. "And *Brooklyn Record* was the first place I ever performed. I was sixteen. For some apparent reason Mr. Davis took a chance on me. He saw potential in this kid who had no plan for his life, no job, and a guitar. He let me perform every single Tuesday. Payed me one hundred a week. More than he paid his damn self. And that was just for gigs, not even the register or nothing. It helped my dad pay for the bills because he would spend his money at the bar. I still performed there even when me, Dallon and Finnick got together. I could care less about losing the Job, I care about Mr. Davis. He told me the city was shutting him down for no apparent reason that we know of. I guess he wasn't making enough money or something. I couldn't let that happen. He did so much for me, and in return, I got the cops called on me and I dragged you into it. And I shouldn't have, and I'm sorry." He purses his lips together. "You know, I always seem to be a few minutes late to the party. These *Vans* don't take me far," he motions towards his sneakers. "always late." He looks up at me after he swallows deeply and gives a chuckle.

"I'm sorry." Is all I can manage to say once again. My hands are just on my sides and I stare up at him, wide eyed. God, now I feel like a piece of shit!

"Nah." He pulls a face and shrugs. "I dragged you into this. Damn it!" He runs his hands through his hair.

"Poppy, I could have gotten you arrested! I...I don't know what I was thinking. If we got arrested--"

"Hey," I begin in a calming whisper. "I was the one that decided to protest with you. It was up to me and my free will. The Paxton jeans finally kicked in." I giggle. "My parents and my sister are always protesting something. But if I didn't want to help you, I sure as hell wouldn't have. But I did and I don't regret it." I say surly.

Atticus then looks back down at me, eyes as big as saucers.

"It was actually kind of fun." I giggle.

He smiles, although I could tell he's still upset with himself.

"I tend to have that effect on people." He says smugly and I laugh.

"And his name was Liam."

"What?"

"My ex," I begin. "His name was Liam. And I met him in school. I was in love with him, I still am in love with him, but it was never good enough. One night, a couple of months ago, we got into a fight and he told me no one wants to be my friend because I'm a priss and no one wants to deal with someone like me. And then he left. You can't expect a snake to be a sheep, huh." I take a deep sigh and look up to see Atticus's expression.

I haven't told that story in months. It still hurts. Will it always? I sure hope not.

Atticus is completely speechless, his lips parted. He just shakes his head and his eyes are squinted in disbelief. He almost looks offended.

"You know that's not true right, Poppy?" He begins. "You do have friends. You have me."

"I know." I shake my head. "But if a person doesn't mean what they say..." and to my dismay I feel a tear escape my eye. "then why say it?"

Atticus is just watching me and his face says it all. I can't tell what he's thinking as I stand here like a fool, but he just looks at me with this pitying look in his eyes. I *hate* when people pity me. I don't need to be pitied.

I just watch as he opens his arms and, without warning, embraces me in a hug.

I don't even think twice about wrapping my arms around him and burying my face in his shirt and gripping on to it. I just sniffle into it. I'm most likely ruining it, but I can't help it. I feel like I haven't got a hug in such a long time. Not even by my parents. Not that they mean not to hug me. I think that everyone's just a little bit too busy in their own world.

He's warm, and smells nice. There is no way to describe the scent, it just smells like Atticus. His grip on me is tight. It's not too gentle, it's one of those good, hardy hugs that hold meaning.

"I'll buy you a new shirt." Is all that comes out of my mouth as I let go of him, along with a bunch of little sniffles. He gives a loud genuine laugh like he did when we were protesting. He props his huge hand on top of my tiny head.

"Don't worry about it," he begins. "there's usually tears on my shirt anyway. Ya know, from my own mental breakdowns." I just roll my eyes as the doorbell rings. "Here," He begins, taking out his wallet and walking towards the door.

"Oh no," I begin. "I'll pay." I grab a twenty off the counter and wipe my tear stained eyes.

"Poppy, you laid in front of a building that was getting bulldozed for me. The least I could do is buy you pizza."

"That's not true! I ordered a rice ball special too."

"Shut up and let me buy the freaking dinner." He huffs and goes to open the door.

"You're so stubborn. It's awfully annoying." I scrunch up my nose.

"*I'm* stubborn? Telling you to put your money away is like taking a fish out of water and telling it to breathe."

"That doesn't even make any sense..." I think for a moment as Atticus opens the door. The delivery guy stands there, everything in his hand. As Atticus holds his arm out in front of me so I can't give the delivery guy the twenty I have.

"Thank you." Says the delivery guy taking his money and Atticus takes the food with one hand.

"Here's your tip!' I say reaching over Atticus's arm and handing the delivery man the twenty. He nods and happily takes it.

"No! Why! Give it back." Atticus practically squeals at me and the delivery man.

"Atticus, no." I state, sternly.

"Give the tip back."

The delivery man looks horrified. I shake my head 'no' behind Atticus as he yells at the delivery man.

"Give the twenty dollars back now…" He says singsongingly.

"No, it's yours. I'm sure you're a fabulous delivery guy. You deserve it."

"No, I bet you're a terrible delivery man and you don't deserve it, give her the money back."

He suddenly puts the food down on the tiny table next to the door, picks me up, and throws me over his shoulder.

"Atticus! Atticus Mckeen, you put me down right now!" All I could do is gasp. I'm shocked by the sudden and brash movement. I barely have time to think.

"Thank you." He says as I hear him take the twenty dollars back from the delivery guy.

I slap his back and kick my legs but he doesn't seem to be bothered.

I hear the door slam as I just continue to hit him. He finally throws me down onto the couch with a loud thud and he puts the twenty back in the exact spot it was in before.

"So," he begins, bringing the food on the coffee table and sitting next to where I am on the couch. "mind if I have half of your rice ball? I *did* pay for it after all." He smirks and I just scowl at him. I almost forgot about my article and the thought of it startles me and it makes me sad.

I don't want to disturb the peace between me and Atticus by asking him about the article but that's why I helped him with the protest, right? Is it? I don't really know anymore.

"Atticus," I begin and he looks up at me cutely, a mouth full of pizza. "I umm… I have a proposition for you…"

CHAPTER FOURTEEN

The Seven Deadly Sins In The Bible According to Men

(Darling, You've Already Committed Two Of Them.)

The next morning I run into work as if I'm being chased by a killer, with both mine and Jane's coffee in my hands. I finally get out of the elevator and make a beeline for my desk.

"I got him." I say out of breath, slamming my hands on my desk.

"You got him? Jeannie looks up with hopeful eyes.

"I got him." I say giddly.

"Did you take my advice?" Riley asks looking up from the book he's reading.

"No Riley, I did it the old fashioned way... I *asked*!" I mock him and gasp.

"As it should be." Jeannie swats Riley's crossed legs off her desk as I take a seat in mine.

"Both of you are no fun."

"How did you end up asking him?" Asks Jeannie just as Jane begins to walk towards us and out of her office.

"Here you go, Ms. DuVull," I give her the coffee that she gives me a down deposit of twenty dollars for every single week. "I'm sorry, I would have brought it to you sooner. I just had to tell Jeannie that I reeled in Atticus to help me with the article."

"Ah, I see..." Jane takes the coffee out of my hand with her newly manicured fingers and black, round sunglasses still on top of her head. "who's Atticus again?"

"The rocker guy that I decided I want to study so he could be the center of the article. You know, how a person like him sees things. Not that he's different from anyone else…" I begin to babble.

"He looks at the world from an angle." Nods Jeannie. "An interesting pop punk angle."

"Oh, that's right," nods Jane. "how exactly did we reel him in? For the love of god, did you take mine and Riley's advice?" She puts her hands on her hips and Riley throws his book down on the desk with a face practically screaming 'I told you so.'

"For the last time you two, I did not and *will not,* prostitute around to get someone to do an article with me."

"Did you mesmerize him with your beauty?" Asks Jane, swiping a piece of hair out of my face.

"No."

"Agree to go on a date with him?"

"No…"

"Do you owe him a favor?"

"No!"

"Well then, what the hell did you do?" Jane slaps her arms out.

"I asked him." I sigh, opening up my laptop.

"Well how? You just don't ask a person if you could do an article on them in one of the biggest lifestyle and fashion magazines in America without some pizazz, Poppyseed!"

"Well, that brings me to the shit show that happened to occur yesterday right after work."

"Oh?" Jeannie props up an eyebrow.

"Here we go." Riley sighs, shaking his blue hair out of his face.

"I have to pull up a chair for this." Jane pulls a chair from a random desk right next to mine.

"Ummm, Ms. DuVull, that's my chair." Says Ginger Lovet from the lifestyle department.

"Get another one." Jane barks, shrugging her off and sipping her coffee expectantly.

"To make a long story short, I'm walking home in one of the rougher areas and…"

"You got mugged?" Jane gasps.

"No, I saw Atticus outside of a record shop protesting."

"Why?" Jeannie asks and everyone leans in.

"Well, some construction company was about to demolish it and it's where he works. He also has a history with the really sweet older man who owns it. So the Paxton blood kicked in and.... I helped him."

"How so?" Asks Jeannie concerned.

"I protested with him. Basically we laid under a bulldozer until the cops were called on us."

"And then you kissed under the bulldozer?" Jane perks up.

"No!" I cry. "Then we ran from the cops."

"Jesus Christ, only you, I swear." Riley shakes his head in disbelief.

"I felt bad!" I retort. "He was so sad! I don't know what came over me."

"Yeah, and what happened afterwards?" Jeannie smirks.

"We went back to my apartment..." I can't even say the rest of my sentence because Jane gasps so loud everyone in the office turns to us.

"Get back to work." She hisses at all of them and like clock work, they get back to what they were doing.

"You took him into your apartment?" Riley whisper shouts.

"We live across from each other!"

"What did you do back in that apartment, *Poppy*?"

"We ordered pizza, *Riley*." I retort which just causes him to laugh even more.

"Please tell me you kissed at some point." Jane begs.

"No!" I practically scream. "Nothing like that happened."

"So, is that when you popped the question?" Jeannie asks.

"Yeah," I nod. "It was right after we had kind of a heart to heart."

"Oh my god." Riley gives an exasperated chuckle.

"About what?" Jeannie leans in even more.

"Liam..." I answer carefully.

"What!" Riley and Jeannie both blurt out.

"Who's Liam?" Jane asks out of the loop.

"My ex."

"The one that left after seven years?"

"Yeah..." I feel an ache in my chest when she says that. "but then I also realized how young and immature we were when we first got together. It should literally be illegal for any freshman to date." I sigh.

"Oh Poppyseed, you never talk about an ex with a potential love interest, dear!"

"He's definitely not a potential love interest--"

"Ok, let's hear Poppy out though please." Jeannie puts her hands up. "Did Atticus bring him up?"

"Yes, he picked up the picture of us and asked who it was."

"Oooooohhhh." All three of them speak at the same time.

"She probably got extremely defensive. It's her coping mechanism." Jane whispers to Jeannie and Riley but I can still hear her.

"Of course I got defensive!" I retort.

"I saw Poppy's hands flying everywhere through the glass windows of the office. What happened?" Arlo walks up to us with a big brown paper bag.

"You don't want to know." Riley states.

"Well I'm on break and I figured I'd bring my favorite people lunch from the bagel place down the street from my job." Arlo props the bag up between me and Jeannie's desk.

"Urgh, do you want to kill me." Jane sighs.

"That's the goal." Arlo jokes and kisses Riley on the top of his head. "Hello, Jane." He then goes to hug her.

"Hello my dear Arlo." She fixes his hair. "I suppose a half of a bagel won't kill me."

"I suppose." Arlo mimics her. "Jeannie." He greets Jeannie by putting his huge hand on top of her small head and shaking it.

"Ah, my favorite asshole." Jeannie smiles up at him.

"I'm offended." Riley mutters.

"And last but not least," Arlo reaches me, puts his arm over my head and kisses it. "my Pops." I cross my arms and slump in his embrace.

"Aw, what's up, cranky pants?" Arlo rubs my arm.

"We'll talk later." Riley says to him.

"Ah, gotcha." He nods.

"What did you do after this boy asked about Liam, babes?" Jane asks continuing the conversation, but I'm quite sure I want to talk about it anymore. I'm finding myself very confused all of the sudden, thinking back to the memory.

"Of course I freaked out on him. Why should he care? But then I realized I got out of line I suppose. He said that we were friends, and that he was just... curious. So I told him everything that happened between me and Liam and the next thing I know I'm in his arms crying." I say all of that a bit above a whisper.

"Once you cry to a guy, it's over." Jane quips. "He either sleeps with you and drops you, or you basically become his wife. Attached to your hips, you meet with parents, ectra, ectra." Jane sighs.

"I thought it was over when you let him into your apartment?" Riley quips.

"The both of you, stop it!" Arlo scolds them.

"Darling, you've already committed two out of the seven deadly sins according to the bible of a man." Jane says, knowingly.

"Oh my god, you're right! I'm such an idiot!" I cry, coming to realization.

"You're not an idiot, Poppy!" Jeannie insists while Riley mouths 'just a little bit' behind her and Arlo gives him a glare.

"I think you should get in touch with him and finally start this article." Riley nods.

"Yeah, and how do I initiate it?" I ask.

"You go with the flow and follow *his* lead." Riley states. "You are following his lifestyle and his fashion. You need to take a step back and let him teach you. I double dare you" Everyone looks at me with a knowing glare.

"What are you, ten?" Jeannie rolls her eyes at him.

"I could easily follow his lead and let loose a bit." I scoff. Jeannie tilts her head and raises an eyebrow and Riley mutters a 'Yeah, Alright.'

"Fine." I lean back into Arlo's arms, mine crossed. "I'll try my best. That's all I can do. All that matters is that we're going to have a fab article."

CHAPTER FIFTEEN
Cigarettes And Crush Syndrome

That next day I find myself fixing my outfit and straightening it out with bated breath.

I'm sporting my white, pleated tennis skirt that falls mid thigh and my matching white bodysuit.

I put my light pink, leather biker jacket over the bodysuit and paired it with my tall, Italian suede, *Christian Louboutin* boots I bought last season. They're pointed toe with leather pink soles. I feel like *such* a rocker.

I finished off the look with my double headband made out of oversized white pearls. Although I look fab, I feel unsure. I'm standing in front of Atticus's door swaying on the heels of my boots and twiddling with my fingers. After three minutes of standing in front of his door, I finally decide to knock on it, using the rusted gold doorknocker attached to every door in the building.

Why am I so nervous? Oh, only because this has the potential to be a groundbreaking article and it's all in my hands! Not to mention that Jeannie is counting on me and so is the whole state to *DuVull and Co.* Get it together Poppy!

I can make a run for it though if I wanted to...

Then the apartment door swings open, taking me out of my thoughts and there stands Atticus.

He's in a pair of skinny black jeans that has one silver chain dripping from the side of them. With it he has on a black, short sleeve button up dress shirt with a long sleeved white shirt underneath with what looks like pretend blood stains splattered all over it. (Or at least I hope it's pretend.) I almost want to grab for his arms and reassure myself it is in fact just a design.

I would definitely consider Atticus my friend now but if you want to know the truth, he still kind of intimidates me even though he's literally a giant teddy bear that dresses like an actual goth mob boss. I'm pretty positive Atticus wouldn't even hurt a fly.

"Pops!" He spreads his arms out in the doorway and has a huge smile on his face, his deep dimples burning a hole in his face almost looking like the Joker. It's the most charming smile I've ever laid eyes upon. Atticus sure is quite the charmer though.

"Hi!" I wave happily and wrap my arms around him. I can't help but smile even wider in his embrace. He gives hugs like no other.

"Well come on in, don't be shy." He begins as I walk into his apartment. It's messy and band equipment is set up right in the center of his living room. He shakes his hair when it falls over his eyes in dirty blonde, messy strands.

His kitchen is the only part of the house that is somewhat clean. It's the same layout of mine of course, but they are polar opposites in style. Kind of like me and Atticus.

He closes the door behind me and gestures towards the apartment.

"Uhhh, mi casa, you casa... or whatever the saying is." He chuckles. "Basically just make yourself at home."

"Thanks!" My eyes meet with the old looking, yellow couch that Atticus was helplessly trying to push into this very apartment when I first met him.

If you told me three months ago that I'd be doing a potentially groundbreaking article with the help of my emo neighbor I would probably tell you to seek help. Maybe I'm the one that needs to seek help though. It's so funny how time flies. It's funny how someone could just pop into your life and suddenly become such a crucial part of it. Not that Atticus is a *crucial* part of my life... but maybe he is right now.

I sit down on the old looking couch and cross one leg over the other.

"You remember that couch, don't ya?" Atticus smiles, walking over to me.

"In fact I do." I grin. "I still can't believe you got it in."

A couple of seconds of silence pass when I hear Atticus gasp beside me.

"Shit! I'm such a horrible host. Can I get you something to drink, to eat, anything else that people usually say..." he stutters frantically, heading towards the kitchen. It's then that I realize he's just as nervous as I am. This is silly. Why are we both so nervous?

It brings me comfort though in some weird way.

"No thank you." I giggle. "I'll be ok. And you're not a horrible host! Not at all--"

"Now what are you crazy kids doing in here?" I hear a familiar voice say from the hallway as Finnick and Dallon come walking into the living room.

"Hi!" I jump up from the couch and immediately go to hug Finnick.

"Hiya, Poppy." Finnick wraps his lanky arms around me. He's so adorable.

He has squared shaped glasses on right now. They shape his face nicely. I've never seen him with glasses before. They rest right above his silver nose ring and his curly black hair is scattered about.

I don't know Finnick that well, but I really like him a lot. He seems so sweet, so genuine.

"We can never leave Mckeen alone with a pretty lady for *too* long." Dallon says with a heavy accent, though when he says that it bothers me. It almost makes my stomach feel a bit queasy.

"Hi, Dallon." I wrap my arms around him as well.

"Hey, Poppy." He says a little bit less enthusiastic then Finnick. Then again, who could be as cute as Finnick?

"Atticus explained everything to us but just so everything's clear, what exactly are what are we doing?" Finnick puts his palms under his chin looking perplexed.

"Well," I begin. "me and my friend Jeannie are doing these adjoining articles on the whole pop punk movement. She's into all that stuff so she really has her whole romance and psyche side covered, but, I for one am not." I giggle. "So, incomes you guys and Atticus. I'll be studying you guys and your fashion. If it's ok with you, you'll be heavily featured in the article. Not to mention it's a great way to promote the band."

"It's extremely smart business wise." Atticus states next to me in agreement and Finnick strokes his chin cutely.

"I like it!" Finnick perks up. "I think it sounds great."

"It really is smart." Dallon shrugs.

"Ok," Atticus claps his hands enthusiastically. "you guys ready?"

Finnick nods as does Dallon.

I dig into my purse and take out my cute, new, pink sparkly notebook I just got with the matching pen so I could take notes.

I watch as Finnick picks up his drumsticks and Atticus and Dallon wrap their guitars around themselves. Atticus has the same green guitar that he had at *The Lounge*. I shiver at the thought of that night.

Atticus readies his mic stand and I open my notebook. I don't even know how I want to start this article. Well, I had an idea, but once I stepped foot in this place I lost it.

I can't help but watch Atticus intensely as I squint my eyes and hold my pen to my lips.

"*ARTICLE IDEAS AND THOUGHTS.*" I write on the top of the page.

"Ummm... Atticus?" I begin. His head pops up from where he was fixing his mic stand and he gives me a closed mouth smile. "There's actually something I meant to tell you...errr... Jeannie is more of a punk fan then I am. I'm doing this article because I really believe in it, and I think it's going to get us a lot of attention from other genres besides fashion, but... I don't really like punk music." I tread carefully and watch Atticus's face immediately fall.

It's as if time has stopped as the drum sticks drop right out of Finnick's hands and Dallon awkwardly gives a weak cough, looking the other way. Oh no.

I knew I shouldn't have said anything.

"I kind of figured that,' Atticus's lips are pursed together in a straight line. "but what do you mean by you 'don't like punk.'"

"I don't know. I don't really care for that pop punk, punk rock, metal, rock genre. All that stuff. Nothing against you! I'm just telling you because I... I don't really understand it. And I need to in order to make this article successful."

Atticus's lips that were in a straight line now form into a slight smile.

"Well, people rarely like things they don't understand. Pop Punk is about freedom, it's about liberation. It's about head-banging guitar riffs and ever changing progression!" His arms are spread wide, passion radiating off of him. You could smell it, you could hear it, and you could see it. "It's about getting your feelings out through beats and sounds, it's about powerful and smart lyrics that inspire and move! I'll teach you everything you need to know." He drops his arms and has a focused gaze on me after his passionate ramble. "What do you want to hear?"

"What do you want to show me?" I ask clueless.

"Ummm..." Atticus swipes his lip across his bottom lip. "ok. I think I got it." He nods and looks at me sitting on the couch.

Finnick just sits looking down at his drums, a cute smile on his face. Dallon is just looking at Finnick nodding his head with an expression on his face I could only read as shocked and impressed.

I take out my cell phone as I get a fab idea.

"Would you mind if I record this? Just for muscle memory. So I could go back and watch it when I eventually type this up?" I ask as if that's the reason.

"Do you even have to ask?" A cute wide smile spreads across Atticus's face. "Ok, we're going pretty heavy now, I promise! I'm going to give you an absolute explosion of pop punk!" He bounces excitedly putting his hands together.

"You're the master. You do what you want. As long as you and Dallon and Finnick are genuinely being yourselves, that's all I want." I start to record.

"Are we rolling?" Atticus looks up at me, but I can't bring myself to look at him. I just look at his face through the phone's camera, my hands shaking slightly. I don't know why.

"Yes." I giggle.

"Hey." He smiles charmingly at the camera. "Sup, I'm Atticus Mckeen, lead singer and guitarist of *The Deadbeats*." He motions towards Finnick and Finnick gives a slight smile while looking into the camera.

"Hey Finnick, how are you?" I laugh as if making a home video.

"I'm doing pretty well today, how are you Poppy? Great writer here, people."

"Well thank you and I'm doing pretty well. What do you do for the band?"

"I'm Finnick Runner, and I'm the drummer for the band *The Deadbeats*." I then turn the camera to Dallon.

"Hey Dallon."

"Hey Poppy. I'm Dallon Frame and I'm guitarist for *The Deadbeats*." He nods.

"What will *The Deadbeats* be playing for us today?"

"I think we'll be playing an original song called 'Golden Boy.' This is a new song I recently wrote. I do write all the songs for this band of course with the help of these two wonderful boys beside me." Atticus shrugs, our eyes meeting through the camera. "I've been getting a lot of inspiration lately and I'm really excited for this... so I hope you love it. Hope it makes you feel something. That's the goal." He smiles and I can't help but think if he's talking to me or the camera.

He sings into his mic as it starts off as just Atticus on the guitar playing a soft electric tune.

"I dreamt about you last night again, so much for being friends.

I might as well just get off your hair, grab my green guitar and bleeding black pens.

You'll be mine, give it time...

But as I bend over backwards for you I'm gonna break my spine."

He looks down and gives an exasperated sigh as the beat now picks up and it officially turns into a punk chorus.

"Deep, deep down in my soul there's a pit dedicated to rock and roll,

A fire for a desire that you can't control.

You wish it was for you, you wish it was for you.

I've set my sights on you and I can't let you leave,

My blood on your hands now, don't you lie to me.

I'm dying in your hands now, don't you see."

Finnick is banging on his drums with his scrawny arms as if it's the last time he'll ever do it. Atticus and Dallon do the same with their guitars. I try my hardest to capture everyone on camera but it seems to only want to focus on Atticus.

"Your voice is velvet and mine is raspy and exasperated,

You're kind and peppy, I'm just... jaded.

You'll be mine, give it time...

But as I look into your eyes I can't even manage a rhyme."

As he repeats the chorus once more, I start to write in my notebook, going into detail about Atticus's voice. I want to make sure I never forget it, I fear I might. People tend to go away a lot and if he ever does,

I'll have this. A distant video and memory of a friend who might not stay because they rarely do. And for the article. Duh! Mostly for the article. Never mind what I said before that! So I write.

"His voice is soft and raspy currently but it has the potential to be loud, extremely loud. When it does get loud, it becomes even raspier. I think in this case Atticus's deep Brooklyn drawl sure is an asset to him."

When I finish writing, the beat picks up like it did before but in a different way. A different tune. An even harder tune.

Then the song ends and all three boys stop completely in unison. It was perfect in every way.

Atticus looks up at the dirty, popcorn ceilings. Finnick drops his drumsticks and Dallon puts his hand on Atticus's shoulder as they both smile, Atticus breathing heavily due to all the singing in his incredibly deep and husky voice.

"You did good." I hear Dallon mumble.

Atticus looks up at me and I continue to film. I can't help but zoom in one his face with his cute little smile, and for the first time ever, I see him blush. A cute little pink flush grazing across his cheeks and nose.

He begins to take wide strides towards me and I curl myself up on the couch as he gets extremely close.

I look at his face through the camera as he brings his lips up to the phone and kisses it. I can't help but giggle uncontrollably.

I shut the phone and toss it beside me. I think I got everything I needed. It's always good to reference, you know.

"Well," Atticus hops on the couch next to me. "what'd ya think?"

"I love it, I thought it was fab. It has meaning." I struggle to find any words to describe what I'm feeling after listening to him sing. He's absolutely amazing. The song was absolutely amazing. Everything about it was just... perfect. "You're not only a fab singer and guitarist, but you're a poet."

Atticus is listening to me with a dazed out smile on his face and his face in the palm of his hands. It goes silent when I finish as I just stare at him.

He looks adorable the way he's sitting, completely engrossed in what I have to say.

I take out my note book and begin to write. I can't help but describe his eyes.

They are too gorgeous not to describe in the article. To share with everyone. Although, a fleeting feeling hits me of not wanting to share. Not wanting to share Atticus with the world. How I want to keep him for myself.

I push down that feeling though and I don't know why I get them. Oh well.

"Atticus looks at me and sometimes, I swear his eyes could look straight through my soul. There is always a constant black halo surrounding them from either exhaustion or the dirty blonde locks sitting in front of his face. I haven't quite figured out which one it is yet.

His stare is cold and uncertain at times, yet his deep brown doe eyes always hold some kind of meaning in them. Kind of like the music he writes." I jot down in my book.

"What are you writing?" He asks dreamly.

"Nothing." I retort looking up at him, trying to hide my smile.

"Come on, let me read it..." he laughs, reaching for my notebook.

"No! You'll read the end result when it's done and published." I hold the book up in the air.

"Come on, let me see!" He pouts, trying to climb on top of me to get the book.

"No!" I giggle. "You're going to crush me." We both begin to burst out into laughter until I hear Dallon clear his throat.

We both immediately look up and with one swift motion. Atticus clears his throat and fixes his chains, getting off the couch. I just sit back up and fix my skirt.

He stalks towards the kitchen as Dallon lifts an eyebrow at him. Atticus just wacks him upside the head.

I look up to Finnick who's sitting by his drums. He cocks his head to the side and a broad smile. I can't help but the blush that creeps on to my cheeks.

"I'm ordering pizza and taking a smoke," begins Atticus, grabbing his phone and walking towards the door.

"I'll come with, pretty boy." Dallon announces next to him, slinging his arm over Atticus.

"Pops, you wanna come?" Atticus looks at me. Come where? To smoke?

During my highschool years I thankfully never got peer-pressured to do anything. Probably because I didn't have many friends, didn't go to any parties and just barely went out overall.

I stayed in on Saturday nights and played board games with my parents while everyone I knew, my sister included, went out to get high or drunk. Jeannie is the only person I know who smokes and it's not like she wants to.

I had a puff of a cigarette once, inhaling the smoke and I literally thought I was gonna die. (What? I'm dramatic.)

"Oh, I don't smoke." I shake my head and give a feeble smile. "I... It scares me a bit. It's not something I ever wanted to do." I babble and try to justify it even though there is no need to. And like that, he gives a little chuckle.

At that moment I feel my heart drop to my stomach and a feeling in my chest I haven't quite felt since Liam broke up with me. There's this lump in my throat that I can't seem to swallow as my breath hitches.

I feel embarrassed, hurt, and humiliated compared to nothing I've ever felt. I don't know why, cause I've been hurt way more before. I've been hurt more by my own sister and Liam, but it feels ten times worse when it's Atticus.

It even feels worse than that one time I tripped and fell flat on my face at *Sephora*. All the posh makeup people were staring at me... urgh. It was horrendous.

"Wha--what's so funny?" I manage to say. Finnick and Dallon are both looking between us. Dallon is amused while Finnick looks discouraged.

"Nothing, I'm sorry..." he smiles but those dimples don't make me blush anymore. I hate them at this moment because those dimples are at my expense. "It's just cute."

I scoff overlooking the compliment. Was it? Did it sound cute? Does he think I'm cute?

No, don't think that Poppy! Don't be consumed by his charm, he's being a jackass!

"Go do what you got to do then just order the pizza, ok?" Finnick retorts.

I turn to look at him. He looks upset as he rips off his glasses and runs his hands through his curly hair. I then hear the door slam behind me.

I'm left with Finnick alone in the apartment which I actually don't mind. He sits carefully beside me unlike Atticus who has too much energy. Finnick has a careful amount.

I find myself starting to sniffle. Oh god, I feel like I'm in highschool once again. Poor Finnick. I hardly even know him!

But I quickly stop sniffling and brashly wipe my eyes. I can't get upset. Why am I even upset? My emotions are all over this place like I'm a teenager again.

"What's the matter?" Finnick asks, sympathetically.

"I feel stupid," I admit. "I'm angry. I don't deserve to be laughed at just because I'm not a pot-head."

Finnick gives a loud laugh.

"Well, I'm not either. Neither are they."

"Yes they are. I *hate* him!" I find the brash words slipping out of my mouth before I could stop them. I immediately regret it. I don't *hate* him… I just strongly dislike him at the moment.

"Poppy--"

"He said he cared about me! He said we were *friends*…" I don't know why I'm opening up to Finnick like this. He's just so easy to talk to.

"You are!"

"Friends don't laugh at each other for being vulnerable!" I erupt. I just can't hold it in. I don't care if Finnick is Atticus's best friend. And I'm well aware I might sound annoying, but I can't help my current outpour of emotions.

"I don't think he meant to hurt you. Atticus is very protective of you."

"I don't want him to protect me!" I retort. "I don't need him, and I don't need this article!"

"Don't say that." Finnick tries to comfort me but it doesn't work. I hear fragments of Dallon and Atticus outside of the apartment.

"You're a fucking idiot, man." I hear Dallon laugh.

"Shut up, what was I supposed to do!"

"Maybe not offer the priss a cig…" and before I could break down at Dallons harsh words I hear a loud crack against the door.

'Priss.' Maybe Liam was right after all. The word just plays over and over again in my head like a song on replay.

Finnick quickly runs towards the door and I find myself getting up with him.

He throws the door open and in falls Dallon, a severe bruise on the side of his cheek. I slap my hand over my mouth as Atticus realizes what he just did, he looks shocked, but doesn't look remorseful.

Finnick runs his hands through his curly, black hair and his eyes go wide.

Atticus's gaze meets mine, hurt and sorrow in his eyes as it should be. I then get in his face, tears in my eyes as I rub them roughly.

"I was *not* put on this earth to amuse you." Is all I could get through bits of sniffles. "I know you probably don't take me seriously. You probably just invested time with me so you could say cruel jokes with Dallon behind my back. Well you know what Atticus, I'm not a joke."

I push past him and walk out of his apartment. Then I hurry into my apartment across the way, slamming the door behind me.

I slide right down the door in tears as soon as it closes. The sad part is, I don't even know exactly why I'm crying.

CHAPTER SIXTEEN
A blooming Poppyseed

"*Poppy, I need to talk* to you." Begins Jeannie, a look of panic on her face all of the sudden.

She's been acting strange all day, but then again, so have I. I'm still confused and hurt about what happened yesterday.

"Of course," I nod. "lay it on me." She takes a deep breath and I suddenly get worried. "Jeannie, what's up?"

"I can't do the article anymore. I'm so, *so* sorry. My mom broke her back a week ago and she needs my help around the house. She can't do anything and she doesn't have my dad anymore. All my energy just can't go into the article right now. God, I can't believe this is happening..."

I'm speechless. I was going to just tell Jeannie that I don't know how I feel about the article now that me and Atticus had a bit of a… well, I don't know what to call it.

Suddenly those problems don't seem to matter to me.

"Jeannie, you didn't tell me your mom broke her back!"

"I'm sorry Pops, I was kind of shocked myself. I didn't know how to tell you because we are working on the article together, but you're my best friend and I should have told you. I'm sorry."

"Don't be sorry! I'm sorry." I take a deep breath. "I got this. I know this is your dream article. I'm going to make you so proud, Jeannie." I almost begin to tear up with all the emotions running through my mind right now.

"I know you will." Jeannie grabs my hands and holds them in hers. "Especially with that little secret weapon of yours." She winks and I have to stop myself from frowning.

"Yeah." Is all I say.

Jeannie is usually who I run to when something crazy like last night happens. I tell her everything and anything but If I tell her what happened, I'll just feel selfish.

So, I'll just keep my mouth shut. What the hell am I going to do now?

"Here's your schedule for next week, Ms. DuVull." I hand Jane her typed out itinerary for the week that took me two hours and a couple of phone calls to make last night.

"Thanks, Poppyseed." She rips it out of my hand, pulling down her glasses as she reads it. "I'm going to need you to run to *Fendi* and get me the three dresses I ordered for the shoot. Make sure to call Vanessa before you go so she could be in the front with the bags ready. Make Riley drive you because I need them back here by twelve."

"Alright, got it." I make a mental note in my head. Call Vanessa, tell Riley, get the skirts. "By the way, I'm on my own now with the article. Jeannie's mom broke her back and she has to help out a lot. She's going to confront you about what she can do later. Try to be considerate." I give a knowing glare.

"I'll try my best. Although we both know being considerate isn't my strong suit." Jane gives a curt smile. I nod my head and begin to turn towards Jane's big glass doors, ready to run some errands.

"Nuh uh," I hear her quip, so I turn back around. What now? "your vibe is off." She stares at me quizzically.

This is Jane's way of saying 'There's obviously something up with you.'

"Oh no! It's really nothing."

"Poppyseed darling," begins Jane as she takes off her glasses and places them beside her. "I know when something is wrong, so don't shrug it off and act like everything is ok when it's not." She throws one hand in the air and leans back in her chair. "Just tell me what's the matter, we'll solve this issue of yours, and we'll be on with our day. Capish?"

"Ms. DuVull, is this really necessary--"

"Patricia, in order to perform your best on an article you are working on, your mind must be clear of everything but that article. Therefore, if your mind is not clear, this big article you are working on is going to be a complete bust and I will be upset. You don't want me to be upset, do you?" She cocks up an eyebrow and it intimidates me.

"No…"

"Fantastic, now pull up a chair and get to talking. I have a lot of work to do." I pull up one of Jane's perfect, fluffy white chairs and bring it to her desk. I sit there awkwardly with my hands in my lap as if I was a child sitting in the principal's office.

"Well," I begin. "I was working on my article last night and I was in Atticus's apartment--" Jane gives me a smirk. "don't be too excited." I add. "Anyway, It was going fab. Atticus's bandmates Dallon and Finnick were there and they were practicing and I was studying them. It was fun. Me and Atticus were getting along just fine. Atticus then asked me if I would like to have a cigarette. I said no. I admitted to Atticus that it scared me and he laughed."

Jane is listening and leaning with her chin in the palm of her right hand and her eyebrows are furrowed together in confusion.

"I was taken aback and I asked him what was so funny. He said it was nothing and it was very 'cute' which I don't quite understand!" I throw my hands in the air, sitting up straight in the chair still confused about the situation as I speak about it. "So to make a long story short, I heard Dallon and Atticus talking in the hallway while Finnick was comforting me. Dallon called me a priss and the next thing I know, Dallon has a bruise on his cheek because Atticus punched him!"

"What happened after that?" Asks Jane seriously.

"I… I told Atticus what was on my mind at that moment. I told him I wasn't a private joke that he and his friends could make fun of after I leave. That I wasn't put on this earth to amuse him."

"Well damn straight." Jane smiles in which I could only describe as proud. She now leans back in her chair and starts to think. "You're very rigid aren't you, Poppyseed." she states more than asks.

"Well yeah."

"He called you cute, this boy?"

"Yes, but--"

"Why did you overlook the compliment?" I think for a moment at the question. I actually pondered over it for quite a while.

"Because it's not a compliment."

"How is being cute not a compliment?" Jane retorts.

"How is not smoking a cigarette 'cute.' I don't get it!" I cry. "Babies are 'cute,' the new blouse I saw at *Express* is 'cute.' *Not* smoking is just... me trying not to get lung cancer!"

"Ok, true..." ponders Jane. "or is it that you don't want to be considered cute?"

I scrunch up my nose and think for a moment. Well, no. I like being cute! Everyone likes to be cute.

"No," I begin when Jane tilts her head. I take a deep sigh. "I don't mind being cute, but I don't understand how that is considered cute. Maybe... maybe I would like to be taken more seriously at times." I break off. "I'm not getting through to people."

"Well," begins Jane, playing with her fingernails. "that's why we write, correct? You say what you believe and what you see and people *do* listen. You *do* get through to people. You just haven't seen it yet. People in your family as well as Atticus might not take you seriously but every single person who reads your articles do! As for Atticus, don't give up on him just yet. Don't get too frustrated with him. You said it yourself, you were having a good time before everything happened." She takes a deep breath. "Poppy, you remind me of someone who used to be very dear to my heart. A young woman I used to know. She went into the world with blinders on, and she wasted her youth because of it. Don't be that girl, Poppyseed. Give this article one more chance, give him one more chance. I don't think you'll regret it."

I'm taken aback at Jane's speech to me. I don't know what I'm going to do, but I know just by talking to Jane I feel better. I want to ask who that girl is but I'm sure I already know the answer.

"Thank you, Ms.DuVull."

"Sure, Poppyseed." She says softly.

It's strange, I never heard Jane speak softly.

"Now, get out of my sight. Everything on this beautiful itinerary ain't gonna do itself." I look down, smile, and nod. Happy that Jane is back to her sarcastic self. I get up off the chair and begin to walk towards the door.

"Oh, and Poppyseed, darling," I turn around to see Jane opening up a granola bar and putting her legs up on her desk. "don't break your brain too much in that article. Enjoy the experience, will you?"

As I walk towards my apartment door I think about me and Jane's talk. I've actually thought about it all day.

I am going to do this article. I'm going to do it for Jeannie, I'm going to do it for Jane, and I'm going to do it for *DuVull and Co.* But most importantly, I'm going to do this article for myself. I'm not giving up just because I'm upset with Atticus. I could interview another person if I want to! I'm sure Jeannie could hook me up with someone.

Now I realize how much I'm doing for this article though. I'm not only covering three pages of fashion, but I'm covering six pages of fashion and lifestyle. It makes me nervous just thinking about it.

I'm then startled by my mom's loud voice booming through my phone.

"We will be having a meeting about the wedding Saturday." To be quite honest, I kind of forgot Diamante was getting married.

"Sounds great, ma." I say exhaustedly.

"Ok dear, well enough of that. How was your day?"

"Oh you know, it was..." as I reach my door I see a big pink piece of construction paper taped to it. I then look down to see a *Dunkin* iced coffee beneath me. "mom... can I call you back?"

"Sure, hon. Is everything ok?"

"Just peachy." I answer without missing a beat. Knowing exactly who it's from, I rip the construction paper off my door and grasp it tightly in my hands and sharply manicured fingers.

My mom hangs up and I begin to read Atticus's note written in his notorious handwriting.

"Blondie, meet me in midtown on Fifth Ave. You'll see me. Bring a pencil and your notebook. -Atty"

I can't help but smile down to myself.

Atty. I love that nickname for him. No, I'm mad at him. I must be stern! God, I'm so easy.

I feel this spark ignite throughout my entire body. Excitement and triumph causes tingles down my spine.

I pick the coffee off the ground and the condensation drips onto the paper. What if I don't go? What if I just left him there? Make him feel like he made me feel the other night. Terrible, used, and completely and utterly alone. I then sigh and put the coffee back on the ground.

Why does he even want to meet on fifth anyway? He's so indecent! Now I have to get back on a bus and go all the way back to Manhattan which is literally where I just came from. You know he could have texted me.

Wait... why am I not doing this? Why am I depriving myself? I have nothing better to do, do I? Unless you count microwavable *Trader Joe's* mac and cheese and a marathon of *My Lottery Dream home* set plans for your Thursday night.

"Damn it." I curse under my breath and turn right back around. Just then I realize I'm forgetting my coffee so I hastily bend down and grab it. A stupid smirk spreads across my face as I do. Poppy stop it! You're mad at him, you're mad at Atticus.

I head into the elevator and out of the apartment, my notebook and pencil already in my bag. It always is.

As I catch the bus to Manhattan I have a feeling that this might just be the start of something big. The article I meant. Not me and Atticus. Of course not.

I get off the bus and head towards fifth avenue. Why the hell does he want to meet here anyway?

I hold my bag in the crook of my arm and look around for him as I reach the spectacle that is fifth. Business men and women are walking around with their fancy briefcases and everyone is arguing with someone over the phone. All the Manhattan IT girls go through here as well. Fifth is so fab.

As I start to walk towards *Saks fifth avenue* I'm stopped in my tracks by the mannequins in the display. They are always *so* gorgeous. I wish I looked like those mannequins sometimes with their porcelain eyes and perfectly painted red lips.

It's November, so of course the holiday season is here, and they are getting everything in place for their famous grand Christmas displays through their windows and lights.

My mom used to take me to look at them every year. Now I pass by it everyday as I go to work.

I spot a purse one of the mannequin is holding through the glass window in her pale, fragile hands. It's light pink leather with gold spiky studs. That *has* to be *Gucci*. I wonder how much it is...

"I knew this is where I'd spot you." I hear a familiar deep Brooklyn tone say, snapping me out of my trance.

I turn to see Atticus standing against the window of the mesmeric display, lighting up a cigarette. I frown as he does so as I remember what happened yesterday.

"You really shouldn't be leaning against those windows." I stand up a bit straighter, looking towards the doors of *Saks* and not paying him any mind. "There are many windows that hold displays here, as you could see. People spend hours cleaning them."

"Oh shit, I'm sorry." He says genuinely, blowing out a puff of smoke and placing himself beside me. We stand in silence, both just staring at the display.

"Oh," I hear him say beside me once again and I glance towards him. "Sorry... again." He rips the cigarette out of his mouth and throws the still burning stick on the floor, crushing it underneath his old looking *Converses*.

I look up at him and I don't quite know what my face looks like, but I'm feeling pretty shocked. I didn't expect him to put out his cigarette for me. He didn't have to do that.

Sometimes I feel as if Atticus might have two sides to him. The rebellious, rude, playboy or the kind, living and breathing teddy bear. It's so strange. I never quite met a guy like him. In a good way though. A very good way.

"What? You have a problem with pollution too?" He lifts an eyebrow but all I could manage is a shake of my head 'no,' and look back at the display, speechless.

"So why did you bring me here?" I finally say.

A tall man dressed in a suit and tie bumps into me and continues to talk on his cell phone.

I lunge forward a bit when Atticus catches me. He huffs and gently grabs my arm, pulling me to the side of the store in this small little nook next to the revolving doors.

It's then when I get a good look at his outfit.

He's in a leather jacket, a tight black turtleneck, ripped black jeans, and a bunch of his signature silver chains. He has one silver earring dangling from his right ear and his hair is in messy dirty blonde locks in front of his face as always. I must say though, that's the most fab outfit I've ever seen on any man, and I don't know why but I'm quite breathless. Whoah.

Maybe it's because we are so close together that our chests are almost touching and I could practically feel his heartbeat and his breath against my skin.

"Why?" I find myself asking.

"Why what?" His intense face now contorts in confusion.

'Why did you laugh in my face when I was vulnerable in front of you?' I'm prepared to say but I fear I'll just cry.

"Why are we here?"

"Well," he tears his deep brown eyes away from mine and looks at the people passing by. "I figured we'd do something for the article. Maybe something we both enjoy being something to do with fashion. Just you and I. To make up for yesterday." He then looks back down at me. He's fidgety and he actually looks worried. Atticus? Worried? Can't be...

There is much more I want to say but all I can murmur is a quiet ok.

CHAPTER SEVENTEEN

New perspectives and big glass balls

As we walk into the department store I feel a sense of euphoria. God, I love shopping. I'm finding that I'm blending in quite easily of course with all the rest as I walk in. Atticus sticks out like a sore thumb though.

I watch as people pass him glares. I don't know whether they are judging him or glancing fondly at his face. Atticus looks like a rockstar. No matter what he wears or how he wears it, he's always going to have that pretty face of his to save him. No matter what.

He is quite the sight though to see in *Saks*. He sure is very fashionable in his own right.

"So, where are we heading?" I look at him but then I catch my reflection in a full body mirror by the cosmetics.

I'm in a light pink sheer top with big puffy sleeves and a big bow on my right shoulder. I have matching light pink high waisted pants. I have some of my favorite *Louboutin* pumps, on them are a whole bunch of different patterns.

The backing is a sparkly hot pink and the heel itself is a dark blue along with silver spikes on the strap. In the crook of my arm I'm holding my *Betsy Johnson* bag that matches my heels perfectly and it has a bunch of cute, little silver charms on it.

"I don't know. This is your territory not mine." Atticus shrugs looking down at me.

I start to fix my ponytail in the mirror and I watch as Atticus bends down to my height, looking through the mirror giving me a skeptical look.

Then he starts to mimic me, fixing his own hair and I giggle. He laughs as well, his chin sitting on my shoulder and his scruff tickling my neck.

"Ok," I turn away from the mirror, getting my thinking face on. "I think I have an Idea!"

"Poppy, darling!" I hear a call across from the mens department. A tall, slim woman with short black hair starts stalking towards me and Atticus.

"Claudia, how are you?" I embrace her in a hug. Claudia is one of the personal shoppers here at *Saks*. She's just great, honestly.

"Oh, I'm so swell! I feel like I haven't seen you in forever!" She practically bounces up and down.

"I know! I have a bit of a task for us today if you don't mind." I say, clasping my hands together.

"Of course not!" I turn to Atticus who is holding up a pair of white, lace underwear between his pointer finger and thumb. He looks so confused and I try to hide my laughter.

"These are 249.00 dollars!" He looks at me as if waiting for an answer as to why. "What the hell are these going to do for you! With that price, it should marry you *and* have your children."

"Claudia... this is Atticus. He's a friend of mine. He is helping me with this groundbreaking article I'm in the process of writing. You see, Atticus is a musician."

"Ohhhh..." Claudia nods, impressed.

"Yes, I must explore his style. I was thinking we could play a bit of dress up with Atticus today and show him some different styles."

"That's *so* fantastique!" she puts out her hand for Atticus. "Hello..." She says a tad bit awkwardly.

I could tell Claudia never really had an interaction with someone with Atticus's style. She's from France and came to America when she was five! How fab is that!

"Well, I say I'm just here for moral and style support because in all actuality, I think Poppy's the real fashion expert." She gives me a wink.

"Well he's a good looking one, ain't he?" Claudia turns to me while we wait outside of the dressing room for Atticus.

"I suppose," I shrug. "he's quite good looking."

"Don't take this the wrong way, but I never expected to see you two together."

"What do you mean?" I question.

"He's just so... goth? I don't know the correct term for it. Oh, don't listen to me!" She shoos. "He's very fine though. Do you think he fancies you?" She asks in a whisper.

"Oh, no." I shake my head. "I'm not his type."

"How do you know?"

"He probably likes girls that could play the guitar and have tattoos. You know, the ones with the crazy colored hair and wear fishnets with *every* outfit."

"The ones with nipple piercings and those big eyeliner wings?" Claudia chides. "I think I know the type you're talking about." We both burst out into a fit of giggles "but don't discriminate, love. You'd be surprised. When people find someone they truly care about, they tend to fall out of that type." And the minute Claudia says that, I begin to think. Does he have feelings for me? No, he wouldn't. Surely he couldn't...

"Yeah, I don't know..." I'm snapped out of my thoughts when Atticus walks out of the dressing room.

He's in a white button up shirt and nice navy blue dress pants. He still has one of his notorious silver chains dangling down his neck as well. He hasn't even buttoned up the shirt the whole way. It's half open and I watch carefully as his long fingers with black painted nails and big silver rings work to close the gap.

"It's nice, but it's really not my style. As I was expecting." He shoots me a tooth filled grin.

I'm the one that picked the outfit out but I'm finding I liked Atticus better in the one he was wearing before. It's just more...him. When someone is confident in their style it makes them more attractive. (Atticus is always very attractive though. No matter what he wears, honestly.)

In this outfit he looks suave. Like some kind of professional business man but with an edge.

I could tell he's struggling with the buttons so I walk over to help him. I hesitate at first when I reach him but he puts his hands down to his sides, letting me assist him. I close the gap between us and begin buttoning up his shirt.

"You look fab." I say a bit below a whisper.

"Thanks." He says and I can practically hear his smile. "Do I look like *James Bond*?"

"For sure." I giggle. "A regular *James Bond*… with black nails." We both begin to laugh.

I finish buttoning up his shirt and leave a couple of buttons open at the top. (You know… for style purposes.)

I tap his chest and back up a bit so I could turn him around and hold his shoulders as he stares into the mirror in front of us. I can't help but rest my head slightly on his shoulder as we look into the mirror. Just like he did to me a couple of minutes ago.

I shake my head and tear myself away from him, grabbing my notebook and pencil out of my bag.

"Hey Poppy," I hear Claudia beside me. "I got an appointment but I'm positive you got this." She smiles.

"Oh Claudia, thank you for all your help." We hug and she blows me a kiss.

"Ciao Pops! I bet you'll have fun with that." She motions towards Atticus and winks as she disappears into the endless amount of clothes and accessories on this floor. I just roll my eyes and choose to ignore the comment.

"So," I hop back over to Atticus. "how do you feel?" I tap my pencil on my chin.

"Ummm…" he screws up his face. "confident I guess." I begin to jot down what he's saying. "Professional, just not like myself. I mean I would definitely wear this. I would just accessorize it."

"How so?"

"Well I would have more chains around my neck for sure. I would probably have one chain attached to my pants. Oh, and I would change the pants from this blue to black. Maybe add a black blazer too. I think that would be pretty dope."

"Would you wear this outfit out?"

"No way…" Atticus chuckles. "yeah no."

I write down what he says word for word.

"Ok." I pop up, happily shutting my book. "You're good to go. You can now turn back into Atticus. I want my Atty Mckeen back." *My* Atty? Since when is he my Atty? He certainly isn't.

He grins and begins to unbutton his shirt.

"What are you doing?" I tense up and quickly shove him in the dressing room. He turns around and looks at me like I'm crazy.

"Unbuttoning my shirt..." he takes off the shirt now and begins to grab the black turtleneck he was wearing before.

"Oh!" I say, taken aback, throwing my hands over my eyes. "I'm not sure if I should take it as an insult or a compliment that you're that comfortable around me."

"Ha." He gives a dark chuckle. "Take it as a compliment." I'm not sure how I feel about that but I get butterflies in the pit of my stomach when he says it.

"Alrighty then," I begin to walk my way out of the dressing room, hands still over my eyes. "I'll uhhhh... I'll wait outside--"

"Poppy wait—" and as I turn around to walk outside I feel myself bang into the wall of the dressing room.

"Ow."

"Do you want my help?" I hear Atticus say dangerously close to me and all of me hopes he is fully dressed.

"No, no... I got this. I'll meet you outside." I say matter of factly as I find my way out of the dressing room and take my hands away from my eyes. Ha, take that dressing room wall and extremely attractive shirtless Atticus!

"Shoes! This is one of my favorite sections!" I gasp, grabbing Atticus's hand, dragging him to a sparkly pair of *Miu Miu* pumps.

"Shoes are necessary. Shoes are an essential part of anyone's style." I nod in agreement and jot down Atticus's words.

"Exactly!" I squeal. "Finally, someone of the male species with style!"

"Oh, stop it." Atticus shoos playfully.

I look up at the ceiling. I always thought the decor over here was so beautiful. There are big, glass bubble-like structures hanging from the ceiling with little strings of diamonds as well. I always can't help but look in awe. It's so ethereal, so elegant.

"I always loved those." I find myself pointing up to the ceiling. "Part of me just wants to reach up and grab them sometimes. Since I was a little girl."

"What's stopping you?" Atticus shrugs.

"Pffff." I can't help but snort. "Are you kidding me?" I jump up and tap him on the head referring to how short I am. Atticus once again just shrugs and wraps his arms around my waist from behind.

"Wha--what are you doing?" I squeak at the surprising contact. He lifts me off the floor with ease, shockingly. "Atticus..."

"Touch them." I hear him say from underneath me. "No ones looking. No one cares." And he's right. No one is looking. Everyone is too preoccupied with their personal shoppers and the tourists are too occupied admiring the beauty of, well, of everything.

I gingerly reach up and watch as my manicured fingernails touch the rim of the glass bubble. It feels just as I thought it would. Like glass.

"How did it feel?" Asks Atticus as he brings me back down to earth, his arms still wrapped around my waist.

I feel as if my face is on fire and the butterflies in my stomach start to fly all around once again. When I'm around him they just never seem to leave. The feeling makes me nervous. Maybe I am nervous. Maybe that's what the feeling means right now.

"How did what feel?" I ask almost as if it's a secret and gasp in shock. "Atticus!" I quickly rip his hands off my waist, turn around and slap him harshly on the arm.

"I meant the glass balls." His face contorts into a smile and he began to laugh. "God, get your mind out of the gutter will ya." He says with faux offence.

"Oh." I begin in embarrassment, my face turning even more red. "It felt like... it felt like glass."

"Did it? Damn, I really thought it was plastic." He snaps his fingers and I giggle. "No, but how did it *feel*? Like how did it feel to do something that you've wanted to do for the longest time." And with that I think. Oh Atticus never ceases to surprise me with his deeper meanings and such.

"Freeing." I find myself saying. "It felt freeing. Something off the life-long bucket list I suppose."

"Write that down in your book." He smirks and I roll my eyes. "I'm serious, write it down." So I open my book with a huff and write it down.

"Freeing?????" Than Atticus takes the book and pencil out of my hand and writes underneath it,

"Being with Atticus I feel free." At that moment something clicks. I kind of do. I actually really do. I blush as he gives me back the book and my pencil.

"So wait, back to the 'how did it feel' thing..."

"No, nope. Stop it..."

"Did that feel good? Was my grip ok? Because I'm--"

"Oh ok. Shut up, please shut up. I bet you have. You're a weirdo." I put my hands over my ears and he continues to laugh even more. His deep voice really does come through when he laughs.

Atticus starts to dance his way towards the middle of the floor where there are expensive leather white couches and a bunch of fancy older women yell at their personal shoppers because the *Gucci's* they wanted don't fit their feet the way they want them to.

None of them pay attention to us though. No one does. No one ever does. We now reach the middle of the floor where not a lot of customers reside and Atticus pushes a couple of shoe boxes to the side.

"What are you doing?" I ask.

"I want to look at the glass bubbles." He points up at them as he lays on his back in the middle of the floor.

"Atticus," I laugh nervously. "You can't..."

"What? I can't do what?" He puts his hands behind his head.

"You're in the middle of a shoe department!"

"And? Look around. No one cares." Oh god, I swear. Atticus is the only person that could ever convince me to lay down in the middle of *Saks's* shoe department like a loon. My attention is completely on him and not on any of the shoes on the floor, and no ones ever been able to do that. Poppy Paxton in a room full of shoes and her attention is on the punk boy she's with instead. What is happening?

So I take a deep breath and slowly and carefully rest beside him. My head hits the rug and we just look up at the ceiling for a couple of seconds. This reminds me of the situation that happened about two weeks ago and I'm just thankful we are not laying on the concrete under a loud bulldozer.

I hear Atticus chuckle beside me.

"What?" I turn to him.

"Nothing." He laughs again.

"What Atticus?" I ask impatiently. "Tell me!"

"Do I have any influence on you? Like, what just happened. Did you lay down next to me because you wanted to or because I told you too?" I'm a bit taken aback by the question and Atticus's usually confident voice is now a little shaky.

"Well you did it. You doing it almost makes me feel like it's ok to do it even if it's not."

"But it *is* ok."

"Is it?"

"Yes. There's no rule saying you can't lay on the floor and look up at the hanging glass bubbles on the ceiling. No one notices anyway."

"No one ever notices people like us." I find myself saying.

"What do you mean?"

"Why would these people focus on me? I'm nobody. You have a lot of stuff going for you though. I'm... I don't know." I give up with a sigh.

"And that's where you're wrong." Atticus smirks and turns his head towards me. "Who's Poppy? Who's Poppy Paxton?" He looks at me with such intensity I feel I might just combust. He says my name is so nice. It holds meaning coming from him.

"She's a fashion journalist."

"That's what you do, not who you are."

"Then what am I?"

"Hmmm..." he thinks for a moment. "well, Poppy Paxton is this kind-hearted, generous, fashionable woman who lives across the way from me. She's funny, she's smart, and she loves her job. She would give you the *Prada* shoes off her feet if you had no shoes. She would give you the *Fendi* scarf she has if you were cold. She's scared to open up her heart to new people because she was hurt really badly. She's very protective of her feelings. She's a great writer. I'm actually quite proud that she calls me her friend. Even if I do come off as a jerk sometimes. A complete idiot, a complete punk. She somehow always knows what to say." I'm at a loss for words, I don't know what to say. I'm absolutely lost in Atticus's deep brown eyes and raspy voice.

How does this beautiful stranger know so much about me? Is it obvious? I mean, Atticus is far from a stranger but sometimes I still do feel he is. I don't think anyones ever figured me out that much in a matter of three months. Not Tiff, not Jeannie, not Riley, not Arlo, and certainly not even Liam. He speaks to me as if we've known each other for years.

"Well she sounds like a fab woman." Is all I could say.

"She is fab. She's the most fab. She's wonderful." He's still looking at me with that intense look and I just wish I knew what the look meant.

He then reaches for my face and I could practically hear my heartbeat. He pulls a strand of hair behind my ear and I offer him a kind smile.

"Hey guys," I hear a familiar French accent above us. "you good? I'm going to have to ask you weirdo's to get up before someone else comes over and isn't as nice as I am about it." Claudia says and Atticus helps me back to my feet. Claudia pulls me by the arm and away from Atticus.

"What has gotten in your head?" She giggles but I could tell it's a nervous giggle.

"I don't know." I answer honestly and she lets go of my arm.

"Oh god, Pop's. She laughs. "What have you gotten yourself into this time?" Well that seems to be the question on everybody's mind, isn't it? Even on mine.

I grab on to Claudia's hand and offer her a kind yet panicked smile.

"Nothing," I shrug. "just an article. That's all it is. Just an article."

CHAPTER EIGHTEEN
He's like a pair of Loui Vutton pumps...

"*'Are you afraid of rejection?'*" Riley reads aloud from Jeannie's new article she's doing that Friday.

By the way, her mom is homebound but she is doing well. I visited her yesterday. She's as fab as ever! Such a sweet lady, really.

"Yes." I answer matter of factly, starting a portion of my article.

I'm plugging in the part about *The Deadbeats* and their song as well as me and Atticus's little escapade at *Saks fifth Avenue* on Wednesday.

I really got to get this article done. Jane is up my ass and rightfully so. The December issue comes out in three weeks.

A wide smile tugs at the corner of my lips when I read Atticus's handwriting in my notebook. *"Being with Atticus I feel free"* I type his words.

"Well it would take a genius to realize that, Poppy!" Riley retorts sarcastically and leans over my desk. "Well in that case you're in luck! 'Five ways to just go for it and stop being afraid of rejection!' By Jeannie Harrison." Of course Jeannie could write about this. She's the most confident person I know.

"Lay them on me." I say, focused on my article.

Jeannie is typing her newest article as well. Jane's really cracking down on her since she had to back out of the article with me.

"'Number one; make sure you have at least some kind of remote interest for said person. Whether it be an attraction to the hottie you met at the club or your bestest friend. Make sure you really are attracted to them and not just forcing yourself. Do *not* chase a fantasy.'"

"Got it." I say.

"'Number two; treat yourself! If you think you look pretty, girl, you stand in front of that mirror and say it out loud. Scream it from the rooftops! 'I look pretty'. I'm pretty, I'm smart, I'm kind, etc.'"

"Oh, totally." I nod in agreement as if I *ever* do it.

"'Number three; practice asking said person out with friends or loved ones. Ask their advice as well, they know you the best.' Poppy?" Riley breaks out of the article for a second.

"Riley?"

"Will you practice with me before you ask out hot goth rocker man?"

"No, and definitely not asking him out." I say stoic not looking up from my article and keyboard.

"Will you practice escaping the restaurant with me in case you have a bad date? Will you also practice having to hit said date over the head with any nearest object if he gets weird?"

"Well, duh."

"Ah, ok. Reality is restored. I taught you well."

Jeannie snorts at us.

"'Number four;'" Riley begins once again. "'STS, honey! (study the situation.) What environment are you in? Make sure to blend in with that environment. Of course you want to stand out, but don't wear that sparkly cocktail dress to a coffee date and try to woo said person with your expensive taste. Instead use your personality.'" There is silence for a moment so I look up. I see Riley and Jeannie staring at me knowingly.

"*I* do that." I say sarcastically and shoot Jeannie a glare.

"'Number Five; make sure he doesn't have a significant other. That would be detrimental.'" And like that, Riley closes the magazine and sighs.

"Well good job, Jeannie. I bet you're going to save thousands of girls from waking up next to the stranger they met at a bar just to find they have a girlfriend."

"Thanks." Sighs Jeannie. "Now I'm up to my eyeballs in articles. Pop's, can you help me?"

"Yeah," I look up from my computer. "what is it?"

"I have to write this thing about what the right man looks like. Not physically but mentally. I could use some help."

"Oh, I got you." I say as I roll my chair next to her. I look at Jeannie's empty doc in front of her and skeptically tap my finger on my chin, putting my thinking heels on.

"What do you look for in a guy?" Asks Jeannie. "I wouldn't say you have a type of any sorts."

"I dunno." I scrunch up my nose. "I guess as long as they're kind? Do I even have any standards after Liam?" I giggle but am actually kind of serious.

"Not one." Laughs Jeannie with me. "Hey after that shitshow, all you could do is go up honestly." I guess she's right.

"What do you mean though? Like, what do you want me to help you with?"

"A quote maybe? I'll quote you. Just give me something that you look for in a man. Something you would advise any woman to look for in a man. What should he be like? Use your wit. You always have a way with words." Jeannie points out.

"Well…" A grin begins to form across my lips. "he's like a pair of *Loui Vutton* pumps, beautiful, sharp, and hard to find. If he's like that he's a keeper…" I think for a moment. "men are stubborn, annoying, and--at times--stupid. Absolutely delirious. Someone will make going through that good-for-nothing ex of yours worth it though. You just have to find him and once you have, you need not be stubborn and let him in! If you don't, how will you know how amazing he is? How will he know how amazing you are?" I finish off with a deep sigh.

"'Said perfectly by Miss Poppy Paxton; fashion journalist here at *DuVull and Co.*" Jeannie finishes off typing with a smile.

"I wonder where that all came from." Riley says with an eye roll, pushing back his teal hair. Jeannie shoots him a glare.

"It wasn't about anyone." I retort. "I had absolutely no one in mind."

"Sure… Riley begins.

"Hola, freaks." I hear an annoying drawl from above us suddenly.

We all look up to see Isla with her golden locks slicked back in a low pony with big hoops hanging from her ears.

She's in black, leather boots with about a six inch heel and black leggings with gold sparkles and designs all over them. She also has a huge, black fur coat. Her green eyes practically bore into Jeannie and Riley's soul but for some apparent reason she's not looking at me.

"Jane wants your article in by two, which is…" she looks down at the gold watch draped around her wrist. "in ten minutes!" She squeaks looking directly at Jeannie. Jeannie just looks up, squinting her eyes evilly at Isla.

"Damn I thought it was Poppy's job to be Jane's assistant." Riley clicks his tongue. "Sorry Poppy, I think Isla's slaving after DuVull now. Looks like you've been promoted." He spits absolute venom at Isla.

Oh, Riley did always have a way with words. No one ever does win a fight with Riley. Not even Arlo.

I watch as Isla swallows thickly and she's practically shaking. Her jaw tightens and I give Riley a look as if to say, 'don't bring me into this!'

"Well, I won't be slaving after Jane once I get promoted to fashion editor." Oh *no.*

I carefully move my head up from my computer and look at Jeannie when I realize Jeannie is already looking at me.

Me and Jeannie have done this thing since we met. It's like she's my soul sister or something. Whenever something happens we give each other this look. It's a somewhat panicked look where my eyes are widened and Jeannie's one eyebrow is almost animatedly raised up. That's the look that's going on right at this moment. Only we are trying to be more discreet about it.

Is that why she's being so mean to all of us? She thinks Jeannie wants the promotion? Jeanie doesn't even work in fashion. Well, she's sadly mistaken. Jeannie isn't the one she needs to be worrying about.

Riley looks at Isla and suddenly starts to laugh. Oh god. I shoot him a warning glare.

I love Riley. So much, but, sometimes his meanness could get the best of him. He'll say anything and everything to hurt someone who attacks his personal circle. Even if that means accidentally hurting someone *in* that circle. Accidentally of course. So I'm praying that he doesn't tell Isla I'm the one who wants the promotion. He gets so heated in the moment sometimes.

"What's so funny, blue?" Isla crosses her arms giving Riley a new, pretty obvious nickname.

"Nothing," Riley wipes the fake tears at the brim of his round, brown eyes. "nothing at all, Isla." I silently sigh in relief and I could see Jeannie does too, as her tense body now practically collapses.

"Well Jeannie, now you have…" Isla once again looks at her watch. "nine minutes…"

"Done." Jeannie clicks on her computer for one last time and now looks up at Isla with a cocky smirk. "And sent to Ms. DuVull." Well, Jeannie always was a fantastic and fast typer.

Isla looks extremely irritated and defeated. I just continue to work on my article minding my own business.

As Isla huffs and begins to walk away she stops beside me and looks over my shoulder reading what I'm typing. I hate every second of it but I don't want unnecessary conflict so I say nothing.

I almost want to throw my hands over the computer so she can't see it as Riley and Jeannie stare at her skeptically.

"Hmmm." She gives a little giggle from behind me. It doesn't sound like a mean giggle though. So I just continue to type. A couple of moments pass as she points to somewhere on my computer with her big, pointy black nails.

"There umm... there should be a coma there." She says kindly, leaning over me a bit.

"Oh." I begin. "Thank you." She's right. I don't know how I missed that.

"Is this just a portion of the article, or the whole thing?" She seems awkward, almost nervous. Her tone in voice completely changes as she talks to me.

"Just a portion." I stop typing for a moment to look up at her. I can't afford for anyone to steal my ideas, although I have a feeling that is not Isla's intention.

Even if it was, I have this article on lockdown. Practically everyone at DuVull knows I'm doing this article. Isla giggles once again as her eyes continue to scan the article.

"I--it's really nice." Her whole body language has changed as she twists her fingers. "You really seem fond of this Atticus guy." She gives me a kind, closed mouth smile. "Is he your... umm... your boyfriend?"

"Oh no..." I laugh. "we're just friends."

"Don't believe her." Riley says and Jeannie slaps him.

"I don't mean to pry," Isla pushes back a strand of her neatly pushed back hair. I don't think there was any hair that needed to be pushed back actually.

"No, no! It's no problem at all." I begin and then my kindness gets the best of me. "Maybe one day we can collaborate on an article." Oh my god! Why would you say that, Poppy?

"Yeah…" nods Isla. "yeah that would be pretty cool." She gives a weirdly shy wave. "Well, I'll see you."

"See ya." I give an enthusiastic wave back as I continue to get lost in my article.

"And she calls us the freaks." Scoffs Riley.

CHAPTER NINETEEN

Purple Mini Dresses Are So Punk Rock (Don't Tell Me Otherwise)

I make my way through Greenwich Village, humming to the beat of my shoes against the concrete and swaying my purse.

Atticus told me to meet him here and text him as soon as I got out of work. He sounded excited. He did mention he loved it over here. It is, afterall, *so* Atticus.

I always loved The Village too. Creativity blossoms here and it's just so cute and artsy! You never know what you're going to find in The Village, it has everything!

I reach the exact spot he told me to wait for him at. Right in the middle of West 4th street. So… here I am.

Atticus said he had some type of surprise for me. He also told me to make sure I bring my notebook. I have no clue what it could be, but my brain is doing cartwheels at the possibilities.

It's a bit chilly outside, and I wish I could find some place inside to sit but I don't want Atticus to miss me. In all fairness, I am a bit early. At least my outfit's fab though! It makes it worth standing outside in the cold just so everyone could see it!

I'm in my dark blue denim top. It's new and from *New York and Company* and so cute! It has a square neckline, thick shoulder straps and three big gold buttons going down the shirt to the flounced hem a bit above my hip.

I'm also in a matching pencil skirt that's the exact color and denim material. It goes exactly below the knee and has a tiny slit by my right leg. It also has two cute little patch pockets on the back of the skirt, just like a pair of jeans.

Then I just have some silver pumps with three big pom poms on the ankle strap. I also have a black fur coat to protect me from the cold.

My hair is up in a tight ponytail with two little strands on the sides. Perfectly even.

I keep a tight grip on my tiny holographic silver bag that is holding my phone, license and notebook.

My eyes land on the mounds of people crossing the street. I see Atticus strutting down the block. He gives me a friendly smile and enthusiastic wave.

He's in this denim jacket with a bunch of different designs on it all in black. Like a row of cheetah print on the arm, a row of a checkerboard design across the chest, and black writing on the other arm. Looks homemade, but in a good way, a chic way. We match with our denim and it's absolutely adorable. We didn't even plan it!

He's also in a black, tight T-shirt and skinny jeans. He has a black beanie on and one silver, dangly earring in the shape of a cross.

As he gets closer I notice the multiple rings on his fingers as well as the little silver chain around his neck.

"Hey." He says as he reaches me, extending his arms. I gladly embrace him in a hug. He's so tall compared to me, my head falls in the middle of his chest.

"Hi!" I look up into the sea of his deep brown eyes. I let go of the hug first and fix my outfit. "So, what's this so-called 'surprise'? What are we doing?" I ask excitedly yet impatiently. I'm kind of nervous, I have to tell you.

"Well if I told you it wouldn't be that much of a surprise, would it?" Atticus cocks up a brow and I smile. What could it be...

"Come on," He motions me with his head. I notice he's a couple of steps away from me already. He's practically bouncing up and down as he puts out his hand for me to take. For a moment I'm taken aback.

I just stand there as I look down at his large hand, scattered with huge, shiny silver rings on his fingers and chipping black nail polish.

I stride towards him and gingerly put my hand out towards him. I don't know why it's shaking. I pull my hand back for a second but Atticus is patient with me.

I haven't really held hands with anyone since Liam. He wasn't very affectionate. I held hands with Atticus once and the only reason we were holding hands was because he was dragging us away from the cops.

Holding hands is platonic though, isn't it? It can be I suppose. I don't know why it's so scary for me. Why am I even overthinking this?

"It's ok." Atticus says cautiously, as if taming an animal at the zoo. I put my hand in his and the minute I do, he holds it in a tight grip. Tighter than Liam ever has.

We just walk as he whisks me away to this so-called "surprise." He playfully swings our arms back and forth and I can't help but giggle.

After a couple of blocks Atticus stops in front of a tiny, brick building.

"Ta da!" He holds his arms out excitedly pointing to the building without letting go of my hand.

I inspect the tiny building and look to see the sign that reads *Village Punk Shop*. There are drawn, purple skulls all over the window next to the sign and it overall looks really dark and mysterious. It almost looks like a tattoo parlor. That type of style.

"Oh my god!" I squeal. "This is absolutely perfect for the article, Atticus!"

"I know!" He says just as excited as I am. "Wait until we go inside and you see all the clothes, and the shoes, and the art..." he breaks off. "It's pretty dope." I take a mental picture in my head of the place. I'll try to remember it. I would usually take out my phone to take a picture but I fear if I let go of Atticus's hand, I won't be able to hold it again. And I'm not sure I want to face rejection when I go to hold his hand again. Not that I think he would reject me but... I don't know! Don't listen to me!

"What are you thinking? Atty tilts his head, trying to read my expression.

"Oh nothing." I shake my head profusely. "Let's go inside!"

When we walk inside the shop, Atticus opens the door for me and I thank him. I feel hot air hit my face as soon as we enter. I still kind of hate heating. Even when it's cold. The heat is just so uncomfortable.

The exact minute we enter, Atticus quickly drops his hand and puts it in his pocket as if he wasn't just holding it. Immediately as he does it, it feels as if my heart just sinks.

He just looks around the shop, avoiding my gaze. Why is he acting so strange right now? You see *this* is why we shouldn't have held hands!

Well I suppose it's my fault as well. What did I expect? For him to hold my hand the whole time? That would be silly.

"Oh look who's here...finally got your ass outta bed huh, Atty boy." I hear an annoying deep New York accent and an even more annoying laugh. Oh...*oh*. That's why.

I see Dallon walk out of, what seems like, the back of the store in a black leather jacket and blue jeans. He chews the toothpick in his mouth and pushes back his sleek, black hair. Great.

At least I know why Atticus let go of my hand.

Atticus clears his throat and suddenly Dallon brings his attention to me.

"Poppy..." Dallon begins. "hi."

"Hi."

"How are you?"

"Fine." I answer in one word statements and Dallon just nods his head in defeat.

I look around the store and it is just dark. There are a couple of installed lights but overall, the only thing keeping the store lit is the windows and the sun from the outside world. It's like the people who come in here are vampires or something.

There is clothing hanging from every nook in the store and a tiny shoe section. There is a velvet purple curtain in the back of the store and a matching couch next to it. I guess that's the dressing area.

There is pop art and graffiti all over the black walls and overall every piece of clothing in the store kind of has a goth, fast fashion look to it.

"What do you think?" Atticus looks at me, expectantly.

"It's errrr... lovely!" I give a tight smile. It's not really my style, but that's the point! That's what makes it great.

"Now, I know it's not really your scene but this will really help your article, won't it? You made me try a different style so... surprise." My tense shoulders relax when I see the excited and hopeful look in Atticus's eyes.

"It's awesome, Atticus." I smile. "Show me around. Have you ever been here?"

"Half my wardrobe is from here." He laughs. "I like taking stuff from here and either rip it, cut it, paint it, make it mine."

"That's cool." I turn to him suddenly.

"I guess." He seems to blush as he looks down, a cute smile on his face.

"No seriously! You design."

"I dabble." We begin to walk around the store and Dallon seems to follow.

"If you were wondering, I work here." Dallon interrupts.

"Yeah no one was wondering." I quip.

"Listen Poppy," I turn to Dallon and out of the corner of my eye could see Atticus giving him a somewhat dangerous glare. "I'm sorry I called you a priss. I really am. I honestly thought you wouldn't hear... but it was wrong as is." He seems genuine as he continues to chew on his toothpick. "Now if there's any way I could make it up to you... I could treat ya to dinner." He looks from me to the floor with a smirk.

"You're a bastard."

"Right."

"Dallon?" I hear Atticus beside me, his voice deep and rigid.

He looks as if he's about to combust. His face has gotten red and his fists are clenched and his knuckles have gone completely white.

"Can I talk to you outside?" It's more of a demand than request. His nostrils start to flare and his tongue is poking the side of his mouth.

"Sure..."

"Great." Atticus begins to stalk outside after he tells me he'll be right back. He slams the door shut behind them. Well, ok then.

I begin to look through the rows of eccentric clothing. There is a lot of black but also quite a lot of color hidden in between the black.

What was *that* all about? Did Dallon really just ask me out to dinner with him? As if!

'Make it up to you,' he said. Gross.

And why was Atticus getting so upset? Mad?

God, I don't think I've ever seen Atticus that pissed off before. I didn't think Atticus was even capable of looking pissed off. But, I must say, he looks quite scary when he is.

I take out my notebook and just write down what I see,

"Lots of black. Like...lots. Pop art, graffiti, no lights. The clothing is edgy. Female clothing could be quite revealing..." I pick up a black mesh top with nothing but two tiny pieces of black tap in the shape of an x covering the... chest area. *"VERY revealing."* I stress. *"Lots of festival-like clothing."*

I hear the ring of a bell as the front door to the store opens. I see Atticus walk in and give him a bright smile.

"Everything ok?" I ask as he reaches my side.

"What? Oh, oh yeah. Everything's fine!" He pulls a face and shrugs as if nothing happened.

"Where's Dallon?" I dare ask.

"He had to go get something. I told him I'd look after the store for him. His boss doesn't care much." He says hitting the points of the follow up questions I was going to ask him.

"Oh." I shrug. "Alright!"

"Why? Did you want him here?" He asks, uncertainty laced in his voice.

"I don't care. Whatever you want!" I beam. Why? Does Atticus not want him here? What's going on? Men are so sneaky, I swear.

Atticus just nods his head. He seems deep in thought.

"See anything you like?" He pops up, changing the subject.

"I mean... it's interesting." I hold a black leather bra with neon green stars in between my fingertips. "Do the girls who shop here not eat or something?" I say as I begin to search through the rack again. "These clothes are so tiny. Atticus, I don't know if anythings gonna fit me. This is literally a size 3." I hold up the tiniest dress I've ever seen. It's tie dyed rainbow and actually kind of cute if it wasn't so short.

Hey, I'm all for a mini dress but when it looks more like a tank top then a dress, that's where I draw the line.

At least I'm not Tiff. She won't even wear anything above her kneecaps. People used to think she was amish.

"Hmmmm..." Atticus hums skeptically. "I'm sure we'll find something."

After a couple of minutes of looking through the endless racks of clothing I hear Atticus take something off the rack beside me.

"What about this?" I turn to him and inspect the mini dress in his hands. It's a dark purple, ruffled dress with a velvet feel. It has puffy sleeves that seem to hang off the shoulder and a pretty deep neckline. It goes a bit below the waist.

It's extremely short but not as short as some other dresses in here. It is way above the knees. It looks curve friendly though, and I do have curves, so at this point I'll take anything.

I walk over to Atticus and hold the dress between my fingers. I look at the size. Not bad. Then I look at the price tag. 45.00 dollars. Fair. So if I ruin it, I'm not going to have to pay 200 dollars for a dress I hate, nor fits me. It's actually a nice dress though.

"Ok." I nod my head, "Ok, deal."

"Yes!" Atticus high fives me excitedly. "Now shoes and accessories."

I find myself standing in the dressing room looking in the full body mirror. I hear Atticus shift about and sit on the purple couch (that ironically matches my dress) outside of the dressing room.

He told me to give him my notebook and purse so he could write what I tell him and how I feel just like I did to him.

I look at the clothing we chose hanging on the hook behind me in fear.

The shoes are these black wedge platform boots. They are *huge* and almost look impossible to walk in. The boots have a whole bunch of intricate buckles and chains on them that make it even more complicated to put on. With it I have a studded choker that Atticus so graciously picked out. The studs are spiky and the material of the choker is pure, black leather.

Here goes nothing I guess.

I begin to shimmy on the mini purple dress. It's tight, but it fits pretty well. I look in the mirror to make sure I look ok. It actually doesn't look half bad. I don't look at myself for too long though. If I do, I'm bound to find some type of unnecessary flaw that will stop me from leaving the dressing room.

I finally manage to get on the platform boots and, of course, trip while doing so.

"Poppy…" I hear outside the dressing room.

"I'm ok!" I assure.

I then put the spiky choker around my neck and once again inspect myself in the mirror.

I sigh and put my hands on my hips. I take out my ponytail and run my hands through my long blonde hair, letting it cascade down my back. I shake it out a bit until it looks quite mental. It still looks good though. Goes with the vibe of the outfit.

I take a deep breath and push aside the curtain of the dressing room before I change my mind. It's for the article, it's for the article, it's for the article, do it for the article...

Atticus's gaze immediately looks up from his chipping black nails and meets mine.

I just stand in front of him awkwardly, fiddling with my hands then swinging my arms back and forth.

His eyes have gone a tad darker than they usually are and he seems like he wants to say something but the words are stuck in the back of his throat.

I stall my movements when I see his expression. His tongue pokes out of the side of his mouth as he goes to wet his lips. I'm suddenly unable to move under his gaze. It makes me feel light-headed and kind of breathless.

There's a general feel in the air, I can feel the tension growing in the room as we stare at each other, dumbfounded. All the thoughts I had in my head, fleeing as soon as Atticus's eyes met mine.

I try to pull down the dress but it just makes the top go even lower, so I decide to just leave it be and huff in frustration.

Atticus suddenly looks away as his leg begins to bounce anxiously. I turn away as well, feeling my cheeks heat up under his stare.

"So, ummmm..." he hastily grabs my notebook and finds an empty page with my pen stuck into it. "how do you feel?" He asks, voice a bit shaky as he seems to snap both of us out of our current daze.

"Well..." I begin with a laugh as I rest my hands on my hips. "It sure is different."

"I can tell." He gives a laugh but it sounds more like an exasperated sigh.

"Ummm..." I motion towards the notebook. "It feels a bit tight." Atticus snorts and begins writing. "It's very different. I don't feel like me. The shoes are a bit uncomfortable. I don't understand how anyone can walk with these... and," I tug at the choker. "this choker makes me feel like a dog." I give a stressed giggle and I hear Atticus chuckle from under his breath.

"I understand that." He says as he writes. "I'm going to ask you the same question you asked me? So it's even. Is that ok?" He flips between pages.

"That's fine. Shoot."

"How would you change the outfit?"

"Hmmmm..." I think for a moment. "I'd probably replace the choker with a necklace. A statement piece for sure. Something big to balance out the plainness of the dress. Not that the dress isn't great, but...it's a little one dimensional besides the ruffles. And a little *too* goth-ish for my liking as well." I watch as Atticus jots down my words. "And I'd replace the shoes with something that matched the necklace. Pumps. Something silver and sparkly. Silver would definitely go well with the purple on the dress." I just stand in the same exact spot for a couple of more seconds while Atticus continues to write.

I move from side to side and cross my legs awkwardly, pursing my lips together.

Atticus looks up as he closes the book and gives a chuckle, watching me struggling to stand on my wedges. I blush as I try to discreetly pull up the dress.

"Are you alright?" He asks.

"Yeah." I just decided to cross my arms over my chest. The amount of cleavage this dress is showing is more than I usually wear. It's not making me feel uncomfortable but it's making me feel self conscious. I doubt I would feel that way in front of anyone but Atticus. Atticus is different for some reason right now.

"I'm gonna..." I motion back to the dressing room.

"Sure." Atticus finishes my sentence, laughing at my awkward behavior.

The minute I enter the dressing room and close the curtain I take a deep breath. Thank god that's over with.

CHAPTER TWENTY

Girls Night

Tiff continues to pour more wine into both our glasses as she walks back to me and plops herself onto the couch.

"I'm absolutely starving." She says as she opens the freshly made, greasy Brooklyn style pizza still in it's box. I'm already engulfed in a slice.

We both just sit in silence as we flip through the channels on the TV in front of us.

"You know," begins Tiff breaking the silence. "that picture is really bothering me, I got to tell you." I follow her gaze but I don't even have to look at the picture to realize that she's talking about the one of me and Liam.

"Why?" I ask, a mouthful of pizza.

"What do you mean 'why'? Both of you aren't a thing anymore. He doesn't deserve that spot on your counter! What's stopping you from taking that picture and chucking it?"

"I like it!"

"No!" Tiff shouts. "You shouldn't! Here," She gets up and reaches the kitchen counter. She grabs the frame and tosses it onto the couch next to me. She then sits back down and I look at her stupidly.

"What the hell do you want me to do with it?"

"Burn it, smash it against the wall, write something vulgar over his face, I don't care, just do something!"

"Are you drunk?"

"No!"

"Then why are you doing this?"

"Let me tell you something," Tiff starts hastily. "you already let him go. You said it yourself, you're not in love with him anymore. I remember it. The hard part is over so in reality, what is this picture really doing for you? Wouldn't it be nice not to have to pass his stupid face every morning?" I usually don't even pay it any mind anymore if I'm being honest.

I fear I might either shatter it against this wall or cling it to my chest and cry. I think back to when Atticus asked me who was in the picture beside me.

I look down at it and I must say, I don't know either of those people. I've changed so much since Liam, I really have.

I take a long swig of my wine finishing every last drop. Two glasses, that's enough for me. Plus, I'm pretty light-weight. We wouldn't want another situation with drinking if you remember correctly. I'm buzzed enough though and so is Tiff.

"Let's do it." I say confidently.

"Let's do what?" Asks Tiff stupidly, sipping her wine.

"Smash the picture! Rip it up, I don't know. Let's just demolish it." I say and I can't believe my own words. Why am I so okay with this? Who is this known and improved Poppy? I like her!

"Oh, I got it!" Gets up Tiff fidgety, grabbing the picture off of the couch. She walks over to the window next to the TV and points to it excitedly as I walk over to her.

"Throw it out the window, Pops!"

"Tiff," I sigh. "we can't throw it out the window..."

"You're right!" Tiff perks up and runs to one of the drawers in my kitchen.

She comes back with a black marker. She hands both the picture and marker to me as if it's a diploma of some sort. I take it and smile.

I rip the marker cap open and write 'You Suck' on top of Liam's far-head while Tiff watches and giggles.

"Genius."

"Should we really throw it out the window?" I ask. "What if someone sees it? Or it hits someone?" I gasp. To my shock this new reckless, drunk Tiff rolls her eyes.

"If they knew Liam, they would understand."

"Ok, ok..." I take a deep breath. I look at the picture one last time, love yet hate filing my veins. I think I'm finally ready to let go.

As I let the picture drop out of my hands, the brisk Brooklyn air hits my face and I feel free as I hear the frame shatter down onto the concrete below us. I don't look down though. I can't. I just close the window as If I'm closing an ending chapter of my life. It feels good. It feels pretty damn good actually.

I sit back down on the couch with Tiff after our little escapade. That's it. It's over. It's really over.

I just finished telling her about all the crazy stuff I've been up to with Atticus. I remember telling her some stuff happened over the phone but I just *had* to tell her in person.

We cuddle up with our matching pillows in our laps watching *Say Yes To The Dress* and judge each dress the bride-to-be tries on, whether we like it or not. That's the thing about Tiff and I, we always have something to say.

Three months ago I couldn't watch one of these shows or listen to a love song without a bitter aftertaste and now I could listen to them with no issue. I could smile at them now, they give me butterflies. What happened, I don't know. Am I really that stupid? Why don't I know? It irks me, it really does. Maybe it's because I'm finally letting go of Liam. That I realize I'm better off without him. Yeah. I'm sure that's it.

"You know," Tiff begins. "I think it's time I meet this Atticus character."

"Oh, you think?" I don't pay it much mind, I rather keep my eyes on the women on the TV in the beautiful, sheer top, drop-waist ball gown. I could never pull that off. When I get married, I wouldn't want any part of my dress to be see-through. You have to keep it somewhat classy.

"I do." Tiff nods.

"Then why don't you knock on his door right now. I saw Dallon and Finnick walk in before you came. I'm sure he's in there practicing" I say sarcastically.

"Oh, so I could catch the man in action?"

"Yep." Before I know what is happening Tiff takes out her phone and looks him up online.

"What are you do--"

"Let's see... Atticus Mckeen on *instagram*, Atticus Mckeen on *Twitter*, Atticus Mckeen on *Facebook*. Gross, who uses *Facebook* anymore..."

"Tiff what are you doing?" I ask cautiously.

"Looking him up." She shrugs. God, she's just like her mom sometimes. Helen stalks everyone. She knows everyone and their mother's business.

"Let's do *instagram.*" She says happily and not a moment later, watch as she pulls a face at her screen.

"Oh god, what?" I throw the pillow over my eyes in fright.

I don't know why this is making me so anxious. Well, everything makes me anxious but that's beside the point! It's not like he can see it, right?

"Can he see it?" I ask.

"No, I'm in incognito mode." Tiff says, squinting down at her phone. What the hell is that? Why do I care if he sees it? I don't. I honestly don't, I swear. "His name is ATTYMCKEEN." She shouts and I put my hands over my ears.

"Ow! What the hell are you screaming for?"

"It was in all caps." She says defensively. "It says here he creates and performs music with his band *The Deadbeats*. It says to follow them on all their social media including *YouTube* and *spotify…*" I giggle to myself. How very hipster of them.

"He also says he is the lead singer of the band, he gives his email for professional purposes only, some random song lyrics at the bottom, the whole nine yards in the backyard, ya know."

"I wanna see!" I toss my pillow to the side.

I get my first glimpse at Atticus's *Instagram* and of course It's filled to the brim with aesthetically pleasing pictures of himself.

If I didn't know Atticus any better, I would think he was already a star. Or If I didn't know Atticus as much as I do, I would think he was quite vain. He's vain, but not as vain as he makes himself seem.

"Let's start at his latest post, shall we?" Tiff clicks happily on the top post.

Atticus is on what looks like the top of a building in his green and black sweater shirt. He's holding up his fingers in the 'rock on' symbol like he always does and his hair is messed up and mental. It's a pretty close up picture, chest up I would say.

You could see every little dimple and birthmark on his face.

He has his one silver earring that dangles down to his defined chin and all his silver chains around his neck.

His deep brown eyes seem to be the focus of the photo though. At least they are for me. The photo is captioned 'Nothing ever completed him, he needed someone to compete with him, but she refused to be the victim of another lonely boy.' Those lyrics sound so familiar to me. I think that they might be his own.

Mmmmm... dramatic.

Like him.

"Wow." breaths Tiff wide-eyed. "*That's* him? That's Atticus?"

"That's Atticus." I say just as breathless.

"He's..." Tiff nods her head. "he's something."

She goes on to the next picture. It's a full body picture. He's in his normal skinny, ripped, black jeans and black Shirt with some random band on it. He has a long sleeved black and white striped shirt underneath it as well.

He's wearing his dirty worn out converses and, once again, multiple silver chains draped around his neck and connected to the loops on his jeans.

He's smiling into the camera with that wide huge, dimpled grin of his like the person taking the picture of him just said something extremely funny. I bet it was Finnick.

The picture looks like it was taken pretty late at night in front of a mural. I know that mural. It's in Soho. He looks stunning, like a punk model or something, I don't know.

All of a sudden I hear Tiff start to chuckle beside me.

"He's..."

"A hipster?" I ask.

"Yeah." Tiff bursts out into laughter. "That's one way to put it." We both just look through his social media for the next twenty minutes and giggle at all his pictures and lyrics he captions every picture with.

No, we don't giggle, we laugh. Tiff laughed so hard at one of the captions she fell off the couch.

In the background plays Atticus and his band. It's quite muffled through the doors, but you could still hear it. As always. Please, the moment Tiff heard them start to play she looked at me and asked if we could go over to listen to them. She called it a 'Private showing.' She is most *definitely* more buzzed than I am.

"I got to say..." begins Tiff sighs longingly. "I kind of like him."

"You do?"

"Oh yes." She nods. "I don't even know him and I like him better than I ever liked Liam."

"Well you can't compare him to Liam." I retort. "Liam was my boyfriend." Tiff just rolls her eyes.

"Mmmm ok."

"Ok what?" I quip.

"Nothing."

"What?" I cry. "Tell me."

"It's just that I find it ironic," Tiff throws her phone to the side and turns her body towards me. "you're always helping Jeannie with these articles about boys and love advice. Have you ever tried to listen to yourself for once? Hmmm?" She purses her lips together and gives me a glare.

"I—" I begin but am cut off by Tiff reaching for the latest issue of *DuVull* on my coffee table. I watch her flip to the romance section.

"You most certainly read the newest issue for a fact, front to back, I know that." She seems to find the page she was looking for and clears her throat. "'He's like a pair of Loui Vutton pumps; beautiful, sharp, and hard to find. If he's like this he's a keeper. Men are stubburn, annoying, and--at times--stupid. Someone will make going through that good-for-nothing ex of yours worth it though. You just have to find him, and once you have, you need not to be stubborn and let him in. If you don't, how will you know how amazing he is? How will he know how amazing you are?" Tiff looks up at me and throws the magazine back on the coffee table. "You wrote those lines for Jeannie. You said it yourself, you helped her."

"So?"

"So? So who was running through your head when you wrote that, Pops?"

"No one!" I retort defensively, but my voice gets higher.

"You're a big fat liar!" Tiff shrieks.

"Am not!"

"You like him! You said it yourself, stop being so stubborn."

"I don't like Atticus." I sneer.

"How do you know?"

"I--"

"You don't. Exactly." Tiff looks me in the eye with a look only a best friend could give you. It's a stare as if to say 'tell me I'm wrong.' Well, I can't. I'm lost in thought.

Do I like Atticus? No, surely I don't. He's very handsome, but I could never. Liking Atticus is impossible, it can't even be an option. Not even a little crush, because a little crush turns into bigger things and I just can't endure that. I just can't get hurt again. I'm not ready.

Just as I'm about to open my mouth and say something there's a knock on the door. Me and Tiff both stand up, looking at each other with skeptical glares.

"Who the hell is that at this hour?" She begins. "I got it."

I stand behind her as she opens the door and to my absolute horror, it's Atticus.

The moment Tiff throws the door open and meets Atticus's tall figure, a somewhat incoherent noise comes out of her mouth, like she was about to say something but stops in her tracks. I didn't even realize the band stopped playing until now.

I move even closer to Tiff now looking over her shoulder and giving Atticus a feebal wave. He sees me behind Tiff and gives me an adorable closed mouth smile--what else is new--and enthusiastic wave back.

"Hi..." begins Tiff calmly as I walk next to her. "I'm guessing you want to talk to Poppy." She turns and gives me a tight smile as she motions towards him with her head.

"Hey." I squeak.

He's in ripped blue jeans with a tucked in green shirt. It has some band logo on it. He also has a single stud earring and a single tiny gold chain.

"Atticus, this is my best friend Tiff. Tiff, this is umm...Is umm... this is my Atticus." Oh *god,* I cringe as soon as I say it. What's wrong with me!

'My Atticus.' Great job, Poppy!

Tiff gives Atticus a friendly wave and Atticus gives one right back.

"Is everything alright?" I ask as I reach him.

Tiff moves out of the way slightly and stands behind me. I could tell she's pretending not to watch as she fiddles with random stuff on my kitchen counter.

Oh god I hope he didn't know we were talking about him? Did he hear? Oh he probably heard! Welp, it's over, that's that.

"Everythings fine," he begins. "I just heard a bunch of shouting. Usually it's quiet on your end. I just wanted to make sure you were ok." He smiles. Oh, he most certainly heard.

"Well, everything is fine! Thanks for checking--" I begin vastly closing the door on him but he catches it and opens it once again.

"Poppy..." Atticus begins. He picks my chin up with his pointer finger and forces me to stare into his big brown eyes. They're stunning. Absolutely stunning. I hate looking him in the eyes because then I remember how stunning they actually are.

The way his finger is holding up my chin forcing me to look at him is making me absolutely breathless. It's such a simple move, but so foreign to me. Liam never did something like that. He hardly ever touched me.

"What's going on?" He gives a laugh but I could tell he's actually concerned.

"Nothing." I begin but then squint my eyes at him. "Why? Did you hear anything... interesting?" I try to get anything I can out of him.

"Not that I know of." He chuckles. "But I did go outside to throw away my garbage and..." he pulls out the shattered frame me and Tiff just threw out from behind his back. It still has the picture of me and Liam inside of it, cracked glass sitting right across his face. "It almost hit me. I gotta say though, I was pleasantly surprised when I picked it up."

"You were?" Asks Tiff behind me. "Sorry..." she mumbles.

"You were?" I ask for myself.

"I was."

"Well..." I swallow deeply. "that's nice."

"Nice?" He asks smirking, his large white teeth and deep dimples on full display now.

"Yeah... nice." I laugh.

We look into each other's eyes for a moment and I feel as if I'm crumbling slowly. I'm suddenly finding myself very confused.

Atticus's soft facial features now turn back into his usual cocky smile and he drops my chin from under his finger, my entire body almost collapsing into itself as he does so.

I snap myself out of the moment but I'm finding myself missing his touch.

"Well, would you like me to throw this out for you?" He asks, waving the picture around.

"Yes, that would be lovely, thank you." I say below a whisper and he just nods.

"Ok we'll do. I'm sure I'll see you around Tiff. It was a pleasure." Atticus salutes her.

"I'm sure you will." Tiff nods confidently.

"Night, Atticus." I say softly, beginning to close the door.

"Night, Blondie." I see him look down and smile and I can't help but smile as well. Is it bad that I missed that nickname?

I lock the door slowly and turn to Tiff. She has a huge excited smile on her face as she begins to squeal.

"Oh my god Pops! He's perfect!"

"Oh please Tiffany…" I sigh as if I don't have crazy butterflies in my stomach. "he's a friend. A good friend. Nothing more, nothing less."

"Oh a friend? Friends don't look at each other like that."

"Such a cliche romance trope." I roll my eyes.

"Ok, I digress." Tiff puts her hands up in mock surrender. "I'll be watching very closely. Don't come running to me when you realize you have feelings for him. I'll tell you I told you so." She warns.

"Well that's the best part isn't it? Tiff's always right. Well not this time" I say yet those damn butterflies remain.

CHAPTER TWENTY-ONE
Inconvenience

My heels click against the concrete steps of my parents house as I walk up the steep stairs. I take a deep breath and compose myself before ringing the new electronic door bell my dad and Carlo installed last weekend.

Supposedly it has cameras in it or something. My dad's always been super paranoid. My mom took a video of them installing it and sent it to me. Apparently Carlo didn't help much. He's not much of a handyman, that's for sure.

I wait outside in the cold for a while and ponder over how it's already December. December! Can you believe it? My mom is already freaking out about Hanukkah preparations.

'ENTERING THE LION'S DEN. WISH ME LUCK.' I text the group chat I have between me, Arlo, Jeannie, and Riley. Immediately I get a reply from Jeannie.

'GOOD LUCK. TELL YOUR SISTER I SAID CONGRATS LMAO.' I just snort at the message and shove my phone into my *Dolce and Gabbana* leather, black crossbody bag.

It has a gold chain as the strap and In the middle of the bag is a huge gold heart made out of crystals. In the very center of the heart is the *DG* symbol in gold, (I got it with my last paycheck! Just... don't ask how much it was.)

I ran into Atticus as I was rushing out of the apartment this morning, (Like... actually ran into him.) He looked down at my bag and took it from me, wrapping the gold chain strap around his neck.

'Wow Poppy, a chain! I must say, I'm in shock. You think I could rock it?' I just giggled and shook my head, still a bit flushed at the events that happened last night. I really hope he didn't hear me and Tiff talking about him.

He followed me down the elevator and asked me why I was in such a rush. I told him it's because I spent way too long getting my outfit together and lost track of time, and If I wasn't on time for this blessed event, my mother and sister would have my head.

He laughed and walked me to the nearest bus stop, telling me to text him when I got here. Just to make sure I got there safely. Which is comforting. The only other person who's ever said that to me was my dad when I went to prom.

So that's my first mission when I get inside. Text Atticus.

As the door finally swings open my mom stands there in her apron and blue jeans. Her bluntly cut bob is in front of her face as she frantically tries to push it away.

"Oh, hi dear." She says with faux calmness. "Come in."

"Hey ma..." I walk into the house as she closes the door behind me and scurries back into the dining room. I follow her and see Diamante and Diamante's best friend Connie at our dining room table. "and everyone." Oh my god is this it? From the sounds of it, mom was throwing this huge mandatory 'wedding meeting.' Is this all the people that made it?

I watch as Diamante plays with the leaves of her chocolate covered strawberry on her plate and Connie gives me a warm smile as she rises up from her seat.

"Hey, girl." She says and kisses me on the cheek. I can't help but smile into her hug. I always loved Connie. She's way too kind to be my sister's best friend.

"Hey Connie!" I bend down to look at my sister who can't seem to make eye contact with me. So I just wrap my arms around her and kiss the top of her head.

She doesn't even move. She's in a blue button up shirt, jeans, and her dirty blonde hair is up in a ponytail.

I look up to Connie who just shrugs her shoulders, so I don't even try.

I find my seat at the end of the table just as my mom walks out of the kitchen with little hors'devours

"Where is Carlo's mom?" I ask. "I thought she was coming?" Both my mom and Connie give me a warning glare.

"Carlo's mother couldn't make it today." States Diamante coldly.

"She's a very busy woman you know." Well apparently she is because she never comes to anything else.

"Ok," my mom takes a seat next to me. "let's get planning, shall we? Now Dia, did you and Carlo find a date…"

"June seventeenth." Diamante answers stone cold with no emotion. All I hear is the silent gasp that comes out of both me and my mom's mouths.

"Darling," begins my mom. "thats six months away! How are you going to find a venue? How are you--"

"You don't think I'm freaking out either!" Diamante erupts. "I want a summer wedding, and I *will* get a summer wedding."

"Why not in July or August?"

"Carlo's parents are going to be on a cruise!" She cries dramatically. Here we go…

"For two months?" I question biting into a pizza roll. Diamante snaps her head towards me viciously.

"Yes, Patricia. Two. Months." She spits and Connie gives her arm a gentle pat.

"Ok." I shrug, not having the energy to care, grabbing a couple more pizza rolls. God, I love these.

"June seventeenth it is then!" Mom scribbles it down in the little notebook titled 'Dia's wedding' beside her.

She's so excited and Diamante could honestly care less about involving her. How could you do that? How could you not want your mother to help you leading up to your *wedding.* Although she's a pain in the ass, she's still our mother.

"Now," begins mom. "I talked to Rabbi John at temple. He said anytime, any place he would be honored to marry you and Carlo…"

"We are not getting married in a temple, ma, and we're surely not getting married by a Rabbi. We don't want to cater to just one religion!" Diamante retorts. I told mom, I *told* her… "I have already decided. I'm getting married at Clove Lake." My mom practically spits out the tea she was drinking and I stifle a snort. Ha! Mom owes me five bucks! I told her it was going to be by a lake!

For those of you who aren't familiar with Staten Island, Clove Lake is a cute little remote park. A lot of people get married there, it's stunning. I just personally wouldn't get married there. Sue me!

"Oh crap!" It suddenly occurs to me that I forgot to text Atticus. "Sorry." I slap my hand over my mouth and apologize for the interruption. I quickly take out my phone and bring up Atticus's number.

ME- 'HEY. GOT TO MY PARENTS HOUSE. JUST LETTING YOU KNOW:)'

"Who are you texting?" Diamante asks, venom filling her voice as she tilts her head.

"My friend." I clutch the phone to my chest as if she were to take Atticus away from me.

"Tiffany?"

"No."

"Then who? What other friends do you even have besides that gay couple and lesbian chick."

"None of your business." I retort quietly. "Leave my friends alone."

"Then put it down. It's disrespectful. We're planning *my* wedding. Not everythings about you."

"Diamante..." mom warns and Diamante crosses her arms like the brat she is.

After Diamante's little tantrum, I just silently put my phone beside me on the table. Mom scribbles 'Clove Lake' in the notebook under the column that says 'venue'

She's looking at it regretfully and I feel this horrible ache for her. Poor mom.

"The dress," mom looks up with new found hope. "Any ideas, love?"

"Something flowy. Something I could wear without shoes." Oh, I'm done! I heard it all. I hate when brides don't wear shoes. Your feet will get dirty!

"Oh dear." I hear mom mumble beside me. "Poppy, you're great at... shopping! Any suggestions?"

"Uh yeah," I begin. Not that she would want it. "there are some boutiques in the village. You probably don't want anything quite grand, so, somewhere in the village for sure."

"Alright. I'll look into it." Diamante surprisingly says.

"Now Poppy," begins mom. "will you get your maid of honor dress there as well or--"

"Wait a minute," Diamante shakes her head. "Poppy is *not* going to be my maid of honor! Connie will be my maid of honor."

"But traditionally the sister is the maid of honor..." stammers mom, slamming her pen down on the notebook completely done. She looks absolutely stunned as she takes off her glasses.

"Yeah," Connie begins. "maid of honor really should go to Poppy."

I just remain quiet.

"No, no, no!" Diamante loses it. "This is my wedding! Stop trying to control me!" Connie rubs her arm and hushes her.

"No one is trying to control you!" Then to my absolute horror, my phone goes off.

I watch as everyone's head snaps towards me and before I could reach it, Diamante rips it off the table.

"Oh this is *exactly* why you're not going to be maid of honor..." she rambles but then looks down at the device in her hands. "who's Atticus?" She asks as her voice gets uncontrollably more shaky as if she's about to completely lose her mind. "And why is he calling you? Is this Atticus more important than *my* wedding?"

"Diamante give me back my phone now!" I rise out of my seat, raising my voice and trying my best to stick up for myself.

"Diamante, you give Poppy her phone back and act like an adult!" Mom shouts.

My heart drops when I helplessly watch Diamante answer the phone, putting it on speaker.

"Hello?" She asks rigidly.

"Uhhh... hi." I hear Atticus's raspy slur. "Is Poppy there?" Thank god he recognizes it's not me. I run over to Diamante but she holds the phone in the air, taunting me.

Ok, now it's on.

"Yes she is. This is her sister and apparently you calling is more important than my wedding. So I hope you're happy! I don't give a damn who you are, but--" I shove her onto the staircase next to us and watch as she loses her balance and falls, the phone dropping out of her hands as she does so.

I manage to grab the phone off the floor and run back towards my seat.

"Atticus? Atticus, this is Poppy. I just ripped the phone out of my sister's hands, I'm..." I suddenly feel tears escape my eyes. "I'm sorry for the inconvenience." And before he can say anything else, I hang up.

I vastly shove my phone back into my purse and get my coat on, watching Connie help Diamante get up.

"Poppy, where are you going?" Asks my mom, grabbing my arm.

"I think I'm going to head back home for the day." I say as I wipe the tears away from my face, already having enough. Damn, now my mascara's running!

"But we haven't even gotten anywhere!"

"Oh, I don't think you care to get anywhere with me." I shoot Diamante a glare. "I'm just an inconvenience."

"Rubbish, sit down!" Tries my mom.

My sister says nothing. Absolutely nothing. She just sits there scowling at me but just for a *mere* second when she sees the tears on my cheek, something flickers behind her eyes. Regret? Sadness prehapes? No, Diamante doesn't experience those emotions. At least not with me.

I wiggle my arm out of my mom's grasp and throw my purse over my shoulder.

Just as I'm about to walk out of the house, I turn back around and everyone watches me with bated breath.

I hastily grab a napkin and put some pizza rolls in them, throwing them into my bag.

And last but never least against my better judgment, I stick both my middle fingers up at Diamante.

Mom loudly gasps but Diamante says nothing.

So, I turn back around leaving the house and slamming the door behind me.

I sit in my apartment at my tiny little missionary desk. The only light shining is the zebra print lamp next to me and the laptop screen in front of me.

I look around at all the bags around me. I went a little crazy after I got home from the whole 'wedding planning party' and told the bus driver to drop me off at fifth avenue. Yes, I stress shop. Shocker, right.

All of a sudden I hear the ping of my phone beside me, picking it up vastly seeing it's Jane.

'POPPY, I NEED YOUR ARTICLE BY 10PM TOMORROW AT THE LATEST! WHAT IS GOING ON WITH YOU!? YOU NEVER GO MIA ON ME!' I slam my phone beside me and throw my head in my hands.

Now I find myself just full on sobbing, hot tears streaming down my cheeks.

Come on Poppy, what the hell is wrong with you? Don't you want that promotion? Get it together!

Ok… take a deep breath.

It is then that I open my word docs. I have five magazine pages already. I just need the opening paragraph, the ending paragraph, and if I could just get some more time with Atticus for one more example that would be ideal.

I could do this, I could do this, come on Poppy, Come on…

I begin the opening paragraph.

"Pop Punk culture is slowly taking the world by storm. It is not only a genre of music but a way of life. Just like any other lifestyle that a person decides to live, pop punk lifestyle is nothing but… well, a lifestyle. A lifestyle that involves very different and risky clothing, piercings, Tattoos, concerts, and, of course, music.

I had the absolute honor of following around a good friend of mine, Atticus Mckeen and taking a look at his lifestyle as well as showing him a bit of mine. Atticus is lead singer and guitarist of the band 'The Deadbeats' and dare I say, future heartthrob of the so-called 'scene' world."

I sit back and admire my opening paragraph for a second.

Ok, Poppy. Not bad. Now get this done!

As I continue typing, I hear a knock on my door. Who the hell is it? It better not be mom…

I stalk towards my door and rip it open only to see Atticus standing there with a container in his hands and a kind smile on his face. The container has some kind of food in it and I avoid his stare, wiping my still glassy eyes with the sleeves of my baggy sweatshirt.

"I made you some of my famous macaroni and meatballs." He's bending his head down to try to reach my eyes but I won't let him. "Ya know…" he begins. "If you insist you're such an inconvenience, then you're my favorite inconvenience."

CHAPTER TWENTY-TWO
The Distractor

Writing and fashion are two of the only things that make sense to me. Writing was a talent I developed young. I remember writing cute little stories for my parents to read. I always flourished in it. It took me away from a cruel world that somewhat always seemed to fail me.

My parents are not cheap but they are quite into thrifting. Not my scene.

So during highschool, I got into high end fashion. It was so easy for me to understand.

When I was younger, me and my mom would walk past stores like *Gucci* and *Dolce and Gabbanna*. I would just stare in awe at the model-like young girls in the window, trying on clothes, and flaunting purses they were about to spend my parent's life savings on.

It was so glamorous, so lux. It was a mere dream. Until I started working for *DuVull and Co.*

I still haven't reached that level of success those women were at. I will though. One day. Hopefully.

But as I was saying, writing is the only thing that just makes sense. Fashion was the missing puzzle piece. I'm good at it, and I'm not good at much.

Nothing *ever* distracts me from my writing. *Nothing.* It's my peace. It just makes sense.

Then *he* came along.

Atticus Mckeen, sitting in front of me crossed legged on my couch with cruel intentions to distract me with his deep set dark eyes and shaggy blonde hair. I don't know if he means to distract me, but he surely is.

I watch as he thinks hard, biting down at his nails and reading off my laptop.

It's nice to get a person's opinion on things. Someone who's not Tiff, and who's not my parents, and who's not Jeannie and Riley because to be quite honest with you, I've asked their opinion on so much over the years, sometimes they just become white noise.

"It's good. Is it true?" Atticus asks in his deep raspy voice.

"Is what true?" I ask stupidly.

"The article. Is what you're telling factual? Isn't the job of a journalist to tell things true and honest."

"I suppose."

"You suppose?"

"Of course it's true! This part of the article is literally about *your* fashion sense."

"Ok," Atticus puts his hands up in mock surrender. "I'm just asking. What I meant was, do you believe in what you're writing? If you were reading this, would you believe you? I'm sorry, I'm not a fashion connoisseur such as yourself." He mocks me.

I'm having Atticus read an excerpt from my article. It's the part when I'm talking about the difference between the current fashion trends and his own sense of fashion.

"You have a good sense of style." I say.

"I think I do."

"I would definitely wear some of your stuff." I immediately cringe when I say that. "Not that you're, like, my boyfriend or anything," I quickly retort. "but say I had nothing else to wear, and I had to stay in your apartment for some reason. I would definitely rock that sweater." Oh god that's even worse. "And I would of course be sleeping on the couch if that were ever to happen. You would be my last resort anyway." Shut up, Poppy! "I'm going to stop babbling... now! Ok." I take a deep breath and look at Atticus to see an amused expression on his face.

"Are you done?" He asks through laughter. I love when he laughs like that. When it's genuine and his accent shines through, and his dimples are practically popping out of his face. It booms and echoes through the room. Like the one he did while we were protesting.

"I think so." I stifle a laugh with him.

"Ok, and thanks. I got it at *Village Punk Shop* actually." It really is a nice sweatshirt.

It's long, baggy, and black. It has what looks like TV static all over it with a big, white skull in the middle of it. On the back of the sweater in big, white writing it states "Punk Is Dead." It pairs nicely with his usual pair of ripped black skinny jeans.

"Of course you did." I give a giggle as I continue to type.

"What do you mean?"

"I dunno. I never really met a guy with a nice sense of style, let alone yours. It's different. All the guys I used to know just wore boring, tight, under armour shirts and basketball shorts." (Outing Liam right there. Ha!)

"By different you mean goth?"

"No, not at all." I shake my head.

"Then what am I?" He stands up and takes a step back so I could get a good look at his outfit.

"Hmmmm…" I hum skeptically and squint my eyes, getting into professional mode. Atticus attempts to do a couple of model poses but fails terribly. I'm actually thinking quite hard about this. I don't know what to call his style.

"Come on, you're the expert." He says.

"I'm thinking!" I quip. "I guess we'll just have to call it… 'The Atticus.'" Atticus looks down at his outfit and shrugs.

"Accurate."

"There's no other way to describe it." I giggle. "It's edgy… but not goth. You wear colors. It's like street style, but a tad bit more put together. I shrug. "You dress like a rocker."

"Yeah." he shrugs. "I guess that's what I go for." He plops back down on the couch with a loud thud, and I practically fall off.

I continue to type on my computer when Atticus starts to annoyingly poke me.

"What?" I look up.

I don't think I've ever been this close to him. That's when I notice something.

I see a tiny hole underneath his lower lip. Then I see one on the right side of his nose, and finally right above his eyebrow. That one is the smallest though.

His nose is the only one that has a ring in it. On his right nostril is a silver hoop. I've noticed that one before, just not the eyebrow and lip.

"What?" Atticus asks, confused.

"Nothing." I shake my head, and look back at my computer embarrassed.

"What?" He laughs. "Tell me, tell me, tell me, tell me..." he keeps poking me.

"Fine!" I erupt. "It's not a big deal. I just never noticed your piercings."

"Oh." He screws up his face. "Yeah. Sometimes I forget they're there."

"Why do you never wear them?"

"I do. You just never notice." He says.

I shouldn't have said anything. I tend to not notice a thing.

Atticus notices my expression though and backtracks.

"I usually don't wear them all at the same time. That's probably why." He points out, probably trying to make me feel not as bad.

"Why don't you wear them all at the same time?" I ask, curious.

"I don't know..." he laughs. "I don't want people to think I'm something I'm not. I'm a nice guy! I don't want people judging me because of holes I put on my face when I was a stupid teenager." He looks down, shaking his head.

I jot down what he says in my notebook. That's important for people to know. That rockers and scene kids aren't just heartless goths. They love, and they have loyalty and compassion like anyone else. And we shouldn't assume they are scary or mean just because of the music they listen to or the clothes they wear. I finally got it! I finally get why Jeannie wanted to do this article so badly. It's all about breaking stereotypes!

"Umm... can I include that in the article? I know it's a bit vulnerable."

"It's your article," Atticus begins. "you do what you have to do to make it great."

"It's our article." I suddenly say and Atticus looks up at me with an expression I can't quite put my finger on. Shocked maybe.

"I got a nose ring when I was sixteen." I say bringing the subject back to piercings. Atticus's face pops up.

"You did not."

"I so did!" I state. "Look." I show him the tiny closed hole where my gold nose ring once laid. "My sister took me one night. I wanted one *so* bad. All my friends had one. We got home at 10:00 that night, my parents were so mad. They got even more mad when they saw the ring in my nose. My sister said she peer pressured me into doing it with her friends, and she should be the one to get grounded, not me. My parents did just that. I always thought my sister hated me. That night I realized maybe she didn't loathe me afterall. Or at least as much as I thought she did. Today showed otherwise though. Just when I think I'm ok with my sister." I click my tongue.

Atticus looks at me and tilts his head, like a lost dog.

"So you don't get along with your sister, do you?" He asks as if not caring, but there is a curious edge to his voice.

"No, I do. Of course I love her, it's just...complicated. We have different ideals."

"Ah, got it." He clicks his tongue. "Only child."

"Lucky you." I scoff.

"Not really." Atticus shakes his head. "A childhood is a lonely one when it's only you and your dad and he's out working day and night to make a living."

"Oh Atticus, I'm sorry."

"You didn't know." Atticus's states. His head suddenly pops up and a smile spreads across his face. "Hey, can I pick your brain on something real fast?" He's got this excited twinkle in his eyes. It reminds me of a twinkle I saw once before.

I know this might sound crazy but It reminds me of the look my Grandpa used to give to my Grandma. My dad's parents. He looked at my grandma like she was his world. She was his world. It was a certain look though. My dad likes to tell me I have the look, but I think Atticus pulls it off better.

"Sure..." and before I could finish, he's out of my apartment. He leaves the door open and I watch as he runs into his own apartment, speedily gets his guitar, then runs back into mine as he closes the door behind him.

He's got his neon green electric guitar in his hands and I could finally see it up close. It's dirty and has writing and crude drawings all over it in sharpie.

He jumps on the couch next to me, guitar in lap. I take out my phone so I could get a picture of the guitar so I could describe it just right.

Atticus notices I'm taking a picture and decides to put his chin in the palm of his hand and give me a big smile.

"Beautiful." I giggle as I snap the picture making sure the guitar is in perfect view as well.

"Can I play you a song?" He begins "I want to perform it at *The Lounge* this weekend." Atticus has this cute little smirk on his face, how can I say no. I just nod my head.

"Of course." I watch as he gets his guitar ready and moves in a position so he's facing me.

He starts to play a surprising soft, almost acoustic, beat on his electric guitar. Every move of his large hands intrigues me, as it goes up and down the guitar and picks at the strings.

"You really do have such talent." I offer a kind smile. He looks shocked, almost speechless. His mouth has fallen agap and his face soft. For a second, he actually looks sad.

Why is he looking at me like that? Has no one ever told him he was good? Does anyone even care?

He just shakes his head and looks down at his guitar.

"Ok..." Is all he says, his voice even more raspy now. He looks down at his guitar and continues playing that soft tune.

"I thought I knew you, did I see you in my dreams?

Because lately it's getting harder and harder, the life of a poet isn't as easy as it seems.

I could go out and catch ya but your heart belongs to someone else,

Every time I talk to you my common sense melts.

Don't worry, she won't treat you like the last two, that is if she notices you..." and like that, he starts a heavy guitar riff.

"And you can't get her out of your head,

And you cling to every word she says,

And you're a goddamn fool,

For liking someone who doesn't like you...back." His eyes are closed when he sings and he sounds as if he means every word he says. You can tell it's his own words. His own experience. He continues with the next verse.

I thought I knew you, did I see you in my dreams?
Because the people I used to know aren't who they seem.
If the bad outweighs the good, then our stories misunderstood.
I was livid but now I'm fine.
People say I'm delusional but I try,
   to understand the lives of others, I just can't understand how people could
be so blind!

His voice raises on the last part. I kind of like it when it rises. It's not annoying, it's just effortless.

"Don't ever tell a person you'd die for the cause they'll slit your throat with their words.

Don't ever tell a person you love them cause they'll give a damn about your concerns."

He repeats those two lines another time and sings the chorus again. He then stops very suddenly and the room isn't filled with the loud sound of his guitar anymore. It's actually kind of depressing. He just looks downwards with a stone cold look on his face.

Those last two lines he sang before the chorus, what does he mean? I know what he means, but it's overall just really depressing. Is that how he *really* feels?

"I love it." I say softly, trying to reach his brown eyes.

He always has dark circles around them, like he hasn't slept in years, or maybe that's just the shadow of his hair. He looks up at me through his hair. He has the look of a fallen angel. When you think about it, Atticus is somewhat of a fallen angel.

"It's stupid..." he laughs to himself shaking his head, his hair swaying as he does so.

"It's not stupid!" I retort. "I--is it true?" I utter the question he asked me a couple of minutes ago when he read that excerpt from the article.

"What?" He looks panicked when I ask him for a moment.

"Is what you're writing about true? Isn't the job of a musician and songwriter to write and sing about what you're feeling? Are those feelings true? Do you feel them?" My smile fades and there is a curious edge to my voice much to my dismay. I don't want to come off nosy, but I still can't quite figure this man out, and I really *really* want to. He's a mystery, and I hate mysteries. They must be solved.

"Yeah..." he thinks for a moment. "yeah, I guess it is." He sits up with his famous closed mouth smile.

"Well good." I nod my head and think for a moment. "Not that the feeling you were singing about is good, because it's not and I'm sorry you feel that way..." I babble. "I meant it's good you're writing what you feel." I nod, matter of factly.

He nods and I could tell he's deep in thought. I look down at my computer and he scooches impossibly closer to me and watches as I edit tonight's little experience into the article.

He puts up his black hood and leans his head on my shoulder. I sigh and giggle a little.

"I'm going to bed. Night." Is all he says and I look at the man snuggled on my shoulder. The man who has no business being there but I don't have the heart to push him off. Something else stops me as well, and I don't know what it is. Some interior force is not letting me.

"You're crazy, Atticus Mckeen." I sigh.

"Absolutely bonkers?" He asks in a fake british accent, eyes closed.

"Certainly."

"Well, all the best people are." He retorts. "And you, Poppy Paxton are completely and utterly sane. We're obviously a match made in heaven." I can't help but smile at his comment.

Before I know it, I hear soft snoring on my shoulder and I look down at his peaceful face.

I shut down my computer and prop my pillows beside me. I lay one blanket over me and Atticus. Before I know it, I'm dozing off too, dreams of award winning articles and one brown eyed rocker runs through my head, whether I want it to or not. And at that moment I realize, I'm in such big trouble.

CHAPTER TWENTY-THREE
Morning Calling

I wake up to the sound of the ringtone and the peach colored Brooklyn sunlight shining through my blackout shades.

I groan as I roll over and a sudden pain shoots up my neck then to my back. It's probably because I'm on the couch...the couch? Why am I on the couch?

And then just like that, memories of last night come flooding back into my mind like a waterfall. Me getting into an argument with my sister. Atticus coming to the apartment and helping me with the article...

I smile thinking back to the memory, resting my face back into the cozy pillow beneath me.

When my ringtone stops it's annoying buzz, I attempt to reach for my phone on the little white, wooden stand next to me.

I finally grasp my phone and squint at the blurry, bright screen. Giving out a deep huff and a roll of the eyes, I reach for my reading glasses that I very conveniently leave on this side table as well.

Once I slip on my glasses the bright light of my phone shines in my face and I see it's Tiff who called and texted me.

The time reads 9:30Am and Tiff called me once an hour ago and texted me once twenty minutes ago and once two minutes ago.

'HEY POPS. YOU DIDN'T ANSWER MY CALL, BUT I WANTED TO KNOW IF YOU NEEDED ANYTHING? YOUR MOM CALLED ME YESTERDAY AND TOLD ME EVERYTHING THAT HAPPENED...' Of course she did. Because my business needs to be everyone else's as well! What else is new? 'JUST CHECKING UP ON YOU? DO YOU WANT ME TO BRING COFFEE AND BAGELS? YOU KNOW WHAT, I'M JUST GONNA COME OVER WHETHER YOU LIKE IT OR NOT. WHAT KIND OF BAGEL DO YOU WANT?'

And then from two minutes ago,

'POPPY, I'M TEN MINUTES AWAY AND I HOPE YOU'RE IN THE MOOD FOR SESAME BAGELS. I GOT, LIKE, TEN. YOU GAVE ME KEYS FOR A REASON, IF YOU'RE NOT UP IN FIVE MINUTES I'M BREAKING AN ENTERING.' Shit. *Shit!*

I slam my phone on the side table and try to get off the couch but my exhaustion gets the best of me. I'm completely burnt out and all I could seem to do is count the little bumps on the white, stained, popcorn ceiling above me. 1, 2, 3...

That's when I feel a sudden lump across from me in the pile of blankets. I continue to kick it harshly to try to decipher what it is, and all the sudden... it moves. Holy shit. Oh. My. GOD.

I feel this sudden lump in my throat as my heart slowly drops. Please don't tell me...

I continue to kick the blankets when I hear an annoyed groan from under them. I scream and fall right off the couch taking the blankets down with me.

"Wha--" a disheveled Atticus lifts his head up from the pillow underneath him with squinted, tired eyes.

I just sit on the floor now fully awake and completely stunned.

Atticus's shaggy hair is now sticking up crazily and he doesn't even look fully up. He's *not* fully up. I'm positive he's not even coherent.

He just rests his head back on the pillow, going back to sleep.

"No, no, no..." I quickly get up off the floor. "Atticus, get up!" I start to shake him but he just groans and ignores me. He grabs the pillow beneath him and covers his ears with it.

He's such a pain in the ass, even in his sleep!

I grab the pillow beside me and begin to whack him with it.

"Atticus! Get. Up. Now." He tries to protect his head from the blows of the pillow but I just keep on hitting him.

"Oh my god, what?" He pops up annoyed and still not fully coherent. He realises who's in front of him, coming to. "Poppy?" He asks, even more confused than usual.

"Yeah?" I manage to croak out.

I watch as his wheels begin to slowly turn.

"We must have just... crashed last night." I could tell he's still thinking, round brown eyes still squinted.

"Yeah we did. I suppose we just fell asleep." The both of us are still in the same clothes we were last night. Nothing more, nothing less. Thank god. He's in his jeans and hoodie, and I'm in my sweatpants and sweater.

"Well that's wholesome." Atticus shoots me a smile and I can't help but nod back, still quite speechless.

I forget about everything and anything going on in my life currently as I watch Atticus rise from the couch and politely fix the pillows and blanket. It's like I get lost in his movements.

"Want some breakfast?" He motions towards the kitchen as I help him with the couch.

I just chuckle, shaking my head.

"You know, I might have to take you up on that offer—" a loud knock on the door interrupts my sentence. Atticus shoots me a curious glare and I feel my face fall. Oh *no*.

"Poppy!" I hear Tiff on the other side of the door. "Poppy Paxton, open this door!"

I shoot Atticus a look of sheer panic.

"Poppy, I'm coming in…" just as Tiff is about to put her spare key into the lock, I run towards the door and rip it open.

"Hey!" I say and put my hand on my hips, trying to play it cool. "I—"

"I don't want to hear it." Begins Tiff moving past me and into the apartment. Oy vey.

She's in her jeans and plain white shirt. Her chocolate brown hair is cascading down her back and she is holding a brown paper bag filled with bagels and a cup holder with two iced coffees in it.

I silently curse under my breath and close the apartment door behind us. Damn!

Tiff stops in her tracks when she sees Atticus standing awkwardly and obviously dishavled fixing the couch.

"Oh my god." Her mouth falls agap in absolute shock.

I quickly grab the bagels and coffees out of her hands so she doesn't drop them, putting them on the dining room table. I then run back to her, putting both my hands on her shoulders, trying to calm her down.

Atticus just waves at Tiff awkwardly, and shoves his hands in his pockets, swaying back and forth. He bites the side of his lip and looks around the apartment, pretending he's not listening to me and Tiff's conversation.

"Tiff, it's not what you think…"

"Oh my god!" She shouts once again, regaining her voice. "I knew it! I knew—" I throw my hands over her mouth and walk her out of the door.

"Help yourself to a bagel, Atticus." I give him a shrill smile as I reach the hallway with Tiff and close the door behind us.

"I knew you liked him, I knew it! I didn't know you were going to be moving this fast! Poppy, did you do something with him? Oh, your mom will kill you…"

"What am I, sixteen? Mom doesn't have to know anything! We don't even live in the same city, and I'm 24! But that's not the point!" I love Tiff, but they call *me* the priss? *Ok.*

"So you *did* do something with him!"

"No! And Shhhh!" I hush her, throwing my pointer finger over my lips.

"Poppy, I don't know about this."

"Tiff, we were finishing up the article and we crashed. We fell asleep. We woke up all the same." I say and I can't quite understand why there is a hint of disappointment in my voice. "Would it be a bad thing if we did do something?" I quirk up an eyebrow.

"I suppose not." Tiff shrugs. "I'm glad you didn't though. It wouldn't be the ideal way to start off a relationship."

"Not that I want to." I make sure to state.

"Oh sure," Tiff nods. "you have no interest in Atticus whatsoever. That's why you let him sleep on your couch last night." She adds sarcastically.

"Shut up, smartass." I retort but I can't help but blush a bit. "That's what friends do, right! Come on," I begin to change the subject. "let's have one of those bagels."

"Actually," begins Tiff. "I think I have to get some groceries…"

"Oh, groceries…" I repete, not buying it.

"Yeah." she nods. "You and Atticus have the bagels and coffee."

"Tiff, no."

"Yes." She suddenly embraces me in a quick hug and begins to walk back towards the elevator. "Knock him dead, Pops. Text me later, I want to hear all about it. Also, don't think I forgot about the fiasco at your parents house yesterday. Apparently we have a lot to talk about." I roll my eyes as I walk back into the apartment.

Atticus is still awkwardly standing by the couch, his hands now clasped together in front of him and he's pursing his lips together. Once he realizes I walked back into the apartment he looks at me almost anxiously.

"Is everything ok?"

"Totally!" I nod my head. "She had an emergency."

"Is she ok?" Atticus asks worriedly.

"Oh, yeah…" I begin to rack my brain for an excuse. I twiddle with my thumbs. "girl problems." I blurt out. "Very sudden. You know how it is." I cringe as soon as the words come out of my mouth.

"Ah, ok. Got you." Atticus nods his head and continues to look around the apartment.

"She said we could have the bagels and coffee though!" I perk up.

I grab the bag of bagels and the cup holder holding both iced coffees and place them on the dining room table.

"Oh cool." Atticus walks over to the table and I could tell he's walking on eggshells, waiting in bated breath.

It's actually quite funny because Atticus is always so cocky and sure of himself and he looks… out of place. Unsure.

He's just standing by one out of the two chairs in the dining room.

I grab some napkins, plates, two knives and butter.

"I'm sorry," I begin walking over to the table and sitting down. "I don't have any cream cheese, I don't really care for it that much. Plus, it's usually just me in the house."

"It's ok," Atticus shakes his head with a smile. He sits across from me once I settle down. "I prefer butter anyway."

I sit criss cross as we both grab a bagel and drop it on our plates. He lets me use the butter first and when I'm done I pass it to him.

We just sit in silence for a couple of seconds.

"You could have a coffee if you want." I take the two iced coffees out of the cup holder and see they are from *Starbucks*. I look on the side of the coffee cups to see what kinds they are but I get nothing. They look pretty identical too.

"What? You can't figure out which ones which?" Atticus laughs, a mouth full of my bagel.

"No." I complain at my lame attempt to figure it out as I lift both up and try to look at the coffees from the bottom.

"Give me." Atticus chuckles and I gladly hand him the two coffees. "Hmmmm…" he looks at them skeptically. "I don't skeeve ya, do I?"

"No." I shake my head and give a shrug. "Tiff loves caramel. One of those might be caramel. I can't try though because it makes me sick. Like, I'll vomit all over you, I can't stand it."

"Ok, ok." He takes a sip out of one and swirls it around his mouth for a moment and dramatically swallows it. I can't help but giggle. "Vanilla." He hands it to me.

"Thank you!" I happily take a sip as Atticus takes a sip of his. "It's good," I begin. "but it's not *Dunkin's* coffee." I see the smile that spreads across Atticus face as well

"No it's not." We sit in silence for another couple of seconds as we eat.

"Did you finish your article last night?" Atticus asks.

"Well," I sigh. "I think so."

"What do you mean 'You think so'?" He asks furrowing his brows together.

"I need to give it in by ten tonight. I just… feel somethings missing." I watch as Atticus thinks and I'm coming to find this situation quite funny. The both of us sitting at the table, eating breakfast and making somewhat mindless small talk. I never thought I would be doing this with Atticus. A day in the life. I haven't woken up and eaten breakfast with anyone in the morning since Liam.

Liam is the only person I ever pictured sitting at the table with, eating breakfast and having mindless conversations. But now I'm not so sure.

I watch as Atticus thinks and chews his now second bagel.

"What do you think is missing?"

"I don't know. I just wish I had more time."

"Well maybe that's the problem." Atticus motions towards me. "Maybe you don't want the article to end,.the experience it brought to you…the experience *I brought* to you. I think you just enjoy my company." He chews and shrugs, looking down at his plate when a little smirk forms across his lips.

He has a point.

"I do..." I nod. "but I still would love to finish the article."

"Well I guess we'll just have to go for one last adventure today, won't we?" He says sipping his coffee.

"I guess we do." I smile. But something tells me this is going to be far from our last adventure.

CHAPTER TWENTY-FOUR
MixTape

I study Atticus as he plays a soft tune on the piano. It's very monotone, but somehow he makes it exciting and sad at the same time.

We're on our last mission for the article this afternoon. I got my notebook and we are including a little last minute example. Just one more.

Atticus told me one of the first instruments he ever learned was the piano. So I called my parents up and asked them if I could use the grand piano in their living room for my new article.

Now here we are. No ones home though. Dad's out at a friend's house and mom went out shopping with Tiff's mom Helen. I'm actually quite thankful no one's home. I wouldn't want to scare Atticus off with my overbearing family.

I study Atticus as if he's a wild animal at the zoo, caged in in the most inhuman way possible. As if I'm a little girl looking at a lion face to face for the first time with no fear. Like he could never hurt her, even though a lion is one of the most dangerous animals on the planet, he looks at the little girl calmly. No intentions to hurt her. Or does he? Afterall, she doesn't know what he's thinking. That's the funny thing about lions, they're calm until they have to strike.

His hair looks pretty. I noticed when I saw him last night it was freshly cut. It's still shaggy and messy, just a tad less unruly. You could see his eyes better now. You could see them fully.

They're so round and brown and huge. They're beautiful, really. I must sound like a broken record when I say that, but they truly are the most fab eyes I've ever seen.

We both parted ways for a little while earlier today so we could both change. I of course took longer than him, so the poor thing had to stand awkwardly outside my door for twenty minutes. Figures.

Atticus has one silver chain today with a big skull on it. He also has a black sweater shirt with a white collar and black ripped jeans, less tight than usual. Just one chain on his pants as well.

He's still wearing his normal *converses* and high socks, but he looks neater today. I don't know if that's the right word, because Atticus always looks neat. He just looks a tad less grungy.

Atticus turns to me, almost innocently with his famous wide smile. There is something different about it though. It's more giddy this time. It's like his smile is permanently tattooed in my brain, I can't get it out of my head. I'm not quite sure I want to. I wish I could find a way to tell him that, but I don't know how so I won't.

It's so strange yet so surreal to have Atticus sitting in my living room playing the piano I used to play when I was a kid. (Or at least attempt to play.) My dad begged me to let him teach me, but I was never musically inclined.

"Here," he hands me a sheet of paper that was on top of the piano. "will you sing while I play?" He halts the music he was playing and looks at me hopefully.

"I can't sing?" I giggle nervously.

"It doesn't matter. I just need someone to just sing this song so I could get a feel of it all. See how I like the piano with it. Come on!" He urges playfully, practically bouncing in his seat. "The best writing is done when you hop in and experience what you are writing about for yourself!" He bites his lip and thinks. "Consider this a learning experience for now on, you know. If you're writing this huge article you might as well enjoy it. Learn something. Anything. Just… let loose, feel the emotion."

I've never been good at "letting loose" and I feel too much emotion sometimes. (Well, most of the time.)

I grab the paper with trembling hands and swallow the lump in my throat. I don't know why I feel so nervous, I couldn't tell you.

He starts up the same soft tune he started off with and continues to do so.

"Where do I hop in?"

"Anywhere."

I clear my throat and begin to sing, my hands shaking gripping to the sheet of paper with the lyrics written in Atticus's handwriting.

"*I know It's late but can you make me a mixtape?*
You're like a replayed song I just can't get out of my head but I should,
No men could, she's just misunderstood.
You're in high demand I know that, but can you make me a mixtape?
You're the only person I don't hate,
And everyone knows your name, and I'm starting to realize through our differences,
our black hearts are quite the same..."

Atticus smiles and bops his head as he plays the piano as I begin the chorus.

"*I wanna come up with a way,*
I just wanna say,
I'm honored to be in your presence,
Being with me is a life long sentence.
I'm honored to be living the same time as you,
I'm honored to live a microscopic part of it too.
And I know the feeling will go away,
I don't want to stay... anyway."

I finish the chorus and jump right into the next verse. The song has a lot of emotion, and you know it's Atticus's work when he bleeds his feelings onto those pages.

"*I feel like I'm constantly heading for a breakdown,*
I wanna be free, I want to see, walking hand and hand on the beach,
I tend to fall for people who don't fall for me.
I'm so out of touch with everyone but you,
I seek attention you are unable to give too,
How can I seek your love when you don't even know I do.
And the pain is I know you're middle name and you don't know mine,
The pain is you didn't do shit and you still make me cry."

I repeat the chorus and see a flicker of sadness in Atticus's eyes as he plays the piano. He is no longer playfully bopping his head along rather he looks deep in thought about something.

I want to ask him if he's ok, I want to ask him what was the matter but I fear I don't want to know the answer. For some reason this song being about some random girl makes me sick to my stomach.

"*Lonely boys could write songs,*

Lonely girls could sit quietly and listen along.

He lives his life as an open book, she glanced at the pages just wanting to take a look.

He's young and he's dumb, smoke filling his lungs,
the words on the tip of her tongue, she can't say them.
He's young and he's dumb, smoke filling his lungs,
If she doesn't want to get hurt, she better run."

I sing the chorus one last time and the sound of my voice and Atticus's piano playing just booms through the house. It's such a pretty noise, I do have to say.

I finish singing and Atticus stops the piano, ending it with a low, dark sounding key. He stares longingly at it and I put my hand on his shoulder.

"Are you ok?"

"Yeah," He looks up at me with that closed mouth smile of his. "I'm fine!"

"Well good." I nod, handing him back the song sheet, feeling guilty that he didn't open up. What do I want, honestly? "It was a beautiful song." I fidget with my necklace.

"You think?"

"Oh, for sure." I'm almost taken aback that he doesn't know how wonderful his work is. Sometimes he's so vain and confident, yet sometimes he proves to me he's so not.

"Wh-- who is it about?" I stumble over my words.

"Oh." Atticus looks taken aback by my question. "It's about some girl I know." He shrugs.

I feel my whole mood change and I'm wondering why I asked. I don't know why my mood changed and I don't know why I feel this way. I don't want to feel this feeling and I don't want to feel anything. Don't ask me what this feeling is because I don't even know. All I know is I feel nauseous and I don't want to be near him anymore.

"That's nice." I say, my voice shaky. "You know, I think I'll make us some coffee…"

"Well I was thinking we could go out. Let's get something to eat. On me." Atticus puts his hands up.

"Where shall we go?"

"Anywhere." He laughs.

"Well ok," I say, my voice still trembling. "I'll get my coat." I go to grab one of my favorite trench coats from *Tanya Taylor*. It's a light wash of purple with mint green accents on the sleeves and waist ties.

As I go to put it on, Atticus comes up from behind and aids me, putting it over my arms and onto my shoulders as I mutter a thank you.

I turn to see Atticus in his black vest and beanie. We look like polar opposites.

"You ready?" He asks, practically jumping up and down.

"Where are we going?" I ask once again.

"Anywhere!" He throws his arms in the air. "And leave *this...*" He carefully takes my notebook out of my hands and throws it on the couch. "at home."

"But I need to finish the article by tonight!"

"No, I don't want to hear it. And you *are* going to finish the article by tonight..." Atticus shoves my notebook now into my purse. "and I don't want to see that notebook out. Stop writing everything down and experience it for yourself. Stop having blinders on when you look at life because there is so much more it could offer!" I sigh in frustration at his lecture, but I don't have the energy to fight with him. "I'll take you anywhere."

"Take me to the moon." I answer, crossing my arms.

"Ok, wise-ass." He rolls his eyes as he starts to walk out the door, me in tow, Atticus singing. "'*Fly me to the moon...*'"

I sit in Atticus's beat up, old, gray Camry. It smells like leather and cigarette smoke.

He has fuzzy dice hanging from his rear view mirror and his back seat is turning the green light on my crippling OCD. It has clothes, band equipment, and strobe lights that makes the car a somewhat bright shade of red.

Atticius is playing the drums on his steering wheel to some pop punk song and that is blasting so loud through the spreaker that I could hardly hear my own thoughts.

I rest my head against the cool glass of the car window, it feels so nice against my temples. I take a deep breath and watch as my breath fogs up the window. Atticus seems to notice and lowers the music quite a bit.

"Are you ok? Is the music too loud?"

"Oh no," I vastly shake my head and pull a face. "just...enjoying the scenery."

I look out at all the headlights and apartments as we drive towards the Verrazano bridge. Every time I drive on this bridge, it takes my breath away. I just love it.

The sun is going down and it's just dark enough to notice the lights of the city. The sky is a crimson blood orange color and it's absolutely stunning.

I feel this anxious surge run through my body though.

What if I don't finish this article? What if I can't. What if I bit off more than I could chew? What if Jane doesn't like the article? I'll never get the promotion and I'll never prove myself. I'm determined though.

I love the article so far, I'm just unsure.

All the sudden I feel a large pair of hands reach my stomach and start to tickle me.

I giggle and snort as Atticus runs his fingers at a rapid pace over me.

"Stop!" I bellow in laughter. I could hardly get my words out.

"Not until you tell me what's the matter." His smile is a mile wide as he balances looking and tickling me, as well as keeping his eyes on the road.

"T--that's such a cliche..."

"What is?" He continues to attack me in tickles.

"'Not until you tell me what's the matter.'" I try to mimic his voice while laughing. "What a cliche!"

"What do you have against cliches?" Atticus says, playfully offended.

"They..." I snort as he reaches under my arm and I squirm uncontrollably in the passenger's seat. "they're not real! Cliches by definition i--is a phrase or opinion that is overused and betrays a lack of original thought..."

"And?"

"And they're stupid!"

"That's a matter of opinion, Poppy."

"Maybe... maybe so *Atticus.*" I mimic him once again as he finally stops tickling me and we pull into a diner.

"So," he begins as he shuts off the car and pulls into a spot. "are you going to tell me what was the matter?" He finally looks me in the eye and raises one of his perfect eyebrows.

"Hmmmm." I screw up my face pretending to think. "Possibly." I rip off the black beanie on the top of his head and all his hair comes cascading down in front of his face. "If you could catch me!"

"Hey!" Atticus shouts as I run out of the car making a beeline for the diner we just pulled into. Let's just say my heels can only take me so far before Atticus grabs me from behind, lifting me off the ground and ripping the beanie out of my hand.

I giggle uncontrollably and squeal in his arms as he throws me over his shoulders and walks towards the door.

"Atticus Mckeen I'm in a dress!" I slap his back.

We reach the door and Atticus puts me down. I almost tumble down the steps of the diner.

He takes a deep breath and slides his beanie on as if nothing happened and opens the doors gesturing towards my now disheveled self as I helplessly try to fix my appearance.

"Well, shall we?" He asks with faux innocence and I just scowl at him.

After dinner me and Atticus end up back at my apartment. I'm sitting at my desk typing hectically.

It's currently 8:30. Atticus is leaning on my chair behind me watching as I put on my last touches. I could practically sense the smile on his face. I could actually see it through the computer screen. And it makes me smile.

As I begin to write my last sentence Atticus playfully pats my head. "Which way is the bathroom?"

"Right over there." I point to the direction of the bathroom without taking my eyes off of the computer screen.

"Ok, I'll be back." Atticus heads to the bathroom and I finally finish the last sentence. (The end statement is *so* good! I'm not reading it to you yet though! Not until it gets published. No spoilers!)

I take a deep breath and press send. Once I send it to Jane I make sure to attach an email as well with it.

'HI JANE. I'M SORRY I'VE BEEN MIA. I'M SORRY I LET YOU DOWN. YOU KNOW THAT'S NEVER MY INTENTION. THIS WEEKEND JUST HAS BEEN... CRAZY. I'LL TALK TO YOU ABOUT IT TOMORROW. THAT IS, IF YOU EVEN WANT TO HEAR FROM ME TOMORROW. I'M SO INCREDIBLY PROUD OF THIS ARTICLE. I THINK IT'S THE BEST WORK I'VE ACTUALLY EVER DONE. SO IF YOU'RE MAD AT ME I UNDERSTAND. TAKE IT OUT ON ME, NOT THE ARTICLE. ONCE AGAIN, THANK YOU FOR THE OPPORTUNITY. I REALLY HOPE YOU ENJOY THE ARTICLE.

WITH LOVE,
POPPY.'

Just as I press send Atticus comes out of the bathroom and I can't help but hop out of my chair and run into his arms.

"We did it, we finished it! And it's sent!" He wraps his arms around me and lifts me up, spinning me around once before putting me down.

"You did it!" He says, still twirling me around. All I could do is giggle, feeling the warmest and flushed I've felt in a very long time. Butterflies erupt in the pit of my stomach from where Atticus picked me up right below my bottom.

It makes me feel all giddy as I rest my hands on his broad shoulders that I just now realize how broad they are.

"Yeah well, if it wasn't for you there wouldn't be an article." I manage after my feet land back onto the floor. I pull back but I'm still quite close to him.

Atticus gives me his cute dimpled smile and I once again wrap my arms around him, overcome with joy and relief. I find myself comfortable in his embrace. Maybe I stay in his embrace a minute too long but Atticus doesn't let go and neither do I, now resting my face in the crook of his neck.

CHAPTER TWENTY-FIVE
BBQ and Monday Morning Gossip

"Don't freak out..." begins *Jeannie* leaning over her desk fixing my hair. "you got the article done in time. Why should there be an issue?"

"Yeah," quips Riley, his foot up on the desk. "luckily for you she's not in the *worst* mood this morning." I just take a deep breath to relieve my nerves as I pick up Jane's coffee and rise out of my seat.

"You got this." Jeannie gives me a thumbs up. I just nervously nod my head as I begin to walk towards Jane's office. Yeah... I got this!

As I open Jane's see-through glass door and close it behind me, I feel my breath quicken.

One of my worst fears is disappointing people. I just hope I didn't disappoint her. It's not even about the stupid promotion crap, Jane's my idol.

The fact that I'm even working for *DuVull and Co* is still a dream to me. No matter how much of a pain in the ass Jane is, I adore her.

"Morning, Ms. DuVull." I begin cautiously walking over to where she sits slouched at her desk on her computer. She pushes her reading glasses down her nose at the sight of me and pushes her long black hair behind her ear.

"Morning, Poppyseed." Is all she says, a tad bit cold as she just looks back down at her computer and continues typing.

"Here is your coffee." I say a bit above a whisper as I wipe away the condensation and place it on her desk. I decide not to say anything else. I don't want to be in more deep than I probably already am.

I think I made myself quite clear in my email last night.

So, I just begin to walk towards the door.

Just as I'm about to open the door, I hear Jane call my name.

"Poppy?"

"Yeah, Ms. DuVull?" I ask. She motions me hurriedly and impatiently to walk over to her so I do.

"So...ummm... your article." she begins and my heart drops.

"Ms. DuVull, I'm sorry I made you wait so long but I gave it in on time--"

"I enjoyed the article, Poppy." She says, suddenly.

"What?"

"I enjoyed the article." She shrugs. "I thought it was informative, I thought it was cute and I thought it was different. Poppy, I never doubted you with this article. If I doubted you, you wouldn't even be doing it. I was worried about you because you weren't responding back." Worried? Jane was worried about me? I try not to look too shocked.

"I'm sorry I made you worried." I say genuinely.

"Well don't be too sorry. You didn't make me *that* worried." There it is.

"Well, I'm glad I didn't make you *too* worried." I respond.

Jane suddenly looks up at me a bit more seriously. A little smile pulling at the ends of her lips.

"I like him."

"Who?"

"That Atticus guy... he's nice isn't he?"

"Yeah!" I nod. "A great friend."

"I liked the ending. About how he gave you a new perspective on life."

"Thanks!"

"You know, I think you should get back out there. I've been thinking about it a lot..."

"Oh have you..." I nod my head and answer sarcastically.

"Yes, and I think Atticus should put his big boy panties on and ask you on a date."

"Ms. DuVull, no." I cross my arms.

"Then you ask him out! I'm not sexist."

"Ms. DuVull, no one is asking anyone out. We are *friends*..."

"Oh yes, Poppy because that article was completely platonic."

"It was!"

"Whatever! You and Atticus aside, this article was amazing. The new issue comes out tomorrow. I believe it will be at the *Barnes and Noble* on fifth. They always usually get it first. Why don't you go and pick up a copy." Jane says, continuing to type on her computer.

"Oh of course." I say surely. "I always do."

"And I expect one to be sent to everyone in your family as well…"

"I don't think that's a good idea."

"And why is that?" Jane retorts. "Doesn't your mother buy it every month?"

"Yes, and everytime I write she mails it around to other family members…"

"So, why the *hell* is this time any different!" Jane rips off her glasses. "Poppyseed, this is your biggest article yet! Do you even understand! This article is going to be huge…"

"I don't know about huge…"

"Of course it's going to be huge! You are meshing two worlds together. In *DuVull and Co* history no one has ever even touched the fashion and lifestyle of pop punk! You could very well be creating a new genre for us." And the moment Jane says that, I think something finally clicked.

I always knew this could be a good article but I never looked at it that way. The fact that Jane has so many expectations for this scares me though.

"I think everyone is a bit too focused on my sister's wedding to stop and read my article." I answer under my breath honestly.

"Speaking of that…" begins Jane starting to look through the stack of papers on her desk. "how did that go? That whole 'wedding meeting' that was on Saturday. You said you would tell me about it, and I have a funny feeling that is why we turned our article in later than we usually do." Jane lifts up a brow at me and motions for me to sit in the white leather chair in front of her desk.

"Well…" I begin and the minute I sit down, the office door opens and Jane's head pops up.

"What?" She asks impatiently and I turn to see Riley at the door.

"Arlo wants to know if you want anything from *Dallas BBQ's*. The one in Times Square. We're splurging today, y'all." He stands at the door impatiently.

"Do you have a menu?" Jane sighs.

"No, I don't have a menu!" Riley says. I've been to the place so many times, I know it by heart.

"Look it up on your computer!" He retorts. Jane groans and starts typing it on her computer.

"Can you get me the pulled pork burger with a side of fries and diet coke?" I pipe up.

"Uh huh." Riley begins typing on his phone.

"Uhhhh… can I have a caesar salad. I'm trying to eat healthy here." Jane sighs. "Oh and you know what, get me an order of the sticky wings and that royale drink made with moscato."

"How's that diet going for you?" Riley asks and smirks to himself.

"How's unemployment going for you?" Jane threatens Riley who's still chuckling.

"What are you two disscussing?" Riley lifts a brow.

He's in a pink sweater shirt with green polka dots all over it and nice black jeans. Everything he wears somehow always compliments his loud blue hair.

"This weekend. The wedding meeting and such…"

"Oh! Oh…" he begins when he opens the door and screams out the office "Jeannie, story time!" Oh here we go.

Jane rolls her eyes and Jeannie comes staggering in.

"What? I'm working."

"If the both of you dimwits are going to be listening in just shut the hell up and sit down." Jane states.

Riley and Jeannie quickly close the door behind them and pull up chairs right beside me.

"Well," I begin once again. "It wasn't that horrible…"

"Oh shut up, yes it was. What happened." Jane proclaims.

"I was trying my hardest really. I always do when it comes to my family. It was only me, my mom, my sister, and my sister's best friend."

"No mother in law?" Jeannie cocks up a brow.

"Carlo's parents are very busy people." I reprete Dia's words.

"Which is code for they don't like Diamante or your family."

"Basically. Well, anyway, that immediately put Diamante in a bad mood. She took it out on me."

"What do you mean she took it out on you?" Asks Riley angrily texting Arlo.

"Well I got a text from someone..." I begin.

"Oh god." Jeannie begins.

"And it's Atticus." An audible gasp falls from all three lips.

"Well I ran into him that morning! He told me to text him when I got to my parents safely. I forgot! So Diamante threw a fit and I didn't answer my phone. So then he called and Diamante decided to rip it out of my reach and answer it." I look up and everyone's face is just in shock. "I know it's a very first world issue but... I feel bad she was very rude to Atticus..." all of a sudden I see a smile on Jane's face.

"Why were you so embarrassed if he's 'just a friend'?"

An hour later we are digging into our lunch and still discussing this. (Because everyone loves to interrupt me and we have no lives.)

"So then the next morning I wake up on the couch and Atticus is on the couch next to me."

"What!" Jeannie yells.

Jane puts her head on her desk to play it off as if she's not laughing and Riley is laughing so hard, I'm convinced the diet coke currently in his mouth is going to come out of his nose.

"Riley, don't you dare spit that out!" Jeannie warns. So Riley throws his head into Arlo's leather jacket.

Arlo's off today so he decided to stay and listen to the story. He just looks shocked, his strikingly blue eyes wide.

Riley's swallowed and now he's laughing so hard into Arlo's jacket, it's making me laugh.

Jane lifts her head up and holds her face in the palms of her hands.

"Just friends, right?" She snorts.

"We are just friends!" I cry. "We didn't do anything! We just got so tired we just crashed I suppose..." I look up at Arlo for reassurance. "that's something friends do, right?" Arlo just takes a big deep breath and looks like he's about to say something.

"Yeah..." begins Jeannie. "I mean, close friends right?"

"Yeah if he's gay." Arlo begins a bit defensively.

"Not necessarily!" I retort.

"Poppy, do you think this guy *likes* you?" Arlo asks. He's dead serious.

"No! Of course not." He can't. No he surely doesn't. I'm not his type.

What even is Atticus's type?

CHAPTER TWENTY-SIX

December

Keep Truckin, Atty

The freezing Manhattan air hits my face and my freshly curled beach waves blow back behind me.

It's that kind of wind where it's so strong that you can't even keep your eyes open.

They're staying open though and they are taking in all the holiday decorations. The lights, the bows, everything.

There is absolutely *nothing* like the holiday season in Manhattan.

More importantly though, Atticus and I's article is here.

It's the fifth of December and Manhattan is even more clustered and packed around here then it usually is. Tonight they're lighting The Rockefeller Center Christmas tree, so that's probably why. God I love the annual Christmas tree lighting. And I don't even celebrate Christmas!

It's all so special, so amazing. The holiday season is just perfection at its finest. I'm the absolute happiest during the holidays (and it's not just because I get to shamelessly shop and not feel bad about it afterwards!)

I push through the crowds as politely as I can. Can I just say, I am wearing the cutest outfit!

I'm in my *Mackage* pure white, wool, wrap coat that has fluffy fur all over it.

Then I have my white trousers and *Mercedes Castillo* white snakeskin ankle boots. I also have my white leather gloves and huge white earmuffs. Wintery yet classy. A bit too sophisticated for my liking but I'm actually digging it!

I usually wear a lot more colors, so this is a tad different for me. I just feel like a winter angel in all my white and fur. So fab!

I hear Christmas music everywhere I pass and everyone just looks… happy. A lot of people have big shopping bags in their hands and all the shops have decorated their windows. If you don't live in the city you might not know this, but the holidays in Manhattan are like, a big deal. Like, a really big deal.

All the shops give everything they have with their store windows. Especially *Saks Fifth Avenue.*

They have a bunch of big windows on the first floor that are usually decorated beautifully, but during the holidays they go so extra.

Every year it's a different type of theme. Like a winter wonderland or something. It's one of my favorite parts of the holidays. Probably because my parents used to take me and Diamante to see the windows every year.

Seeing the beautiful mannequins all dressed up in their finest, holding ornaments or having some kind of elebret background behind them kind of pushed me into fashion. That's at least one of the things that did so.

The windows are just breathtaking. Something you have to see for yourself. Oh, and don't even get me started on their light show…

"Here we are." I hear an excited, deep voice beside me.

Atticus's arms are crossed and his hands are moving up and down his arms to fight against the cold, but it doesn't stop from the genuinely excited smile on his face.

He has his black beanie on top of his head and a long black, buttoned up coat. He's in black dress jeans with embroidered silver crosses down the side of the leg and black *Vans* with one stud in his right ear.

He has his normal silver chains under his coat and a silver ring on almost everyone of his fingers. We look like complete opposites as per usual.

I look up to see the 5th avenue *Barnes and Noble* right in front of us.

I'd like to take Atticus to see the *Saks* windows. Show him something for once.

"Are you ready?" He asks, giddily. "Yeah." I nod as we both push through the revolving doors.

When we enter the building, warmth finally washes over the both of us. We both take a deep breath and the heat, for once, feels good. I hate the heat. But on a freezing day like today, I don't mind it.

Right in front of us are the new releases and as I begin to move towards them, I get shoved and almost fall onto the display. Typical. What is it with me always getting shoved when I'm with Atticus!

"Yo, watch where you're going." Atticus barks at the middle aged man who just shoved me. His voice is even deeper than usual and that Brooklyn accent really shines through his tone.

The man just continues walking, not paying any mind. Atticus takes me by the shoulders and we move out of the way and into the autobiography section.

"You ok?" He asks. I just nod my head with a thankful closed mouth smile.

I can't bring myself to look at him. This whole time I've been so awkward. I feel it's because of the conversation I had yesterday with Jane, Riley, Jeannie, and Arlo.

I know for a fact that Atticus considers me a good friend, he's said it himself.

So, there must be nothing there, right? Same with me. Yeah sure, Atticus is very good looking but he's a *good* friend of mine. That's that. Ok, so why am I being so weird! God, get it together Poppy!

"Hey…" he begins in a gentle tone as he grabs my chin in between his thumb and pointer finger, forcing me to look up at him. That same gesture he did a couple of days ago made me completely weak. That's something friends do, right?

The cold of the ring on his thumb is so frigid, it makes me jolt a bit. It feels good against my now warmed up skin.

"What's the matter?" He looks perplexed. Quite frankly, so am I.

I snap myself out of it though.

"Just nervous." That's not a lie. I am a tad bit nervous. I hope he likes the article. This will be his first time reading it fully. I made him wait.

"Why?" My chin is still grasped between his thumb and pointer finger.

"I want you to like it." I just shrug and say below a whisper. Atticus gives a harmless laugh.

"I'll love it, Poppy. I'm sure I will." I try to escape his grasp to hide my cheeks that are growing red but he keeps his firm hold on my chin.

I could see the little smirk starting to form on Atticus's lips and his brown eyes are more dilated than they usually are when he's looking down at me. They're just these huge brown saucers.

"Come on, don't get shy on me. I stayed at your place the other night..." he can't even say the sentence without cracking up. "that's about as intimate as it gets."

"Shut up." I slap his chest, grab his hand, and drag him towards the magazine section.

"Ok..." I begin singsongly, dragging Atticus by the hand, all the uncomfort and awkwardness there before has now dissipated.

My heart is now beating out of my chest but it's not only because Atticus is beside me, it's because I'm about to read the published version of what's been my life for the past couple of months. My supposed biggest article yet.

"Let's see..." Atticus begins excitedly as he starts to look through the fashion section of the magazine racks. He's practically bouncing up and down. He's always so hyper. It's absolutely adorable.

I watch as he gains this magnetic smile on his face as he reaches the top of the shelf, grabbing a copy of *DuVull* effortlessly. I usually have to stand on my tippy toes to reach it.

Atticus passes me the magazine with hopeful eyes and I take it out of his grasp with shaky hands. I look up at him for a moment with sudden fright.

"What?" He asks, crossing his arms and squinting his eyes skeptically, trying to figure out my look of fright.

"Atticus..." I begin holding the magazine to my chest thinking about how I'm going to utter the words I want to come out of my mouth. To think of a clever way to say them. I am, afterall, a writer for a living. "I often try not to but... I tend to have a habit of disappointing people. Whether it be at work because I'm too ambitious, or at home with my parents, or because I was born according to my sister. Even with Tiff! And I don't know why I'm being extremely vulnerable in front of you right now, chances or it's a mistake, but--" Atticus suddenly playfully pinches my top and bottom lip together with his thumb and pointer finger to get me to stop talking.

He looks gentle but he's also trying not to laugh at the sight.

"Too much babbling?" I mutter best I can with him pinching my lips shut.

"I love your babbling... get to the point though." He chuckles and lets go of my lips.

"I don't want to disappoint you with this article."

His face suddenly gets soft and a bit confused.

"You never do." He smiles. "And you never will."

"Oh, ok." I snort more goofily than I thought I would.

I stand next to him as I start to flip the pages of the magazine looking intently for my article. I try to avoid Atticus's gaze.

Atticus is looking carefully as well, the smile not leaving his face.

"Here it is!" I squeal excitedly as we reach the cover page. Oh my god. Jane really did make the art department go off on the cover page.

"Holy shit, it's my guitar!" Atticus laughs pointing to the drawn green guitar on the page.

The design and art of the article is somewhat punk but still very *DuVull and Co.* It's like glam meets goth. (Ohhhhh... that's good.)

It's a black background with silver sparkles and Atticus's green guitar that one of the artists drew. I'm the one that really pushed for it, that's why I got a picture of the guitar. I wanted it to be very personalized for him.

It's very playful. I titled the article, '*Pop Punk is all the rage. Hop on the musical lifestyle.*'

The article ended up being a total of six pages and me and Atticus point at each one in disbelief. We really did it...we really did it! I can't remember the last time I was this proud of one of my articles.

The minute I see the 'By Poppy Paxton' at the bottom I feel a sense of relief and accomplishment. It's indescribable. Any writer could understand the feeling. The feeling of 'wow... I did that.' And you did, and you have every right to be proud!

We sit on the lone bench in the middle of the magazine aisle and laugh and smile as we read through the article. Atticus points at every little detail like a child in awe of something. It's so sweet. It's satisfying and a relief. I'm glad he likes it.

As we reach the last page of the article and the last paragraph, I make sure to look next to me the whole time at Atticus to grasp his reaction.

His wide smile now turns into a soft one as he reads the heartfelt message I wrote for him. How he's changed my perspective on so many things. Opened and broadened my horizons. It's the paragraph I wrote when he was in the bathroom the other night while he was in my apartment.

I can't help but blush when I think back to what I wrote. It states,

"It's truly amazing to listen and watch how someone else lives their life. The Pop Punk genre is not only a music style, but a lifestyle. A lifestyle I've actually surprisingly learned to like.

Atticus truly has a talent and I wouldn't want anyone else to show me their lifestyle. I'm not sure if I even find anyone interesting enough to go through their lifestyle. If I'm being quite honest, Atticus is the most interesting, most talented, and kindest person I know. There is no other person I rather spend my time with, no other person I would sing for while they play the piano.

Not only did this article open and broaden my horizons, but it created a beautiful friendship. Atticus, when you read this, know I appreciate you. When you make it big and you are playing stages around the world, send a postcard. Keep truckin, Atty. -Poppy."

Atticus looks stunned as he reads it, almost breathless.

He looks up from the magazine as if he could cry at any moment.

He won't though, I know he won't. Atticus is very in touch with his feelings but one thing to know about men is they never cry in front of you. Happy tears, sad tears, never.

I remember my senior year of highschool Liam's Grandmother passed away. It was the first Grandparent he had lost. I myself had my fair share of experiences with losses.

I remember standing behind him, rubbing his arms as he just stared angrily down at the coffin.

God knows why, he was always angry.

'You know, we've been together for almost four years now, you *can* cry in front of me. You could be vulnerable. It's ok.' I offered with a kind smile. He just looked down at me as if I just said the most offensive thing he's ever heard.

'I'm not a little bitch, Patricia.' Is all he spat.

So… yeah. Guy's don't cry. And Atticus is no exception.

"It's amazing, Poppy." I'm snapped out of the memory when I hear Atticus's deep drawl, now even more deep. He's looking at me dumbstruck, and his eyes are soft.

"Thank you." I rasp out. Atticus can't seem to keep his eyes off of the article. He looks up once again, his chocolate doe brown eyes looking straight into my soul.

His look is gentle. For all the hardcore music he play's and all the dark clothes he wears, Atticus truly is just...a gentle soul.

"Come here." He suddenly says but before I could lean into him, he wraps his arms around me and pulls me into his chest in a tight hug. One out of the many things I adore about Atticus is his hugs. "This article is amazing! You totally have this promotion in the bag."

I giggle as he keeps me in a tight bear hug. I lean into his chest and lay my hand there as well. He rests his chin on the top of my head and keeps his hands on my waist.

Neither of us are giggling anymore though. Now it's just silent as I bury the side of my cheek in his chest. Usually I would worry about my makeup rubbing off but currently I could care less.

I feel Atticus's fingertips gently go up and down the small of my back. At that moment, I think my heart has officially just dropped to my stomach. I feel this overwhelming pang in my chest. I feel safe. As one of his fingers inch lower down the small of my back, my breath hitches in the back of my throat and sparks of tingles ensue.

"You know," he begins, breaking the silence. "If me and the boys ever *do* make it big, you'll be getting more than a postcard, right?"

"Oh yeah?" I look up at him with a bright smile. "What are you going to bring me back?"

"Whatever you want." He laughs, but it comes out as more of an exasperated sigh. He seems to be searching for something in my eyes and I don't exactly know what he's searching for.

No one else is in the magazine section but me and Atticus and it suddenly gets extremely quiet. I could feel his heartbeat where my hand rests on his chest, it's beating insanely fast and I could only imagine how fast mine is beating.

To make things less heated in the moment, I poke his little silver nose ring, adding a slight 'boop' sound at the end.

He scrunches up his nose and it causes me to bite my lip and giggle even more.

Out of nowhere he gently grabs a hold on the back of my neck and places his forehead again against mine. I look into his eyes and swallow thickly, the playful mood fleeing as soon as it came.

The way Atticus puts his forehead against mine, the way he's holding the back of my neck, it makes me feel like we're more than friends. That's how couples hold each other, and I don't know how I feel about Atticus holding me this way.

Why is he holding me this way? The only reason you hold someone this way is if you're about too... oh my god, if you're about to kiss them! Oh... my *god*.

I lick my lips and watch as Atticus does the same. I close my eyes as I feel his nose brush up against mine.

"Excuse me?" Interrupts a fraggle, kind voice behind us and I give a frightened jolt, Atticus's hand still on the back of my neck. My face is bright red as an older woman, maybe around 70 years old, stands in front of us.

"I don't mean to interrupt, but where did you get that *DuVull* magazine?"

"Oh," I say, a bit taken back by her question. Atticus just gives a shy smile and looks down at his lap, letting go of the back of my neck.

I get up and rush towards the shelf I got it from.

"It's right here! Do you normally read it?" I ask kindly as I stand on my tippy toes to reach for the magazine. I struggle a bit trying to reach the top of the shelf.

"Oh yes, for years now. It's wonderful. Do you?" I giggle. Oh she doesn't know half of it.

"She writes for them." I hear Atticus behind me as he grabs the magazine I was reaching for with ease and hands it to the older woman.

"Do you, love? Oh my!" The older woman gasps in excitement. "Do you have an article this month?"

"I do!" I state excitedly. She opens her magazine and motions me to show her my article. I help her turn the pages and look up to see Atticus staring fondly. He throws a wink at me and I can't help but blush and shake my head as I look back down and continue to help the lady.

"There it is!" I point excitedly. "He's in the article too." I point to Atticus who gives a shy wave and smiles at the older lady. "Actually, the article surrounds him."

"Oh, well I will make sure to read it." The lady says in awe. "Well thank you." She gives a kind smile and waves and walks out of the asle.

Atticus slowly walks up to me and it's now just us once again. It makes me nervous and it makes me anxious. He's standing in front of me now and looking down at me as I look up at him. What do I say, what do I do? Are we going to pick up from where we left off? Should I lean into him?

"Do you want to get a coffee?" I ask, my voice cracking trying to relive any of the awkwardness. I don't know if awkwardness is the right word, it's something else, I just can't put my finger on the emotion. Tension maybe?

"Ok." He nods and we begin to walk towards the *Starbucks* on the other side of the upstairs floor.

We don't really talk as we get on line for coffee. We just stand there for a while.

God, he must think I'm such a fool! Imagine if I *did* kiss him. Our friendship would be over! But... didn't he make the first move? Was that *even* a move? Did I just take it the wrong way? Probably. Go figure. Well at least nothing happened.

As me and Atticus sit down with our drinks in hand, nothing is really awkward anymore. I don't know what I was expecting after that. We just sit and talk and laugh after a while as we sip our coffees and look through the magazine.

"I was meaning to ask you," I begin. "Tiff plays in the girls league for a pretty popular softball team around here. She's playing a really huge game tomorrow. The softball season is over but it's for a holiday fundraiser. It's going to be at a pretty well known stadium too...would you like to go with me?" My voice is high pitched and nervous. "Just a last minute thought, you know. I have two tickets. I kind of wouldn't want to bring anyone else." I could see the sudden huge smile spread across Atticus's face.

"I'd love to."

CHAPTER TWENTY-SEVEN
Baseball and Bras

I feel panic starting to rise as the car hits multiple speed bumps at the same time. It's not because of the unsafe speed bumps Staten Island desperately needs to fix, it's because of the unusual circumstance I currently got myself into.

I hop on my phone to tell Tiff we are currently on our way to the stadium, although she is probably practicing, It makes me feel better to tell her.

It also makes me feel better to say *we* because she doesn't know Atticus is joining me. I hope she's not upset, disappointed or sees me as selfish for wanting his company during the game.

I'm proud of Tiff and her athletic abilities. If I could show it off to the world, I would.

But as I sit in the car and the GPS from Atticus's phone goes off over and over again, I feel my stomach go a wee bit funny. It's a nervous and anxious feeling that I get all too often when around him. What the *hell* was I thinking?

I just have to keep reminding myself, this is not--

"Ok," begins Atticus turning to me, an amused smirk on his face. "you're quiet, and you're *never* quiet. What's up?"

"Nothing." I pop up, bringing my attention to him.

He looks through his rear view mirror and keeps his eye on the domestic Staten Island blocks.

One thing I *do* love about Staten Island is that each house you pass looks different. No house is the same. Each has its own personality, you know. It doesn't matter if they have the same layout, they all have a different type of look judging by who lives in them.

"Nothing, huh?" He repeats.

"Nothing at all!" I give a fake bright smile. I don't know if it's fake because I'm happy, I am! I'm just... confused. I brought this amongst myself though. I'm the one that asked Atticus to come to this game with me. Of course I don't regret it, not one bit. There is one thing I have to keep in mind though, this is *not* a date. No sir, not even close. Just dudes being dudes, friends being friends.

"Ok!" Atticus begins as we pull into the field and he turns off his music playing at an ear shattering volume. I've said it before though, I don't mind it.

We pull into the parking lot of the Richmond County Bank Ballpark. God, It's so exciting to see Tiff play at such an Iconic place! She deserves it.

Everything is all decorated with mostly Christmas decorations. So cute. I love how they host a fundraiser. We go every year. Tiff's team plays against another league and whoever wins gets money donated to the charity of the team's choice.

Of course Tiff's team always wins!

They have the best softball player of all time. Duh!

"Ok." I say back playfully. I can't hide my nervous smile.

As we get out of the car I see that the parking lot is almost completely filled to the brim with other cars, and I'm thankful we found a spot. It's not terribly cold today like it was yesterday. It's just a bit windy.

I made sure to dress appropriately for the venue and the weather.

I'm in light, baggy white sweatpants and a baby pink oversized hoodie. I paired it with a matching pink baseball cap and mini baby blue, *Gucci* crossbody bag.

It has the two big double G's in the middle and a chain shoulder strap too.

I also made sure to slip on my new pink, white, and black checkered denim jacket. It's cozy and goes with the outfit.

To finish it all off, I'm in these huge white platform sneakers. They're surprisingly comfortable.

I'm dressed surprisingly comfortable.

I can't remember the last time I dressed even remotely cozy.

My idea of comfort these days is a skirt that's not too tight and five inch heels opposed to seven.

But I'm dressed softball appropriate and that's all that matters. There are certain things you have to wear to certain places. That is one of the many rules of fashion!

You're not going to wear your new *Balmain* skirt to a softball game. What happens if it gets dirty? It's just unheard of!

When Atticus gets out of the car I can't help but marvel at how cool he looks as well.

He's in blue jeans that are purposely rolled up to show his long white socks.

He's wearing new immaculately clean, black converses and a plain black shirt tucked into his jeans. Under the plan black T-shirt is a black and red striped, long sleeved shirt.

He has one silver chain around his neck and a matching one attached to his jeans. His hair is all messed up on top of his head but it doesn't necessarily look... messy. It just looks like Atticus.

"Atticus Mckeen," I begin to scold. "where's your jacket!" He just gives a little smile and pulls out a long, black coat out of his backseat. He holds it up victoriously with a proud smile.

I just chuckle and shake my head.

We begin to walk towards the stadium and I put my hair up into a ponytail.

"Hey, Atty?" I say cautiously, as we walk in. We stroll through all the concessions then down to the hundreds of seats facing the field. "I need to talk to you."

So funny story, Atticus doesn't know my family is here either. We're both looking around and I could tell Atticus is very out of his element as am I.

He finally looks down at me with a curious smile.

"What is it?" He asks, but when we reach our seats it's too late.

"Oh my god!" I hear my mom's brooklyn jewish accent begin and I immediately cringe. I just turn to Atticus with a forced smile on my face.

"Surprise!"

Atticus looks absolutely speechless. I can't seem to face him so I turn back to my parents, Tiff's mom Helen and her dad Dave, and Diamante and Carlo. They look just as shocked.

Mom clasps her hands together with her big, pink bonet on her head and Helen has a matching orange one. They're absolutely horrendous. Bonnets are for spring, not winter. Everyone knows that!

Mom starts to hit Helen's shoulder and Helen rolls her glasses down her nose to get a better look at me and Atticus.

Dad and Dave look Atticus up and down skeptically and Diamante violently hits Carlo's shoulder, looking at Atticus in complete disgust.

She better keep her mouth shut and be respectful, because I'll jump over these seats and punch her, I swear.

"Hi…" Atticus begins, friendly. "everyone." I turn to him with a sudden saddened frown.

"I'm *so* sorry." I mouth.

"Sneaky bastard." He mouths back but I could tell he's not mad due to the growing grin on his face.

I say my hello's to everyone and mom grabs me by the cheeks, kissing me on the sides of my face. Helen does the same. I kiss my dad's cheek as well.

"How's my favorite youngest daughter?" He asks and I give a stressed half laugh at his dad joke.

I give both Diamante and Carlo a kiss on the cheek as well. Diamante looks annoyed. (What else is new.)

When I give Carlo his kiss on the cheek, I grab his face in both my hands and whisper quietly in his ear.

"Don't you let her intimidate you. She's your fiance now." I nod my head when I sit back up. Carlo just nods and gives me a closed mouth smile.

I've never been close to Carlo. If I'm being quite honest, I think he's a little standoffish and he's quite the mute. He is going to be my brother-in-law though, and I always did hate the way Diamante treated him. How she just bosses him around and constantly mistreats him verbally. I tap him on the side of the face and resume to my spot next to Atticus.

"Sit, sit, don't be shy…" begins mom, patting the last two seats in the row.

I sit next to my mom and Atticus sits next to me on the end.

"Poppy," she begins once again. "are you going to introduce us to your friend?"

'You already know who it is!' I want to scream. But instead I press my lips together into a tight smile and put my hand on Atticus's arm.

"Atticus," I begin. "This is my mom Molly, my dad Geoff, Tiff's mom Helen and her dad Dave, and my sister Diamante, and my future brother-in-law Carlo. Guys, this is Atticus."

"Hello, ma'am." Atticus says respectfully and holds his hand out to my mom with that contagious smile. My mom excitedly takes his hand and shakes it. "Sir." He holds his hand out for dad to shake as well.

Dad takes Atticus's hand with a curt smile and shakes it.

Something about Atticus calling my mom 'ma'am' and my dad 'sir' is just so adorable. Especially with his accent. That Brooklyn drawl always makes him sound so intimidating.

"Hi Helen, Dave. Hi Diamante, sup Carlo." Atticus gives them a friendly wave as well.

"Oh hi, love!" Helen is holding onto my mom's shoulder happily as if she's never seen me with a man before.

"Nice to meet you, Atticus." Dave gives a tiny wave of the hand.

"Hi." Carlo puts his weak hand out for Atticus to shake and I can't help but smile. Atticus gladly shakes his hand more on the rough side, not meaning too of course. Carlo's just...well, weak.

Diamante stares at Carlo as if he *dare* shake Atticus's hand without her giving the ok. Atticus gives Dia a bright smile and Diamante just looks him up and down, crosses her arms, and turns back to the playing field.

Atticus sits back in his seat defeated and I can't help but roll my eyes at my bitchy sister. The game is about to begin and I spot Tiff in the dugout.

I excitedly tap Atticus's shoulder and point towards her. He looks at me, smiling at my enthusiasm.

"Great job on the article. The both of you." Says my mom to me and Atticus. "I've sent it to so many people, right Geoff?"

"Oh yeah..." begins my dad. "great job with the... uh... different styles and what not." He motions towards me and Atticus, continuing to eat his popcorn. "Very impressive."

"Don't listen to him," whispers my mom to us. "he knows nothing about fashion." And she does?

"The article was so enjoyable, Poppy!" Helen squeals. "Oh and I'm so honored. Meeting the famous Atticus. Tiff has told me so much about you! I was reading the article and I looked at my Tiff and I said, 'Tiff! Who's this boy?' and Tiffany said you were Poppy's little goth friend. How cute--" mom puts her hand over Helen's mouth and I sink impossibly deeper in my seat.

"Oh god, Helen, will you stop." Murmurs Dave. "Let the kids get ready for the game in peace will ya? It's gonna be a hell of a ride!" He turns to my dad excitedly.

"Well I'm glad you enjoyed it." Atticus states. Helen and my mom blush quite a bit when he shoots them his signature smirk. Urgh. They're so embarrassing.

"Oh Poppy, he's cute." Mom says as her and Helen lean in closer to me. I can see Atticus's smile grow even wider as he pretends he can't hear them, facing the starting game. I just give them a stressed smile and nod slowly.

"He's very different from Liam." Helen nods. "He's got a ring on the side of his nose."

"It's a nose ring, Helen!" Retorts my mom. "God, didn't you read the article?"

"I'm so sorry." I suddenly look up at Atticus. He just laughs and sinks in his chair to my level.

"It's fine!" He laughs once again. "Why didn't you tell me your family was going to be here?"

"I thought you wouldn't want to come." I answer honestly. "Look at them!" He just chuckles once again and pokes my cheek with his pointer finger.

"I would've still come." He says surly.

All the sudden I see Tiff come out of the dugout and I quickly stand up and bounce up and down.

"Tiffy!" I start to wave my hands in the air to try to get her attention.

She's swinging her bat back and forth practicing when she finally looks up at where I'm seated not too far away from her. She gives a little laugh and an embarrassed wave.

Her eyes wander next to me where Atticus sits. He gives her a friendly wave and she immediately turns back to me mouthing,

"What the hell?"

"We'll talk later." I shoo her and the look of both astonishment and confusion is quite funny. She just rolls her eyes, slaps her hands on her sides and heads back into the dugout. Typical Tiff.

After the game begins, me and Atticus only really watch when Tiff comes on.

When Tiff is not on we talk amongst ourselves and I can't help but giggle and snort at the story he's telling me about the time he, Dallon, and Finnick were playing a gig in a Manhattan hotel and they got stuck in the elevator.

I catch a couple of squinted glances from my sister but I don't think too much into it. Finally she speaks up. I knew that big mouth couldn't stay quiet for too long.

"What's so funny?" She suddenly asks, leaning over a timid Carlo.

"What?" I ask as if I can't be bothered. Oh, and does that bother her.

"I said, 'what's so funny?'" She draws it out as if I'm stupid. "Surely something must be. Mom and dad always scold me for talking to Carlo alone during family outings. Why are the rules different for *you?*" I bite the side of my mouth so I don't say anything I might regret.

Something like, 'because you're a hoe and mom and dad don't trust you because the both of you are a bunch of weirdos. So in retrospect, you're perfect for eachother!' But thankfully I stop myself from saying that.

"I'm just telling Poppy a story about the time me and my bandmates got stuck in an elevator." Atticus gives her a friendly smile.

"How endeering." Diamante says sarcastically.

"Dia!" Mom snaps.

"I'm just creating conversation." Diamante then gets a wicked smirk on her face. "I got a story..." she pops up.

My dad and Dave just roll their eyes, trying to focus on the game.

Helen and mom are on the edge of their seats. I just give Diamante a warning glare.

"So," Diamante begins facing everyone. "Poppy was in ninth grade. She was going on her first date with Liam... you remember Liam, right Poppy?" Diamante cocks up a brow evilly.

"Of course I do." I retort angrily. Oh god, please don't talk about Liam...

"Just checking." Diamante begins. "He broke up with you *ages* ago anyway. What was it, a couple of months now? Plus, you got a new toy anyway..." she motions to Atticus. I scold her completely speechless. "I taught you well." She gives a proud smirk.

"Ok," begins my dad getting up. "I'm getting more popcorn. Dave?"

"I'm with ya, pal." They both walk past us and out to the concession stands.

"Anyway, Poppy was this cute little thing in ninth grade and she was going on her first date with Liam. Well obviously me, being the good sister I am, gave her all the info she needed to know when going on a date." She winks and I feel my face begin to turn red with anger and embarrassment. "Well I obviously told her she needed a push-up bra. Little ninth grade Poppy didn't have any money, she had no Job and of course I wasn't buying it for her. So, she scurried to *Victoria Secrets* and *stole* a push-up bra. Luckily she didn't get caught..."

"Is that true, Poppy?" My mom gasps.

"Diamante told me to do so!" I retort, almost in tears. I can't even look at Atticus. "I was young, she took advantage of me. She told me Liam wouldn't like me unless I had one!"

"And you followed my instructions and had lots of fun with Liam that night, didn't you?" She retorts and I swallow thickly so the tears that are threatening to pour out of my eyes don't. I give her the satisfaction of seeing me cry all too much.

"Don't you doubt for one minute Patrica that I'm a good sister. I'm the best sister because I am, and always will be, one step ahead of you. You learned most of what you know today from me, me! Don't you *dare* forget it." She states.

I turn away to wipe the tears from my eyes and everyone goes silent.

I feel a hand on my back and turn to look at Atticus. He's giving my sister a look I never seen Atticus give before. It's intense, it's angry. It's different from the look he gave Dallon. He almost looks hurt, affected by her words.

He looks at me and his whole face softens as he rubs my back soothingly.

"You ok?" He asks worriedly and I just nod.

"Well, I think that was a little uncalled for." I hear Helen say facing the game. She then looks to my mom, prompting her to say something.

"I agree." States mom, saddened and in a low voice. "We have a guest. You're only embarrassing yourself, Diamante." She talks to Diamante as if she's fourteen years old and not getting her way.

"You're right, mom..." pops up Diamante suddenly. "It was a horrible decision for me to say those things." It doesn't take a genius to decipher the condescending tone in her voice.

I just remain in Atticus's arms.

"Poppy dear, I'm *so* sorry." She gives me a slight raise of her brow and a little smirk she makes sure no one else sees. Me and Atticus do though. I look up to see him glaring at her.

Diamante looks to mom and Helen for some kind of approval but she gets none. My mom's eyes remain slightly glassy and on the game and Helen turns to me and Atticus, giving us a little kind smile and wink.

I have a sudden feeling of adoration and appreciation for Helen as I give her a smile back.

I turn my vision back to the game but make sure not to move. I don't want Atticus to move his arm from around me.

Dad and Dave eventually come back and sit in their seats.

"Can we sit back down? Is the girl talk over?" Dave jokes but no one even responds. We just stay stoic, our eyes on the game.

"I'll take that as a yes." My dad and Dave roll their eyes and shake their heads in typical middle aged dad fashion.

We sit and watch the game go by for a couple of minutes in silence. Atticus's arm is around my chair like a protective shield. Suddenly I feel him lean in towards me and his breath tickles against my ear.

"Do you understand any of this?"

"Not one bit." I look up at his somewhat worried expression and give a giggle. I look towards Helen and mom who are both showing each other something on their phones and Helen has her knitting set on her lap.

"It's ok though, they don't either." I tell him with a laugh.

"Popcorn?" Dave reaches across Helen and my mom to me and Atticus, holding his bucket of popcorn to us.

"Dave!" Helen squeals, practically pushing the popcorn out of his hands. She gives a curt smile, then mom and her both turn to him. "Will you stop! Don't you see that this is a *date*..." A date! No, no it's not! "stop bothering them." I turn to Atticus to make sure he didn't hear Helen but he doesn't seem like he hasn't. I sigh in relief.

Thank god. Then I would have to go on this whole spiel to everyone about how this is in fact *not* a date. Mom and Helen could believe what they want to believe all day long. As long as they're happy.

All of the sudden someone on Tiff's team hits the ball with their bat at the speed of light and it heads up into the air. I watch carefully as it heads towards us. It comes directly towards me and Atticus and I squeal and duck, but I watch as Atticus catches it with ease.

Victorious cheers erupt throughout the stadium and Atticus turns to me innocently and proudly. He has this cute little smile on his face.

"I caught it!" He says excitedly. I nod, smiling back at Atticus not having the heart to tell him he did nothing useful. I watch as the couple of girls on Tiff's team shrug and clap while Tiff looks up at us, chuckling and shaking her head.

"Good job, guitar boy." Dave murmurs.

"Did Tiff just get a home run? I jump out of my seat.

"Did I help?" Atticus pops up the same, waving the ball he caught in the air.

"Yes, Tiff got a home run..." Dad begins. Then he turns to Atticus. "and sure, pal. Whatever makes you happy."

"You helped!" I squeal, jumping up and down, clapping my hands.

After the game is done and over with, the masses start to leave the stadium. Mom, dad, Helen, Dave, Diamante, and Carlo all stand up. I look at Atticus and shrug, as we both stand up as well. The both of us follow the bulk down to the field where Tiff and her team are.

Once we reach the field I hear my mom and Helen whispering about something and I could tell it's about Atticus.

My dad and Dave are talking about the route they are taking for their fishing trip next week, and Diamante is typing something on her phone as Carlo looks lost.

Me and Atticus are just standing behind everyone and I feel quite unsure. I really didn't mean to spring my family on him. I wish I knew what he thinks of this. Is he angry? I don't think so. He doesn't seem it. Friends meet each other's parents. It's totally normal! Jeannie, Riley, and Arlo know my family. I just wish I knew what was running through his mind right now.

I feel Atticus playfully nudge my side with his elbow. I look towards him as he looks down at me, a grin on his face.

"What?" I ask, my own smile growing.

"Nothing." He screws his face up and shrugs. "Care to share what you're thinking about."

"No." I answer honestly.

"Is it about how devastatingly handsome I am?"

"No." I snort.

"Are you sure?"

"Yes."

"Positive?"

"Hundred percent."

"Come on," he begins when he leans towards me. "I won't tell anybody."

I just look up at him, scrunch up my nose and shake my head.

"No... I think I'll keep you guessing."

"Ah, I see," Atticus clicks his tongue with a cheeky smile. "In true female fashion."

I try to debunk his statement but I honestly can't.

"I'll keep guessing though." He suddenly looks back down at me. "I don't mind a challenge."

"In true Atticus fashion." I can't help but say and give a little smile.

"Do you have an answer for everything?"

"Don't you?" We both begin to laugh.

Diamante turns to us strangely when she hears our laughter and we both immediately stop like children who just got reprimanded. As soon as she turns back to her phone we just laugh even more as silently as we can.

"What I want to know is how a sixteen year old Poppy Paxton got away with stealing a push-up bra?" I hear Atticus ask beside me and I give a giggle.

"I snuck into the dressing room, ripped off the tag, and put it over the bra I already had on. Just in case the store alarm went off. Not like they could ask me to lift up my shirt." I say bluntly.

I look up to see an amused smile on Atticus's face, mouth agape. He can't seem to believe what he's hearing.

"I would have never guessed you were a kleptomaniac." He teases.

"Am not!" I retort. "And it was one time. Have you ever stolen something."

"Oh yeah..." Atticus pulls a face and nods. "gum, drinks, cookies, cigarettes. All when I was younger though."

"You couldn't afford it?" I ask, sympathetically.

"Nah, it was for the thrill." He laughs with a wide smile and I gasp, swatting his arm.

"And to think, I felt bad for you..."

"Hey, I'm not the one who stole a bra."

Tiff comes out of the dugout with her big bag of softball equipment as she wipes her sweat off of her forehead with her arm. She looks exhausted as always after a game. Who could blame her? I couldn't do half of what she does!

A kind smile spreads across her face as she hugs her mom and dad, my mom and dad, and Diamante and Carlo. Finally she reaches me and Atticus and all she does is shake her head at us, a little giggle coming out of her mouth.

We wrap our arms around each other and I can't help the huge smile that spreads across my face.

When she lets go of me she then hugs Atticus. Atticus doesn't even hesitate.

Tiff then faces the both of us, putting her hands on her hips.

"I wasn't expecting to see the both of you today." She looks at me with not-so-subtle wide eyes.

"Yes well," I shrug trying to avoid her glance. "I had bought an extra ticket by accident."

"By accident?"

"Yes." I give a manic smile, trying to stay calm. Tiff seems to pick up on it, then turns to Atticus.

"It was nice of you to join Pops. Thanks for coming." She gives him a grateful smile.

"Of course." Atticus nods. "By the way... you're welcome for catching the ball." He says with faux cockiness.

"Ah yes, couldn't have done it without you." Tiff laughs.

"I'm sure you could have." Atticus snorts. "I don't know anything about softball."

"It's ok. Pop's doesn't either."

"I so do!" I retort.

"Ok then," begins Tiff challengingly. "what's a Foul Tip?"

I polk the side of my mouth with my tongue, look the other way, and cross my arms thinking.

"I--it's a... foul tip. A tip that's...foul." I shrug my shoulders and purse my lips together.

"You're cute." Tiff shakes her head and laughs. I turn to Atticus still in my defensive state.

He's just looking down at me, a wide smile on his face as he laughs.

"I have no clue what it is either." He turns to Tiff and all three of us start to laugh.

As everyone begins to walk back to their cars, I stand next to my mom and Atticus is beside me. Tiff swings her bat back and forth standing next to Helen, as mom and Helen whisper something amongst themselves. (As always.)

"So Atticus,' begins mom. "the holidays are coming up. What are you doing?"

"Oh..." begins Atticus a bit shyly. "I really don't know. I might be going to my dad's, but we really aren't on the same page with anything ever, so, probably not." Like that, I hear Helen's very loud gasp from here.

"You're not spending the holidays alone, are you? You can't do that! What about your mom--"

"Uh, mom..." begins Tiff. "not appropriate."

"What! It was a *question* Tiffany..."

"It's ok." Atticus shakes his head with a smile, looking towards the two older women. "my mom left when I was tiny, I never met her. My dad doesn't talk about her so I never bring her up. I'm not sure I want to anyway. I've lived my life without her so far, so... yeah."

Both women look at him with sudden shock and remorse. I just rub my hand up and down Atticus's arm for comfort.

He looks down at me and nods his head with a reassuring smile. I really can't get a read on Atticus about his mom. How he truly feels that is. He acts like he could care less but an absent mother would upset anyone, wouldn't it?

"How old were you when she left?" Asks Helen and my mom hits her arm.

"It's a *question* Molly..."

"I'm so sorry." I mumble to Atticus.

"It's ok," and to my suprise, he laughs. "I was six months old." He says to my mom and Helen. "Me and my father haven't heard from her since then. I'm not too tight with my dad either. It is what it is though." He says as if it doesn't bother him.

"You didn't have to tell them all of that. It's none of their business." I whisper to him, embarrassed. God, mom and Helen could be so damn pushy sometimes.

"It's ok, Pops. It really doesn't bother me." He laughs and shrugs, not bothered.

"Well then you're a saint." murmurs Tiff and all three of us chuckle.

"Atticus," pops up my mom suddenly and I pray she doesn't say anything offensive or embarrassing. Her and Helen really do have no filter. "would you like to join us for Hanukkah dinner?" I instinctively tighten my grip on Atticus's arm. I didn't even realize I was still holding onto it.

Oh *damn* my mom and her caring and kind self! Why does she have to be so loving!

I turn to Tiff, my eyes wide. She gives me a bit of a glare and a shrug. She doesn't seem to know what to say either. God, I hope Atticus didn't find that weird.

I can't make out Atticus's expression because he's facing my mom untill he turns to look down at me. I give him a kind smile and shrug.

I don't quite know what to say. Of *course* I would like to have Atticus at Hanukkah dinner. The idea of him being alone for the holidays makes my stomach turn and I suddenly feel sick.

It's like the song says, 'Nobody ought to be alone on Christmas.'

But instead it will be... 'Nobody ought to be alone on Hanukkah.' Or any holiday for that matter. No one should be alone.

I don't get my hopes up that he'll say yes though.

"I didn't know you celebrated Hanukkah." Atticus smirks down at me.

"Well to be fair, I don't walk around leisurely telling people." I say.

"When is it?" Atticus turns to my mom.

"Oh, it's late this year hon..." she takes her calendar out of her bag and checks. I can't even remember the day it is this year. "the 22nd, love." Mom pops up happily. "That's the day of our little celebration. The start of Hanukkah."

Atticus once again looks down at me. He lifts up his brows and smiles.

"What do you say?" He asks under his breath so no one could really hear us. I could see Helen and my mom gaping towards Tiff and I could only *imagine* the glare she's giving them.

"I don't want you to feel obligated to." I give a nervous laugh, matching his tone of voice.

"I don't..." Atticus shakes his head. "not at all. I just don't want *you* to feel obligated in letting me accompany you to the party."

"I don't!" I say, maybe a bit too fast. "I mean...errrr, yeah. No, not at all." I recover.

"The 22nd, right?" Atticus turns to my mom.

"Yes, love." And as she says that Atticus gets out his phone and seems to be typing something on it. He suddenly stops typing and shoves it back into his back pocket.

"I'll be there." He gives the two women his contagious smile and I swear the both of them melt a bit on the inside. You could tell. Everyone does. "Thank you so much for inviting me. I honestly can't wait. I've never been to a Hanukkah party before." He has the widest, happiest smile and it makes me happy and smile. I'm just happy he won't be alone.

I turn to Tiff and see she has a smile on her face too. She looks at me and raises her eyebrows skeptically.

As me and Atticus reach his car I realize how close everyone has parked to each other. Figures.

I give my hugs and kisses to everyone and almost forget that Diamante and Carlo are here. She's going to have a stroke when she finds out Atticus is coming to Hanukkah dinner. I don't think she likes him very much. (But who the hell *does* Diamante like anyway.)

I watch Atticus shake my dad's hand and I watch him hug my mom. Something inside of me arises and comes to the surface. A feeling. I can't put my hand on the exact feeling but It feels like my heart is in my throat.

After we say our goodbyes, me and Atticus hops in his car and we begin to pull out.

"Well that was fun. I'm sorry your sister was being such a bitch to you."

"To be quite honest, I kind of forgot about it." Of course I didn't.

"No you didn't." Atticus says, turning to me, as if reading my mind.

"No, I didn't." I admit.

"It's ok," Atticus begins, turning back to the road ahead of us. "I got you."

It's such a simple statement. Why am I thinking so much into it? It's just so... so comforting.

Although he's next to me, Atticus's voice keeps running through my head. 'I got you, I got you.'

I shake my head and open my mouth to say something when my phone buzzes on my lap. I immediately look down to see a new text from Tiff.

'HOW DO YOU CONSTANTLY MANAGE TO DIG HOLES YOU CAN'T GET YOURSELF OUT OF????'

I just sigh and look up to Atticus tapping his finger on his leather steering wheel to the beat of the metal song on the radio.

"You ok?" He asks me, a cute little dimpled smile on his face.

"Yeah, oh yeah. Perfect!" I smile but then look down at my phone.

'I KNOW.' Is all I could manage to type.

CHAPTER TWENTY-EIGHT
International preparations

"*Why don't I believe you?*" My mom's voice booms through my phone.

I look in front of me to see Jeannie trying not to eavesdrop as she flips through a random magazine and Riley shamelessly eavesdrops as he's sitting next to me, his ear on the other side of my phone. 'Put her on speaker?' he retorted in a whisper. Jeannie widened her eyes and pushed him off the chair. And now he's sitting here being nosy-magee.

"I told you," I sigh and roll my eyes towards Jeannie. "me and Atticus are *not* dating. I would tell you if we were…"

"He seems very taken with you, Poppy." Mom quips, voice a bit muffled.

Riley nods his head in agreement.

"Well I think you're just excited that you're having an extra guest for Hanukkah dinner, aren't you?" I counter.

"Not true!" Mom cries.

"I'm at work, can I go--"

"Oh, so now Jane DuVull is more important than this family. What else is new?"

"Ok ma, stop." I sigh. "Wha--what's the problem here?"

"Everything Poppy!" Mom shrieks and me and Riley cringe. "Does Atticus like latkes?"

"Everyone likes latkes, ma."

"Does he like brisket?"

"Stop worrying so much about Atticus!" I cry helplessly, maybe a little too loud because a couple of other people briefly stop and look at me.

I give them all a friendly smile as Riley gives them all a threatening look. At that, they get back to work.

"Stop worrying about Atticus." I try again, calmly.

I'm honestly worried enough about having Atticus at dinner with my whole family. I don't need my mom freaking out either. One of us needs to stay calm!

I hear my mom take a breath over the phone.

"Poppy, you *would* tell me if you two were dating, wouldn't you?" She finally asks and I can't quite tell what her tone is.

I watch Riley as he shakes his head 'no', and I sigh.

"Yes mom, of course. I have to go, I have work to do. I love you, goodbye." I hang up and throw my phone onto my desk, slumping back into my chair.

"I still can't believe you took that Atticus guy to meet your parents." Riley shakes his head.

"Yeah…" begins Jeannie throwing her magazine down. "you know you can't keep us in the dark too long. Plus, I'm confused."

"About what?" I retort, typing up Jane's itinerary for next week.

"Why did you take Atticus to meet your parents!" Jeannie remarks.

"When you could have brought me!" Riley then retorts. "I'm much better company."

All I could do is snort.

"But all jokes aside," begins Jeannie. "what happened?"

"I… I don't know." I answer honestly. "I really don't know."

"Did it come up in a conversation?"

"Did he invite himself?" Riley prys. "Cause that's a red flag."

"No, no, no…" I shake my head and look away from my computer as I rapidly stop typing and look down at my desk.

"What's the matter, babes?" Jeannie frowns.

"Do you remember the day the Winter issue of *DuVull* came out, and me and Atticus went to go pick it up?"

"Yeah…" Jeannie nods nervously.

God, I'm surprised I kept this from them for this long. I usually tell Jeannie and Riley *everything* the moment it happens. Like, literally. One time I was riding in a taxi and I saw a dog running out of a pizzeria with a slice of pizza in it's mouth, and the owner of the shop was running after him. I texted Jeannie and Riley about it the moment it happened.

My point made.

"Well, me and Atticus were sitting in the magazine aisle reading my article. You read it, I wrote him a little letter at the end, it was cute or whatever..." I motion with my hands. "but all of a sudden we got to talking, and in my article I said that if he ever got famous to send me a postcard, right? Then Atticus said he would bring me back more than a postcard if he got famous, so I said 'Oh Atticus, what will you bring me back?' You know, like a moron. And then he said, 'Whatever you want...' In that attractive raspy voice, you know the one..."

"Poppy!" Riley shouts, cutting off my helpless babbling. "Get to the point!"

"I think he was going to kiss me." I say so fast I secretly hope they can't understand.

Jeannie sits in her seat frozen and so does Riley.

"How do you know?" Asks Jeannie, even more wary than before.

"Jeannie," I whisper shout. "you act like I've never been kissed before! H—he put his hand on the back of my neck, a pretty good grip. He leaned in very close, and he looked down at my lips and licked his! Then he leaned and our noses were practically touching!"

"Sounds like he was making a move." Riley ponders.

"Yeah but what happened?" Jeannie cries.

"Some sweet older women came behind us at the exact moment he was about to kiss me! She asked where I found my issue of *DuVull*, so I got up and showed her!"

"You should have just ignored her and made out with him." Jeannie sighs and murmurs quietly lifting a brow.

"Jeannie!"

"You're life's an unfortunate tacky romcom. You know that, right?" Riley says, still rubbing his temples in shock.

I just give an exasperated whine.

"So, what..." begins Riley. "he tried to make a move so you blackmail him into going to a family outing with you?"

"No dumbass!" Jeannie answers for me.

"Rough crowd today." Riley huffs.

"I didn't know what to do." I utter desperately. "After the supposed attempted kiss happened we didn't *act* awkward. I'm always so lonely at Tiff's games. I love watching Tiff play but it's not like she could have a conversation with me as she's getting a homerun! And it's not like I have a good relationship with my sister! I can't have a normal conversation with her. And my mom talks to Helen and my dad talks to Dave. And I'm alone. Atticus *never* makes me feel alone..." I can't quite decipher the looks on Jeannie and Riley's faces. Riley's eyes knit together and Jeannie frowns.

"I don't know." I sigh, shoulders slumping.

"It's ok." nods Jeannie, putting her hand over mine. "What kind of friends would we be if we didn't help you figure out your feelings." She says with a slight chuckle. "But seriously though. You got us. Always."

"I know."

"So..." begins Riley. "the question is, do you want him to make it to first base?"

Me and Jeannie just glare at him.

"Get it, cause you took him to a baseball game..."

"I get it."

About two hours pass and I finally print out Jane's itinerary. I organize it and staple it as I stand, getting ready to walk it to Jane's office when Ginger Lovett, from the romance department gasps so loud that it goes around the whole office.

I look up to Riley and Jeannie skeptically.

Riley just rolls his eyes and Jeannie doesn't even look up from her computer.

"I wonder if her boyfriend finally broke up with her again." Riley murmurs.

"We've gone to France!" She shouts.

Like that, me Jeannie and Riley lock eyes. I watch everyone in the room look towards each other with stunned expressions.

Did she come to work high again?

"What the hell are you talking about?" Riley sneers.

"One of our articles has made it to other countries! It made it to Japan!" Ginger cries, excitedly. "It's even translated to Japanese! Made it to Britain too. And now France! They're praising it!"

"Holy shit." Jeannie says in shock.

"This is the first time we've gone international in a year!" Ginger begins. "Poppy, it's *your* article. And in France! That's such an honor for any fashion journalist!" And like that, I feel I may pass out. What? Did she just say it was *my* article?

In France, Britain, and Japan! What!

All eyes turn to me.

"Oh my god, Pops!" Jeannie puts her hands over mine.

"You really did it, Pops." Riley laughs in disbelief.

"It's the pop punk one. With your little rocker friend!" Ginger squeals. "Everyone thinks it's genius! You should see the praise you're getting." Me, Riley and Jeannie immediately run over to Ginger's desk. We all lean over it.

"Look," she begins. "Britain says 'an absolute marvelous look on a different lifestyle in a fun way. Praise for *DuVull* magazine and Poppy Paxton.'".

"Oh my god..." I begin, breathless. "Is this a joke?"

"Not one bit!" Ginger Lovett puts her hand on my shoulder. "Congrats, Poppy!"

Suddenly everyone hears the doors of the office open and we snap our heads towards it. Then in walks Isla Hattie coming back from her lunch break in her perfect pin straight golden hair, her leather jacket with silver spikes, high heeled boots and tight leather pants. All in black. Always in black.

"Anyone mind telling me what's going on?" Her high-pitched voice almost shouts and Riley chuckles under his breath.

She pushes her way towards Riley, me, and Jeannie and Ginger. She rests her hands on Ginger's desk reading intensely the article on her computer.

I watch her eyes carefully as the computer mirrors through her round, hazel orbs. She stands up straight in absolute shock and turns to me, Jeannie, and Riley.

"Congratulations." Her voice cracks but she says it kindly.

"Thanks." I nod and say quietly.

"What in the hell..." Jane's voice suddenly booms through the office. Everyone's heads pop up in fear.

"Ms. DuVull, look!" Ginger turns around her computer to Jane. "Poppy's article traveled to France!!"

"Just say went international." Jeannie murmurs, exhausted.

Jane's eyes widen as she takes her glasses down from the top of her head and places them on her nose. She looks towards me as if to confirm it. I nod slowly, still in shock. I can't even think straight. I... I can't believe this.

Jane shoves Ginger Lovet to the side and bends down, beginning to read the article.

"Would you look at that..." she begins. She doesn't seem in shock though. Why isn't she in shock? "Poppy, my office. Now." And like that, she starts to stalk towards her office. I take that as my cue to follow her.

The office is quiet as all eyes turn to me.

I look at Riley and Jeannie. Riley gives me a nervous smile and Jeannie gives me an encouraging thumbs up. So with that, I follow Jane into her office with bated breath and close the door behind us. Jane sits at her desk and I sit in one of her chairs in front of her.

Suddenly a huge smile spreads across her face.

"I honestly can't say I'm surprised."

"What?" I ask, still in a daze.

"I told you it was going to be huge." Jane shrugs, an even bigger smile growing.

"Thank you, Ms. DuVull." I say but can't stop myself from getting a bit choked up. It's all so overwhelming! An article going international is a huge honor. I can't believe this is actually happening.

"What are you thanking me for?" She squints her eyes.

"Everything." I answer honestly.

"Well..." Jane looks towards her computer, typing something. "you're welcome. I'm going to get in touch with that article from the UK. Get Ginger for me." I quickly get up and call Ginger into the office.

I sit back into the seat as Ginger stands in the doorway.

"Where was that British article from?" Jane demands from Ginger.

"Uh, *British Vogue,* Ms. DuVull." She says.

British Vogue! Holy crap...

"Thank you..." Jane shoos Ginger and she quickly leaves.

"I'll get in touch with them. Simple enough." Jane nods and I stare at her in amazement.

"What do you mean get in touch with them?" I rasp out.

"If they want an interview with you and Atticus or something."

I'm floored. If it could, my open mouth would be touching the floor.

"Don't be so shocked, Poppyseed..." Jane winks. "I told ya so."

CHAPTER TWENTY-NINE
Hanukkah

"Now this recipe has been in the family for four generations..." I begin getting all the ingredients in order, standing in my parents tiny townhouse kitchen.

I rest the food processor on the granite table top as I try to purposely talk over my mom and dad bickering in the sunroom. Thank god the electric shredder is louder than them.

"So basically what you're saying is 'don't screw this up, Atty.'" He jokes, leaning on the doorway of the kitchen.

"No!" I say but my voice says otherwise as it goes a tad bit higher. "Would you like to shred potatoes and onions? You just have to put it in the little machine and it, you know, goes through and shreds it."

"I would love to." I watch as Atticus unfolds his arms and walks next to me into the tiny space.

He takes the tiny bowl of potatoes and onions, along with the food processor to the other side of the kitchen directly behind me, setting it onto the opposite countertop.

Me and Atticus arrived at my parents house around fifteen minutes ago. The minute we walked in, my mom threw me into the kitchen. At least she doesn't insist on doing it all herself anymore.

Mom is currently straightening up the house and arguing with dad whether or not *The Beatles* and *The Rolling Stones* got along or not.

Obviously we came before anyone else to help with preparations and what not. Diamante and Carlo were supposed to be here to help out as well, but alas, they're not here. Are you honestly shocked though?

Me and Atticus stand back to back for a few seconds in silence, doing our own thing.

"You alright back there?" I hear Atticus chuckle over the loud shredder. He catches me off guard for a moment then I giggle.

"Oh...oh yeah. Fine. Just setting everything up." I shout.

"You know Geoff, *Beatles* and *Stones* fans never liked each other, So we're quite rare."

"Who the hell told you that, Molly?" My parent's muffled bickering is heard through the sliding doors of the sunroom next to the kitchen.

I hear Atticus try to suppress a laugh but it comes out as a cough. It makes me smile as well.

Atticus looks really nice today. He's in that tight black turtleneck I like on him and a black blazer, with a silver chain attached to it.

He's in black slacks and black combat boots. He also has one tiny chain around his neck followed by a bucky long one. Both silver. As per usual.

I'm in this fab mini, baby blue dress by *Alexia Maria*. I bought it just for Hanukkah and it's so perfect.

It lays a bit above my knees and is strapless with a straightneck cut at the bust. It's silk too, and the best part... It has this absolutely humongous oversized baby blue bow one the back. It's like *I'm* the Hanukkah present!

The dress is surprisingly snug and short though. If I knew it would be *this* form fitting, I would have gotten a size up. Sure didn't look this tight on the maiquine. But then again, I'm far from a mannequin figure.

"So, what are we making again?" Asks Atticus, breaking yet another silence.

"Latkes." I pipe up. "Tradition. They're like potato pancakes."

"That sounds really good."

"Mine are awesome. The best." I can't help but add.

"Are they now?" I hear him challenge me from behind.

"Yes! Well, I suppose they'll be ours now." I curse my tongue as soon as it comes out of my mouth. "You know, because you're helping out."

He all but chuckles as the shredding stops. Atticus turns around and walks next to me, placing the shredder down and pouring the shreds of onions and potatoes into the bowl they were in before.

"Ok..." I begin. "I'm going to try to finish them in time for dinner. Thanks for your help--"

"Hey, what happened to *our* latkes, huh?" I look up to see a little smile on Atticus's face. "You know, I was so excited... I thought you were gonna teach me how to make these things."

I can't help but match his smile.

"Well alright then, but no fooling around." I playfully swat his arm with the towel in my hands. "The key to a crispy latke is to draw out all the moisture in the shredded potatoes and onions." Atticus watches as I get a paper towel and my mom's strainer out of the cabinet.

I pour the potatoes and onions into the strainer with the paper towel under them. I then take the salt next to me and sprinkle just a pinch into the strainer.

"Now we must be patient," I state. "we need to wait for all the moisture to leave the onions and potatoes so we can have a crispy Latke."

I anxiously study my surroundings to make sure we have everything we need to continue cooking.

Atticus seems to catch on to what I'm doing and his eyes wander wherever mine do. He has an amused smirk on his face at my anxious behavior.

"Ok," I clasp my hands together and look up at him. "we're going to take this bowl," I pat yet another big, dark blue bowl beside me. "and we're going to finish off the latke mixture." I hand him four eggs in a tiny bowl. Every ingredient I made sure had its own little bowl so everything is organized.

"You're going to crack the eggs into the big blue bowl while I whisk at the same time. All these ingredients we are currently putting in this bowl is just to keep the latkes together and add a bit more flavor."

"Got you." Atticus nods as he starts to crack the eggs and adds them into the bowl. I immediately start whisking the cracked eggs as he does so.

"I hate cracking eggs." I scrunch up my nose.

"Do you?" Atticus asks, a hint of amusement in his voice.

"Yeah." I pull a face. "The yolk always gets under my nails. These nails take work, you know. Very hard work."

"I'm sure."

"Yeah, my nail lady Frane takes at *least* an hour to do them. Look at this…" I hold up my long manicured tips that are coffin shaped and dark blue with little yellow dreidels on the ring finger. So. Fab. "Hard. Work."

Atticus chuckles as he cracks his last egg and I continue to whisk them.

"Tell Frane I said I think they're lit."

"I will!" I smile. "She'll be so honored. She loves the article too."

I didn't tell Atticus that the article went international yet. It's so hard to keep it a secret! But I really want to wait till we're alone. Maybe we could go out for dinner or something. And I'll tell him there. Something nice for him. For us.

Then I'll tell my family and Tiff. Although part of me desperately wants to gloat about it at the dinner table tonight *just* to see my sister's face. I won't though. Of course not.

"Well, I'll gladly crack eggs for you anytime." Atticus says as he throws the egg shells into the garbage and washes his hands.

That's when a silly little smile spreads across my face but I quickly shake it off.

"I might have to take you up on that." I quip. "Now let's pour the potatoes and onions in the big bowl with eggs." I say, and Atticus does just that. He then puts the food processor and excess bowls into the sink.

"Now I'll squeeze some of these sliced lemons into the bowl." I say as I do so. When I'm done, I toss it into the garbage. "The lemon juice will prevent the potatoes from turning grey, as weird as it sounds." I say.

"And you know this off the top of your head?" Asks Atticus, watching me reach for the knife to my side and three scallions.

"Mhmm…" I nod as I start to chop them. "my aunt Florence and mom taught me. As I said, the recipe has been in the family for ages but when I make them, I change them up a bit. My mom was pissed when she first found out I tweaked the recipe, but she's used to it now. Can you pour some of that oil into the frying pan?"

Atticus nods his head as he does just that.

"That's pretty cool." Atticus looks at me again, leaning on the counter.

"Yeah it is." I laugh. "It's honestly a miracle I can memorize any recipe." Just as I say it, I bite my tongue. God Poppy, shut up!

"Why?" Atticus squints.

"I… uh… have a memorization issue." I nod, not bothering to look up at him, still a tad ashamed of it till this day.

"Really?" I hear the slight shock in Atticus's voice.

"Yeah." I nod as I start to season the mixture with some paper. "Since I was tiny. Born with it I suppose. It's like a form of short term memory loss but not really. I don't know. I used to have to be in special classes for it when I was little. You could imagine I struggled with math. I always loved to write though. Came easy to me. One of the only things that did. So I pursued Journalism." I give a stressed chuckle. "When this group of girls found out I had a memorization issue, well, they thought it would be funny to start to call me Dory. You know, because of *Finding Nemo*." I admit, and I can't believe I'm telling him this.

A couple of moments of silence pass when Atticus finally speaks.

"When I was in middle school the kids used to make fun of me and call me a weirdo because I wrote songs and played the guitar. I wasn't on the football team... I--I didn't belong to anything. They would call me a freak and try to kick my ass. My dad threw me in a boxing class and that's where I learned to fight. No one fucked with me after that."

"Thirteen year olds are horrible." I murmur softly, my heart slowly breaking knowing a little Atticus was bullied.

"Pre teens suck." He laughs. "They really do suck."

"Well anyway," I perk up, trying to change the subject. "I'm just going to add these breadcrumbs in." I pour ⅔ of a cup of breadcrumbs into the mixture and mix it up a bit.

Me and Atticus both turn around towards the pan to see it sizzling.

"Alright, when it sizzles that means we're ready to fry!" I state, excited. "Can you get me that scooper?" I motion towards the scooper on Atticus's side.

"Yes, chef." He hands it to me hastily.

"Thank you." I put it next to my shredded potatoes and onions. "Now we're going to scoop this mixture up and drop it in the frying pan." I say as I do it. Atticus's watches, his arms folded and his brows knitted focusing. "Then I take this spatula and push the latke mixture down to a hockey puck size." After a few minutes of frying I turn it over. "You just want to wait a couple of minutes until each side is golden brown." I then take the now fried Latke off the frying pan and onto the iron rack next to the stove. "There we go!"

The latke looks amazingly crispy and golden brown. It's also a pretty nice size. Not to toot my horn but... toot toot!

"Now to finish it off, we will garnish the top of the latke with just a *tad* of salt." I sprinkle a pinch of salt onto the beautiful latke. "Perfect! Now you try. Just don't crowd the pan." I stand behind Atticus as he repeats my steps and I can't help but smile.

"Is this a good size?" He asks. He's so tall compared to me, I have to grab his arms, stand on my tippy toes and rest my head over his shoulder to see the pan.

"A little bigger." I say as Atticus pushes the latke down just a bit more. "Perfect."

I keep my stance so I could watch what he's doing.

After he finishes his first latke he turns to me with a proud smile.

"It's perfect." I giggle. "You're a great student."

"Well, I did have a wonderful teacher."

When we finish we have about fifteen latkes and I place them all on a platter with a bowl of applesauce in the middle.

"There. Beautiful!" I giggle and look up to Atticus.

"I call dibs on that one." Atticus points to an extremely crispy and thick looking latke on the far left side of the platter.

"No!" I squeak. "That's the one I wanted!"

"Damn... that's too bad." I see the sly smirk form on Atticus's face.

I bite the side of my mouth as my eyes begin to idly wander around the kitchen when I suddenly get an idea.

I quickly reach for the platter and that one certain latke but before I can reach it, Atticus arms wrap around my waist and lift me off my feet.

"No!" I laugh uncontrollably. "Atticus, stop this right now!" I try to be stern but my laugh deceives me.

I hear his laugh from behind me and feel it vibrate against my back. It just makes me laugh harder.

I grab a kitchen towel laying in front of me on the counter, and with all my might, try to hit Atticus with it. We're both laughing so loud, I could hear it echo through the kitchen.

Just then, mom comes strutting in.

"What are you two doing?" she scolds.

Atticus puts me down and I look up at him just as he looks down at me. I could tell he's trying to suppress a giggle and I can't help but snort.

"Look at those latkes!" Mom gasps. "How wonderful they look! Poppy, you really did outdo yourself, although they're not exactly like me and Grandma's--"

"Thanks Mom!" I interrupt her before she could completely debunk her statement that the latkes do in fact look good.

"So, the table is all set..." she begins. "you guys really were such a great help, thank you."

"Of course, ma." I say as she hugs me. She hesitates for a moment then hugs Atticus.

"I'm glad you came, darling." She says to him. "No one should be alone for the Holidays."

"Thanks for inviting me Mrs Paxton." He then turns to me. "And thank you for letting her." As his brown eyes stare down at me, I see that little glimmer in them. I glimmer I've never seen in anyone else's eyes ever before.

We all sit around the table that is way too huge for my parent's dining room. It's decorated pretty though.

Mom put down a dark blue tablecloth with a sparkly silver table runner across it. Every one of us has white plates and our silverware wrapped in silver cloth, matching the table runner. We also have two big candelabras in the middle of the table. It really does look pretty.

My dad sits at the head of the table as my mom sits at the other end. I sit in the middle of Aunt Eva and Atticus. Diamante Carlo and Uncle Duncan across from us. That's dad's brother. He couldn't make it for Rosh Hashanah because he was working. Uncle Duncan's a travel agent. He's ten years younger than dad.

"We have to light the menorah tonight. It's the first night. Does anyone want to volunteer to do it?" Mom begins, standing up from her seat and starting to cut the roast.

"I always do it." My dad's head pops up in confusion and he almost looks offended. (In true dad fashion, honestly.)

"Yes I know Geoffrey, but maybe we ought to change things up this year." Mom gives a tight smile. I instantly know what she is referring to. She obviously wants Atticus to light the first candle.

I shoot her a knowing glare and she just gives an innocent smile.

"Dad, you always light the candle," I begin. "I think you should just continue to do so. It's tradition."

"Thank you, Poppy. See Molly, Tradition." My dad nods his head and mom scowls at him.

"Well, sue me for wanting to shake things up a bit!"

"Poppy shook things up enough by changing the latke recipe." My dad retorts. Great! We're back to this!

"Thanks, dad." I sigh under my breath. Atticus rubs my back encouragingly.

"Can we please eat?" Diamante sighs impatiently. Carlo just sits next to her, hands in lap and eyes like a deer in headlights.

"Be patient, we have to read first." Aunt Eva retorts.

After dad reads the history of Hanukkah (like he does every year), we could finally eat.

"Wonderful pot roast, Molly." Dad nods as we all begin to dig into the food.

"Thanks, hon." Mom says happily. Everyone has the latkes that me and Atticus made, yet no one comments on it.

"Wonderful latkes, Poppy." Atticus says, a smirk smile on his face as if he just read my mind.

"Thank you." I smile triumphantly. "Thanks for helping me."

"Of course." out of the corner of my eye, I could see every single person at this table staring at us. As soon as I pick my head up, everyone looks down and away.

"The pot roast is great as well, Mrs. Paxton." Atticus smiles as he takes another bite.

"Oh! Thanks, dear." Mom's lips form the widest smile. We have the pot roast, we have the latkes, we have the applesauce and a big bowl of matzo ball soup.

"What did you make Diamante?" Atticus asks looking up at her.

I give a weak cough. He doesn't say it condescendingly at all, he says it almost innocently. Like Diamante would do anything but anyone besides herself. As if!

Everyone immediately tenses in their seat and I watch as Diamante looks up at Atticus and-- if looks could kill-- Atticus would be ten feet underground right now.

Carlo looks like he wants to hide under the table and honestly, I do too. Uncle Duncan puts his face in his napkin trying not to laugh, and it causes me to slap my hand over my mouth.

"Ha!" Aunt Eva reaches over me and pats Atticus's shoulder. "She didn't make anything, babe."

I look at Atticus to see he's absolutely frozen in his seat, biting the inside of his mouth.

"I'm sorry."

"Don't apologize, darling. You didn't know." My mom says to him. Diamante snaps her head at my mom, scowling.

"Don't you choose winners, Poppy." She chides. I just give her a glare, warning her not to continue.

"Be quiet!" Aunt Eva retorts to Diamante.

"Aren't you a bit too old to be chewing out your sister." Uncle Duncan adds.

Diamante has that stupid, entitled, shocked expression on her face as if anyone correct her behavior.

I look at Atticus, my cheeks burning with embarrassment. He just shrugs without a care in the world and shakes his head.

"Who cares..." he mouths. "let it go." He pretends to meditate and I just huff, shaking my head.

I truly wish I could be as carefree as Atticus. Not care what anyone says or thinks about me.

We all continue eating and dad and Diamante argue about politics (like always), and Aunt Eva tells us about what her physic told her last week (like always) and mom complains that no one ever appreciates what she does around this house. What else is new?

Suddenly I feel a light tap on my shoulder and I look up to see Atty very sneakily pointing to Diamante.

I look towards her to see the way that her head is looking at mom as she talks, it looks as if she has big horns at the top of her head due to the glass bullhead mom and dad have in the china cabinet behind her seat. (Uncle Dunacan brought that back for us when he visited

London. Out of all the things he could have bought for us. We keep it up to be polite.)

I almost spit out my wine as I immediately look away trying my hardest not to make a sound. Atticus's face scrunches up in half suppressed laughter and I can't help but put my head in his shoulder. I'm laughing so hard, tears are coming out of my eyes now.

"What is so funny!" Diamante turns to me and Atticus and shouts. "Should I have mom make a kids table and sit the both of you at it? Immature little brats. We're talking about politics--what the world is controlled by--and you *laugh?*" Her face has turned beat red and now the horns behind her are even more perfectly positioned on top of her head.

Without total reservation whatsoever, me and Atticus just burst out in a fit of laughter.

"You're not helping your case, my darling." Aunt Eva says, chuckling and I realized she's picked up on what we are laughing at. I look around to see everyone has seemed to have picked up on it as well.

Dad is practically choking on his pot roast, mom has her hand slapped over her mouth, Carlo has a little smile on his face, and Uncle Duncan is just shamelessly snickering.

"Behind you, love." Mom says, suppressing her laugh. Diamante vastly turns around and realizes the way the horns were sitting on top of her head.

"Pretty accurate, huh Dia?" Dad jokes.

"Are you kidding me?" She turns to me and Atticus in rage.

"It was funny." Uncle Duncan shrugs.

"You're all making fun of me!" Diamante crys, slamming her spoon into her matzo ball soup.

"No one's making fun of you..." begins dad.

"Carlo, are they making fun of me?" She asks him. "I'm not crazy, they're mocking me!"

"Ummm... I..." Carlo begins.

"Oh for shits sake Carlo, be a man for once and stick up for me!"

"You seem to be sticking up for yourself just fine." I hear Atticus say beside me, and everyone grows quiet in shock.

Oh no...

He doesn't say it rudley or anything, he just says it matter of factly. Diamante turns to him with furey in her eyes.

"And who are *you* to tell me that?" She retorts.

"He's one of the poor bastards who have to witness your crappy behavior." Aunt Eva remarks.

"Ok, ok, please..." begins mom. "let's not. Aren't we such a great example of a family! We have a guest here, you know."

"I'm so sorry." I mouth to Atticus for the second time tonight.

"Listen," Atticus begins to everyone. "I really don't judge. I never had much of a family dynamic growing up, so this is a breath of fresh air." I give a slight frown when he says that. I don't know the whole story of his childhood, but I could tell it wasn't great.

"Well good, because if you judged, this family would be no place for you." Dad chuckles and I just roll my eyes at him.

Diamante mutters something under her breath I can't quite pick up on.

"Carlo, what do you do for work?" Atticus takes a sip of his wine.

Carlo looks up in shock, as if he can't believe Atticus is talking to him.

"I...um... I'm an accountant. It's boring, but it pays well." He chuckles and gives back a kind smile.

I could tell he's just thankful that someone is talking to him. He's usually such a mute, you know Carlo. I can't help but give him a proud nod. Diamante glares at Carlo as if he *dare* talk to Atticus.

"That's dope, man." Atticus says as he shoves a latke in his mouth.

"I mean, I guess..."

"Hey we need accountants in this world, dude." Atticus points his fork at Carlo. "Don't let anyone tell you otherwise."

"Yeah, thanks." Carlo shrugs. "You're a musician right?"

"I am!" He absolutely lights up.

"That's pretty neat how you could make a career out of that."

"Carlo, don't be ignorant." Diamante retorts. "Being a musician isn't a career." I watch Atticus's face fall and I suddenly feel as if I might jump over this table and ring my hands around her skinny throat.

"Diamante, that's not true!" My mom retorts before I can say something. "You should be ashamed, treating a guest like that!"

"Well, would you consider Poppy's job a *real* job?" She asks.

"Are you dumb?" I quip.

"No, I'm a lawyer."

"I make money from my job, don't I?"

"You write."

"I'm a journalist, dumbass!" I practically squeak. "And as for Atticus, he is ten times more talented than you'll ever be!"

"Poppy real talk, how much money do you make?"

"Is that really your business though?" Atticus puts his hand on the small of my back and squints his eyes at her.

"Ok, then Atticus, how much do you make?"

"Me and Atticus's article went international!" I suddenly burst out, and immediately curse myself.

Everyone goes quiet and looks at me.

"What?" Atticus looks at me, his eyes growing wide.

"We uhh... went international. Only our article. Some other countries have taken a liking to it as well. It's kind of becoming this... phenomenon."

A sudden wide smile spreads across Atticus's face and he gives a shocked laugh.

"Are you serious?" He asks.

"Yes, of course!" I nod happily. "I wanted to find a better way to tell you... but it slipped." I glare at Diamante who looks utterly speechless.

"Darling, what does it mean you've gone international?" Asks mom.

"It means our article has reached other countries. The article was printed in Japanese, as well as hit the UK."

"Oh my god, that's amazing you two!" Mom claps her hands. "Oh I'm so proud!"

"Well done." Dad nods, with a smile. "That's quite the accomplishment. Well deserved."

Atticus looks at me, still in shock, an amazed smile on his face.

Diamante sits back in her chair, dumbfounded. Everyone says congratulations but her. Although she's a bitch she's still my sister, and no matter what I do, she will still never be proud. And although I feel pride in everyone's praises, she still manages to hurt me.

As we hop into Atticu's car after a long night, he quickly turns on the heat.

"I know my family's not the most ideal one, but I hope you had fun." I shiver as Atticus puts his jacket over me. "Thanks." God, it's freezing.

He smiles and warms me up with his arms as the radio practically whispers through the speakers of the car.

"You know there's no such thing as a perfect family, right?" Atticus quirks up a brow, warming me up but nearly melting my insides.

"Tiff has a pretty perfect family. Well, not perfect, but you know what I mean."

"Perfects boring, you know." Atticus gives a chuckle and I watch as his whole face scrunches up into a smile. He looks so adorable when that happens. His smile is just utterly stunning.

"I suppose." I shrug, warming up a bit.

"By the way, I got a present for you." He begins reaching into the backseat of his car. "I was going to give it to you when I gave your mom her flowers but... I figured it may be better between me and you." He suddenly pulls out a little black box from the backseat. It has a little hot pink bow on top.

"I was thinking the same thing!" I squeak, digging through my purse finding his present. I wrapped it in black wrapping paper and took it upon myself to draw skulls all over it in silver sharpie. It also has a black bow on top.

"You didn't have to buy me anything." I shake my head as we exchange gifts.

"Touche'. It's not even my holiday." Atticus smirks.

Wait until you see what I bought him, you're gonna freak out!

"Open yours first." He says excitedly.

I carefully untie the pink bow on top and take the top of the black box. Laying in the box I see two medium sized, gold hoop earrings. On the sides of them are a whole bunch of tiny little rhinestones. I can't help but grow absolutely speechless.

"Oh my god, Atticus." I breathe out. "They're beautiful."

"So I did good?"

"Yes!" I laugh, breathlessly.

"Ok, good. I always noticed you have quite a lot of ear piercings, so I figured you'd like a pair of earrings." He's right, I do. I have about six piercings in my ears. I'm just obsessed with jewelry.

"I'm putting them in right now!" I declare, taking out the pair of little silver hoops in my ear lobes and put in the gold hoops. They're absolutely stunning!

"Atticus, you really didn't have to do that."

"I—I know. I wanted to though." Atticus glances up at me and we lock eyes suddenly. He runs his fingers over the hoop earring now in my ear and gives a little smile. Then his eyes meet mine once again and I quickly turn away, growing quite flushed.

"Open your present." I say and motion to the box on his lap. He nods his head with an eager smile and begins to unwrap my gift towards him.

I watch on the edge of my seat as his bright smile lights up the car when he pulls out the silver necklace I bought for him.

It's a silver chain with a little tiny silver lock on it. He has a lot of those, but none that look like this. The lock has a rhinestone in the middle, but still manages to be manly with the tiny little gold spikes around the rhinestone. (It was... very expensive, let's just say that. But you can't put a price on friendship, can you?)

"Oh my god, Poppy are you freaking kidding me! This is so awesome, holy shit!" I laugh at the way he reacts to the gift. "This is by far the best chain *ever*. Thank you."

"It's because it's from me." I joke playfully.

"Especially because it's from you." He nods truthfully. "Would you help me put it on?" He asks. I motion for him to twist around and when he does, I clasp the necklace together.

He turns back around, looking down at the neckless still. It looks wonderful where it hangs right on the chest. It looks lovely with his black turtleneck. It looks lovely on him anyways, like anything usually does.

It has completely warmed up in the car so Atticus turns down the heat all the way. We're still parked in front of my parent's small driveway. In Staten Island you can never park *in* a driveway. You're lucky you could get a spot in your own.

Me and Atticus lock eyes once again when he looks up from his necklace and his face falls from a wide smile to more of a soft one.

I'm completely warmed up but I still keep Atticus's coat around me, holding it tightly against my body.

I lean my head against the seat and give Atticus a tired smile, watching as he moves a bit closer and leaning against the dashboard.

He gives a gentle grin as his eyes trail down to my own then to my lips.

At the moment I immediately tense up. He smells like the mint gum he was chewing as he somehow gets impossibly closer to me, the only thing separating us is the dashboard.

Atticus purses his lips together as he continues staring at mine, seeming to be deep in thought. Like he's contemplating something. I can't help but wonder if he's thinking about me. Is there something on my face? Has my makeup gone a tad wonky?

Atticus seems to snap out of whatever he's thinking when he brings his hand up to the side of my face and brings his gaze back to my eyes.

When his dark butterscotch colored eyes nearly go black, I find myself not being able to move. I don't even say a sound, my mouth slightly parting as he takes his thumbs and gently runs it over my bottom lip. My heart is beating so fast that it might as well explode and my stomach is in knots.

I don't even know what to think, and I don't quite want to think about it, but... does this mean when we were at *Barnes and Nobles* he did after all try to kiss me? That it wasn't just me looking too much into this?

I'm absolutely terrified I'm reading the situation wrong, but how can I be? He's surely going to kiss me, he has to be! Why else would he be this close? Why would his thumb be on my lip! Oh, what do I know!

He grips my chin in tight hold and pulls himself impossibly closer to me as his own lips part.

The minute our noses touch and I feel his lips brush against mine, there's a loud honk of a horn behind us that causes both me and Atticus to jump out of our skins. We both quickly separate out of fright.

"Jesus Christ!" Atticus slaps his hand on the steering wheel, frustrated. I slam my head on the back of my seat, annoyed as well.

We both turn around to see my sister and Carlo in the car behind us. I motion for them to go around us and Diamante yells something in her car.

I obviously can't hear, so I tap my ears and motion to the fact that I have no freaking clue what she's saying. So, for our listening pleasure, she rolls down her window.

"If you want to makeout or do other *things,* go to a abandoned parking lot like they do in those stupid cliche movies!" She screams and reaches over Carlo, honking the horn again, annoyingly

Atticus just rolls his eyes as do I.

I huff as we both turn back around and put our seatbelts on. He begins to drive away and I can't help but blush in embarrassment and cross my arms.

"Isn't she great." I mutter.

Atticus turns to me, a growing smile on his face as he laughs. And like that, things are back to normal. At least on the outside. Internally I actually find myself wondering what would've happened if we did in fact kiss. I can't speak for him though.

CHAPTER THIRTY

March

Are you flirting or are you *flirting*

You know, after the holidays I always seem to get this seasonal depression. Since I was little even. From late January to early March I just don't feel... right. Luckily this year I'm far too busy for seasonal depression. End of holiday depression, be gone!

Life has been absolutely off the wall. In a good way though!

In the past couple of months, Atticus and I's article has just blown up! It's literally become a phenomenon. It's everywhere!

Ok don't get the wrong Idea, we're not famous or anything, but the article keeps spreading around the world and America. The response has just gotten better and better.

DuVull also keeps getting praise for the article over and over and over. Which is crazy, because we haven't gotten that kind of praise in a long time. And it's for *my* article! Can you believe it! The success of the article has also encouraged all the other journalists to try their hardest as well and I'm so proud because of that.

Atticus's band has gotten a lot more popular as well. They are trying to find management currently because they've gotten *so* popular. I'm so proud of him. He did that all himself though with his talent and determination. And Dallon and Finn's talent as well of course.

"So, superstar," begins Jeannie across from me eating a bagel. "what are you doing for the March issue?" She hands me a half of her buttered everything bagel and I gladly begin to dig into it.

"I don't know. I have a lot to live up to, don't I?" I ask anxiously, sipping my iced coffee.

Jeannie shoots me a knowing glare and quirks up one of her bushy brows.

"You think." She snorts. "What did you do for February and March again?"

"Oh, I just did some articles regarding some of the new trends in Jewelry. Little mini articles. Jane has told me she didn't want me to do something that would take long. I don't know why. So yeah, I just wrote about some trends in jewelry."

"Did we now? Well, how could I forget that." Jeannie gives a big smirk and lifts her eyebrows a couple of times as she motions to the gold hoop earrings in my ears that Atticus gave me. I put them in literally everyday. I just love them.

"I still can't believe the poor jerk bought you a 70 dollar pair of earrings." Riley comes back from Jane's office and sits in his normal spot.

"I know." I sigh. The moment I came into work after Hanakkuh, I had to show off my earrings to Jeannie and Riley. Not only are they beautiful, but Atticus bought them for me. That's what makes them the most special.

The both of them absolutely freaked out and teased the hell out of me. All they did was chant 'Atticus and Poppy sitting in a tree, K.I.S.S.I.N.G!' like they were a bunch of ten years old.

"Uh... to be fair," Jeannie puts her manicured finger tip up. "Poppy bought him a 110 dollar necklace, even though I told her she could buy a similar one at *HotTopic* for 12 bucks."

"You can't put a price on friendship!" I retort. "During the holidays me, you, Arlo, and Riley always splurge on eachother."

"'Friendship.'" Riley uses air quotes and makes his voice a tad higher to mimic mine. "Friends have never tried to kiss each other, have they now? You don't see me trying to make out with you! Twice Poppy, twice he tried!"

"And what do you say I do about it?" I quip.

"The both of you are beating around the bush," begins Jeannie. "just take Atticus's face and smooch him! Grab him by his face and go for it. Honestly, he's tried two times. What do you have to lose, Pops?"

"What if he regrets trying to kiss me?" I ask, below a whisper.

"Then he's stupid." Riley shrugs. "No other way to put it." Jeannie nods her head in agreement.

"But you'll never know unless you try, right?" Jeannie says.

"I guess." I shrug. "God, I feel like I'm in highschool again. With all these mixed emotions."

"Like, all jokes aside, do you honestly think you're catching feelings for this guy?" Riley asks and he and Jeannie both look at me expectantly.

"I know we talk about him trying to kiss you, and the cute little flirting, but are you flirting or are you *flirting*. Ya know what I mean?" Jeannie adds. "Because he seems like he's *flirting.*"

"I don't know!" I shrug desperately. "I don't know what I want. That's why I said I feel like I'm back in highschool. I still sometimes find myself missing Liam. It's not often, but still!"

"Liam was your first love, Pops. You're always going to love him in a way. This isn't about Liam though." She says matter of factly, shoving the last piece of her bagel in her mouth.

"I get this feeling when I'm around Atticus, and I'll admit, it's the feeling I used to get around Liam. I'll admit it! I had it from the moment I met him. His personality is contagious, he's kind, he's funny, and he's definitely not bad to look at..." I find myself breathless just thinking of him. Jeannie and Riley both smirk at my statement. "but look is all I'll do." I admit, matter of factly.

"Why?" Riley practically squeaks. "Shoot your shot, make your move!"

"He doesn't do relationships! We were talking when he first met because I was convinced his friend Finnick was trying to set us up. Come to think of it, I remember that day. A couple of days after *The Lounge*. Atticus was so off that day, he just wasn't himself. Anyway, no one was making any moves, we were just talking. I remember his exact words. He said he wasn't exactly 'into the dating game' and that he 'wasn't good at it.'" I sigh. "What does that even mean?"

"He sleeps around." Answers Riley blatantly.

"I know that!" I retort, almost throwing up at the thought of any other girl with him. "It was a rhetorical question!"

"Oh God Pops, are you serious?" Jeannie takes her eyes fully away from her computer and puts all her attention on me. "Guys absolutely love to say that shit! 'I'm not into the dating game.' These men-- for some reason--they seem to enjoy this cat and mouse game. You know it, and I know it. It's hard to get, and you need to play the game."

"I don't want to play any games!" I practically cry. "Not anymore. I played enough of the cat and the mouse game with Liam. I'm over it. I don't like Atticus, I really don't! I don't know what I'm thinking. And he doesn't like me. He... doesn't date."

"Those damn earrings in your ears say otherwise." RIley tilts his head and pulls a face.

"Just don't fear falling for someone. Don't keep these feelings inside and deny them because you think he feels some way. Chances are, he feels differently." Jeannie notes.

I just nod my head. I look on my computer typing Jane's itinerary for next week so far. Just trying to get a head start on it.

I'm confused as to why Jane has told me to write little articles. Atticus and I's article has literally gone viral. Does she not trust that I could top it? That's fair I suppose. I don't even know if I could top it, but I could try with all I have. I'll have to have a chat with her.

All that is currently heard is the taping of me and Jeannie's fingers against our keyboards and Riley typing something on his phone. And of course the chatter around the office is heard in muffles as well.

As I type Jane's itinerary I think, and think and think, even having to fix a few typos because my brain is just so scattered. Somehow, my mind floats back to Atticus.

How do I feel about Atticus? At the most this is a tiny crush right? If even. If I did like Atticus, would he like me back? Would he reciprocate the same feelings? That's the scariest part. Are these feelings I have for Atticus platonic love, or is it something else?

I have no clue. I haven't really gotten these feelings in a long time. Maybe ever.

I fiddle with the gold earrings he bought for me when I finally decide to speak. I don't even look up though, I just continue typing.

"Atticus and his band are performing at *The Lounge* tonight."

I hear Jeannie and Riley's typing both stop and I know I got their attention.

I look up from my computer and I watch as the wheels in both their heads turn. A little smirk forms on both their faces. Shit. I don't even know why I said that. It kind of just came out. Why did I have to open my big mouth!

"Well then, I guess we're going back to *The Lounge* tonight." Jeannie declares.

"Jeannie, *The Lounge* is more of a weekend thing, wouldn't you say? It's a fancy alternative bar restaurant." I try to rationalize with her.

"I know. So?"

"So? Jeannie, it's Wednesday."

"So?"

"The band is performing at 9:30."

"Text Atticus and tell him we'll be there." Riley looks up from his phone.

"With bells on." Jeannie responds.

"And my new *Gucci* heels!"

CHAPTER THIRTY-ONE

Eleven Eleven

It feels like just yesterday when we went to *The Lounge* last. I can't believe it was literally months ago. Time has flown, it really has.

To think, I didn't even *like* Atticus back then. I kind of couldn't stand him. Now I'm going to *The Lounge* to watch and support his band. It's crazy how things could change in just five months.

I can't help but think back to my fuzzy, drunken memory of that night. I was trying to table hop and I drunkenly spotted Atticus and talked to him. (And drunkenly asked for a *Dunkin* iced coffee he later bought for me.) I also met Dallon and Finn for the first time that night.

I cringe at the memory of that night but also find myself stupidly smiling about it as I stare down at the five outfits I have picked out on my bed.

"Poppy, what are you--" Jeannie walks into my room and stops mid sentence when she sees all those clothes and shoes and jewelry neatly paired in five different options. "Are you serious?" She stands in my doorway, resting her hand on her hip.

"It's not my fault you came at 7:00 and and Riley and Arlo are supposed to be picking us up at 8:00. You know I spend a lot of time on my outfits as is."

"And if I wasn't here, would you be ready on time?" Jeannie quirks a brow and rolls her eyes. "You know, you weren't this indecisive and picky with your outfit the first time we went to *The Lounge.*" She plops down on my bed next to my new pairs of *Jimmy Choos.*

"I'm always indecisive and picky when choosing my outfits." I cross my arms.

"True, but I've never seen you *this* upsest with it. What the hell, Pops!" Jeannie slowly picks up my new *Alexander Wang* dress in between her thumb and her pointer finger, very carefully.

"495.00 dollars!" She practically squeaks. "Did you just buy this! Is this new?"

"No..." I shake my head. "It's something I found in my closet. I actually forgot I had it." Jeannie shakes her head at me, carefully placing the dress down.

The dress is fab, but very plain. It's just a short, tight, mini black dress with spaghetti straps and a deep neckline.

"What about this one?" Jeannie begins, reaching for the favorite on the bed.

"No, no, no." I give a stressed giggle and push it behind me. "It's old." Oh my god it's *so* fab!

It's *Pamella Roland* and I bought it two months ago. I just haven't found an event to wear it to yet.

It's this light pink fur and squareneck. It's strapless and scattered with Marabou ostrich feathers. A matching pink, banded waist separates the bottom and top of the dress.

It is just the most beautiful dress I've ever seen in my life! Is it *Lounge* appropriate though?

I sneakily rip the price tag off of the dress and throw it in the garbage beside my bed. The price isn't important!

"Well whatever." Jeannie pops up. "We have to get you ready." Jeannie starts looking through the jewelry laid out by the clothes.

I'm just standing over my bed weighing my options in my silk robe and matching furry slippers.

Jeannie already has on her outfit. She's in this strapless, straight neck mini dress. It's super short and way above the knees. It goes so well with her tall and skinny figure. That style is just so great on her.

The dress is all black with sequins all over it. There's not one part of the dress that does not have black sequins on it. She's also in these amazing neon green pumps.

"I say we match by both wearing black dresses." I finally decide. "I mean, Atticus always wears black, so..."

"That would be sick!" Cries Jeannie.

"I know!" I squeal back.

"What about this one?" Jeannie holds up the *Jay Godfrey* dress I had on my bed as one of my options.

"Oh my god yes, It's perfect!" I exclaim.

"It really is." Agrees Jeannie. It might be even shorter than Jeannie's dress, but I suppose the puffiness of it makes up for the length. It's not very poofy, but just enough.

It has this ruffled texture on the top of the dress. It's strapless and almost looks like an open fan. Around the waist is a velour trim. Just to separate everything.

The outfit is going to be so great. And when the outfit is great, the night is great. Logic!

"Oh my god, Pops..." begins Jeannie as we walk down the streets of Tribeca, arm in arm. "you really do look great."

I'm of course in my *Jay Godfrey* dress, but it wouldn't be me if I didn't excessorize it. I'm wearing the gold hoops Atticus bought for me (what else). I'm also in this gold necklace with a huge, gold bow made of rhinestones.

And the shoes... oh my god they're perfect. They bring the splash of color this outfit so desperately needed.

They're these *Sophia Webster* black pumps with these black butterfly wings sticking out on the back.

It's satin, suede and pointed toe. The wings on the back have pink, yellow and blue rhinestones on it, making a pattern a butterfly's wing might have. The whole back of the black heels have little bits of pink, yellow, and blue rhinestones as well. There are also two ankle straps overlapping each other.

I do like heels with straps on them. I mean, of course I could walk in heels without the strap but, I'm kind of a cluts so I rather not.

"You're gonna knock him dead." Arlo says, walking in front of us. I blush at the thought of Atticus even finding me remotely attractive. I don't understand why they have to mention it though!

"There's no stopping him from kissing you tonight." Riley murmurs.

"No one's kissing..." I begin. "we're all just...gonna have fun. And be home at a reasonable hour." I can't help but add, but all that's running through my head is Atticus currently. I can't even take in the complete nuance and beauty of Tribeca.

I'm not nervous, I'm actually quite excited!

Ok, maybe I'm just a tinsey bit nervous. I don't know why though! I'm going with my friends to a fancy bar, to support my other friend who I may or may not have feelings for. What could go wrong!

I think I just have to keep reminding myself that I don't in fact like Atticus. He's just a very good friend who also so happens to be very good looking. Ok, so what? You know what I'm saying? Like, I'm making a big deal out of nothing, really!

"You did tell Atticus we were coming, didn't you?" Jeannie asks, snapping me out of my thoughts.

"Yes." I nod.

"What did he say?" Riley questions.

"I mean, he sounded excited over the text. I was going to knock on his door and tell him in person, but he was taking Mr. Davis to a doctor's appointment."

"Who's Mr. Davis?" Jeannie asks.

"Oh, that nice older man Atticus is close to. The one whose record shop got shut down, the one that Atticus worked at. The one we protested for."

"Well who could forget that." Scoffs Riley.

We reach *The Lounge* and walk down the concrete stairs and into the restaurant. It really is so fab. As I said before, it's more like a bar and restaurant in one. It hasn't changed one bit.

Even on a Wednesday night, it's crazy crowded. A little less crowded than it was the last time, but still crowded for a Wednesday night.

"Hi," says Arlo politely to the hostess. "Is it ok if we just hang out by the bar and not get a table. Is that something we could do?"

"Oh of course!" She nods her head. "That may actually be a good idea, it's not as crowded as the bar usually is."

We walk past everyone and finally get to the bar. The tables are packed but the bar really isn't. It's just me, Arlo, Jeannie, Riley, and some other Manhattan IT girls and fancy looking men.

We all find four stools next to each other and each take a seat. We end up ordering our drinks and an appetizer platter to split.

"Are they coming in through the back?" Riley asks, drinking his beer.

"Probably?" I shrug, sipping on my cosmopolitan, already feeling tipsy. This is my second and last one, I promise!

"Yeah, It's almost time for them to perform, and Poppy's nervous drinking." Jeannie points out, eating the olive out of her martini.

"That's true." I nod my head agreeing.

"There is no reason to be nervous drinking, there is no reason to be nervous in general." Arlo rubs my shoulder while standing up.

He's been standing for the past couple of minutes, like the watchdog of the group. He has his coke in his hand and is picking at the appetizer platter like the rest of us.

Him and Riley both look so handsome and cute together. (As always.)

Arlo is in this nice white T-shirt and green cargo pants. His light brown hair is pushed to the side in a nice wave as always. As soon as a strand falls over his eye, he pushes it back.

Riley is in tight, black skinny jeans covering his thin legs, and the huge leather combat boots on his feet are practically bigger than his body. He has a baby pink, baggy sweatshirt tucked into his pants with a *Louis Vuitton* belt.

He fiddles with his blue hair as he munches on a mozzarella stick.

The funny thing about Riley and Arlo is that you would never assume they were a couple.

They never hold hands in public, they never hug nor kiss. Riley does hate public displays of affection though. It grosses him out. If Arlo grabbed his hand in public, I'm positive Riley would punch him the gut.

"We should go by the stage." I tell them and finish off my drink.

Everyone does the same as we walk towards the relatively big stage *The Lounge* has. It's very grungy yet rustic. There are lit up light bulbs drilled around the rim of the stage and beat up wood floors.

I notice that Finn's drums are already set up on the stage. I didn't even realize he came out to set them up. There are also speakers and a mic stand.

It actually looks really cool. Suddenly I feel this wave of pride.

I have a friend who gets to perform at *The Lounge*. How cool is that! I'm just proud of Atticus though. Proud to call someone with so much talent such a good friend of mine.

Just then the lights dim and Jeannie starts to hit me on the arm.

I watch as Atticus, Finnick, and Dallon all walk on stage. Quite a crowd has gathered behind us, it almost looks like a club a little.

I can't help but wonder if they're here just to be here, or if they actually came to see Atticus's band. I hope it's because they actually came to see his band. Wouldn't that be great? He deserves all the fans in the world. He's so talented!

The minute he and the band get on stage, I immediately notice his outfit.

He's wearing these skinny jeans. One leg is black denim while the other half is light blue denim. He's got on a belt and a silver chain that hangs from the belt up to his upper thigh. He also has on some kind of graphic T Shirt and a dark denim jacket.

A lot of denim, but somehow he could completely rock it. It just looks right on him.

He's in leather combat boots, and his hair is shaggy and messy as usual and hangs a bit above his eyes, some strands falling in front of them.

He's wearing his normal silver nose ring, but this time I notice he has a silver ring in the corner of his mouth. I've never seen his lip piercing before, but it looks absolutely stunning on him. I didn't think it wouldn't.

The one thing that sticks out though is the silver chain around his neck. It's not any silver necklace, it's the one I bought for him. And it's the only one he's wearing.

Instead of his green guitar, he has the white one with all the writing on it. I like that one too. Goes better with his outfit.

Unfortunately, I hardly even notice Dallon and Finnick and what they are wearing, to enthrawled with Atticus and just his mere presence.

"Checking, checking, 1,2,3..." Atticus says into the mic leaning down just a bit. Not a lot, but enough for his hair to fall in front of his eyes, forming a dark shadow around them.

His voice sounds even deeper than usual. He has this cocky smirk on his face the minute he says those words into the mic.

It's that smirk where one side of his mouth quirks up and then it slowly turns to both. The look appears even more devious than usual with his lip ring and the wideness of his grin.

There is chatter and hums around the place, especially from the restaurant side, but a lot of the hubbub around us has dialed down and even stopped.

"Oh... oh he's hot." Jeannie leans towards me and murmurs. "And you *know* he's hot when your lesbian best friend says something."

"I'm shook." I hear Riley say on the other side of me. "I mean, we've seen him, but we haven't seen him this close. I honestly thought he was going to be ugly up close. This man is out here proving me wrong."

"I approve in the looks department." Arlo pulls a face and shrugs.

"Shhhhh!" I shush them as if they all were a pair of embarrassing and overbearing parents.

Finally, Atticus's eyes meet mine.

If I couldn't move before, I'm certainly paryliyzed now. His eyes were just so intimidating and smug but now they're soft and gentle, almost unsure.

The smirk on his face now turns into a little closed mouth smile. A genuine one. And it's just for me.

I feel this intense heat spread through my cheeks and I bite my lip.

"Hi." I mouth and give a shy wave.

"Hi." He mouths back with that sudden contagious smile and little wink, his whole demeanor changing under seeing me.

It's almost like it's just us in the room for a moment but I thankfully snap myself out of that.

"Oh my god, he mouthed 'hi' to her! And winked!" Jeannie squeals like a school girl under her breath to Riley.

Riley just rolls his eyes and nods, chewing his gum.

Atticus looks down for his moment, his tongue poking the inside of his mouth as he gives a little chuckle.

God, I hope he didn't hear that.

He looks back up, regaining that arrogant look he wears so well.

"Welcome, welcome..." He begins.

Wow, when he speaks into that mic his voice becomes so dark, so deep, even more raspy. Kind of dangerous. (If that's ever a word to describe Atticus.) But something tells me he becomes a bit of a different person on stage.

Not too much, but I could already tell. It's just a little bit.

"We're *The Deadbeats* and I hope you don't mind if we play you a couple of songs tonight..." he begins over the chatter and some claps here and there. "this ones called 'Eleven Eleven.'"

"I bet you ten bucks it's *super* angsty." RIley murmurs to Arlo.

"You're on." Arlo chuckles.

Suddenly a loud beat begins to blare through the restaurant. it's practically shaking the whole place. Or maybe that's because we're so close to the stage.

The beat is rough, almost hard rock. Something I never really heard Atticus play before. Punk rock, yeah, but not hard rock.

I don't quite know how to describe it. It's definitely not metal, but it's rock. I could hear every instrument they're playing. Atticus's guitar, then Dallons guitar, and Finnick banging on his drums.

Then suddenly the beat goes soft, almost not here anymore.

"I have a habit of ignoring the warning signs with this fleeting illusion that everything will be fine.

He's your world still but you're mine,

And eleven eleven is nothing but a time,

So happy eleven eleven.

It's just self expression, it's just depression, it's just self recession you left an impression on." He begins, his voice raspy as usual.

"You owe me ten bucks." I hear Riley murmur and Arlo sigh, as he takes a ten out of his pocket and throws it in Riley's outstretched hand.

The beat is mellow but then begins to pick up a bit.

Finnick begins back gently and slowly with the drums as both Atticus and Dallon's guitars begin to ramp up and get louder.

"I want you to fix this gloom, Want to drown myself in the scent of your expensive perfume.

When I met you, my morals cracked,

Put yourself in my shoes for a day,

And watch the colors in your life fade to black..." And there it is, the beat picks back up to the way it was in the beginning as we reach the chorus.

"My dear I died a long time ago, but now I'm coming back from the dead.

Take me away from this curse, everlasting seeing red.

I know it might not always feel this way and it might just be in my head...

But can I just rest my head on your shoulder cause I want to be with you instead." After the chorus the beat goes soft once again.

I love when he sings, he truly looks stunning. He looks angelic. The way he's playing his guitar and bouncing up and down energetically.

The way he closes his eyes when he sings and his eyebrows furrow as if he's focusing is absolutely mesmerizing. It's as if nothing but him and the beat are in the room as he loses himself in the song.

I know it sounds mean, but I don't even notice nor see Dallon and Finnick. My eyes are completely transfixed on Atty and just... well... just the utter beauty of him.

"*I'll be eleven sharp nails in your hopes and dreams coffin as I start to disappoint more and more often.*

"*I'll be eleven stabs to your colorful heart, Come on, I know a place where we can get a fresh start.*

And everytime you talk about him it sounds like Shakespearean literature, and nothing runs through my veins like bitterness and constant anger..." I do have to say, I love the song.

I love the lyrics, and the beat. I can't help but wonder who it's about. Sounds pretty specific to me.

I rack my brain as Atticus continues the song, repeating the chorus.

I remember when we were at my parents house and he was playing the piano and singing one of his songs for the article. I wondered who that song was about. That song really was beautiful. He said it was some girl.

The minute I remember that moment, the strange pang in my heart I got when he said that comes back. Who is this girl? Maybe an ex? Who knows, maybe I'll ask him. Will I? I almost feel angry at the thought of Atticus singing about some random girl.

He doesn't date though He's so confusing! I honestly can't keep up with this man.

I'm snapped out of my thoughts as Atticus and the band finishes the song. Claps go around the restaurant but mine is definitely the loudest as I do a bunch of little claps and I bounce up and down as much as I can in my heels.

"Thank you, thank you." Atticus says, voice deep with that smug smile of his.

His eyes meet mine again. The cocky smile is still cocky but it fades slightly as he gives me a little wink. My heart absolutely flutters and practically beats out of my chest. All I could do is bite my lip and give a little giggle.

I turn next to me to see Jeannie, Arlo, and Riley all staring at me as if I have two heads.

"What?" I ask.

"We'll talk later." Jeannie assures and Arlo nods in agreement.

What did I do? Already? Really?

When the performance is over, Atticus and the band thank everyone as they go into the back.

"Pops..." Jeannie turns to me as soon as the band enters the backroom.

"Hmmm?" I turn to her with a giddy smile on my face. I'm feeling quite giddy now that I think of it.

"I have this funny feeling—"

"Are you, like, stupid?" Riley interrupts Jeannie, turning from Arlo to us.

"What?" I ask defensively.

"That song. The first one. It was so blatantly about you it made my ears hurt."

"What?" I ask for the twentieth time tonight but this time my voice is a bit higher.

"Well, we don't know!" Begins Jeannie. "Maybe it's just... the way we heard it!"

"The way we heard is correct!" Sighs Riley, his hands on his hips. "Right Arlo?"

"Whatever you're conspiring, I'm not involved." Arlo says, typing on his phone.

"Maybe we should talk about this tomorrow." I state. "Let's get out of here, we have work in the morning." I suddenly watch as Riley, Jeannie, and Arlo's faces fall and they all get quite pale.

Jeannie puts her arm up weakly and points behind me.

"Wha—" Everything in front of me goes black as a pair of big hands cover my eyes.

"Guess who."

"Uhhhh *Tom Ford*?" I joke and hear a very familiar, raspy chuckle.

I feel Atticus against my back and his laughter vibrates against me. I can't help but crack a smile myself.

He releases his hands and I'm faced with a shocked Arlo, Riley and Jeannie once again. I give them a pleading glare not to embarrass me the turn to Atticus.

He has this glowing, most radiant smile that only Atticus could have. His straight white teeth are out on display and his dimples are engraved on the sides of his mouth, his huge smile lines up to his nose.

"Hey! You look great." He motions to my dress.

"Thanks! So do you!" I blush. Thank god I'm wearing lots of makeup so he can't really tell. "These are my friends, Riley, Arlo, and Jeannie." I point to each of them.

Arlo and Atticus shake hands and Jeannie and Riley exchange little waves with him.

"We've heard so many great things about you." Jeannie says, kindly.

"Same here." Atticus gives them his contagious grin.

"Where's Dallon and Finn?" I ask Atty.

"They both have to work tomorrow but they send their love." he gives a deep sigh. "I, for one, do not have to work tomorrow morning so I think I'm gonna have a drink. Would you like to get one with me?" He motions to the bar and asks.

The world has suddenly stopped just like in the movies. I find myself in an internal battle between what I want to do and what I should do. I want to have a drink with Atticus. I should go home and get to bed. Like Dallon and Finnick, I have work in the morning. Responsibility sucks. It sucks even more than the ripoff *Gucci* belt Riley recently ordered.

I close my eyes and look down as I shake my head, deciding my fate for the night. (No matter how painful it is.)

I finally look up to face Atticus, my left arm crossed over, my hand holding onto my right one in distress.

"I'm sorry Atticus, I wish I could. I got work tomorrow though." I hear three collective sighs behind me. "I don't want you to just sit there and drink alone. Do you want to come home with us? You and I are going to the same place after all." I give a nervous giggle.

"No, no, it's fine..." Atticus shakes his head. "text me when you get home? So I know you're safe."

"Yeah, of course." I nod.

"Nice show man. My girlfriend told me about your article. Huge punk fans. You were great." Some random guy and, who seems to be his girlfriend around his shoulder, taps Atticus's arm.

"Thanks..." Atticus stutters breathlessly. "glad you enjoyed it."

Once they walk away, me and Atticus look at each other and both our mouths drop. We then both burst out in laughter.

"Oh my god!" I look at him in disbelief.

"Holy shit!" His smile is the brightest I've ever seen. "When I said you were going to change things for me, I meant it."

"And you me." I give a little smile and nod. I can't believe that just happened!

For a second Atticus stares deeply into my eyes, his smile fading to a straight line. He looks like he's about to lean into me but he seems to decide against it.

He settles for putting his big, veiny, amazing hands on the side of my face, his rings cold against my hot skin.

I lean into his touch and give a little closed mouth smile and he gives the same one back, looking down at me.

Once he lets go of my face, he looks down at the floor with the same shy grin.

"Get some rest." He nods, pushing a piece of my hair behind my ear. It suddenly feels as if it's just us in the room now even though the restaurant is ridiculously rowdy and we have three spectators behind us.

"You need some as well." I remind him.

"I'll sleep when I'm dead." He retorts, giving me tired eyes and an exhausted smile.

"Typical." I snort. "Don't drink too much. And don't drive home. Take the transit. Obvi."

"Ok." Atticus chuckles and gives me a little salute. "Thanks for coming to see me... all of you." He motions to Riley, Arlo and Jeannie. I don't even turn around to grasp their reaction.

Suddenly I throw myself at Atticus, embracing him in a huge hug. He stumbles back in shock but fastly recovers by wrapping his arms around me securely. Tightly.

"Get home safe, ok?" I whisper into his neck, feeling a bit weary about leaving him here to drink without a drive home. But he promised he would take the bus. And I can't force him to come home with us if he doesn't want to. Should I try to pry more? No, no. He's a grown man. He can handle himself.

"Ok." I just nod, feeling as if I'm abandoning him. "Alright." I look down and give him a tiny wave as I begin to walk out of the restaurant, Riley, Arlo, and Jeannie behind me.

As we walk out of the rowdy restaurant and into the warm spring night Tribeca and Manhattan has to offer us, Jeannie rubs my back, seeming to know something is the matter, I give out a deep sigh.

I feel this fleeting feeling of sadness, of disappointment.

The question is, why am I so disappointed?

CHAPTER THIRTY-TWO

The Bonnie and Clyde of the fashion industry

"So, are we going to talk about what happened yesterday or..."

"You say it like it's an option." Riley utters to Jeannie. I just sigh, continuing to type in my horoscope on the computer.

"I honestly don't know what there is to discuss." I shrug. "Why is it always about me? There is absolutely nothing to discuss."

"Well lets see," begins Riley. "you have three witnesses that caught you and Atticus flirting with each other *majorly*. As well as, the so painfully obvious song that *Atty* wrote about you. Care to discuss? Because I was under the impression that we didn't think we had romantic feelings for Atticus?" He says condescendingly.

I look up to see Riley and Jeannie glaring at me expectantly through the gray lenses of my *Gucci* Sunglasses.

"I don't know what you're talking about." I say, trying to sound emotionless.

I got about three hours of sleep last night, my eyes are absolutely bloodshot. Hence, the huge, round sunglasses I'm wearing inside.

"He's obviously extremely into you." Shrugs Jeannie.

"You should have stayed and had that drink with him last night." Riley crosses his arms. "Who knows what could have happened."

"We had work! What, you wanted me to stay at the bar with Atticus till three in the morning?"

"Arlo would have picked you up." Riley shrugs.

"Riley! I wake up at 5:30 for work."

"If it was a weekend it would be different, right?" Jeannie asks, leaning in, her eyebrows raised in expectation.

"I..." I begin to think. If it was a Saturday or Friday night and Atticus asked to have a drink with me, would I stay with him? Is it the right thing? Well, why would it be the wrong thing? "I don't know." I answer honestly.

"What do you mean you don't know?" Riley asks, shrill.

"Why?" Asks Jeannie softly, putting her chin in the palm of her hand.

"I would go out with him," I begin. "but--"

"You're scared that if you go out to dinner with him, you'll fall for him." Jeannie finishes for me. Is that really what I'm scared of? Yes. Yes it is.

I'm absolutely positively petrified that if I do something remotely intimate with Atticus, such as dinner, my feelings won't be platonic anymore. The fact that I have to worry about that means my feelings towards him are already borderline not platonic. And that scares the shit out of me.

"No..." I say, my voice growing higher. Jeannie and Riley both tilt their heads and roll their eyes as if to say 'Poppy, you're a big, fat liar.' "ok maybe, but it doesn't matter!" I retort. "Maybe it looked like flirting to you, and maybe it was flirting but it wasn't on my side. Surely not."

"Ok, Pops." Jeannie chuckles.

"Fifty bucks they'll hook up." Riley whispers to Jeannie. But the whisper isn't a whisper at all even if he has his hand over his mouth and is leaning into her. He does know you have to talk quietly as well, right?

"My lovelife is not a bet." I chide in a murmur.

"Ha."

"Poppyseed!" I hear Jane's voice boom from behind me. I give a little jolt and quickly turn around. "My office. Thank you." She walks back into her office. Jeannie and Riley both give me quizzical glares.

I get up, take a sip of my iced coffee, and begin to walk towards Jane's towards the big glass doors.

I step into Jane's office in my *Del Mar* dress from the Eva Mendes collection at *New York and Company*. It's a cute, strapless, straightneck that's light pink with white polka dots.

It flows out at the waist and falls a bit above my knees. It's nice and comfy. Usually comfort isn't my top priority but today it was.

I close the glass door behind me and sit in Jane's chair. I cross my right leg over my left and sit up. I can't help but notice how similar we look right now. Not looks that much but with other things.

We're both sitting in the same position, both wearing our oversized, black sunglasses, and we're both in very similar hairstyles.

Jane has always been my idol, always been my mentor, always been my hero. There's a moment in your life when someone will always tell you 'don't meet your heroes.' When I first met Jane I was scared that would apply to her. And it did.

Jane DuVull is a *Prada* wearing, money hungry, most of the time ruthless girl boss, who will get her way at all costs. No matter what. I wanted nothing more but to be Jane DuVull.

Jane DuVull is one of my favorite people on this planet, even if she's not the saint sixteen year old Poppy thought she was. No one's a saint though, no one.

And now looking at our similarities as she sits in front of me, despite all the money she has, despite the multi billion dollar magazine she owns, I realize we're not that different after all.

"What's with your sunglasses?" She motions with her head. I rip off my sunglasses and show her my bloodshot eyes that I can't even put contacts in, with the dark blue bags under both of them.

At the same time Jane takes off her glasses and her eyes look identical to mine.

"Why did *you* get no sleep?" She puts her sunglasses back on and looks down at the paper she was reading before.

"I went out." I admit, somewhat ashamed.

"Where?" Jane asks, sounding actually curious.

"*The Lounge.*"

"Really?" She looks up and gives me a knowing smirk. "Was it to see that Atticus guy? Who even names their child Atticus anyway? God, people are so goddamn stupid."

I snort.

"Well did you at least have fun?" Jane now moves to another paper.

"I guess. I mean, I watched him perform. Went with Riley, Arlo, and Jeannie. Maybe I'm just tired."

"Well your eyebags could have told me that." Jane scribbles something on the paper she's reading. "But I'm glad you're getting out more often. It's been months since that ex boyfriend of yours left you and it's still like pulling teeth to get you out of the house. It's like you're a freakin vampire."

"Not true!" I retort. "I've been out. I just need to… get out a little more. Never mind that though," I shake my head. "what do you need? Why did you call me?"

"Well," begins Jane, putting down the papers she was reading and looking at me. "I hope you're aware how much your article has blown up."

"Yes of course." I nod.

"To tell you the truth, we haven't gotten recognition like this in quite a while. We have gone international, rock magazines have been getting in touch, the praise has been crazy, ya know." She lifts a brow and I nod.

God, I wonder what she's going to ask me? Is she going to put me in charge of another article? I hope so. I'm so tired of writing tiny little filler articles. I proved myself, haven't I? So why hasn't Jane given me the permission to write anything worth writing about.

"You must be confused because I haven't given you any big articles…" 'Yes, I am!' I want to shout. "well as you know I always have my reasons."

"Mrs. DuVull, with all due respect, I think I proved myself exponentially and I don't know what I did but I could do better--"

"Poppy, I want you to attend the FTSC." Jane says, cutting me off and typing something on her computer.

"What?" I ask, feeling like I've just been hit with a ton of bricks and my breath has been taken out of my lungs.

"The FTSC. Fashion Trade show and Conference. It's in Atlantic City this year. It's one of the biggest trade shows in the game."

"Y--yeah, I know." I say in shock. "I remember helping you pack for the one that was in London last year."

"Exactly right, Poppyseed." Jane turns her attention to me. "I go sponsoring *DuVull* every year, but I honestly don't feel like dealing with it. So, I decided you'd be the best runner up to sponsor the company."

"Mrs. DuVull, I'm honored! I don't even know what to say." Am I dreaming? I secretly pinch myself on my thigh just to make sure. But I'm not waking up. This is actually happening.

"People in the industry have really taken a liking to you and your article. I've gotten praise from multiple designers as well. They think your take on lifestyle and fashion is fun and fresh and that's just what we need." She shrugs. "What do you say? I mean, you don't really have a choice, but I'd like to make it seem like you do."

Everything around me is blurred though and an overwhelming feeling of happiness rushes over me. I'm finally getting recognition for my passion. It's... it's amazing!

"I'd, well... I would love to go..." I stumble upon my words.

"Ok, good, great, fantastic, superb!" Jane nods, as she heads back to the papers she was working on. "Clear up your calendar and get packing because you're heading out next Friday. I suggest you and Atticus start packing--"

"Wait..." I shake my head. "what about Atticus?" Jane rolls down her glasses and looks at me like I'm crazy.

"You're really not looking at all the praise for the article are you?"

"I've seen some. My mom always said praise isn't good for the soul nor the ego."

"What kind of backwards, hippie bullshit is that?" Jane scoffs, typing something vastly on her computer. "Praise is part of where I've gotten today. Look at this," she turns her computer towards me. "'Beautifully written, amazing way to look at other types of fashion trends, could this be the first Bonnie and Clyde of the fashion industry?' That's from the creative director of *Vogue*. You're taking the boy with you. Everyones crazy about him."

"I'm aware." I nod, and give a little smile at the thought. I don't think I know a person who doesn't like Atticus. "What if he has something to do though. It's kind of last minute, don't you think?"

"Oh trust me," Jane snorts. "I wouldn't worry your tiny little mind about that, Poppyseed. He'll gladly pause his oh so exciting life to spend two days in Atlantic City with you."

I roll my eyes and cross my arms.

"You can count on me to represent *DuVull* in the best and most elegant way possible." I nod, matter of factly but on the inside I'm squealing and jumping up and down!

"Oh please," begins Jane. "since when is *DuVull* elegant in any way, shape or form."

I nod my head in agreement.

"What do we even do though, what's the itinerary, what--"

"Hey, hey, hey, slow down. I only had one cup of coffee so far." Jane puts her hands up. "I'll hook you up with the itinerary and the details later. I'll FaceTime you or something and text you all the details. Good? Good. Great. Now, I have a photography department to whip into shape."

"Ok!" I get up out of the leather chair and begin to walk out the door. "Oh, and Ms. DuVull?" She picks her head up. "Thank you. I--I won't let you down."

Jane looks soft for a moment but then sits up and looks back at her papers.

"I know you won't, Poppyseed." She nods. "Make sure you and Atticus dress extra extravagantly. You're representing me, after all."

CHAPTER THIRTY-THREE
Sleep talking and (one) bed

"And are you sure you have everything?" Tiff's voice rings through my ears.

"Almost." I say throwing my fifth skirt into my *Betsy Johnson* suitcase. (You know...who knows what I'm going to feel like wearing once we're there. I don't!)

"That's probably an understatement." Tiff snorts and I scowl at her comment through the phone.

"I have to be prepared!" I tell her. "This is one of the biggest fashion events for every brand in the world." I say a tad bit smugly.

"I know, you've only told me fifteen times." Tiff jokes.

"Well whatever..." I shrug it off. "I will be prepared no matter what. I have no choice!" I hold the phone between my shoulder and the crook of my neck and begin to push down on my suitcase when it won't close. Why. Won't. This. Thing. Close!

"Yeah and in Poppy language that means bring ten pairs of shoes when we're only there for two days."

"Not true!" I retort. "I brought four pairs of shoes. I learned my lesson when we went to Florida." Oh my god. Let's not talk about Florida. They 'lost' my *Loui Vuitton's* on the plane. I call bullshit, that's what it is. I still think about them everyday...

"Well that's great to hear." Tiff sighs sarcastically.

"I'd bring my whole closet if I could!" I exclaim. "The people that are going to be there are very high up in the industry, Tiffy. Brand owners, models, owners of other magazines, fashion IT girls. This could be my chance, my connection. I could *be* one of them."

I hop on top of my suitcase and put my whole body on it. I push down and try to get it to zipper up but it won't budge.

Ok, I can't lose it. It's just a suitcase... What should I do!

I refuse to take anything out of this suitcase. My overnight bag is already filled! With the important things of course. Makeup, hygiene products, and more clothes... and maybe two more pairs of shoes. Ok, maybe three. The point is, I can't take anything out of my suitcase!

"Wow," begins Tiff. "I guess you're right. What's a trade show anyway? What's the conference even for?"

"Uh, a trade show is like an event where brand owners and fashion designers show off their new stuff to businesses or possible consumers. And Jane just described the conference as a little get together for brands and people in the fashion industry to network. They're back to back. Both days." I get off the suitcase, still holding the phone in the crook of my neck.

I get a running start and bodyslam the suitcase. Well ouch!

I immediately fall off of it and onto my bed in pain.

"Are you excited?" Asks Tiff. I can hear her own excitement through the phone.

"Yes!" I exclaim. "It's going to be so fab." I get back on my suitcase, hopping up and down on it repeatedly and trying to zip it.

"Is Atticus driving down?"

"Yeah, he's the one with the car. We'll have fun on the way down I bet." A two hour car ride? I don't know. But a two hour car ride with Atticus I could definitely do.

"What's the hotel situation?" Asks Tiff and I could hear her skeptical tone through the phone.

"Same room. Hopefully two beds." Oh I give up! I now just sit criss-cross on top of the suitcase, resting my face in the palm of my hand.

"That's probably not going to happen."

"I know."

"Did you look up the room Jane had booked?"

"Yes!" I squeal. "The people running the event booked the room since Jane was going to be one of the most valued people there. The room has a mini fridge, a flat screen television--"

"And two beds?"

"No." I huff. Way to ruin the moment, Tiff.

"I'm just being rational, I'm sorry. It's a curse!" She giggles. "Tell him to bring a sleeping bag."

"Yeah and win the award for biggest bitch of the year." A sleeping bag, Tiff. Really? That is so something she would do. "We slept on the same couch before. How different could sleeping in a bed be?" As I say it though, my voice goes high. Could it be bad? Yes. It could be very, *very* bad.

"It's honestly a recipe for disaster."

"How so?" I retort defensively. (Although I know exactly why, I'll never admit it out loud.)

"Don't you think it's funny..." begins Tiff as I finally get my suitcase zipped. I flop onto my back and hit the soft cushions on my bed, exhausted. "It's so typical! A romantic trope if I've ever seen one. 'Oh! There's only one bed? Guess we'll have to sleep together!' We all know how that ends!"

"It's a romantic trope you're even talking about that." I make fun of the situation, but in reality she's right. As flipping always!

"I'm serious, Pops."

"You're always serious, Tiff." I murmur and—I don't mean it—but with a tad bit of an attitude.

"Would it be so bad if we slept together?"

"In what contexts?" Asks Tiff, shrill.

"In any contexts, why should it matter!"

"Do you like the boy, Poppy? Like, all jokes aside."

"I...I don't know. But if I don't like him like that, then why would platonically sleeping with him be a big deal?"

"Because I know you better than that?"

"How so?"

"I'm not getting into this with you." Tiff sighs. "Did you guys plan what you're wearing both days?"

"We have an idea." I smile. "I'll send you pictures."

"Promise?"

"Swear." I say, surly. "And who cares about the bed situation! I'm sure we'll have a great time."

"Very true. I'm sure it will be fine. It's always an adventure with the two of you anyway."

"It is." I nod in agreement. "Well alright. I love you. I'll text you when we get there. And mom, and Helen, and Riley, and Jeannie, and Jane, and Arlo. I should honestly just make a group chat!"

"I love you too." Tiff chuckles. "Be safe. Tell Atticus I said hi."

After we say our goodbyes, I hang up and sigh.

Now Tiff has me worrying and thinking about things that I wasn't concerned about before. I can't be like that though.

Breath... It's supposed to be fun! It's business, but it's also supposed to be a great time. I'm going to one of the biggest fashion events of the year for God's sake! I won't let minior worries get me down. Yes. Perfect. We'll solve it when we get there. Nothing to worry about.

I hop off my bed and grab my suitcase and overnight bag, dragging the heavy luggage off the bed. It practically weighs me down but I manage to roll the suitcase out of my room and my apartment and throw my overnight bag over my shoulder.

I close and lock the apartment door behind me as I drag my feet to Atticus's door just a couple of feet away, directly in front of me.

God, what a workout!

I take the palm of my hand and bang against the metal door, hearing the loud song echo throughout the building's 7th floor we're on.

"Atticus?" I complain. "Are you done?" Suddenly the door swings open and he motions me into his apartment.

He's in a black button up shirt that has the design of white barbed wire all around it. He's also in black skinny jeans with different sized chains draped from his black leather belt. He has a total of, like, four chains. Makes me wonder how he doesn't tip over!

I plop onto his couch, utterly worn out. I give an exaggerated sigh as Atticus grabs his own suitcase.

"What's the matter, Poppy?" Atticus asks sarcastically, amusement dripping from his tone.

"My bags are heavy, Tiff got me in a mood, and you take longer than me to get ready!" I cry and cross my arms like a child.

"Well..." Atticus walks up behind me and fix's the straw hat on top of my head. "why did you pack so much stuff?" He thinks for a moment then continues. "Wait, that's a stupid question. I forgot who I was talking to." He leans towards my head and pokes the side of my cheek. He then walks to his suitcase, seeming to be putting last minute things in it.

"Why did Tiff upset you though?"

"I guess she didn't upset me." I huff, crossing my leg over my other and playing with the hem of my dress. "We just had a conversation I suppose." I'm in my *Milly* pink and white, striped wrap. It's low cut, flowy, and lands a bit above the knees. So fab as a going away outfit. It says, 'I'm going on holiday. But I'm not there yet, I'm on my way though!'

"About?" Atticus fixes his shirt and lifts his suitcase. I get off the couch and before I could grab my suitcase, he's already rolling it out the door.

"Thanks." I motion to my suitcase he's rolling. "Ummm… just the trip. You know… things." I finish off as we reach the elevator. Atticus presses the button and we begin to go down.

"Things?" He asks, a smirk on his face.

"Yeah… things." I fix the overnight bag on my shoulder and stand up straighter. I just look at the rusted, silver metal door of the elevator in front of us, keeping us closed in.

"Come on," begins Atticus suddenly bumping his shoulder into mine. "don't put so much pressure on yourself with this trip."

"Easy for you to say." I begin, mumbled. "Everyone loves you. They haven't even met you and they love you."

"And the fashion entrepreneurs and enthusiasts love you too." He says surly. Sure enough it almost convinces me. "The praise is for *your* article, not me."

A million thoughts are running through my head at once and honestly, I really don't want to worry about them right now. I just bite my lip and look down at the dirty elevator floors covered in suspicious stains and candy wrappers.

"Hey," Atticus begins gently and taps under my chin with his pointer finger. It forces me to look up at him. "you're ok. I'm here." He gives a kind grin and it warms my heart completely. I just give a closed mouthed smile and nod, but from the corner of my eye I could see him still looking at me worried, concerned.

I see him put his hand up to touch my arm but he quickly puts it down, not seeming to know what to do. I feel this awkward tension surge that has never been between us before. I wish I could make it stop but I can't. I feel so weird right now. I'm worried but excited. Sure yet confused.

As the elevator door pings and opens with a squeak, Atticus awkwardly motions for me to go in front of him. When we walk out of the building, he walks slightly in front of me. I have a feeling if we keep this awkward tension up, the whole weekend we'll be ruined. And if me and Atticus are anything around each other, it surely isn't awkward.

All of a sudden I feel inclined to catch up to his side and put my arm in the crook of his. I feel the sturdy fabric of his dress shirt against my arm. Atticus looks down at me with a raised eyebrow.

"Brooklyn streets are dangerous." I shrug and snort at my lame excuse to put my arm in his. He just makes me feel protected. I mean, I of course feel protected and secure without him, but with him I feel a lot of my anxiety dissipate. Less anxiety about life, less like the world is closing in on me, less like someone would run up and snatch my *Gucci* purse. (Chances are though if anyone ever did that, they'd get a *Jimmy Choo* shoe to the throat.)

As we get to Atticus's car, I hop in the passenger's seat while Atticus shoves our luggage in the trunk. He then gets in the car and starts it, the cool air conditioner blowing in my face and the buzz of the radio floating through my ears.

I can't help but yawn due to the lack of much needed sleep I got last night. I rub my eyes, leaving a tiny coat and crumbles of mascara underneath but I don't care much right now. I probably will later though.

I close my eyes and rest my head on Atticus's shoulder, feeling the slight twist and turns of the car as he drives.

"Sorry." I murmur, yawning once again as I feel myself begin to relax.

"For what?" He asks softly, putting his big hand on top of my hat, taking it off and throwing it in the back seat. He begins to run his hands through my hair bringing me much needed calmness and comfort.

Usually I would scold him for throwing a fifty dollar hat in the back of his dirty, old car carelessly but I really don't have the energy. So, I just nuzzle my head on his shoulder as he plays with my hair and I slowly find myself drifting off.

"Poppy?" I hear a soft, raspy voice cut through the black void I'm currently facing.

I feel the peach colored sunset begin to dance across my eyelids as I slowly begin to bat them open.

"Pops, we're here." I come to and realize who's next to me and where we are.

I feel Atticus gently put his hand on my arm and I sigh, opening my eyes.

The sharp Atlantic City sunset hits immediately and I start to tear up from the brightness. I rub my eyes once again and yawn, turning to Atticus who is currently looking quite blurry. I think I'm still half asleep.

I hear him chuckle and bring his huge hand up to my face, wiping under my eyes. He takes his thumb, dawning a huge silver ring and wipes the small nooks that have gotten absolutely ruined with black mascara, making my eyebags look ten times worse than they already were.

"How many hours of sleep did you get last night?" Atticus asks concerned, leaving his hand on the side of my face.

"I haven't gotten any sleep as of late." I begin groggily. "I got maybe an hour of sleep last night."

"Poppy..."

"I'm fine," I answer, my voice going a tad higher than usual. "I was planning the itinerary for the weekend. And worrying about everything. As usual."

"I don't understand what you're so worried about." Atticus shakes his head and his face contorts in confusion. I feel my eyes keep closing and I can't quite seem to keep them open.

"Are you ready to go inside? The hotel looks beautiful."

"Yeah," I yawn. "let's go."

As soon as I step out of the car, I rub my eyes and the cool night breeze hits me.

A new wave of exhaustion washes over me and I feel my knees buckle as I almost fall face first onto the concrete. Ok, maybe I'm not fully awake yet.

"Oh my god, Pops!" I hear Atticus yell from the otherside of the car and before I hit the concrete, he wraps his arms around me pulling me up.

I'm going to be honest, I was fine this morning, but I think the exhaustion has finally hit. I haven't slept the whole week. Recurring thoughts have been running through my head, a lot of them about Atticus.

"I'm good." I rasp out, eyes closed and falling into Atticus's embrace.

"Is that so?" He questions and I could only imagine his face.

"Mhhmm." I feel him begin to move me around in his arms and get ready to pick me up. "Don't carry me over your shoulder." I mumble, absolutely spent, beginning to relax in his arms.

"Why?"

"It's going to look like you drugged and kidnaped me." I answer as matter of factly as I can.

"You have makeup smudged under your eye, you could barely even stand, and you're hardly even coherent. It's going to look pretty questionable anyway."

"Mmmm... ok." I hardly even manage to say that. I feel Atticus scoop me up with ease and practically cradle me in his arms.

I weakly wrap one arm around him and rest my head on the side of his shirt. It's two layers of black. The black behind my eyelids and Atticus's shirt. It makes me extra drowsy.

"You're getting rest tonight whether you like it or not." I hear Atticus mumble, beginning to walk. I'm in no place to argue with him. "I'll get our stuff after I drop you off in the room." I hear Atticus kick the door to the hotel open. We're staying at *Harrahs*. When I looked it up online it looked so stunning! I'll explore it tomorrow I suppose.

A brisk breeze follows us as we walk into the hotel. It's a frigid cold in the hotel which I love, and it just makes me more comfortable in Atticus's arms as I almost feel giddy with exhaustion.

"Hi..." begins Atticus and that's how I know we've reached the front desk. "we're booked under *DuVull and Co.* Poppy Paxton and Atticus Mckeen."

"Got you guys." says the woman at the front desk, not even a moment later. "Here's your keys, just sign right there." I feel Atticus lean in and sign something. "You guys are here for the conference right?"

"Yes we are." I hear Atticus put down the pen and stand normally again.

After the woman talks to Atticus about room service and other little things I barely could make out, we finally end up in our room. It's actually quite blurry everything, as I drift in and out of sleep.

He places me gently on the bed and sits beside me for a moment. I feel him take off my shoes and as soon as he does it, my legs plop back down on the sheets with a thud. The bed dips as he plops down beside me again.

"Thanks... thanks for carrying me. You're the best." I say groggily, eyes closed as I lazily pick up my arm and pat him on the thigh.

"You're welcome." He chuckles and says below a whisper, taking a piece of hair out of my face and then getting up off the bed. I hear him shuffle about in the hotel room.

I get comfortable and find myself drifting off once again.

CHAPTER THIRTY–FOUR
The Morning After

"It's absolutely fab Jeannie. Absolutely stunning." I look back down at my phone on FaceTime after giving the barista in *Starbucks* a thank you and kind smile.

"I wish I was there." Jeannie looks up from the chocolate muffin she's munching on and the article she's writing.

"You would love it." I take a sip of my freshly brewed iced coffee. It definitely isn't the same as the *Starbucks* I usually go to in Manhattan, but it's pretty good nonetheless. I immediately feel a bit of a caffeine buzz. Thank god.

"Well I'm stuck here with this." She turns the camera around to show Riley, who just walked in.

"How many beds are in the room?" Riley demands, not even seated yet.

Well apparently that's everyone's question, isn't it.

"One." I say as if caring less.

"What's up with that?" Jeannie's eyebrows are raised when she turns the camera back to her.

"I woke up to see him snuggled up on the floor below the bed with a blanket and pillow." I sigh guiltily. "I don't want Atticus sleeping on the floor. I know it's clean, but who knows what happened on there! And if he sleeps on the floor surely his back will hurt. I don't want his back to hurt. Maybe we could switch it up! I slept on the bed last night, he'll sleep on it tonight, and tomorrow I'll sleep on it again. Or..." I trail off carefully. "maybe we could sleep together. Meaning sleep of course! Not... ya know. Would it be right for him to sleep in the same bed as me?"

"Oh?" Jeannie says, taken aback. "You're considering letting him..."

"Yeah."

"Let him sleep with you." I hear Riley in the background. "If you want to get back to New York and act like nothing happened, do that. I mean, if he does like you and you seem to have a thing for him...who knows what will happen. But with your crippling sense of self-discipline and control, you should be fine."

"I do not have 'a thing' for him." I scoff.

Ok, I'm well aware I suck at lying. I could see that now. I'm just not exactly sure what the 'thing' is yet.

"Can we not talk about this please?" I grumble, biting on my straw anxiously.

"You brought it up." Retorts Jeannie, mouthful of muffin. "But how was the ride down yesterday?"

"Oh god..." I groan. "you don't want to know. My lack of sleep had finally reached its breaking point. I guess the result of four hours of sleep over the course of seven days is passing out in a car and having to be carried into a hotel."

"Oh really?" Jeannie says, trying to hide her laughter.

"Yep"

"I bet you're never going without your much needed eight hours of sleep ever again, huh?" I hear Riley.

"Basically."

"Do you want to talk to Jane? She just came in?"

"No," I shake my head. "I'm fine. She's probably super busy anyway."

She just got in. I'm not going to bother her with my anxiety fueled multitude of questions. Yet.

"I'll let you guys get back to work. I'm going back to the room anyway. See if Atticus is up yet."

I hear Riley chuckle and catch Jeannie's cheeky smile.

"Have fun!" Riley practically yells.

"Have fun." Jeannie says, a bit more calm. "Be safe, take it easy. Have a good time today. Try not to stress. Have a drink for me."

"We'll do." I lift my *Starbucks* to salute her as we all say our goodbyes and I hang up.

Thanks to Atticus I got a pretty good sleep last night. More sleep than I've gotten in months probably.

Am I heavily embarrassed that Atticus had to carry me into the hotel yesterday because of my lack of sleep? Yes.

Am I avoiding eye contact with the people at the front desk because of it? Yes.

I still can't believe what happened yesterday. I can't believe Atticus had to carry me into this hotel as if I was inebriated with alcohol like a girl at her 21st birthday party. What is wrong with me? God, why couldn't I just shake myself awake!

Trust me though, lesson learned.

The trade show is today and the conference is tomorrow and I am absolutely ecstatic! I still feel like I'm in some type of dream. I honestly thought I was going to wake up in my apartment this morning.

So, as of now I'm just walking around and exploring the casino and hotel. I'm not really a gambler but I still think casinos are quite cool to hang out in. Not at 8:30 in the morning of course, but I needed to look around. I couldn't wait anymore!

The hotel looks just like the pictures. It's beautiful. Truly stunning. I checked out the pool, oh my god. I don't even know what to say.

It's breathtaking with humongous palm trees and lounge chairs all around. Palm trees! Palm trees in an indoor pool in Atlantic City. Can you believe it! I packed a bathing suit just in case. I mean, not that I'm *expecting* us to have downtime, but who knows!

The room is stunning as well. And yes, I woke up this morning to find the room only has one bed. (What did you expect?)

We can't get another room either unless there is something horribly wrong with it. I mean, It was the room booked for Jane. I don't want to be an inconvenience and ask for another one. I honestly don't know what the hell to do.

I'm just walking aimlessly through the hotel as if walking on air, feeling kind of giddy I have to say.

I make awkward eye contact with the occasional early morning gamblers (all five of them.) and somehow manage to almost trip over my own two feet multiple times, my brain scattered and focused on plans for today.

Where shall we eat for dinner? What are me and Atticus going to wear to the trade show? Now the real question we all want to know; what shops do they have?

Speaking of shops and clothes, I'm in my floral print maxi dress.

It has these long, puffy sleeves and the dress touches the floor. Different types of flowers coat it and the different colors make it vibrant.

When I woke up this morning I decided to change into this. I'm not going to waste a perfectly good outfit!

Once I get out of the elevator and back back onto the floor of me and Atticus's room, I walk slowly down the classy hallways.

As I reach our hotel room I take out my card and have the scanner thingy scan it. I walk into the room and close the door behind me quietly, making sure not to wake Atticus from his slumber. That's when I see that he's not on the floor anymore, hearing the shower running.

So I plop down onto the bed I neatened up a bit earlier this morning. It's absolutely huge and the most comfy thing ever.

There are four pillows scattered about from where I slept and the white sheets are lazily thrown together, the best I could muster myself up to do so.

At the end of the bed is a little, red, cushioned bench. Now that I think of it, the room is absolutely humongous. It's tremendously modern and chic.

On each side of the bed are little wooden, brown nightstands that are built into the wall and connected to the very end of the head of the bed.

Two fancy lamps are on each nightstand and directly next to the bed is a full body mirror. It practically takes up that one whole wall. You could see the whole room through it's reflection. There is also a weirdly shaped, curved chair next to the bed that makes it look like we're in the Museum of Modern Art.

In front of the bed is a flat screen TV and next to the TV is a long desk and chair. I absolutely adore the classy yet modern and funky edge this whole hotel has to it.

The closet in the room is filled with my clothes and there weren't enough hangers, so I had to call down this morning and ask for some more.

I tried to shove my *Louis Vuitton's* in the safe, but they wouldn't fit. So, I think it's safe to say all expensive shoes will be kept in the suitcase. (As much as it hurts me not to put them on display in the closet.)

I also made some room for Atticus in the closet. It's the least I could do, honestly. I was going to buy him a coffee too, but I don't remember what he likes.

I still feel so guilty about him sleeping on the floor. The chair isn't big enough for him to sleep on, none of the chairs in the room are. I don't know what the hell to do.

I just sip my coffee in the attempt to ease some of today's nerves and flip aimlessly through the TV channels.

Suddenly I hear the door to the bathroom open not far after I heard the shower stop. I can't help but tear my eyes away from the TV and towards the opening bathroom door. I immediately regret it.

I practically spit my iced coffee back into its cup when Atticus walks out of the bathroom in nothing but the white hotel towel wrapped around his waist. He looks at me in sudden shock

"I...uhh... you weren't here, so I figured I..." he motions towards the bathroom.

"Ye—Yeah, Of course." I nod vastly. He looks around the room awkwardly for a second and gives a fake cough.

His dirty blonde hair is now even darker and hangs loosely in front of his face in wet strands. The heat from the shower is still radiating off his chest and evaporating into the air. (But I'm *not* staring at his chest. I swear!)

I quickly and belatedly slap my hands over my eyes and hear Atticus chuckle as he shuffles around the room, sounding to be grabbing clothes.

"Don't change yet!" I cry. "We have to decide what outfits we are both wearing together to make sure they coincide properly!" I babble and my voice raises to an obnoxious tone.

I hear Atticus give another laugh, and zip his suitcase.

"Ok, well can you at least let me change into sweats for now? Or would you rather me walk around in this?" He says, and I could practically sense the cocky smile on his face.

I roll my eyes behind my hands and scoff.

"Don't talk to me." I turn around and throw myself into the nearest pillow, my face blushing like crazy.

I walk out of the trade show defeated. Maybe I didn't properly understand the point of a trade show. No one really talked to me and Atticus besides the people who were trying to network or sell us something. Hence, the trade show.

Don't get me wrong, seeing sneak peaks of what fashion has to bring us this year is totally fab! It was absolutely amazing! Everyone just kind of kept to themselves though. I didn't expect that. Maybe that's naive on my part though.

On the bright side, we met some really nice girl, Emma.

Emma owns a new and upcoming brand and recognized me and Atticus. Her brand is kind of gothic and eccentric. Some of the stuff was really cute though!

She absolutely freaked out when she saw me and Atty. She called us over and said she was a huge fan of the article and that she's been selling so much more ever since it came out. She gave us a whole bunch of free stuff. How amazeballs is that!

Me and Atticus walk out of the trade show, holding a bunch of shopping bags (most of them mine.) I suddenly find it extremely hard to walk in these heels. I'm usually a pro, but these are the highest heels I've ever worn.

They're thick platforms with a block heel and a round toe. There is a little buckle around the ankles so I don't trip and bust my face open. (But let's face it, if anyone was to trip in a pair of heels here it would be me.)

The heels are also a baby pink color with little cherries all over them.

My dress matches them. It's this flowy mini dress with the same design and same color. My hair is in wavy locks down my back and sitting on the top of my head is a pink beret with a huge pink bow on it.

Atticus is in a black, button up dress shirt, and to follow the cherry theme, one single cherry patch on the right side of his chest. He also has on these black, somewhat baggy jeans rolled up so you could see his pink socks that match my dress. He has black boots and chains going down both sides of his jeans.

"I don't understand," I begin. "Jane said to socialize, but no one was socializing. No one talked, they just tried to sell each other things. I'm very confused."

"Maybe she meant at the conference tomorrow." Atticus squints his eyes as we walk into the elevator.

"I still don't get it." I huff. "What is it, some kind of rule that you can't even smile at someone unless you're trying to sell them something?"

"So you're basically just describing human interaction on a daily basis." He looks down at me and smirks.

"Touche." I scoff. "But still. I felt like I was in some cult or something." I give a dramatic shiver.

"That's because you're a social butterfly and everyone else in there were either rich, middle aged silent bidders of the fashion world, or brand owners." The elevator door dings open and we reach our floor. (Me and Atticus are still amazed by how fast it is compared to our apartments.)

"Don't they know we're from *DuVull* though. We have name tags!" I state excitedly. They're so adorable. I bedazzled mine!

"You're so cute." Atticus smiles, shaking his head and opening up our hotel room door. I blush at the complement and give a little giddy smile like a schoolgirl.

I finally feel happy being called cute.

Once we get inside the room we drop all the bags on to the floor. I plop down on the bed and Atticus plops down beside me.

We just lay in silence for a couple of moments and I can't help but wonder what's going through that wild head of his.

"Hey Poppy?" Atticus asks, his eyes looking up at the hotel ceiling.

"Yeah?" I pipe up, giving him a kind smile. He takes a deep breath still not facing me and looks as if he's debating on saying something.

"What is it?" I ask, my smile fading and suddenly worried. He turns to look at me and then offers a closed mouth smile.

"Where do you want to eat for dinner?" I could tell he wanted to say something else but he doesn't.

CHAPTER THIRTY-FIVE
His Poppy

"I don't know about this." I begin anxiously. Me and Atticus just entered the conference room and of course it's beautiful, with an amazing bar overlooking the ocean and everything.

The room is filled to the brim with people dressed to impress, drinking, mingling, and laughing amongst one another. (It seems much friendlier than the trade show yesterday. Or at least I hope so.)

"What do you mean?" Asks Atticus looking down at me, squinting his eyes skeptically.

"I dunno..." I talk over the loud buzz in the room. "I just hope it goes better than yesterday. What if they think we're stupid? What if they think our articles stupid? Look at them! These people are the real deal, Atticus."

"And so are you. Plus, half these people are drunk off their asses anyway. It will probably be real easy to talk to them." He chuckles.

I talked to Jane this morning. She said we have nothing to worry about because most of the people here know of me and Atticus and our article. We did go viral after all. Although it's still hard to bebelive sometimes. Jane basically just said to mingle and be ourselves. Find people to talk to. Easy enough, right?

By the way, our outfits are so fab! We obviously are the best dressed in the room. I'm in this black satin, cropped tank top with a straight neckline made up of black feathers. Right below my exposed belly button is where my mini skirt begins. It's the yellow and black *Burberry* stripe design. I'm also wearing white thigh highs and black, opened toe platforms. They match my shirt to a T, with the ankle strap made up of black feathers as well.

I have a silver choker with a diamond heart in the middle and matching hoop earrings. My hair is in a half up half down pony, with a big furry, black scrunchie sitting on top of my head.

I'm feeling Cher from *Clueless* vibes, if you know what I mean. I feel like I should be driving around in a white jeep, carelessly crashing into stop signs and claiming, 'I like, totally paused.'

Atticus looks even more fab than me in our matching outfits. He is wearing pants that match my skirt perfectly, with the same black and yellow *Burberry* design. He has a black belt with three layered silver chains draped down his leg. He has a plan black button up dress shirt with long sleeves he's currently rolling up as if he means business.

He also has a couple of layered silver chains around his neck as well. (Including the one I bought for him.)

On his feet are his big, black combat boots with silver spikes on them and his hair is wild and in front of his face. But in a good way. As usual. He looks so handsome.

The day before we left for the trip, we went to *The Village Punk Shop* and picked up our outfits from yesterday and for today. I might actually shop there more often. There are some real good finds!

After we bought our stuff we went to lunch. It was fun. Not that I thought it wouldn't be, but I think when I'm around Atticus I enjoy myself more than I always expect to. Sometimes more than I want to.

We walk straight towards the crowded bar and Atticus orders his drink as I take a glass of champagne off of the waiter's tray he's walking passing around. As Atticus waits for his drink, I look down at the floor, twiddling with my fingers and biting my lip.

"Hey…" Atticus begins and I hear his soothing tone beside me. He taps his pointer finger against the bottom of my chin, playfully. "they'll love you. I bet we'll find someone to talk to." He offers a kind smile as the bartender hands him his drink.

We walk around, heading towards the sea of fashion entrepreneurs, business owners, and designers. The people I've always wanted to be amongst. Yet as it's happening, I'm having a hard time enjoying it.

"We'll be fine." Atticus assures.

"Easy for you to say." I look up at his tall figure. He's so confident without even trying. It's one of the many things I admire about him. I watch as he walks. He always holds his head up high and has this cute little bounce when he walks. Confidently clumsy is a good way to describe him at times. He's always just so... adorable! Yet he also has this extremely sexy and suave confidence.

"You're the one that wrote the article. This is all you. They're gonna wanna see you." He holds his hands up in mock surrender.

"They all seem to love you too." 'Who wouldn't' I want to add, but I don't. I suddenly gain the confidence to hook my arm through his. He doesn't budge, rather he looks down at me with a cute little smirk smile. I give a bright smile back, taking a sip of my champagne and beginning to calm down.

I see a woman holding a limited edition, clear silver *Birkin* bag between the crook of her arm. I'd know that bag anywhere, it's absolutely stunning. Mustering up the confidence, I slowly drag Atticus towards the woman who is talking to two other women and one other man, all of them professionally dressed.

"Excuse me..." I begin just as all four people turn to face me and Atticus. "I love your bag. That limited edition *Birkin* is so fab!" I say kindly. Atticus looks down at me, a proud smile on his face. I feel a hint of triumph.

"Well thank you." Says the woman who seems to be dressed head to toe in *Prada*.

She seems to do an obvious fashion once over on me and Atticus, looking us up and down skeptically. I didn't expect anything less. You get those once over's quite a lot in Manhattan, especially working in the fashion field.

Although, everytime someone does it to me I always feel this amance amount of pressure. I mean, I do it all the time to other people as well, but still. I don't judge, I actually just want to see who and what they're wearing. Like a runway show!

Her eyes land on both mine and Atticus's nametag and her face drops, a smile spreading across her lips.

"Miss. Paxton and Mr. Mckeen with *DuVull* magazine." She says taken aback as she puts her hand out for us to shake.

Oh my god! Whoever this lady is, she wants to shake our hand! Oh my god, it's happening!

I (maybe too enthusiastically) shake her hand and look at her nametag. It says her name is Tori and that... oh my god. She's the retail buyer for *Barneys New York!* How cool is that? I'm shaking hands with the retail buyer for *Barneys New York!* Ha!

I put my arm right back into the crook of Atticus's once I let go of the woman's hand.

"Oh my god," I begin. "what an honor. The new *Barney's* spring collection is such a stunner! I love *Barney's,* I shop there all the time…" I babble.

"Well I'm glad to hear it," Tori gives a nod. "and it's an honor to meet you two as well. What a fabulous article you've written, Miss. Paxton. Quite superb. I actually enjoyed reading it. And I don't usually buy into all that magazine shit, but you… you're different."

"Thank you." I say breathlessly. "It's honestly an honor to be here. He's my other creative half though." I giggle, motioning towards Atticus. I suddenly bite my tongue. 'Creative other half?' Real subtle Poppy…

"So I've heard." Tori gives Atticus another skeptical once over. "So tell me…" she leans in a bit closer to me. "should I go pop punk? Is it better?" she gives me a knowing smirk and wink.

I suddenly begin to choke on the champagne I was sipping on and finally manage to swallow it.

"I—I'm sorry, what?" My eyes widen as I give a scared chuckle. Oh. oh she better not mean…

I vastly shoot my head up towards Atticus. He's looking down at me with arched eyebrows and a lopsided grin. I give him an anxious and desperate glare at him as if to say. Did she really just say that!

"Aren't you two together?" She says without missing a beat, looking down at my arm intertwined with Atticus's.

I just keep on looking at her, wide eyed and a stressed smile on my face. Well apparently everyone thinks me and Atticus are together, now don't they!

I look up at Atticus once again desperately, hoping he'll get my signal for him to speak, cause quite frankly, I'm at a loss with this one.

I look back down at Tori with faux calmness and zen.

"Uhhhh… we…" I begin to stutter.

"Yeah," says Atticus interrupting me in a carefree manner. I snap my head back up to him and he furrows his eyebrows at me, giving a casual shrug. "Yep!" He looks down at Tori and snakes his hand around my waist, pulling me into his side. "This is my... this my Poppy."

"'Should I go pop punk? Is it better?'" Atticus mimics Tori from the conference and we both begin to laugh uncontrollably.

The conference was amazing, don't get me wrong! But now I know why Jane always complains about going to them. Some of the people there were...well... in a league of their own, let's just say that!

It was a chance of a lifetime, truly. I guess I expected something different. To be quite honest though, I don't even know what I was expecting. It was a good different though, a great different.

Everyone was really fond of me and Atticus, we were such a hit! After Atticus told Tori we were a 'couple,' she took us around and introduced us to practically everyone. It was like being a couple made us valid or something. Or maybe it just made the sea of workaholics there believe in love just a tad. Or 'love.'

"Here, give me your shoes." Says Atticus as we walk towards a bench on the edge of the boardwalk.

I look out towards the ocean, watching the waves ripple and crash against each other, creating a line of little bubbles.

There are a lot of people on the beach today, crowded with families, couples, and friends. Not a care in the world. Very Alantic City of them.

The beach is beautiful today, an apricot colored haze surrounding it. I can't help but stare. (And examine people's bathing suits.) I hope that guy with the oddly hairy back and ice cream cone doesn't think I'm staring at him...

Suddenly I hear a little rustle beside me and watch as Atticus hops over the small railing with ease and lands on the sand of the beach. He gives me his wild, contagious smile and holds his hand out.

"Come on, give me your shoes." He says suddenly becoming an impatient child, playfully jumping up and down. I rest my hands on the hot railing and lean in a bit, shaking my head and scrunching up my nose.

"Come on!" He practically begs.

"Fine." I huff, leaning on the railing in the hopes it will help me keep my balance as I unstrap my shoes. I give them to Atticus when they're fully off as my feet hit the boiling boardwalk.

"Just jump over it." Says Atticus as if it's no big feat. (Which I'm considering doing because my feet are going to fry off if I don't!)

"Atticus, I'm wearing a tight mini skirt..."

"So?"

"So!" I practically squeak. "You're lucky I can even walk in this skirt, let alone jump feet first over a railing in it."

Atticus purses his lips together and puts his hands on his hips. He looks away, seeming to have his thinking face on.

"Stand on the first step of the railing then sit on the second one. I'll help you with the rest." He turns back to me. I sigh and look around to make sure no one sees. Are we even allowed to do this?

I stand on the warm railing like he said to do so and watch as Atticus throws my shoes next to him onto the sand.

"Atticus!" I screech. "Those were expensive!"

"Oh shit, sorry!" He bends down, dusting off some of the sand on them and lining them up neatly next to each other.

He stands back up looking at me expectantly. I sit on the second railing and carefully swing my legs around to him and the beach.

Atticus firmly grips my waist to transport me on to the beach. His hands are strong and I could feel his cold rings through the thin fabric of my dress. Even though the gesture is just meant to help me onto the beach, I wonder if his hands rest on my hips for a little *too* long. But I surely don't mind. It makes butterflies erupt in the pit of my stomach.

Once I land on the beach, Atticus takes his hands off my waist and I can't help but feel quite empty when he does so.

He picks up my shoes, dusting them off once again and holding them by their straps. I straighten my skirt as my feet hit the scolding hot sand which is not much of a relief from the boardwalk or railing.

We walk and wander aimlessly around, the ocean bringing a cool breeze as the sun begins to get ready to set.

I usually hate the feeling of sand between my toes. Come to think of it, I'm not too fond of the beach as it is. Something about right now is changing my mind though. Right now, I don't hate the beach, nor the feeling of sand between my toes. I actually quite like it.

"So how do you think today went? Think it went well?" Atticus asks, squinting his eyes. The sun is no doubt shining right into them.

"I think it went well!" I nod. "Everyone seemed to like us. That's a start."

"Oh for sure. I'm positive you have this promotion in the bag."

"You think?" I give a blissful smile.

"Of course! Why else would Jane send you here? It couldn't be just about the article. She probably wants to see how you get on with all those people."

"I never thought of it like that." I suddenly start to think. Could I really have this promotion? Is this really why Jane sent me here?

"You know if you get this promotion, you'll probably be doing this more often." He points out.

"Yeah. I never quite thought about how many things might change if I do get this promotion." I trail off. "All good things. I just suppose…"

"With the high title comes high responsibility, and with high responsibility comes pressure."

"Exactly." He took the words right out of my mouth. "I want this more than anything, I do! I just… hate change."

"Well when you get this promotion—"

"If."

"*When* you get this promotion," he repeats. "It will all be good changes. Good adjustments."

"Yeah." I nod still a tad anxious at just the word change. "Atticus?" I begin as we pass a family on the beach. A mother holding her child close to her, a big umbrella above them. The father playing with the other two children in the sand.

"Hmmm?" He turns to me.

"Why did you tell everyone we were a couple at the conference?" I wanted to sound nonchalant, like I don't care. But I hear my voice crack a bit when I ask the question. A curious edge to my tone much to my dismay.

Atticus looks the other way, avoiding eye contact with me. I could see the little smirk growing on his face though.

"Marketing strategy." He says, still looking away from me.

"Ah, marketing strategy…" I repeat, a smile spreading across my face. "ok."

"Why? Would you be embarrassed if I was your boyfriend?" He looks down at me with a raised eyebrow and a crooked grin.

The neon orange sunset lands right on his face, causing a tangerine shadow to form from his now shining blonde hair to defined jawline.

His deep brown eyes have impossibly even more of a twinkle when the suns in them. The radiance that Atticus brings to people's lives is no comparison to the sun at all though.

"Of course not!" I chuckle. "I actually think whatever girl you end up with should consider herself lucky. She somehow managed to get one of the best guys out there." I say, my voice lowering quite a bit.

At the thought of Atticus being happy and in love with some girl brings this sudden intense pit to my stomach. It brings a strong surge of jealousy running through my veins.

I'll try my hardest to ignore it.

I watch as Atticus's cocky smirk fades at my words and a rather soft smile spreads across his face instead. He looks down and through the sun, could see a little blush on his cheeks.

"Atticus Mckeen?" I begin. "Are you blushing?" I tease.

"Maybe!" He looks up, reaching in front of me and beginning to walk backwards. "Come on, race ya to that umbrella!" He runs, sand kicking up behind him.

"You're on!" I giggle running after him, the wind ruining my hair. I don't quite mind it though.

CHAPTER THIRTY-SIX

The Boy with the Mac eyeliner

Once we get back into the hotel room, Atticus heads downstairs for the search of food.

I make a beeline straight for the hotel's gorgeous bathroom to take a much needed shower. The bathroom is so stunning with all its gold and white marble and elegant feel.

I stand in front of the sink and stare into the brightly lit mirror, starting to take off my makeup and waiting for the shower to get hot.

I feel strange taking a shower while Atticus is in the hotel room. Not for any particular reason just because it feels... strange. Not in a bad or uncomfortable way! It just feels out of place I guess. I don't know, it just feels weird, ok!

When I step into the shower I try to let the hot water relieve some of my stress. I'm under constant stress. One of the joys of being me. What am I even stressing about? I have no clue! Everything's great! Everyone loves Atticus and I's article, I'm in a *beautiful* hotel room. Why am I stressed out!

I rinse out my hair and get out not even twenty minutes later. I wrap one of the hotel's white towels around myself and wipe the fog off of the bathroom mirror above the sink. I take a deep breath as I stare at myself in the reflection. How'd I even get here?

Yes, I worked hard on the article. Yes, I worked *very* hard on the article. Is it really that good though? I'm proud of it. So is everyone else apparently. Why me though? Anyone else could have written that right? Or maybe I just look down upon myself too much? I don't know. Do we all do that? Is it normal to look down on ourselves that much?

These days I'm not sure of much. I'm in a hotel room with this punk guitarist I've known for seven months for God's sake! I mean, Atticus has grown to be a great friend and I really do care for him. I just don't know what the hell I'm doing and where I'm heading. Does this article mean bigger things for me, for us? What even are me and Atticus? Where am I heading in my job now that Jane is giving me this opportunity?

If there is one thing I don't like it's uncertainty and although I'm enjoying all this time, I'm not certain about it. What lies ahead? I hate not knowing. I thought I had everything mapped out, but now my plans for life are going in a completely different direction. Dare I say I like the direction it's going in.

I continue to look in the mirror and start to judge every tiny little crease in my face and question if I should in fact get botox. Can't hurt that much, can it? I'll ask Jane what she thinks. She gets it, like, every two months anyway.

I mean my creases aren't that bad under my eyes but why do I have them anyway! Is it normal? I'm 24! Whatever.

I take the tweezer sitting on the sink and start to pluck my eyebrows. They're not the most bushy and full but they're also not that squirmy. They are a little sparse though so whenever I see a stray hair I immediately pluck it.

All the sudden I hear a weird knocking noise outside of the hotel room and instantly tense up. It can't be. Atticus *can't* be back already. Well, he probably can, but still!

I'd like to think I'm a bit of a modest person. I mean, I have boundaries. I can't answer the door like this! I would if it was anybody else I knew, but this is Atticus we're talking about.

I also can't leave Atticus out there though. Does he have his card? Well, If he had his card he wouldn't knock! Goddamnit!

I pace around the bathroom for a couple of seconds and then finally tighten the knot holding the towel around me together. I check in the mirror to make sure the towel is covering all the parts it needs to be, then I rip the bathroom door open.

Ok, I'll just peak through to make sure it's Atticus, then run back into the bathroom. Perfect! He won't even realize.

I grab my phone and unlock the door and peek out to realize no one is in front of the door. I sigh then peek out to both sides.

"I swear Atticus…" I make sure no one is in the hallway and walk out to look on both sides of the elegant looking walkways.

I don't see Attiicus and I groan in frustration. It must have been the room next door. Damn it!

Before I can even turn around and head back into the room, I hear the door slam shut. I sigh and twist the knob to open the door when it doesn't open. *Shit!* My card is in the damn hotel room and I need it to open the door. How can I be so *Stupid!*

I drop my phone onto the hotel carpet and desperately try to open the door as if it might miraculously open. You never know!

When It doesn't open I keep my hand on the gold handle and start to kick the door. I don't even know why!

When I'm not successful in my little fit, I hold onto my white towel (The only thing currently on me) and sink down onto the floor in front of the door. I can't believe this is happening right now. I can't believe that I let this happen. I slam my head with my now stringy, long wet hair on to the door. I helplessly look around the hallway from my spot on the floor and pray no one comes over here.

I look down at my phone. I could call Atticus! Yes, yes perfect! Oh thank god I took it out with me. I quickly go to Atticus's contect number and plan to tell him the embarrassing event occurring.

Me and Atticus are close friends though! He's no different then Riley or Arlo right? Well he kind of is. He's straight, and extremely attractive (not that Arlo and Riley aren't), and flirty, and I'm staying at a hotel with him.

You know what, I take that back. He is very different from Riley and Arlo. Especially from the point where I am attracted to him. (Don't mind that though!)

But what's worse, getting caught by a stranger or calling Atticus in order to prevent that? I'm just gonna call him! I click call and after, I'm put on voicemail. Are you kidding me! The one time he doesn't answer his phone!

I look through my contacts when I see the perfect two people that will both get a rise out of me, and help me with this situation. The only two people that before Atticus, I would know to call in a situation like this.

"Come on, pick up, pick up..."

"Hello?" I hear a forever annoyed voice ask over the phone.

"Riley, It's Poppy!"

"I know who it is, Pops." It's around 4:30 and Jeannie and Riley usually leave by six or seven today. Riley has to stay with Jane and Jeannie usually stays with him, finishing up the last of her article. So, this is absolutely perfect!

"Riley I need your help," I say desperately. "Is Jeannie by you? Are you by anyone else? Can you put me on speaker?"

"Woah, slow your roll. It's just me and Jeannie at her desk. I'm putting you on speaker..." He pauses for a minute.

"Hey, Pops." I hear Jeannie.

"Ok, you're on speaker. What's the matter now?" Riley sighs.

"Listen to me," I say in the most quiet yet urgent tone I can. "I am locked outside of the hotel room and Atticus is not here yet. He went to get food."

"Really? That's what you called for?" Riley huffs.

"It's ok, Pops." Jeannie laughs. "Go on your phone for a while, chill in the hallway. If it's really bothering you—"

"No, I'm in the hallway in nothing but a towel! Like, I just took a shower and I am in *nothing* but the towel wrapped around me!"

"How the hell did that happen?" Riley asks, his voice raising to a squeak.

"Just don't ask. Don't. Ask."

"Ok," begins Jeannie's voice of reason. "call Atticus now."

"I did!" I cry in a whisper. "The one time he doesn't answer!" I hear Riley giggling in the background. "It's not funny, Riley!" I retort.

"It kinda is."

"Ok, just breath..." starts Jeannie. "and pray no one sees you." I hear her murmur and I give a helpless cry.

"If it's any consolation, at least you're good looking. You're pretty. I mean, you're not in bad shape. You're curvy, you're kind. Anyone would be lucky to run into you in only a towel." States Riley.

"That really doesn't help." I shake my head.

"Riley, all those things just give a person more of a reason to kidnap her. Why would you say that?" Exclaims Jeannie.

"Uh, reassurance. You could be kidnaped but still pretty."

"The both of you are horrible at this." I sigh.

"Uh... ok! I got it! Is there a curtain anywhere?" Riley asks.

"Yeah, there's a window with a curtain a few steps away from me."

"Take it down and wrap the rest of your body in it."

"Are you stupid?" Jeannie questions him.

"It's a solution, Jeannie!" He retorts. "At this point we're desperate!" And then suddenly I hear footsteps.

"Guys, I hear someone!" I whisper.

"Ok, on second thought, maybe the curtain isn't so bad. Hide behind the curtain!" Jeannie whisper screams.

I do just that. I quickly get up off the floor and bolt towards the silk curtain by the window. I jump past the window and right behind the curtain praying no one notices I'm behind it.

"Are you behind the curtain?" Riley asks.

"Yes." I answer as quietly as I possibly can.

"So I'm not stupid afterall..."

"Shhhhhh!" Jeannie shushes him as if they are here with me. The footsteps get closer and closer and I stay as still as I possibly can, darkness covering my face and my back against the wall, Jeannie and Riley dead silent on the other end.

"What's going on?" Asks Riley suddenly.

"Riley, Shhh!" I whisper shout.

I hear the footsteps get impossibly closer towards me and my curtain. Whatever higher being is up there, God, Budda, whatever... Please, *Please* let this person not look behind this curtain. They will be unpleasantly surprised. So, do it for their sake!

The part of the curtain by my head is pulled away. I give a terrified shriek when I hear a comforting familiar voice.

"Pops?" I see Atticus now standing in front of me, the silk curtain separating us.

"Atticus?" I ask stupidly. As his name comes out of my mouth I hear short little murmurs from Jeannie and Riley as they hang up the phone. If I wasn't so petrified, I would laugh.

"What are you doing?" He gives an amused smile as he tries to pull the curtain away. I just yank it closer to me. He looks at me with confusion.

"What are you--"

"Atticus, listen to me," I begin eagerly leaning closer to him. Here goes nothing. "I'm currently not in any clothes." Ok, that came out a little wrong. Atticus's eyes widen as He goes to open his mouth to say something but I quickly interrupt him.

"I'm in a towel though!" I assure him. "I am locked outside of the hotel room. Do you have your card?" I question with bated breath.

"Of course I have my card! How did this happen..."

"Great! Then how are we going to do this?" I interrupt his question not feeling like going over the embarrassing ordeal.

"Uhhh... let's see," begins Atticus. "I'm going to show the scanner thingy on the door my card, it's going to scan my card, and we're going to walk into our hotel." He says sarcastically and gives his cute little closed mouth smile. Urgh. I hate that cocky, annoying side of him. (No matter how attractive it may be.)

"Ok fine. Can you at least close your eyes though?"

"How am I going to be able to open the door with my eyes closed?"

"Just find a way!" I shout.

"Ok," begins Atticus turning around. "I'm not facing you and I'm walking towards the door." He puts the card in the scanner and I hear the clicking sound of the door opening. It is absolute music to my ears.

"Now my eyes are closed," he says agitated. "run into the apartment before I open them." With a roll of my eyes I do just that.

"You're good." I say as I enter the safety of the bathroom.

I hear the door to the hotel close and the shifting of Atticus's feet. I lean against the bathroom door, slipping down it until I reach a sitting position. I just cling my knees to my chest. Well, that was something.

I lay on the comfortable hotel bed with my head and eyes towards the ceiling counting the cracks. There's, like, one. One itty bitty one. Of course there's hardly any cracks in this ceiling, why would I even try counting them. Unlike my ceiling back home which has 22. And that's just in the bedroom.

My hair has dried and I've straightened it to filth. I've become a master at straightening over the years. If you want to know the truth, my hair is actually naturally wavy. My natural curls are pretty, it has its place... in the morning as bedhead.

I straighten my hair every two days and curl it when I want to. When it's straight and I curl it, I can place the curls where I want to. Where I can control them.

You know what's funny? I just started really straightening my hair when Liam left. I started putting on more makeup too. I think in some warped way Liam leaving taught me to take care of myself more. Hmmmm. How about that!

It's not completely dark in the room, not at all. All the lights are still on but it's about 8:30 and the nightlife of AC is shining through the big hotel window in bright neon colors.

I give a deep sigh and tap my finger against the blanket. What are we doing? Atticus is on the floor by the end of the bed with his pillow and blanket. We're just laying here in silence.

After the whole fiasco happened I realized Atticus managed to bring home *Wendy's*.

We sat down on the bed and had dinner and after that Atticus went into the shower. I just sat on the bed awkwardly while he was in there, not knowing what to do with myself. So I turned on the TV. Nothing good was on. So now we're here.

"Hey," I hear a whisper from Atticus over the bed. It's so funny because I can't see him over the bed but I can hear his voice. I try to hold in my giggle. "are you awake?" He asks.

"Of course I'm awake." I snort. "Why? You sound like that one really annoying kid at a sleepover who thinks that falling asleep last will win him some kind of prize." Atticus starts to laugh. "Like you know, the one that gets straight A's and still insists on putting in his retainer."

"That couldn't be farther from what I was." Atticus chuckles.

"I could only imagine…" I nod. "I'd actually be quite scared of Atticus the teenager." I give a playful shudder.

"I'm the same." He laughs. "the only thing that's changed is that I have to pay bills and I don't wear my piercings all at the same time."

"Really?"

"Yeah! I mean, I was a really hard worker. I had to be. I didn't do great in school though. I was a good kid. I just hated it. I'm not good with order. I'm all over the place! You know that though. No adult really understood that but Mr. Davis at the record shop. I don't know where I would be if it wasn't for him. I'd literally probably be dead right now." That response both scares and intrigues me, but before I can ask him what he means, he continues. "What kind of kid were you?"

"The kid that didn't understand kids like you." I chuckle. "I was a nerd. Always in my sister's shadow. I worked extremely hard. I actually really enjoyed school."

"Ya see, I got my homework from kids like you." He quips and I just shake my head.

"Were you popular?" I ask.

"Hell no. Were you?"

"*Hell* no!" And then I think for a moment. "You know, I feel I know so much about you yet nothing. I don't know..." I shrug. "like I'm here with you but I'm still lacking tiny little details good friends should know about each other." Then I backtrack. "You know what, that was stupid. I'm sorry."

"Hmmmmm." I hear Atticus mumble. "I got my first guitar when I was 12. My dad bought it for me. That's where the obsession for music started. Not long after that I taught myself the piano. I tried DJing..." he begins to laugh. "gave that up real fast. I found that I was much better with my instruments and voice. Performing live basically. I was told my whole life I had 'stage presence.' Whatever that means." He thinks for a moment but then continues to ramble on. "I started to sing in my Freshman year of highschool. I figured I might as well. I found there was nothing more I loved in the world than writing songs. Although it emotionally takes the life out of me. I grew up with bands like *Kiss* and *Aerosmith*. Bands my dad liked. As I got older though I started to develop my own taste. I got my paycheck from the record shop and I went straight to the mall and into *Mac*. I remember buying a jet black, cole eyeliner..." the both of us burst out into a fit of giggles. "I wore that damn eyeliner every single day of highschool. I'm wearing eyeliner in literally every single one of my yearbook pictures."

"Do you still wear it?" I ask, twiddling my fingers.

"When I'm performing, yeah." Atticus begins. "My dad was so happy. He was a rocker in his day. Had a band and everything. He says he gave it up for my mom though. She didn't like him touring and leaving her all the time... ironic, right." He chuckles but it slightly breaks my heart for him. "My dad drank though. So when he was good he was great, when he was bad he was horrible. Not gonna bore you with those details."

"I'm sorry." I say below a whisper. It brings anger and an ample amount of emotion over me everytime I hear Atty talk about his dad.

"It's ok, Pop's. Nothing you could do." He begins again. "I struggled with addiction. I smoked and drank a lot. I still smoke, so I can't say '*struggled.*' I still struggle. It's all fun and games until it catches up to you though. I rather smoke a cig then smoke that stupid vape shit. I also had a multitude of substance issues with other drugs. I would love to say it was thanks to the assholes I used to hang out with in highschool but at the end of the day, I did it to myself."

There's a silence around the room. I knew Atticus smoked but I didn't know he had all those other issues. It brings tears to my eyes at even the thought of Atticus struggling with substance addiction. I quickly wipe them away and hold in my sniffles. I don't want him to think he upset me or anything. I did tell him to talk to me afterall.

"Is that what you meant before?" I ask. "When you said if it wasn't for Mr. Davis you would probably be dead by now?"

"Yeah." Atticus rasps out. "And Finnick. All four years of highschool me and Finnick were friendly. He helped me with my work in math and I attempted to help him flirt with a couple of girls. He never really got them though." He gives a deep sigh. "One day in early senior year I stopped by Finnick's house to get my homework. I had never been to Finnick's house before. At the time I was just using him, really." You could hear the pain in Atticus's voice when he says that. "I was... let's say under the influence when I walked to Finnick's house. We lived relatively close. I reached Finn's house and went straight to his room. I don't remember much. I remember being out of it. I was more ditzy than I usually am. The world looked a little too fuzzy for my liking and so did Finnick. I remember him asking me if I was ok and looked at me strangely when I told him no. Before he could answer him back I blacked out on his bedroom floor. I was out before my head even hit his rug. I woke up at the hospital to find out I overdosed. My dad wasn't sitting next to my hospital bed, it was Finnick and Mr. Davis. As typical as it sounds, that was my wake up call. After that, I stopped hanging out with the group I was hanging out with. I spent the rest of my year struggling to make sure I graduated. If it wasn't for Finnick, I wouldn't have passed. He tutored me and I got him a job at the record shop. I kind of insisted I teach him how to play drums because he took quite an interest in it. I knew I finally found my best friend. It's so funny because he was always there, and I just didn't take notice. I wish I did sooner. As horrible as that sounds."

Now I'm really crying. I'm biting down on my lip so Atticus doesn't hear. I'm borderline bawling as silently as I can. How do I even respond to that?

"Onto other random things. Hopefully more positive..." Atticus gives a stressed laugh. "I hate holding grudges. It makes me feel guilty. I don't know why. I love Italian food. My dad used to take me to *Warped Tour* every year and I have really happy memories when it comes to that. I love to read even though it doesn't hold my attention for too long. I told you I hate holding grudges but to this day it still makes my blood boil that Dallon called you a priss..." He passes by it so fast, like I wouldn't think twice about it but I do.

He holds a grudge against Dallon for hurting my feelings? For calling me the hurtful words Liam once called me? Atticus holds a grudge on his close friend for *me?* My heart drops to my stomach at the thought.

"And since I could remember, my dream was to have the *Loui Vutton* guitar that Pete Wentz had in *Fall Out Boys* 'This Ain't A Scene, It's An Arms Race' music video." My head pops up at the words *Loui Vutton*.

"Atticus," I begin seriously. "I must see this guitar." All I see is his head pop up at the end of the bed and I'm thrown into a fit of giggles. A little floating Atticus head. He has that stupid, smirk on his face.

"May I join you?" He motions to the bed.

"If you must." I joke as he gets up and jumps on the bed next to me, practically lifting me off the bed. I yelp as I almost go flying off. I make sure to wipe my eyes so he doesn't know I was crying before.

I needed to change the subject fast, I didn't want Atticus to dwell on his past for too long. I want him to enjoy his time here. His time with me. I don't want him to think I was prying about his childhood or his personal life because I surely wasn't. I just wanted to know some more things about him. Things friends should know about each other. But I'm glad he told me those things actually.

Am I a bad person for saying Atticus's past with drugs doesn't shock me. Yes. No?

I fight with myself for a moment. I assumed he was a troubled teen. Is that bad as well? I'll forget about it for now. For the sake of my sanity but the question in my head still stands, If Atticus was such a troubled person at one point in his life... could people ever really change?

CHAPTER THIRTY-SEVEN
Back To Brooklyn

I laugh with Atticus as we get out of his car. As we walk up to the apartment building, I take a deep breath and let the fresh air of Brooklyn that I have missed so much engulf me whole.

I hear the rolling of my luggage and the clanking of my heels against the concrete. Atticus also has one of my bags in his hands as well as his own. If you don't remember we packed... pretty heavily, let's just say that.

The kids from the apartment are outside playing basketball as usual. I even missed them. They all stop and stare at me and Atticus. The little ones just stare at us in shock and awe and the ones a bit older than them start to cheer.

"Get it, Atticus!" One kid says.

I just roll my eyes and snort as Atticus cocks up an eyebrow at the boys and tries to give them a stern look but he can't stop from snickering.

He opens the apartment door for me and for once I don't have to wipe the residue of the dirty, taped up handle on my expensive jacket. (This ones a pink spring coat from *Barney's*. 50 percent off!)

I kindly say thank you and he nods as we walk into the stuffy, smoke smelling apartment building. It's home though. Is it bad that I love it?

He clicks on the button on the elevator and the red light appears meaning it's coming down. He turns to me with an electric smile on his face that ignites something deep within me. I give him one back.

"I had fun." He says as the steel elevator door creaks open the fastest it's ever been. Ironic, huh. The day you wish the elevator was broken.

"I did too." I step in the elevator, Atticus in tow. A couple of seconds of silence pass when Atticus swiftly wraps his left arm around me, embracing me into his side.

"Come here!" He rasps and I giggle as he buries his head in my hair.

"I enjoyed being your fake girlfriend." I rest the side of my face on his denim jacket. It's quite uncomfortable against my rosy cheeks and irritable skin but I don't mind it. I like being in his embrace. I'll take the uncomfortableness any day.

I don't know why I'm being so mushy, we literally live across the way from each other. Nothing is ending. Why is Atticus being so mushy?

"Atticus?"

"Yes?" I don't why I just said his name. I guess I just lost my train of thought.

"Never mind."

"What? You can't do that to me. You say it yourself, you hate it when people do that to you." He smiles down at me shaking his head, his hair swaying about with it. I rack my brain for something to say.

"I… I just really like your denim jacket." I smile up at him and then look in the mirror of the elevator that I hardly ever notice is there. (Shocking, I know.)

We look like a couple. A real couple. A happy couple.

"Oh, thanks." He laughs, his eyes squinting and his dimples popping out.

"Yep." I nod, turning my eyes away from him.

He gently grabs a string of my blonde hair and begins to twirl it on his finger. I just smile and repay the cute gesture by putting my hand on top of his completely lost in the beauty that is him. That is Atticus.

Everything he does just seems to hold a meaning, it just seems to capture the beauty of an old renaissance painting. Instead of a portrait of angels flying around fluffy clouds and an orange sky it's Atticus in his black ensemble holding that neon green guitar and looking as ethereal as ever.

I have a sudden fleeting fear that I don't want this moment to end. That I'd do anything just to stay in here with Atticus for just one more second because that second could be fatal, that second could change fate.

I don't think I would have any issue whatsoever if this elevator got stuck right now. I would actually be overjoyed.

When the elevator door opens real life seems to set in though. It seems to hit me like a ton of bricks. Atticus has no issue walking out of the elevator. Maybe that's because he already lives in a dream.

I slowly follow after him and turn around to watch the elevator door close and head back down to the first floor to bring someone else up to reality.

You know, it's funny. I tend to think about this a lot lately. Atticus walked into my life like he was always there.

Here I was, just trying to get through this all too ordinary world and then in comes Atticus Mckeen with his piercings, guitar, and magnetic personality. No matter how hard I try, I can't shake him. I don't think I want to.

As we reach my decorated door I'm finding that I don't want this to end. *This.* I just don't know what *this* is.

I fiddle with one of the strings of decorated orange and pink beads that hang from my door in between my fingers. I look into his eyes and squint mine to see if I could get the exact color, to see if I could get that shade of brown just right to describe to you.

"I don't want to go inside." I find the words slipping off my tongue.

"Why?" Atticus squints playing with the string of beads as well. He's wrapping himself in them, almost getting stuck and I giggle as he untangles himself.

"I dunno..." I shrug. "I'm just not ready. I had fun this weekend, and I feel like when I walk back into that apartment..." I click my tongue. "reality will set back in."

"Reality is good sometimes. You taught me that." Atticus smiles but my heart breaks. Out of all the things he's taught me, that's what he got out of me? That a healthy dose of reality is good sometimes. God why am I like that! So I crushed his spirit. Great.

"Reality is great," I nod. "but sometimes you have to let loose. Look at the world through a different lens. You taught me that."

"You already looked at the world through a different lens, Poppy." Atticus chuckles. He looks deep in thought and solem for a moment, gazing at me until he shakes himself out of it. "I mean... If you don't want to go back into your apartment you could always stay at mine. What's the big deal? You literally live across from me. Grab some clothes and I'll sleep on the couch."

I find myself actually pondering over the offer. I'm scared of what will happen if I do so though. That I may make a move. You might ask 'what's so bad about that, Poppy?' Well I'll tell you! Does Atticus even like me like that? Is he just being a friend? A really nice friend.

I bet he doesn't like me like that. Also, the whole order of my life will be turned upside down by the punk boy I fell for. It already is but imagine if something was actually to happen. No, no it could never.

"I think I might take you up on that offer." I say. What the hell, Poppy! Stop chasing a dream!

"Ok." He smiles brightly and his dimples light up my world. "Ok! Well get a pair of clothes and we'll order pizza--"

And like clock work, my phone dings. I squint my eyes and take it out of my purse. I open my phone and the breath is knocked out of me. My heart absolutely plummets to my stomach and heat runs to my cheeks.

LIAM: HEY PATRICIA. I DIDN'T KNOW IF YOU HAD MY NUMBER ANYMORE (I COMPLETELY GET IF YOU DON'T) I DON'T EVEN KNOW WHAT TO SAY. I WAS THINKING ABOUT YOU, AND I KNOW IT'S BEEN A WHILE. I THINK WE NEED TO TALK. PLEASE GET BACK TO ME WHEN YOU CAN. I LOVE YOU. I'VE ALWAYS LOVED YOU. -LIAM

The text suddenly blurs just as a puddle sized tear splashes onto my phone. It drops right on to Liams name, practically magnifying it.

"Poppy?" Begins Atticus, worry evident in his voice.

I look up at him but he gets all jumbled by tears until a blink and they all stream down my cheeks at the same time. "Pops, what the hell happened?" Atticus stammers, eyes wide in fear. I've actually never quite seen Atticus look this worried. He actually looks panicked.

I want to desperately gather my words to tell him what's the matter, but I can't. I hear my quiet sobs, as hot tears keep streaming from my cheeks, down to my jawline and to my neck.

"Hey, hey, hey..." Atticus puts both his huge hands on each of my cheeks, the cold sting of his silver rings bringing relief to my hot skin. Atticus seems to be searching for something in my eyes, as if it will give him any hint of what's the matter.

He takes his hands away from my cheeks and quickly opens his door. I try to hold back my tears as he motions for me to walk into his apartment. He takes all my luggage and his, dropping it by the couch motions me too.

I sit on the couch, that when I first met him, he was helplessly trying to get into the apartment door.

The fond memory almost brings a smile to my face, but not quite.

"This mascara is too expensive to ruin." I say in a squeaky sob as I rub my hand across my eye, a black smudge running straight across my hand.

The couch dips as Atticus sits beside me, handing me a box of tissues.

"Thanks." I sniffle taking one. I look up to Atticus, finally being able to see him clear. He looks on edge, concerned, and I want to convince him not to be, but my mouth just doesn't open. I don't want him to worry about me. How could I be so selfish!

"Poppy, please tell me what's the matter... Is it something I said..." I just hand him my phone as he looks at me in confusion.

He carefully takes the phone out of my hand as he reads the text.

After, he hands my phone back to me and just shrugs, looking down. But when he looks back up at me and deeper into my eyes, I could tell something changes in his expression.

It's not soft anymore. It's just cold.

"What's the matter? It's just a text." He says, shaking his head. Just a text?

Well when he says that, it does indeed simplify it. It's not just a text though. It screws up everything.

"A text that completely messes up and changes everything." I say. At this point, I thought I wasn't going to hear from Liam ever again. I'm not sure I wanted to.

"It doesn't have to." Atticus says, his voice even deeper than usual.

"What do you mean?"

"Why do you even have to text him back? Why can't you just ignore him. Do you even want to talk to him?" Atticus voices, seeming as confused as I am. He's squinting his eyes, almost looking frustrated.

"I mean, I don't..." I think for a moment. "what do you think I should do?" I manage to ask.

There is silence for a moment but then he takes a deep breath and speaks.

"I couldn't tell you." He shakes his head. "You have to do what's good for you. What do you feel?" He's looking at me, almost desprestly. Why is he looking at me like that?

"I don't know. I thought I was over him." I fiddle with the hem at the end of my jacket.

"I thought so too." Atticus purses his lips together and nods, as he avoids eye contact with me and slouches over the couch.

I feel another tear fall down my cheek at his disappointed tone. Why is he so confusing! Why is he disappointed? Guys are shit, honestly. It's all a scam. I want my money back.

He doesn't even have a right to be upset! Liam doesn't have a right to want to talk to me either. It's all fun and games until they can't play with your feelings anymore.

Is that what Atticus is doing though?

"I should go." I say below a whisper, my voice raspy from the silent tears and cries.

"Yeah." Atticus says just as quietly. He just sits there on the couch as I grab my luggage and open his door. He doesn't even face me nor move. So I just leave, closing his door behind me.

Immediately as I get out of the apartment, I'm faced with mine. How did things go so sour so fast? I feel anger, confusion and sadness boil through my veins. I want to smash my phone against my door and watch the notification for Liam's text smash with it. I keep my cool though. God knows my insurance doesn't cover 'guy problems.'

So I just bang my head against my steel apartment door, the colorful hanging beading I hung on it is no doubt making an indent on my far-head. Lovely.

CHAPTER THIRTY-EIGHT

April

Promotions and Stolen Kisses

"*That's ugly, that's horrendous, I* hate it. That makes me want to throw up in the Sheepshead Bay *Target* bathroom like you did." Riley says to me, typing on his laptop and looking up directions to Jane's new yoga class.

"I mean, I agree, but that's a little dramatic." Jeannie shrugs, looking into a topic she might do for the April issue. For once not keeping it last minute.

"We had a great time up until... you know."

"Yeah, up until your ugly ass ex texted you and screwed everything up."

"As he does best." Jeannie agrees.

"Listen," I look up from my computer. "It's been two weeks since me and Atticus came back from the conference. I thought we already discussed this whole fiasco."

"We've known Jeannie for five years, we still need to talk to her about her weird fashion sense."

"Hey!" Jeannie quips.

"Point is," Riley rolls his eyes. "you're acting a fool."

"What do you mean!"

"Liam texted me... whoa is me! I don't know what to do!'" Riley fake cries and pretends to pass out, impersonating me. (A horrible impersonation, really.)

"I haven't even texted him back yet." I huff.

"Good to see you're showing restraint." Riley states sarcastically.

"Well I'm confused, are you really going to text him back?" Jeannie asks.

"I don't know!"

"Poppy..." she sighs, tearing her eyes away from her computer and leaning back into her chair. "are you serious?"

"Well what am I going to do! I was with the guy for almost nine years. This wasn't some fling, Jeannie. I thought we were going to get married. You know that. I could text him back when he says he misses me."

"That's a shit reason." Jeannie argues. "The words 'I miss you' uttered by any jerky ex like Liam are secretly code for 'let's hook up' or 'I kind of miss someone constantly taking my crap, so let's give it a go again!' I don't think he deserves anything from you. Do you remember how he treated you? How he talked to you? You want to go back to that?"

"I never said I wanted to go back to him, I said I wanted to see what he has to say." I nod, matter of factly.

"Not all closure is good closure." Jeannie points out. It makes me think. She does have a point. "The only reason this text and Liam are pulling you back in is because the relationship is unfinished. Everyone loves an unfinished relationship. It makes the situation ten times more steamy because we want what we can't have. And what you don't have is closure."

I think about what Jeannie's said for a moment. No wonder why she works for the love department! She's absolutely right! I don't miss Liam, I miss the ideology of the unfinished relationship and what it *could* have been.

"I don't know..." Riley clicks his tongue. "what does your horoscope say about it?" He teases and I scowl, blocking my computer from him.

"It says Riley's a pain in the ass."

"Oddly specific."

"Not to mention, you haven't talked to Atticus." Riley gives me a knowing glare. And he's right. I haven't talked to Atticus since we got home from the conference and Liam texted me. I can't exactly pinpoint my feelings for Atty. He's grown to be one of the closest friends but there is something else to him. Something *more*.

God, I can't even explain it correctly. You know what I mean though, right? I know it sounds silly and adolescent but it's true.

Maybe it's a coincidence on Atticus's end. I haven't seen him around the apartment building. Maybe he's just busy. I miss him. Maybe I'll text him today. Just to hear from him.

"I don't know." Jeannie shakes her head. "At the end of the day, you have to do what makes you happy."

"Yeah." I just bite my lip.

Suddenly my phone dings beside me and I feel this nervous pit grow in my stomach. What if it's Liam again? Maybe it's Atticus.

I look up to see Riley and Jeannie wide eyed and on the edge of their seats as well.

I take a deep sigh of relief when I see Jane's name instead. I feel this intense disappointment that it's not Atticus though.

"It's Jane." I say and hear Riley and Jeannie both give a collective sigh of relief.

MS. DUVULL- 'POPPY, I NEED TO TALK TO YOU. IT'S EXTREMELY IMPORTANT. COME TO MY OFFICE NOW.'

I look back up again, panicked. Am I in trouble? Did I say or do something wrong at the conference? This doesn't sound good...

I hold up the phone to Jeannie and Riley. They squint their eyes and read it. Jeannie looks just as panicked as I do but Riley just shakes his head.

"Watch her scold you for the barista getting her order wrong this morning or something." He sneers.

"I hope that's all it is." I rasp out. Could this week get any worse! Like, honestly.

"You'll be fine..." Jeannie rapidly nods her head. "I bet it's something silly as always."

"She never sends texts though."

"She's lazy."

"True." I give out a shaky breath and get out of my seat.

Jeannie and Riley both give me a supportive thumbs up but I can't seem to give them one back, suddenly paralyzed by fear.

I walk towards the clear glass doors of Jane's office as I judge my reflection through it. I look as scared as I feel.

Come to think of it, Jeannie was right. I do look quite haggard. I didn't put on any makeup besides mascara and lip gloss, and I couldn't bring myself to dress fab this morning either. (I know, shocker for me.)

I'm in some slightly ripped, blue jeans and a light pink bodysuit tucked into them. The bodysuit has long sleeves but the fabric is pretty thin, so it's comfy and airy. Yet still quite nice. It has a pretty deep neckline as well. With it I paired some white heels I found in my closet. They're probably *Alexander McQueen*.

I didn't even put my contacts in today so I have my big, round, clear glasses sitting on my nose.

I look ok. Presentable just... not fully myself. At least my hair looks nice, in it's long wavy locks down my back.

I pry my eyes away from my failed appearance and take a deep breath, knocking on Jane's door as I open it.

"Ms. DuVull? You wanted to see me."

"Yeah. Come in." Jane says shortly. I walk in carefully, closing the door behind me. "Sit down." She orders and I do just that.

I sit on one of her huge, white leather chairs across her desk. I'm practically on the edge of it. She takes her eyes away from her paperwork on her desk and lifts up her glasses.

She looks over me and squints her eyes.

"You're not dressed like yourself." She points out.

"I don't feel like myself."

"And that's because?"

"It's nothing." I shake my head. "Tired. But I'm fine! What do you need?"

"Well..." Jane sighs, reaching below her desk and dropping her black, leather *Prada* purse on top of it. (Not to mention her desk is already a mess and we took three hours organizing it last week.)

She begins to dig through her bag when she finally pulls out an envelope.

"Here." She hands the envelope to me. It's probably the most classy and the most expensive looking envelope I've ever seen. It's black with smooth gold spirals all over.

I grasp it in between my hands and look up at Jane, who starts working through her paperwork once again.

"What is this?" I give a slight nervous chuckle.

"Don't make a big deal out of it." Jane begins in a tone I can't quite read. "I'm not great with words. As you know. So, hence the card. Open it if you want, wait till you get home, I don't care."

"Can I open it now?" I can't mask the curious undertone to my voice.

"Sure." Says Jane, still not looking up at me.

I trace one of the gold spirals on the envelope as I carefully open it and take out a card. The card looks even more expensive than the envelope. It's all black with gold spirals matching the envelope it was encased in. In the middle of the card it reads 'congratulations' in white cursive.

I look up at Jane squinting my eyes. What's going on?

She's just knowingly smirking as she continues on her work. I open the card to see Jane's immaculately neat cursive handwriting that I seem to know so well.

> *Dearest Poppyseed,*
>
> *I haven't been good with words for quite some time now. (Or at least words involving any type of emotion and not a business deal.) You, my dear, have the unfortunate advantage of knowing more about me than my ex husband ever had. (And we were together for four years. Urgh.)*

I didn't know Jane was married…

> *Anyway, that was years ago. What I'm trying to say is that you know me better than anyone. And that's some feat, let me tell you. You are truly the best assistant anyone could ever ask for. I knew I had to give you the job of a fashion journalist though. You had too much talent to just be making up my schedules and buying my iced coffees. Yet, you still do that because I can't seem to let you go. I'm slowly realizing that I need to though. Therefore, I'm firing you as my assistant.*

I look at Jane, shock probably evident in my eyes. She's firing me as her assistant? In one way I'm relieved, on the other hand I'm actually quite sad. Did she even find someone else yet?

"Ms. DuVull..."

"Keep reading it, will you?" She instructs, motioning to the card.

> *I finally understand that being both a journalist and my*
> *assistant could be quite taxing. I was selfish. (What else*
> *is new?) So upon much deliberation, I decided to fire you*
> *as a journalist as well.*

And like that, my heart drops to my heels and the world stops. What? Wait... no, no, no, this can't be happening... what did I do! She can't do this! She can't do this to me! I thought we were close, I thought we had a relationship. I thought she cared for me. This job is my world!

I look up at Jane, tears pouring out of my eyes. What did I do? She can't do this to me...

"Jane, don't do this... you know this job is my world! What did I do..."

"No, no, read the rest! Stop pausing!" Jane whales.

My eyes are now glassy and I could barely read, a huge tear drop falls onto the card and smudges the black pen Jane wrote in. I keep reading as panic continues to arise in me.

> *Did I give you a fright? Good. Fears good sometimes.*
> *You should be on your toes at all times anyway. Besides,*
> *I have to fire you as a journalist if you're going to be*
> *fashion editor. What's that called again...ah, that's*
> *right. A promotion. Can't think of anyone who deserves*
> *it more,*
>
> *With love my dearest Poppyseed,*
> *JD*

I look up at Jane once again, even more tears streaming down my face now. I'm stuck to the chair, I'm frozen. I got it. I really did. I got the promotion! I'm going to be fashion editor for *DuVull and Co*! Ha!

I could feel my mascara burning my eyes but I don't care. I try to gather myself together enough to even speak, say anything.

Jane is just looking at me, a proud smile tugging at the corners of her lips. I drop the card, shooting up out of my seat and towards Jane. I practically attacked her in a bear hug.

"You better not get tears on my *Gucci* blazer." She says in a joking tone, embracing me just as tight. I've never gotten a hug from Jane. She gives amazing hugs. "You've done good, Poppyseed."

"Thank you, Ms. DuVull." I sob. I can't believe it. This is crazy. Me, Poppy Paxton, is going to be fashion editor of *DuVull* magazine. I feel as if I'm dreaming.

I run out of the apartment elevator in a frenzy holding two *Dunkin* iced coffees in my hands. I feel as if I'm walking on air as I rush straight towards Atticus's apartment. I've had this huge smile plastered to my face all day, it actually hurts.

I reach Atticus's door and start kicking it with my heels, praying I don't knock out a rhinestone.

"Atticus, Atticus, you won't believe it--" But just then my eyes land on the notorious big piece of yellow construction paper he leaves on his door when he's either out or practicing. It's cute and always makes me chuckle.

'DO NOT DISTURB, EITHER OUT OR PRACTICING!!!!!! (IF I'M OUT, PLEASE DON'T ROB ME. I PROMISE I HAVE NOTHING VALUABLE, I'M KINDA POOR. THANKS!'

I don't hear an annoying guitar riff, or the echo of drums, nor Atticus's beautiful, raspy singing voice. He must be out.

I give a sigh of defeat, quite literally feeling my whole body sink within itself. I just blow a stray hair out of my face and huff. Damn. What am I going to do with two iced coffees...

I shrug and take a sip out of each of them, walking back towards my own apartment. Just as I do that though, Atticus's door swings open.

Finnick stands in the doorway, his curly black hair now freshly cut.

"Hey, Pops." He says, almost shocked at the sight of me. "What's up? How are you?" He quickly recovers, embracing me in a hug.

"I--I'm ok. Where's Atticus?"

"He went to his dad's house believe it or not." Finnick puts his hands on his hips and motions me into the apartment. "Come sit. I'm sure he won't mind." I gladly step into the apartment and put one of the iced coffees on the kitchen counter.

Atticus is at his dad's house? I'm shocked. Well, that sounds bad. I mean it just because I know they don't talk much.

"Really?" I say, my voice rising to a squeak. I sit on the couch and curse myself for not being able to mask my surprised tone.

"Yeah." Finnick nods and puts the iced coffee on the counter in the fridge. "Please, I was shocked too. He's been in a mood lately. We were practicing and you could tell something was bugging him. He said he needed to talk to his dad and just left. Dallon left a little while after and I'm staying here just in case... just in case."

I bite on the straw in my coffee anxiously.

"Just in case he comes back drunk." I finish off, suddenly saddened. I feel like before the weekend of the conference, I would have never thought that. Now I suddenly find myself worrying about it.

"Yeah." Finn says with glazed eyes. "He has a habit of doing that after he goes and sees his dad. He'll go to the bar there and... you know." He seems to be avoiding eye contact with me, scared of saying too much.

"Atty told me everything basically." I manage.

"Ok, got it." Finnick chuckles. "Had to watch my P's and Q's there for a moment."

"I understand." I lift up my glasses a bit as they begin to slip down my nose. God, I wish I had my contacts.

"He'll be happy you came by though! And I'm sure he'll appreciate the coffee. Returning the favor, huh?" Finnick smirks, putting the iced coffee in the fridge.

"Basically." I snort. "I feel like I haven't talked to him in ages yet it's only been two weeks."

"Did you get into an argument with him or something?" Finn squints, starting to tidy up Atticus's messy apartment. Much like his car. It represents Atticus perfectly.

"No, no. My ex boyfriend texted me when we got back from the conference. I haven't heard from him in a while, all my feelings got jumbled up and I think Atticus got upset for some reason. I don't know."

"That I heard." Finnick begins to fix the pillows on the chair across from me. "He was going on about it. You know him. When he gets his horns twisted." I actually don't. I've never seen Atticus when he gets his horns severely twisted. Only when he punched Dallon for calling me a priss. But even that I fully didn't see. "He seemed pretty upset." Finn nods.

'Yeah, I'm aware' I want to say. He has no right to be upset. This is my life. I'll text Liam back if I want to. There is no reason for him to be upset! Why am I upset? I'm supposed to be happy! This is supposed to be a happy day!

"Well," I get up off the couch, dusting off my jeans. "I just came here to see how Atticus was. Tell him I got promoted to fashion editor--"

"You got the promotion?" Finn pops up. I nod excitedly as Finnick rushes over to me and embraces me in another tight hug.

"You deserve it, Pops. Atticus is going to be so proud!" But at the mention of Atticus, I frown again, feeling this ache in my chest.

"Well ok," I sigh, walking towards the door. "tell Atticus I said…" a bunch of thoughts run through my head. What do I want to tell him? Well, I want to tell him a lot-- "tell him I said hi."

I clumsily stumble through the hallways of the apartment building, heading back from a quite long night out. It's about one in the morning and I just got back from dinner with Riley, Jeannie, and Arlo. They insisted we go out to celebrate. I was in absolutely no position to decline.

We went to some fancy Italian restaurant with this beautiful outside patio. So. Fab! They had gold fairy lights hanging from the white drapes that were above us. It was very 'aesthetically pleasing' as Atticus would say. They had the best calamari too. I should have taken some home...

I love eating outside in Manhattan. It's so beautiful watching the cars pass by and listening to the natural sounds and smells of the urban jungle. (Being construction work, angry drivers, pine nuts and smoke.)

So after dinner we all decided to go to *Starbucks* to get a coffee, attempting to fight off all the wine we drank with dinner to stop a possible massive hangover. Which it honestly won't fight off anything. We kind of just wanted *Starbucks*.

I hold my heels loosely in my right hand, hearing the rubber of them bang against each other.

My feet are absolutely killing me. I shouldn't have worn seven inch *Kate Spades* though knowing I would be walking around manhattan all night. So... that's on me.

Brings me back to the night Liam and I broke up. My feet are just as sore as when I walked home alone in the rain that night. At this point I don't even care how dirty and gross these old apartment tiles are. The cold of it feels amazing against my blistered and heel indented feet.

I feel my baby pink, latex mini dress I got from *Pretty Little Thing* ride up my thighs. But as I continue to pull the dress down, the already extremely low neckline continues to pull down with it. I just decide to leave it with an annoyed huff.

It's actually a really cute dress. It has thick straps and is a clingy uncomfortable material, now all bunched up. (Well, duh. It's latex!)

I fight to keep my white leather, mini *Loui Vutton* purse up on my shoulders as I rub my eyes. Crap. I had mascara on. Urgh. It's now probably smudged all under my eye along with my light pink lipstick that has turned into a mere stain throughout the night.

I run my hands through my straightened hair and give a huge yawn.

Ok, maybe I'm a little drunk. Not as drunk as the night at *The Lounge* though. Definitely not. A dignified buzz is what I'd like to call it. (She says walking barefoot and a mess towards her apartment.)

I quickly decide to dial Tiff's number. Things were so crazy today that I didn't even get to tell her about my promotion.

I of course called mom and dad and they kept me on the phone for two hours. I practically had to walk them through my whole day. Then I went out with Jeannie, Riley, and Arlo. I just never got a chance to phone Tiff.

She's always busy anyway though.

I put my phone up to my ear, hitting my (a little too expensive) bunch of earrings. I hear the horribly loud ringing that sounds ten times worse currently as I lean against my apartment door, no desire of unlocking it just yet.

"This is Tiffany Chase. Sorry I can't get to the phone right now, but leave a message and I'll get back to you!" Her reasonable and businesslike voicemail plays and I roll my eyes. Oh wait. It's like, one in the morning. She's probably asleep. Duh!

"Uhhh... hi Tiffy. It's Pops. Obvi. Sorry it's late... well early..." I slur. "I got the promotion. I'm going to be fashion editor. Yeah... I got it. Alright. Call me back when you get a chance. I know you're like, single handedly teaching the youth and being the female version of Jackie Robinson at the same time. When you hang up your cape, don't forget to phone me." I sigh, hanging up.

I begin to aimlessly scroll through my messages and once again, land on Liam's.

It's still not responded to. Unfortunately I don't think this issue us going to solve itself this time. I don't think this message is going away anytime soon either. I mean, I could just delete it. I could block his number, can't I?

Although not responding feels like an injustice to me. Liam may not deserve an answer, but I deserve to tell him I'm happy without him. I'm better without him. I mean, maybe not at this exact moment, but in retrospect!

My head goes through what thousands of women go through a day; is he worth it? But the 'he' I'm referencing isn't who my head is thinking of.

I bang my head against my door in frustration. Well ouch!

I groan, annoyed and angered just by the mere presence of the text.

'We need to talk.' Liam said. Ha! Bastard. We need to talk, huh? Oh, I'll put a stop to that real quick pal!

'I DON'T THINK THERE IS ANYTHING TO TALK ABOUT, LIAM. I'M HAPPY NOW. I'LL BE EVEN HAPPIER IF I NEVER SEE YOU'RE GODDAMN FACE EVER AGAIN. GOOD DAY!' I type and send back to him.

Ok, maybe the 'good day' was a little much, but I got my point across!

I feel this huge weight lifted off my shoulders. Whoa! That felt good!

I scroll through my phone once again, now heading to my camera roll. One of the pictures that pop up is of me and Atticus. I remember the moment that photo was taken.

It was when we were on the beach. After the trade show we went to dinner, then to the beach. He took my phone and I was fighting him and chasing him, trying to make him give it back to me. He just kept taking pictures.

In the picture he is carrying me on his back because I claimed my heels hurt. They really didn't. If I'm being honest... I wanted to see what he would do about it. Liam never carried me on his back. Atticus did though.

Then my eyes land on the video I took of Atticus and the band. I play it and watch as he bounces around and sings. He's so passionate, so quirky and energetic. Even the most simple things he does seem like utter perfection. As if everyone who has the honor of running into him has been grazed by an angel.

And then when he makes eye contact with the camera, it's as if his eyes are pouring into my soul. I could just about faint against this door at the sight.

I bang the back of my head against my door once again. Ouch! Why did I do that again!

What am I waiting for though. It's like some interior force is not letting me unlock my door. But my eyes land on Atticus's door directly across from me.

What if Liam didn't text me the day we got back from the conference? What if he did text me, but I just didn't get so freaking caught up in it? What would have happened? I almost slept at Atticus's place. Platonically of course. But would it have stayed platonic...

All these thoughts are running through my head at once.

I shove my phone in my purse and push against my door, beginning to walk towards his. As if some gravitational pull is pulling me towards it. He has to be home by now, right? And I need to talk to him. I don't need to talk to Liam, I need to talk to Atticus.

I want to know why he got so upset that Liam texted me, why he started acting differently after I told him. Why hasn't he talked to me? I need to know a lot of things.

I knock on his door feeling a tad bit worried. What Atticus am I walking into now? Did he just get home? Is he drunk? Is he ok? Part of me wants answers here and now at 1:00 in the morning. Yet part of me just wants to make sure he's alright.

I just continue banging on his door annoyingly.

It rapidly swings open and I almost fall in. I'm faced with an Atticus I've never quite seen before.

His hair is messy as usual but his eyes are glassy and salmon pink. His face almost looks sunken in and he has dark blue bags surrounding his eyes.

He has a harsh and violent glare, one I've never seen nor recognize on him. It almost makes me flinch and shrivel up beneath his gaze.

But once his tired eyes come to, and realize it's me in front of them, they grow gentle.

He purses his lips together as he rubs his temples, seeming confused. He pinches the top of his nose between his thumb and pointer finger.

"Hey, Pops. Uh...What are you--"

"I came to see you. I was worried about you." I cut him off. "I haven't heard from you."

"Yeah. Finn said you came." He rubs his eyes, still obviously half asleep.

"Are you alright? Have you been drinking?" I could tell he has been. I stumble over my own two feet as I attempt to pull down my dress.

I watch as his eyes move away from my own and begin to scan up and down my body. He smirks down at my dress and my cheeks suddenly feel as if they're on fire.

"You should talk." He sneers as his eyes glaze over me, coldly. Is he kidding me? Well he's right, but still! I'm not the one with the past drinking and drug problem here.

"Now is that anyway to treat a guest at your doorstep?" I slur.

"At one thirty in the morning? Yes." He snaps back.

"What a shame. It seems as if you went to sleep yet you still didn't sober up." I tsk.

I scan over his body just as he did to me. He's only in black sweats and a single silver chain he seems to have fallen asleep in. My eyes are fixated on his toned chest though, absolutely no shame.

He doesn't have muscles but he's not lanky either. He's actually perfect. Is there even any faults to him? Well, yes, but even his heavy flaws and insecurities are just... perfect to me.

My eyes go from the shiny silver chain in the middle of his chest to his somewhat thick arms.

Wow, I almost feel breathless.

I take a shaky breath and take my eyes away from his chest before... well, before the staring gets weird and before I think he's a little *too hot* right now. He's absolutely intoxicating.

"Get some sleep Poppy." He snarls. "Congratulations on the promotion. Looks like you got everything you wanted..." he begins to close the door on me.

"Atticus!" I slam my hands against his steel door, hearing my rings echo and bang against it. He rolls his eyes, swinging it open wide once again.

"What?" He quips.

"I texted Liam." I blurt out. It's the first thing that comes to my drunken mind to say. "I texted him back. Just now. I said I want no part of him."

Atticus's stare goes from a cold drunken one to a confused sympathetic one.

"Pops, listen--"

"Atticus, I don't want anything to do with him. I really don't." I say. I have no clue why I think I have to tell him any of this. Well actually, I do.

"What are you trying to say?" He shakes his head, as he looks deeply into my eyes, squinting his.

I suddenly feel this panic arise in me. What am I trying to say?

"What I'm trying to say is I don't want Liam! I don't even want closure anymore. I'm over it. Like, I honestly don't care..." I slap my arms against my sides. "I don't care about Liam. I was worried about you. I came to see you earlier on but Finnick said you were at your dad's. Even when I was out at dinner and everyone was celebrating me, all I could think about was you! If you were ok, if you stumbled home drunk. So to stop worrying, I got drunk! Now, I know that's not the best coping mechanism but we're not here to judge, are we. God... I'm such a freaking idiot." I begin to babble on.

"It's like my brain is filled with cobwebs, and you're the freaking annoying spider that created them! Even drunk I still think about you! I think about you even more..." I trail off, not being able to look Atticus

in the eye. "but I see you're absolutely fine without me. With your..."
I point to his shirtless chest, annoyed. "and you're stupid silver chains.
Where's the one I bought for you? At some girl's house?" I sneer angrily.

I feel all these stupid emotions rush over me all at the same time.

Anger, confusion, frustration, sadness. Why does he have to be so
attractive? Why do I have to be attracted to him? I hate this. I just want
these feelings to piss off. What are these exact feelings though?

He probably did leave my necklace at some random girl's house.
Some random girl he hardly even knows. Absolutely forgetting about
me and in return forgetting the necklace. She's probably prancing
around wearing it for him. It's probably the girl he sings about all the
time. Well if she means so goddamn much to him, where hell is she
now? Huh?

I feel even more anger rise to the surface and rush to my cheeks,
now even more rosy and red with frustration.

"Figures. You have nothing to say." I cross my arms and quirk up
a brow, looking up at him.

His eyebrows are furrowed together and his lips are in an 'o'. He
can't even seem to gather up his words.

"You really need to go to bed. I'll talk to you tomorrow..."

"Don't tell me what to do!" I retort. "You're just as drunk as me!"

"Oh really?"

"Yes. If not drunk-er... is that even a word? Oh you know what I
mean!" I slap my hands to my sides and feel my heels hit my exposed
upper thigh.

"I think your babbling sobered me up quite a bit. As well as woke
up everyone on the floor of the apartment building." I could see he's
trying to hide the little smirk that's growing on his face.

I lean against his door frame and roll my eyes. He mimics my
movements and crosses his arms.

"What made you come to that conclusion? Telling off your ex."
Atticus asks, a wicked grin spreading across his face. The grin that is
ridiculously breathtaking.

I realize how close we are. We're practically chest to chest. It makes
butterflies erupt in my stomach.

My eyes slowly move down to his pink lips that are in that tight smirk and the little scruff that lands under his chin and jawline. If you blink, you'll miss it. I like it. I like it a lot.

"Just some...unspoken, stupid thing." I rasp out, eyes still on his lips. "Yeah?"

"Yeah," I hum, leaning impossibly closer to him. "some stupid, stupid thing..." I watch as Atticus's smirk now turns to a straight line and his whole face drops.

"Pops," he begins, arms dropping to his sides. "listen, you're drunk..."

I just roll my eyes. God, why is he being such a buzzkill right now?

"Blah, blah, blah, shut up." I'm no longer in control of my body as I carelessly drop my heels on to the tile floor with a thud.

I knowingly smirk at his furrowed eyebrows and stunned expression as I lean in and smash my lip on to his.

I could tell he's obviously shocked because there isn't much movement on his side at first but he soon recovers as he moves his lips in sync with mine and rests his hands on my hips, moving me impossibly closer to him.

I tug on his silver single chain roughly to bring him down to my height so I don't have to stand on my tippy toes any longer. (Damn my small stature!)

Just as Atticus begins to deepen the kiss, I pull away. I can't help the little arrogant smirk begin to form on my lips.

"Who's the player now?" I say, eyes half closed feeling woozy and suddenly drowsy. Just as Atticus is about to say something, my knees buckle underneath me.

CHAPTER THIRTY-NINE

Head Over Heels

My hot pink, SJP heels with it's crystal embellished straps sink into the grass ofthe softball field.

I silently curse out the grass for not being sturdy enough. Does the grass even recognize that these heels are *Sarah Jessica Parker* originals? Like, seriously.

I figured if there was any day to bust out the new *SJP* heels, It would be today. Cause honestly, what gets more Carrie Bradshaw then meeting your best friend to discuss how you practically pounced on your other friend who you also seem to be attracted to. Oh, and who is also your freaking neighbor! Not to mention, I just got back from stress shopping.

So the answer is nothing. Nothing gets more Carrie Bradshaw than that.

I woke up this morning to see I was in the same clothes as last night. (Which I'm not complaining about. Did you see the outfit I was in?) My shoes were taken off and I was tucked underneath my sheets.

Of course my head was pounding but I wasn't focused on that. I was more or less shaken up by the craziest dream I had. In my dream I kissed Atticus. (Well, practically jumped at him.) The strangest part is… he kissed back. *Vigorously.*

I was just about to take my phone out it's charger and text the group chat between me, Riley, Arlo, and Jeannie about the dream when I saw a piece of paper taped to my closet.

Turns out that 'dream' wasn't a dream at all. I swear, I almost passed out.

I kissed Atticus and he kissed me back. (Like he *kissed* me, ya know.)

I feel heat rush to my cheeks and butterflies in my stomach at the thought of it. Well, memory technically.

I feel embarrassed, I feel flustered and fazed. I'm rattled. But more importantly, I feel confused. Lately I feel I'm in a state of constant confusion when it comes to Atticus. When it comes to everything.

I find the cold and uncomfortable metal bleachers and sit on it, carefully making sure it doesn't mess up my pink ruffled *Miu Miu* skirt.

I put my white *Chanel* bag next to me as well as the coffee and takeout I brought for me and Tiff to munch on.

I haven't told anyone about what happened last night. Not even Riley and Jeannie. I figured before I do anything I have to consult the voice of reason in my life.

I watch as the little girls in their softball uniforms giggle and play as they practice swinging their bats. Tiff cheers them on even if they miss the ball. That's one thing I always envied about Tiff. Her patience.

She high fives each of them and says her 'see you laters' to every single one of their parents. She doesn't miss one.

After everyone leaves she begins to walk over to me in her softball uniform. She hops on the bleachers beside me and gives me a look as if to say, 'what did you get yourself into now?'

"So..." she begins. "how are you?"

"I'm ok." I shrug and nod my head.

"Ok? That's it?" Tiff looks at me suspiciously as she puts one of her legs up on the higher bleacher to change into her slides.

"Yeah... ok." I nod once again with false confidence.

"Ok." All of a sudden we burst out into a fit of giggles. "Let's see what we got here..." begins Tiff sipping the coffee I ordered for her and rummaging through the takeout bag. "What the hell Pops, did you order everything on *Pronto's* menu?"

"I'm hungry!" I retort.

She takes out the salad she asked for and hands me the fifteen bucks she owes me. I'm honestly in no mood to do the 'no, it's on me' argument. So I just thank her and shove it into my purse.

"Congrats on the promotion." Tiff smirks. "I got your voicemail at one in the morning. Typical Poppy."

"Yeah, I'm sorry."

"Don't be." Tiff laughs. "When does Miss Poppy Paxton officially become editor of *DuVull magazine?*"

"July." I blush excitedly.

"Ok, then why don't we look happy?" She sips her drink, quirking up an eyebrow. Her eyes land on my shoes.

"Oh no, you got your Carrie Bradshaw shoes on. What happened?" She pulls a face and sighs.

I shove a piece of my cheesy rice ball in my mouth as I begin to dig through my purse. I slowly hand her the note Atticus left for me, my hands extremely shaky.

Tiff grabs it out of my hand, squinting her eyes. She takes a huge bite of her salad then unfolds the note.

"'Dear Poppy,'" she begins to read it outloud and I anxiously bite at my acrylics. "'I don't even know where to begin. I'm sitting at your dining room table racking my brain, trying to form a cohesive sentence. Hope you don't mind. I'm still kind of drunk though and I don't want to say anything I might regret. I'm usually never straight forward, but I figure straight forward is the best way to be right now as I drunkenly try to write you this note. I can't form some beautiful poem turned melody because that may be how I feel, but you're a completely different story. You're probably tired and confused and would prefer straight forward at this moment anyway. So here I am. We kissed. There's no other way to put it...'" Tiff continues on but then stops when she realizes what just came out of her mouth. She snaps her head up at me.

"Just keep reading it!" I shoo her. God, why does she have to read it outloud! The vivid memory of me and Atticus's kiss keeps popping in and out of my head and I can't get rid of it.

Tiff clears her throat and continues reading the note, her voice now shaky.

"'Right after we kissed, you passed out. I didn't know what to do so I dug through your purse to get your keys. I'm sorry! I figured if you woke up in my bed you would freak out even more. So...now here we are. Call me. Or I'll call you. Whatever you want. I'll leave a coffee in front of your door in the morning. You probably need it. Sleep well, Pops. Love, Atty. P.S, you're a good kisser. I'm still better though." Tiff throws the note back at me and looks at me stunned.

I quickly fold it up and shove it back into my purse, almost scared to look at it.

"Oh my god, Pops!"

"Ssshhhh!" I shush her desperately.

"Don't tell me to shhh! We're in a freaking field! And you kissed Atticus! What happened? Wha--what..."

"Stop!" I cry. "You're going to freak me out even more! You're supposed to be the calm one!"

"Ok, ok..." Tiff takes a deep breath. "what happened?"

"Well after I left you your voicemail, I saw Liam's text. I got angry and frustrated so I texted him that I wanted nothing to do with him."

"Good for you." Tiff nods matter of factly.

"But then I happened to stumble across pictures of me and Atticus. I began to wonder what it would be like if I didn't get caught up in Liam's text. So I knocked on his door, we were both drunkenly bickering and then I kissed him! I just kissed him."

"And he kissed back?"

"Mmmhhmm," I nod. "vigorously. It was very intense. Let me tell you, It was so good that I thought it was a dream..."

"Ok, I get it." Tiff cringes.

"Tiff, I was so drunk..." I lean in closer to her. "I grabbed him by his chains."

"Who are you?" She says sarcastically.

"Tiff, this is serious!" I whine.

"I know." She sighs. "Oh Poppy Paxton, keeping me on my toes since we were in diapers. You never fail to surprise me."

I just roll my eyes, taking another huge bite of my rice ball.

"I'm confused though, why was *he* drunk?"

"Well, when I got home from work I went to his apartment to tell him I got promoted to fashion editor. He wasn't there though, his best friend Finnick was. Finn said he went to go see his dad. Now here I am thinking, 'wow, good for him!' Because remember, he said he and his dad don't really get along. But Finn seemed pretty on edge. I began to put two and two together because one night when we were at the conference, he told me he used to have an issue with..." I try to find the right words without giving too much info. "substance abuse.

Atticus tends to have a tendency to come back drunk after seeing his dad. Probably because he gets frustrated or something. I don't know."

Tiff just rubs her temples, eyes closed. She looks even more stressed out than I do.

"Wow... ok, yeah. Two drunk people doesn't make one whole sober person, Pops." Tiff chuckles.

"I'm aware." I munch on my food. "I was worried about him though. The whole night. I was out with Jeannie, Riley, and Arlo but all I could think about was Atticus. I didn't walk up to his apartment with the intention of making out with him. Obvi. I just wanted to make sure he was ok."

"How did we go from worrying about him to jumping him though. How did that transition occur."

"I dunno!" I cry. "I was drunk, and we were bickering. He didn't have a shirt on, so that didn't help one bit. I just kissed him."

"Well," Tiff begins. "how do you feel now?"

"Uh... I don't know. How about awkward, confused, embarrassed. Everything in that whole spectrum."

Tiff sips her coffee and gives out her huge sigh, moving her salad to the side.

"Well let me put it to you this way, if you were writing an article about this, what would you say?"

I think for a moment, lost in thought. I know what I'm thinking, but do I want to admit it? That's the issue.

"What if..." I begin, trying to gather my words. "what if your life is finally sorting itself out. What if you finally are reaching a point in life where you just got your dream job, just everything. But there is something missing. Something vidal. And I screwed it up and now that vidal thing probably wants nothing to do with me. Where does this vidal thing belong in my life though? That's the real question. If I go chase after this so-called 'vidal thing', will it just run away?" I sigh. I sound so confusing, yet, I know Tiff understands exactly what I'm saying.

"Well, why are you so scared to chase after this 'vidal thing?'" She lifts a brow. Suddenly I feel this ping in my heart and tears begin to form.

"What if the vidal thing doesn't want anything to do with me anymore."

"Then it's the vidal things loss. It'll be the worst regret of his life." A little smile forms on Tiff's face. "You haven't called him today, have you?"

"No." I shake my head. "What do I even say?"

"Whatever you feel." Tiff shrugs. "As I said, think of it as an article. Word it like that if it helps you."

I wipe the single tear off my cheek and give a warm smile, embracing Tiff in a tight hug.

"Thanks Tiffy, you're a star!"

"Call me back and tell me what happened. I'm on the edge of my seat here."

I run towards Atticus's apartment door, trying to form what I'm going to say in my head.

'Atticus, about last night…' Nah.

'Atticus, pertaining to last night…' Ugh gross.What am I, 95?

'Atticus, what happened between us…' Oh screw it! For once in my life I suppose I'm just going to have to go off on a whim here. Wing it. In true Atticus fashion.

I take a deep breath as I become face to face with his door. It has that cute little sign he always leaves on it whenever he's out or practicing.

I hear a loud song playing and hear Atticus's voice. I can't help but pull a little smile. His voice is so fab. It's all deep, and raspy. Even more so when he sings.

I shake my head at the thought and knock on the door a couple of times.

'Atticus, we need to talk…' Gross! Who am I, Liam?

'Atticus, can you step outside for a moment…' Oh my god, get it together Poppy! You're his friend, not his high school principal…

Suddenly the door swings open and before I could babble out what I'm going to say, I'm faced with a beautiful tall stranger.

She's skinny, practically, a stick and at least 5'10. She has long purple hair practically down to her bum and the palest skin I've ever seen. Her skin seems to look practically glass with little freckles by her button nose and her huge round, brown eyes. She has an eyebrow ring and a sleeve of tattoos as well.

She's absolutely stunning.

Her legs seem to go on for ages and that's when I realize, she's in only an oversized band T Shirt. You could barely see it, but she has *very* tiny black shorts on. (If that's even what they are.)

I feel my heart drop to my stomach when I see her little ensemble. Oh.

"Hi." The girl gives me a kind smile. "Can I help you?" I try to look past her to see if I could spot Atticus, but her annoyingly perfect body is blocking my view.

I feel my whole body sink into itself and I look down at my *SJP* heels. It's in times like these you wonder what Sarah Jessica Parker would do...

I suddenly can't speak, it's like I've lost my voice. I actually feel quite sick as a rush of anger takes over me. Humiliation perhaps. It's like my veins are rattling and the ground has completely fallen from beneath me, and I'm falling. Falling. Falling.

"I..." I begin, my voice sounding hoarse. The girl is looking at me patiently and kindly, which for some reason makes me even more frustrated.

Is this the girl Atticus is always singing about? Is there even a girl he's singing about?

The music is still playing in the background and the worst part is, I could still hear Atticus's voice.

He has a girl over while the band is there? Typical! He truly is *such* a fuck boy. I should have known better, I really should have.

Has he kissed her? Has he done things with her after he kissed me last night? Why should I care? Why do I care?

A feeling washes over me that I never quite felt before. There's no name nor description for the feeling. There's just this pit in my stomach and knot in my throat that indicates I'm about to get quite choked up.

I want to push past this girl and talk to Atticus, I want to scream at him. Why am I feeling this way?

"Can you just please tell Atticus Poppy came by? Uhh... thanks." And before the girl could say anything, I walk away with an angered tear streaming down my face.

I don't walk into my apartment, rather I just head back into the elevator to hop back onto the transit. Mom, Helen, and Tiff invited me out for dinner tonight anyway. I don't have time to go back into my apartment anyway. I'll be three hours early, but who cares, right?

I feel this overwhelming feeling of blah. I just feel...blah. I feel icky, I feel uneasy, and I feel unwanted.

I run my hand through my long blonde hair and with my other hand hold my two new, shiny *Barney's* bags. I *obviously* couldn't just sit and wait at the diner for three hours. So ideally I went shopping. I mean, come on, are you shocked? It's stress relief ok?

I walk past the bus stop and towards the diner slowly, my feet absolutely aching. I'm probably limping right now.

What does Atticus even see in her anyway? Yeah, this nameless woman might be beautiful, and tatted up, and have a cute little silver eyebrow ring. She may have gorg, flowy red locks and a cute little button nose. She may be Atticus's exact type, but who cares! That means nothing!

Why do I care? Why do I give a flying crap if Atticus slept with someone! Maybe I'll sleep with someone! Someone way cuter and smarter than Atticus. Maybe one of Diamante's lawyer friends! And I'll make sure he hears all about it...

"Hey cutie." Begins some random, scrawny guy with a mustache and white tank top.

"Urgh! No thank you!" I fume and scrunch up my nose. "I come back to Staten Island and get fucking cat called? I don't deserve this!" I flail my arms and cry.

The guy puts his hands up in surrender, backing away in shock.

"Thank you..." I huff. "good day!" Ok, maybe I won't sleep with someone. Safer decision.

Urgh. Back to Atticus.

I don't understand why I care if he's sleeping around. In fact, I knew he slept around, so why has it suddenly gotten to me so much?

He's called me about five times in the past three hours. I did what any mature adult would do; I didn't answer.

He doesn't need me. He's with *her.* Whatever her name is. I bet it's something super basic. Like...like Steph! Or one of those gender neutral names like Jordan. Yeah. I bet it's something like that.

Do I find Atticus attractive? Yes, I am extremely attracted to Atticus. But it's obviously just not about looks. He made me look at the world from a whole new angle, he's kind, talented, and compassionate, and so much more.

All the times me and Atticus have spent together come flooding through my head. From the moment we met, from the moment we protested together, to the moment I got that stupid text from Liam. Everything comes back to me.

And then it hits me, the invisible little lightbulb pops on top of my head. I find myself now suddenly full on sobbing. It feels as if my heart has just dropped down to my heels.

All the buildings around me become blurry with tears and my breath has been knocked out of me.

I feel like I might throw up right here in front of the diner and a wave of panic yet euphoria rushes over me. It's like a rollercoaster.

You know, when you go up and up for so long and then you finally drop down. That's what it feels like.

You know the feeling. You *have* to know the feeling. I feel my shopping bags slip out of my hands and hit against the concrete streets.

How could I have been so blinded this whole time? How could I have been this naive towards my own damn feelings!

From the moment I met *him,* since I first heard *his* absolutely angelic raspy tone, from the moment I just merely landed my eyes on *him.* It's always been *him.*

I am completely, in definitely, utterly, absolutely, to the hilt in love with Atticus Mckeen.

I'm in love with Atticus. There is no doubt in my mind. I feel like screaming it to everyone!

I'm absolutely head over heels for the punk rocker who walked into my life with his shaggy blonde hair and neon green guitar.

The man who walked into my life like he's always been there, with his chains and piercings.

Every bone, every fiber, every cell in my body is telling me what I wish I realized a long time ago. I feel as if heart shaped fireworks should go off behind me at any second right now.

I remember a couple of months ago when Tiff uttered the exact words, 'Don't come running to me when you realize you have feelings for him. I'll tell you I told you so.'

I quickly dust off my *Barney's* bags and pick them up off the floor, frazzled as I run into the diner. I want to hear nothing more but 'I told you so.'

CHAPTER FORTY

A completely and utterly Fab idea

(That only Poppy Paxton would think of.)

"What the hell am I going to do now?" I bang my head against my desk with a loud thud.

"Well, now Atticus will never want you because you're gonna have a huge ass bump on your head if you don't stop banging it on your desk." I hear Riley huff.

"Thanks Riley." I remark sarcastically, lifting my head. I just finished telling Riley and Jeannie about how I came to the very sudden realization that I'm in love with Atticus. (God, saying it makes it sound so real.) How I was walking down the streets of Great Kills, trying to get to the diner and it just hit me!

But with that came the bad news. The worst news. That there was some girl in his apartment. Just thinking about it makes my stomach go funny.

"Well," Jeannie begins. "It could have been his… cousin."

"Jeannie, the girl was practically in nothing but a T-Shirt. She wasn't his cousin. Trust me."

"Uhh, stranger things have happened, babes."

"I think it's safe to say this chick wasn't his cousin." Riley snorts.

"Do you think he's going out with this girl?" Jeannie asks.

"No." I shake my head surly. "Atticus Mckeen doesn't date, remember?" I sneer. So what's the point of telling him I love him?

"Urgh, what did we talk about? Men only say that because they are emotionally closed off."

"That's a huge issue!" I cry, biting down anxiously on the straw in my iced coffee.

"I thought you said he called you." Jeannie says.

"He did." I sigh. "Multiple times over the weekend. I stayed at my parents house. He called me this morning too."

"Pops!" Jeannie cries. "Call him back!"

"And say what? I already ruined everything."

"He has feelings for you. It's so obvious! The night we all went to *The Lounge,* Those songs were about you! Not to mention he tried to kiss you twice! Oh, and I almost forgot, when you drunkenly kissed him he kissed back. 'Vigorously.'" She uses air quotes.

"Don't speak too loud!" I hiss. "That was between us."

"Point is, he has strong feelings for you. You know it, I know it, we all know it. Maybe he even loves you back. The question is, how are you going to tell him you love him."

"That's what I'm trying to ask you two!" I retort. Jeannie forms her thinking face. Her eyebrows furrowed and she purses her lips together. Riley just scrunches up his nose and looks at her strangely.

"I think we need to bring in reinforcements."

"You three do realize I do have work to do, right?" Jane looks at us, hands under her chin.

I just finished babbling to her about everything that happened in a fast and panicked ramble.

"Yes, but we need your... expertise with this situation." Jeannie gives a tight smile.

"What the hell is that supposed to mean?"

"It means we need your advice!" Riley slaps his hands against his sides. "You're wise aren't you."

I watch Jane think for a moment, pursuing her lips together. She blows a strand of her long black hair out of her face and finally gives in with a deep sigh and a roll of her eyes.

"Sit down." And as she says it, Riley and Jeannie immediately hop in the two chairs beside me.

"Ms. DuVull," I begin to babble. "I know this doesn't have anything to do with work, I'm sorry. I know you're a busy woman. I admire that very much about you! I--I look at you like my mentor. I've looked up to you since I was sixteen years old, and...please, Ms. DuVull. I just don't know what to do. You're smart! You always have the most fab ideas!"

I look in Jane's eyes as they slowly go a bit softer than usual. She sits forward in her chair a bit.

"Alright." She nods. "What's the plan?"

"That's what we came to you for." Jeannie says.

"There is no plan! Nothing. Nada. Zilch. Zero plan. We need to get Atticus, that's the plan." Riley remarks.

"I knew you were taken with this boy." Jane smirks. "When are you going to realize Poppyseed, I know everything. But what's our issue? The whore that was in his apartment?" I practically spit out the iced coffee I was sipping on. "Well I'm right!" She retorts. "Plus, that word never goes out of style anyway, hunny."

"She is right." Jeannie points out with a shrug.

"I mean think logically, are you sure he slept with her?" Jane asks. "I mean, it could be his cousin."

"That's what I said!" Jeannie states.

"Oh my god, it wasn't his cousin!" Riley cries.

"Nevermind..." I sigh, suddenly feeling a lump in my throat. I lean back in the leather chair, crossing my legs. "I had my chance. I had it this whole time. I was too stupid to realize what was in front of my face. Now it's too late." I wipe the tears daring to roll down my cheek. "I screwed it all up Even our friendship. For heaven's sake, I drunkenly pounced on him the other night. At least now I know why. I can't believe this." I sniffle.

Jeannie rubs my arm soothingly and Riley runs his hands through his blue hair, deep in thought.

There are a couple of moments of silence, the only sounds heard are my sniffles and shaky breaths.

"Are you done yet?" I hear Jane's somewhat annoyed voice ask.

I look up at her through glassy eyes.

"Listen here, there is zero time for self pity. It's obvious by your article and everything that you tell me that this boy has been trying to win your heart for the past couple of months. It looks like it finally worked. Now it's your turn to chase after him and assure him you want this. Guys are idiots! Believe it or not you have to *tell* him how you feel." Jane rips off her reading glasses.

"Both of you..." Jane motions to Jeannie and Riley. "skedaddle. I need to knock some sense into her." Riley gives an eyeroll walking towards the room and Jeannie just gives me a warm smile.

Jane waits until both of them are out of the office and sits up in her chair just a tad, clearing her throat. She almost looks a bit weary of what she's about to say.

"Poppy, I was once like you. And believe it or not, I was married to someone exactly like this boy you like." She says so fast, I'm not even sure I understand her.

"What do you mean?" I squint my eyes.

"Well... he was charming, he was quirky, he was funny. He loved me and I loved him. And we got married. Overall we were together for a couple of years. He was nothing like me..." she chuckles deep in thought. "he wore eyeliner, he played guitar, he was kind. We were complete opposites. I think that's why I was so on bored with the article. Not everyone gets their happily ever after with the person they love though, and that's that. You need to tell this boy how you feel though. You'll regret it forever if you don't."

My mind wanders back to the first time I met Jane DuVull and it was a chance meeting. I was out with my family at The Brookfield Place. I was sixteen. I met her in *Gucci*. Typical.

But before that, not knowing it was her, I was listening to a conversation she was having with some man. (In my defence, they were standing super close to me.) I don't remember much of the conversation though.

The man was in a leather jacket and he was grungy... well shit. That may have been her ex husband!

"Atticus doesn't date." I say below a whisper.

"Neither did my ex husband." Jane smirks. "He made an exception." I smile back at her through a couple of tears that begin to shed.

"He likes you back, believe me, I'm wise."

"It comes with age."

"Don't push it."

"Yeah, but how can I tell him how I feel? The only time I'm ever good with words is when I write..." And suddenly it hits me. It hits me like a bus. It may just be the most fab idea I've ever had.

"What?" Jane looks at me, a weary glare spreading over her features.

"The April issue just came out..." I think out loud for a moment.

"Yeah..."

"Is there any room for an extra article in the May issue?"

CHAPTER FORTY-ONE

May

Love on fifth avenue

I stand on fifth avenue tiddling with my fingers and biting the side of my mouth. I'm nervous. Can you tell?

What if he doesn't show? At the very least I just want to talk with him. (I say it as if he hasn't been in touch with me like a thousand before I called him to meet me here. He's left multiple notes on my door as well. God, I'm such a jerk.)

I just want to clear things up. I'm sure he does as well. I don't know whether he's upset with me or not. I'm willing to bet he's not. I think he'll show up. He cares about me, that's for sure. Therefore, he should show up. Oh what do I know!

I have questions and queries I need answered though. I think I have every right to know them. Or do I? I want to know who that girl was in his apartment. I thought he at least had some type of feelings for me that weren't completely platonic. So what was *she* doing there? Although, he couldn't wait for me forever, could he?

I just thought something was there. Some type of feelings. Maybe? Maybe I was wrong though. Maybe he was just... being a friend.

Nothing is worse than coming to the realization that you love someone just to find out you're too late.

I'm not looking to win him over by impressing him with my wit or with some kind of grand gesture. (Well I guess I'll leave that up to you whether my little surprise I have planned is grand or not.)

I shouldn't have to do any of that though according to Jeannie and Riley. Although I thought about it. Balloons, chocolates, a hot air balloon company...(don't ask.) But then Jeannie said, 'If someone loves you, your mere presence impresses them. What you've done is enough.'

Maybe she's right. But does Atticus love me? I know he cares for me, but love is a strong word. Does he feel exactly how I feel? I don't like him, I *love* him. In a romantic way. It's the strongest feeling of love I've ever felt in my life. Maybe that's why I didn't know what it was at first.

I've never been so sure of anything in my life though. I'm utterly in love with Atticus Mckeen.

Does he know what he's getting himself into coming here today? Being the playboy Atticus is described to be by everyone around him, can he settle down?

I know he said he doesn't date, but hearing the story about Jane and her ex husband gave me a tad bit of hope.

So as I stand on fifth avenue I just feel out of place. And I never feel out of place on fifth. They have such great shops! But it feels just a tad more dull without Atticus by my side.

I suddenly catch myself in the reflection of a shop window.

I'm in a hot pink, ruffled long maxi dress with thin little spaghetti straps. I honestly don't even remember the brand. It's quite old, come to think of it.

My blonde hair is clipped back with two little strands in front, dangling on the sides of my face. And of course I'm wearing the gold hoops Atticus bought for me.

I wanted to look my best today but as I was leaving work, Jeannie and Riley said not to try too hard. Which--as you could assume-- shakes things up for me. So everything just feels natural. Like I didn't put days of planning into the meeting, you know?

Immediately as I look up from my gold watch, I see Atticus striding down the streets. Fashionably late as usual. Only five minutes though.

The moment he sees me his intimidating exterior falters and he gives a huge smile. It's so cute, so wide, so genuine. I truly do wish you could see it. It breaks me completely. Suddenly I feel this pit in my stomach. It grows larger and larger as he inches closer and closer.

He's wearing more of a plain outfit than usual just like me. He's in a tight black T-shirt and ripped black jeans. No chains attached to them. He's still wearing all the huge rings he usually wears though and the chain I bought for him.

I feel like I haven't seen him in forever. It's been a month. A month since I've seen his face, heard his voice, been in his arms. I haven't seen him by the apartment at all either. I've heard him and the band practicing late into the nights and I just basked in the sound of his angelic, raspy, drawl.

Some part of me wondered if he was playing so loud in the hopes I would come knock on his door, asking him to be quieter. I would just shake the thought out of my head.

A month may not be a long time in retrospect, but a month without Atticus is like Dolce without Gabbana. It just doesn't work!

Although it sounds stupid, I don't think any amount of preparing could prepare me for this moment.

"I'm sorry I'm late, Pops. The train was ridiculously crowded as usual--" the minute he's within my reach I just throw my arms around him, embracing him in what might be the biggest hug I've ever given.

I rest my chin in the crook of his neck to stop me from crying. Although it sounds dramatic, I missed him so much.

I can tell he's a bit taken aback by the sudden display of affection as he stumbles back a bit but quickly regains composure and tightly wraps his arms around me. I feel his wide smile grow against my neck.

"Well I've missed you too." He chuckles.

I relish in the hug, eyes closed. I just take in the mere scent that is Atticus.

I'm well aware that this could be our last hug if he doesn't reciprocate my strong feelings back and does not want to continue with this friendship. Although I can see him not being in love with me, I can't see him not wanting to continue with our friendship. But who knows at this point.

I abruptly let go of the hug and look him deep in his big brown eyes. He lands each of his huge hands on my cheeks and it makes my heart flutter.

"Are you ok?" He asks anxiously. "How have you been? I've been trying to get in touch with you..."

"I--I'm fine. I'm sorry. I haven't been a good friend, have I?"

"No! I was just worried about you."

"I'm sorry, I just... needed time."

Atticus drops his hands to his sides and gives a tired sigh.

"Last month when you came by the apartment, Casey answered the door…" Casey must be the girl. "she said you seemed distraught. She told me to run after you and I did, but by that time I was too late. I was pounding on your apartment door… you weren't in there either. You didn't come back for the whole weekend. I assumed you were in your parents house. I've called you so many times--"

"I know. I'm sorry. I was just taken aback." I begin. "I didn't know you were…ummm…staying with someone that afternoon. I didn't want to interrupt." I can't help but say.

Atticus's face scrunches up in confusion.

"What do you mean?"

"Uh, Casey right? That's what you said? I came to visit you…I uhhh…I had something to tell you. But then I saw her and that's that. I didn't want to interrupt since you were… occupied."

"Occupied? Woah, woah, woah, hold up. You think I'm seeing Casey?" He gives a chuckle and an amused smile dawns on his face. What? What did I say?

"That's what I assumed."

"Poppy, Casey is Dallon's girlfriend. The boys were over and she came with Dallon. She just so have happened to answer the door."

"Yeah, ok…" I snort. "then why was she in only a T-shirt and tiny little short shorts?" My voice rises to a squeak.

"Wha--Poppy, she spilled a drink all over herself. She was already wearing those shorts. Dallon gave her his shirt."

Well, I wasn't expecting that. I trust him but how do I know…

"Look," Atticus pulls out his phone as if reading my mind. He shows me a picture of Casey kissing Dallon on the cheek on Dallon's social media.

Well ha! Would you look at that!

"You never told me Dallon had a girlfriend."

"You never asked." Atticus crosses his arms, remaining calm. "They met around two months ago. They've been inseparable ever since." Atticus shoves his phone back in his pocket. "Why? Would you be upset if I was seeing Casey?" He lifts a brow and gives a smirk.

The thought of him dating her makes me absolutely sick. I can't say that to him though. Not yet.

"No..." I look down, a sly smile growing on my face as well. "It's not an option. Atticus Mckeen doesn't date, right?" I look back up at him to see his smile growing wider and his tongue slightly poking out of his mouth.

"Well, I'm finding that the theory of not dating is slowly turning into bullshit." He says, voice lower than his usual loud one.

"I have something to show you." I say vastly. He looks at me skeptically with an eyebrow raised. He then nods his head with a quiet 'well ok.'

I desperately want to take my arm and put it in his. I won't do that though. It's not the right time.

As we reach the magazine stand a smile creeps across my face. I realize what I did. What I'm about to do. It makes me absolutely terrified, he might think I'm crazy. But I'm hoping he doesn't. I've prepared myself for any possible scenario where he could run for the hills and freak out. So I won't be ok... but I guess I'm prepared for the worst.

My eyes carefully scan the stand, and there it is. The new issue of *DuVull and Co* on every other shelf. It's scattered everywhere amongst *Forbes, New York Times, Vogue, Cosmopolitan,* and *Brides.*

I grab Atticus's arm gently and guide him closer to the stand. I then point to the latest issue of *DuVull.*

"I kind of strayed away from the fashion spectrum of things. I decided to write about something that means a lot to me since it's probably going to be my last article as just a fashion journalist."

Under the white title of the magazine and two other articles lay the title of mine. But this time it's not about fashion. First and last time.

In big white writing it states, '***How I fell in love with punk(and a person who embodies it perfectly.)***

Ta da! Isn't it fab! I just hope he thinks so!

I wrote an article about how I fell in love with Atticus. Writing is the easiest way I could get my feelings out and I figured, well, straightforward is the way to go.

I instantly turn my head to Atticus, anxiously.

His eyebrows are furrowed when he first begins to read the magazine cover. They soon widen and his jaw drops and I assume he sees the title of my article.

He grabs the magazine off the stand and handles it as if it's fine china. He squints his eyes and brings the magazine closer to his face. Probably making sure he got it right.

He speechlessly holds the magazine up to me in absolute confusion then looks back down at it, opening his mouth but then shutting instantly. It scares me.

He puts the magazine down on the stand and pulls a ten dollar bill out of his pocket.

"Just the magazine… thank you." He stammers, almost sounding out of breath.

I can't tell if his reaction is good or bad. I mean, he's buying the magazine right? How bad could his reaction be?

I can't take the suspense anymore, so I decide to speak first.

"Atticus…" I move closer to him and he doesn't budge as the man behind the stand hands Atticus his change and the magazine back. He's watching me and Atticus excitedly like we're some kind of daytime soap opera.

Atticus slowly turns me with a reaction I can not fully grasp, so I just decide to continue to speak.

"I dare to dream because of you…" I begin. "you taught me so much about life…and love. You've grown to be one of my best friends, and I don't think I can live my life without you. You're the missing puzzle piece. It's not Liam, it's you. It's been you since the moment I saw you trying to squeeze that huge couch into your tiny apartment door." I giggle. "I was just scared that you were too good to be true, and you are, but you're here with me. A--and I love you. I'm in love with you." I manage to say the last sentence below a whisper. Much to my dismay, I begin to sniffle.

I can't believe I'm admitting this to him. I can't believe I actually gathered the strength to tell him I love him. Absolutely adore him.

Atticus shakes his head when, suddenly, a smile spreads across his face. Is that a good smile? Is he amused? Is he laughing at me? Oh god…

I don't know what the hell to do, so I begin to ramble again.

"I know this is random and I know you might have not seen it coming. I actually have no idea how you feel and I'm not willing to lose you as a friend, but I'm willing to fight for what I love and--" suddenly Atticus moves impossibly closer to me and puts both his hands on the sides of my face like he did earlier.

His hands are soft and the cold rings on his fingers graze against my cheeks. The words I was just about to ramble now getting stuck in the back of my throat.

My mouth parts slightly as I look him in his round brown eyes in utter amazement. It's like he's staring into my soul at this very moment. He's looking at me as if searching for something in my own eyes. What he's searching for, I still don't know.

Suddenly his lips abruptly and hastily meet mine in this fierce collision.

It's as if time has stopped right here and now in the middle of fifth avenue in front of this magazine stand and mexican food truck.

I honestly wasn't expecting this. I *really* wasn't expecting this, nor did I prepare for it. I can't help this feeling of panic and shock shoot through me.

I'm kissing Atticus.

And Atticus is kissing me.

And we're both not drunk this time!

Get it together, Poppy!

I close my eyes and part my lips, kissing him back as if my life absolutely depends on it. I rest my hands on top of each of his hands holding the sides of my face.

Atticus has this eagerness about him in the kiss that I just can't keep up with and I absolutely love it. My heart feels like it just skipped thousands of beats and my knees are weak. If Atticus didn't have such a strong grip on both sides of my face, I'm positive my knees would probably buckle underneath me.

Now I could finally understand why people describe kissing the way they do. Breathtaking, heated, fervent, all that good stuff. It's all of that and more.

All the kisses I've had with Liam in the past can't even be compared to one kiss with Atticus. It just makes Atticus well worth the wait.

He has the tiniest bit of scruff along his jawline and under his chin like he hasn't shaved in awhile. It's hardly noticeable but I could feel it though. It stings a bit as it hashly sits against my own skin. It's a welcomed sting. A sting I rather enjoy.

I bask in the way he tastes like mint and smells like a mix of cigarette smoke and a light cologne. It's surprisingly a pleasant smell.

Atticus's lips keep up it's urgent and demanding pace against mine as if he's been waiting for years to do this. It makes my stomach go in knots. I swear, he's holding on to me as if I might disappear at any moment.

Every inch of my body just melts into his as he pulls me impossibly closer. I never wanted to be with someone as much as I do Atticus. Just to be near him. I want to breathe him in, I want to bask in every stolen touch and glance we share. I want to bask in every lingering song lyric he recites and every word spoken through his raspy Brooklyn drawl.

I want to be the blood that runs through his veins. I absolutely just want him and him alone.

I let go of the kiss first, resting my forehead against his. Atticus's hands still have a tight grip on the sides of my face as we both breath heavily.

"I love you too, Blondie." Is all he says, his voice hoarse as he opens his eyes to once again look at me in mine.

The moment he says that, it's like everything around us has disappeared. It's just us.

"Really?" I squeak in shock.

"Yes," His face scrunches up into a wide smile, his dimples the deepest I've ever seen them. We're so close together that I could feel the vibration from his chuckle. "I actually thought it was kind of obvious."

"I had no clue what you thought." I laugh with him.

I'm honestly shocked. I didn't think he would reciprocate those exact strong feelings back. Love isn't a word that should just be thrown around lightly when it comes to romance. At least I don't think so.

I feel this dip in my stomach, dizzy with happiness and excitement.

"Well I don't know what to say…" I begin. "what do we do now?"

Atticus pulls a face and shrugs.

"Want another magazine?" He motions to the stand in front of us, grabbing the *DuVull and Co* he bought, forgotten on the counter when he kissed me. "*Forbes,* probably not. *Cosmopolitan?* Nope, nevermind. We don't give money to the competitors. *Brides?* Don't get any ideas..."

I giggle and shake my head, looking up at him with utmost adortion. God, he's perfect.

"Seriously though. What about--" and before I could finish, Atticus's lips are on mine again, shutting me up.

When he lets go of this kiss I can't help but keep my eyes closed for an extra couple of seconds. Just basking in the bliss. When I open my eyes, Atticus is just grinning down at me.

"Well," he begins looking around us. His eyes then land back on me. "I think I should take you on a date, shouldn't I?"

How I Fell In Love With Punk(And A Person Who Embodies It Perfectly.)

Atticus, this article is for you.

By Poppy Paxton   May 28

I once wrote that the perfect man was like a pair of *Loui Vuitton* pumps. 'Rare, sharp, hard to find, etc.' Well I'm here to drive that point even further.

Now, I know, I know, I know, 'But Poppy, you don't write about romance!' Trust me, I *know*. But what I do know is fashion.

Men come in all shapes and sizes. Different bells and whistles and different prices to pay. Men are like shoes.

You could go to a sample sale and get a rip-off of *Gucci,* You could go down to *TJMaxx* and get a pair hundreds of girls tried on before you, or you could spend a tad bit more and get shoes that will last forever. Lux shoes that will never fail you. Shoes that may cut your feet but never leave a scar, shoes with crystals that don't pop off one by one the week after you get them, and shoes with heels that don't snap like twigs.

A strong, sturdy pair of shoes with soft soles that comfort your heels. Shoes you could look at and be proud you have them.

Men are like shoes.

And the man I'm in love with is... well, I'm sure you know the quote by now.

A couple of months ago I wrote an article that went quite viral. (If I do say so myself!)

Some of you may remember it was about pop punk, and the lifestyle of an upcoming rockstar. Study how someone very different from me lives their life. How they dress, what they listen to, how they look at life, everything.

I had the honor of following around and studying a neighbor grown friend, Atticus Mckeen.

I've never met someone so kind, so passionate about what he does, so quirky and silly yet so smart when it comes to his expertise.

He is someone you want to introduce to everyone.

I was immediately drawn to him. The wannabe rockstar with two left feet still has two left feet, but the wannabe rockstar is becoming less and less apparent.

He *is* a rockstar.

His mentality, everything he does, says, murmurs, breathes, eats, drinks, sings, plays on his guitar, everything he does just oozes perfection. He wears all this black, he wears all these chains, he wears this seductive and cocky smirk yet he bleeds rainbows! I think that's what I was drawn to.

I've known Atticus for such little time, yet, I feel as if I've known him forever. And there is a very good chance I may not know Atticus forever. He might read this and move out next week, wanting nothing to do with me or the dreaded 'L word.' But I'm willing to bet he's not.

It might seem strange to some that I'm confessing my love in an article. It might seem even stranger that it's in the biggest fashion and lifestyle magazine in the country.

Well, too late to back down I guess! Welcome to my world!

Atticus, you're my rare pair of *Loui Vuitton* pumps. You're the steal I never saw coming and wouldn't return for the world. Truth be told, I don't want a refund on you. You're perfect exactly the way you are.

I hope to inspire everyone reading this to confess their love for whomever they feel it for. To be proud of it. To find their pair of rare pumps.(Or, to just go out and buy that nice pair of shoes you saw the other day!)

All jokes aside, I think you all get what I'm saying. And I think you do too, Atticus.

If you don't love me back, so be it. That's ok. But it beats not writing to or about you.

Because honestly some people walk into your life, whether it be short term or long term, and are just too damn special not to write about.

Sincerely all yours and the utmost love,
Your friend Poppy.

PS, I'm the new fashion editor by the way. Hi!

CHAPTER FORTY–TWO
The Morning After Pt 2

My eyes flutter open carefully as the city morning sunlight dances across my eyelids and the tangerine colored sunrise beams through the apartment window, dancing across my lashes.

I hear the familiar sound of passing cars and the loud beeping of their horns. My eyes land on the window from which that sound is coming from. It's the same as mine but it just has a different view.

I just sink back into the comfortable bed sheets and pillows, not wanting to get out of this comfy bed just yet.

I'm covered in black sheets and surrounded by dark brown walls. Posters of bands I've never even heard of flood me as well as messed up LED lights that lazily hang around the lamp beside me and the dresser holding a little flatscreen.

I turn beside me but the bed is empty. Where has he gone? Oh god, did I push him off? I'm a kicker…

I then hear the running of a sink on the other side of the door and sigh deeply. I pinch myself to make sure this is real, and it is. It is very much real and I couldn't be happier.

I reach the nightstand next to me and grab my phone that sits on it. Luckily it's pretty charged. It reads 9:30 in the morning.

I have a bunch of messages and I just keep scrolling up and down, dumbstruck while I groggily rub my eye.

I look down to see my bag on the floor next to the dresser as well. I pick it up and start rummaging through it for my reading glasses. (Obvi still out of contacts.)

When I find my round, oversized, clear glasses I pop them on and frantically look through my messages.

MOM- 'ME AND DAD JUST RECEIVED THE NEW ISSUE! THE ARTICLE WAS DIVINE,

DARLING! LET'S DO LUNCH TODAY! ME AND HELEN WANT TO HEAR EVERYTHING!'

HELEN- 'WHAT HAPPENED YESTERDAY??? TEXT BACK ASAP!"

TIFF- 'HEY! HOW ARE YOU? DID EVERYTHING WORK OUT YESTERDAY? DO YOU WANT TO DO LUNCH WITH OUR MOMS? THEY SAID YOU WEREN'T ANSWERING BACK:)'

Oh my god, can I have a minute?

JEANNIE- 'HEY, HEY, HEY. JUST CHECKING IN ON YA. DON'T WORRY, I'M NOT DUMB. I KNOW YOU STAYED WITH ATTICUS. JUST GET BACK TO ME WHEN YOU CAN... NO RUSH LOL.'

RILEY- 'WHY AREN'T YOU ANSWERING MY PHONE CALLS, DUMBASS????'

I roll my eyes annoyed as I suddenly realize there is a big folded T-Shirt on the bed beside me. I look at the oversized T-shirt with some random band on it and slip it on without hesitation.

I shove my phone back into my bag and leave it on the nightstand as I walk out of the bedroom.

This time is for me and I don't have to share it with anyone but Atticus. (Except for when I tell Jeannie and Riley *everything!*)

I walk outside the bedroom and feel oddly comfortable. It's the same exact layout as my apartment but it's decorated the exact opposite.

As I reach the adjoining living room, dining room, and kitchen I see Atticus behind the kitchen counter fully dressed and cursing under his breath as he attempts to flip a pancake.

I cross my arms and lean in the hallway, observing.

"Shit." He mutters as he flips the pancake too high and it falls out of the pan and onto the tile floors.

I can't help but giggle and at that, his head immediately pops up to look at me. He picks up the pancake and tosses it in the garbage.

"Why does this keep happening to me..." he pulls a face and complains.

"I think you're just stressing yourself out." I begin to walk over to him.

The TV in the living room speaks in whispers and you could practically feel the vibrations from the commotion of the busy Brooklyn streets beneath us. Cars zoom by and construction is heard through Atticus's open window.

When I reach Atty, I wrap my arms around his stomach from behind and I can tell he's quite shocked by the way he tenses up. Only slightly though.

He probably doesn't know how to react. Atticus hasn't really ever been in a serious relationship. Ever. He expressed last night that he wanted to be serious with me. I'll teach him.

I think he might just feel a bit awkward. No, not awkward. He just doesn't know how to react. I'm positive he's not used to little acts of innocent intimacy such as a hug from behind.

"Maybe next time try not flipping it so high?"

"Yeah..." He finally says, leaning into my touch. "I can cook though! I swear!" He gives a false cocky chuckle. "Trust me."

"I know you can." I say, crashing my head on to his back and nuzzle my nose in his shirt, feeling the cotton material rubbing against me.

We just stay in that stance for a couple of moments until Atticus turns around and wraps his hands around my waist, lifting me up onto the counter.

I giggle as I land on the granite table top. Atticus leans against it and I can't help but poke one of his deep dimples as he smiles.

"Are you ok?" He asks, a sympathetic edge to his tone.

"Yeah, why?" I scrunch up my nose as I anxiously swing my legs back and forth.

"Well..." he begins, putting a halt to my swinging legs with both his big hands when I accidentally almost kick him.

"Sorry." I mouth with a little nervous smile. He just gives me another one of his cute, wide grins and shakes his head.

"I like that shirt." He regains his cocky composure, motioning his head towards the oversized T-shirt he left for me.

"Oh thanks..." I shrug and begin to mimic him. "I got it at *HotTopic*. You know, my favorite store." I peek down at the band, trying to read the name backwards.

"Is it now?"

"Oh, for sure." We burst into a fit of laughter. "I've never shopped there." I admit.

"I would have never guessed." Atticus gasps and says sarcastically, leaning in closer and pinching my nose. He leans in a bit more until his lips meet mine.

I happily kiss him back as he gently places his hand on the side of my face.

All the sudden a loud beeping sound interrupts us along with a horrible burnt smell. Atticus quickly tears away from me and reaches the oven.

I jump off the counter quickly as he opens the oven. We both cough as a puff of smoke begins to surface. He pulls out what seems to be a burnt casserole.

Atty just looks down at it in absolute horror as the smoke from the oven begins to fade away.

I go to open my mouth to attempt to complement his efforts.

"At least you tried." I give a trying smile and slight cringe. Atticus pokes the side of his mouth with his tongue and looks at me, annoyed. I just give a nervous smile and shrug.

"So... *Dunkin?*" He sighs and walks over to me, wrapping his arms around my waist once again. I wrap my arms around his neck in return and nod.

"Dunkin."

10:00PM
SEND TO: RILEY, ARLO, JEANNE

'OH MY GOD, OH MY GOD, TEXT BACK ASAP!
I HAVE SO MUCH TO TELL YOU GUYS!'

CHAPTER FORTY–THREE

June

On A Very Special Chapter...

"*Just breathe*..." *Atticus rubs my* arms. "It's gonna be fine." he doesn't sound so sure though.

I'll paint you a picture, me and Atticus are holding our luggage and both are in all black. We both have big black sunglasses on and look like we're heading for a funeral.

Yeah, the death of love, no doubt.

I can't believe it's June already. I can't believe Diamante is actually getting married. (Not that she let us get involved in much of it at all.)

I take a deep breath as Atticus said, take out my old house keys and open the front door.

We walk into the house and I see white balloons everywhere. There are dresses laying on the couch and presents on the piano bench. Atticus helps me take my black, fur coat off and we both hang our jackets up on the coat rack you see the minute you walk in.

"Mom! Mom..." I hear the scream of the blushing bride as soon as me and Atty enter the house.

"Sweetheart, I'm upstairs!" I hear my mom shout.

I take that as my cue to grab Atticus's hand and run upstairs with him.

I look for my mom and find her in the bathroom with Helen. There are curlers in both their hair and Helen is shoving some blue eyeshadow on mom's eye.

"Helen, I don't think this is the right way to do this..." my mom's Brooklyn Jewish drawl begins.

"Oh hush..."

I shoot my head up to Atticus and he gives a trying smile.

"Hi, mom." I say and drop my bags in the hallway leaving it next to Atticus. I then tap Helen's shoulder. "Hi Helen, may I..."

"Oh sure, hon." Helen kisses me on the cheek and gets out of my way. I cringe when she gives me the Q tip with the blue eyeshadow all over it.

"No, this isn't gonna work." I mumble to mom about the eyeshadow. What the hell did Helen do? Who wears bright blue eyeshadow to a wedding anyway? Newsflash, we're not in the 80's anymore.

Mom kisses me as well, gingerly wiping the lip gloss stain she left off my cheek.

I gently wipe off my mom's god awful blue eyeshadow and grab the black eyeliner on the counter. I run it over my mom's eyes carefully, making a straight black line.

Way better.

After that, I help her apply the nude lipstick that was sitting on the bathroom counter along with more of her lovely lip gloss.

"There you go, ma." I smile. I'm actually impressed with my work! She looks fab!

"Oh, it is lovely Poppy!" Helen squeals.

"Let me see!" Says my mom as she gets off of the rim of the bathtub and rushes to the mirror above the sink.

"I love it, Poppy!" She cries.

"I'm glad." I give a little bit of a giggle. "It's really nothing--"

"Atticus, darling!" Mom cuts me off running towards Atticus, arms wide.

"Hi, Molly." Atty gives her a hardy hug. "You have a lovely house."

"Oh, look at you..." begins Helen, not even letting him finish. Both women begin to mob him, looking up at his tall figure in awe.

"Look at that scruff on you! You're not going to temple like that, are you?" Helen puts both hands on Atticus's arms and I roll my eyes. Good news though, Diamante agreed to have her ceremony at a temple.

The party is at a park though. I'm happy she compromised with mom because let's just say... she was stressed out.

"Will the both of you stop!" I begin. "I happen to like the scruff--"

"Don't worry," Atticus chuckles at the two women. "I brought my razor."

"Really, cause I quite like the scruff." My mom puts her hands on her hips. "Shapes his face."

"It's lovely to see the both of you too." I murmur under my breath.

"What the hell is this, a funeral? What's with all the black?" Helen motions to us.

"Well if you would let us change..." I give an annoyed laugh. "where is everyone else? Tiffy, Aunt Eva, Dave, dad, Uncle Duncan, Lottie?"

Mom and Helen give each other knowing glares.

Truth be told, Paxton weddings never quite go to plan. Ever. Not that they go great, something just always seems to happen though. And Diamante not doing anything traditional is jinx enough.

"Well, Tiffy and Dave are getting ready at our house." Nods Helen. "Unfortunately Lottie can't make it. She has an exam today and couldn't get out of it. We'll FaceTime her at the ceremony."

"And your dad and Uncle Duncan and Aunt Helen went to go get more decorations for the house. Diamante didn't think there was enough."

"The wedding is not at the house though!"

"We know." My mom states exhaustively. "Ok, you two get ready. You are staying the night, right? Of course you are, the spare bedroom is all yours."

"Mom!" I jolt when I hear the voice of the blushing bride behind me.

I turn to see Diamante in only an oversized T-Shirt, silk bathrobe, and a messy bun. She has a look of sheer panic on her face. Connie stands behind her in a nice white T-shirt and blue jeans.

"Mom!" She cries again. "The hairdresser is here but I told her to be here at four *not* three! The makeup artist is coming at four so they could do it at the *same* time, but the stupid, *stupid* hairdresser got it wrong!" Me, mom, Atticus, and Helen just stare at Diamante in awe as Connie gently rubs her back. "How is the makeup artist going to put bronzer by my hairline if my hair is already done and layed!" She's practically in tears.

"Oh stop it." Shoos Helen. "You know what makeup and hair I had done for my wedding? Nothing. I was nineteen years old, curled my own hair, and every ounce of my teenage acne prone skin was showing. *And* I had purple eyeliner." She shakes her head. "Stop acting like a brat. Be a bride, not a brat." I put my head on Atticus shoulder to stop myself from laughing yet I hear him shamelessly chuckle. Diamante scowls at him.

Her eyes light up though when she sees me and I have to tell you, It worries me.

What did I do!

"Poppy, I need you in the spare bedroom asap!" She gives me a look of urgency.

"Uh... ok..." but as I say that, I realise she's already walking out of the bathroom. I roll my eyes and follow her.

As soon as we enter the safety of the spare bedroom, I realize Connie isn't with us. So... she just wanted me? What did I do now?

Diamante closes and locks the door. She looks around the spare bedroom and opens and closes the closet as if someone's hiding in there. She looks absolutely manic.

"Diamante, your wedding is literally four hours away, you need to start getting ready with Connie--"

"I'm pregnant." She blurts out. I watch her mouth move and I hear the words come out, yet I can't quite believe it. I just stare, shocked.

"What?" I ask stupidly.

Diamante gives an exasperated sigh and runs towards the wooden dresser on the side of the bed. She opens the top wooden drawer as she starts to speak once again.

"I was hoping no one would see it. No one really comes in here anyway besides to clean." See what? Oh my god, I can't believe this is happening...

I watch Diamante turn around and hold up a little pink stick. It's the pregnancy test. I lean in and look at it as it reads positive.

I look up at Diamante with absolute shock. Well, at least she's getting married!

I don't know what to say, I don't want to say anything she believes is wrong. I don't want to upset her. I'm kind of just frozen. I can't help the little excitement that ignites within me though. I'm gonna be an Aunt! I could picture it now, Auntie Poppy...

"Is Carlo the father?" Is all that manages to come out of my mouth.

"Yes Carlo is the father, dumbass!" She squeals.

"Does mom and dad know?"

"No." She shakes her head. "No one knows. Not even Carlo." Oh shit! Why, *why* do I always have the burden of keeping everyone's secrets! Why! She never tells me anything and *this* is what she decides to tell me before anyone else!

"When did you find this out?" I manage to regain my composure as I look up at Diamante's absolutely horrified expression.

"Two days ago. I'm two months along." I watch slowly as she begins to tear up. A panic starts to arise in me when she does so. Oh god, oh god, oh my god… "What am I going to do Poppy?" She begins to bawl. Oh. My. *God,* what do *I* do?

"It's ok…" I bring Diamante to sit next to me on the bed. "It's great news… right?"

"Is it?" Diamante asks.

"Can you fit into your dress?"

"Yes."

"Ok…" then what's the issue?

"What about everyone else?" Cries Diamante. "Carlo, mom, dad, Connie! Mom and dad will die if they ever found out I was pregnant on my wedding day--"

"Easy," I cut her off. "tell them after the honeymoon. If anyone asks, you say you found out *on* the honeymoon."

"I'm two months along, Poppy! They'll figure it out when the baby comes two months earlier than it should!"

"Say it's premature."

"No!"

"Ok…" I think. "well then just say you didn't *know* you were pregnant on your wedding day. I got you!" I grasp her hands in mine and look through her scared, glassy eyes. "It will be between you and me. Always."

"You would do that for me?" Diamante asks, crying even more.

"Of course!" I wrap my arms around her. "You're my sister!"

"Urgh," Diamante shakes her head as she let's go of my embrace. "Now don't go all *Frozen* Disney bullshit with that sister's crap." I can't help but giggle.

"I agree." I nod. "I don't think Elsa ever completely belittled Anna at a baseball game in front of the man she loves… or told him about the time she stole a bra from *Victoria Secrets*." I say as I joke but I watch as Diamante's face drops once again.

"Poppy, I'm sorry about that. I'm sorry about... yeah." She says sadly walking on eggshells.

"It's ok." I nod my head. "We all say things we wish we didn't, I suppose." I can't help the hurt in my voice.

"Yeah." Diamante says quietly.

Both me and Diamante's heads pop up at the little knock we hear on the door.

"You guys good?" I sigh in relief when I hear Atticus's deep slur.

"Yeah." I squeak. "One minute." Diamante gets up off the bed with a deep sigh and starts to walk towards the door.

Suddenly I can't help but wrap my arms around her from behind.

"I love you." I say. She pats my hand that's ironically on her stomach. I hear her chuckle.

"Yeah... me too, Pops." Diamante swings open the door as I let go of her, regaining her sassy composure as she stands in front of Atticus.

"They're waiting for you downstairs. Not to fear, the makeup artist came early too. Your dad made a call." Atticus says, a tight smile on his face.

"Thanks..." Diamante begins then squints her eyes at him. "and shave that weird scruffy thing you have going on, will you?" There it is. She huffs and puffs and moves past him as Atticus enters the room with our overnight bags.

"Have fun!." Diamante waves and sways off. I roll my eyes and slam the door behind her.

As Atticus puts down our overnight bags, I spot the pregnancy test on the bed. I dive directly for it, and when Atticus turns the other way, I throw it deep into my purse. Whoa, that was a close one.

"You ok?" Atticus asks with an innocent smile as I yelp and jump up from where my purse now lays on the bed.

"Oh, oh yeah! Never better." I could be better, actually.

"We should start a mosh pit."

"No, Atticus." I sigh, fanning myself with the pink fan I put in my bag. God, why couldn't Diamante have a wedding somewhere that has air conditioning. Maybe not a public park perhaps?

The reception just started. The ceremony was great, I did shed a couple of tears. Who wouldn't when your sister is getting married. And the newfound news of her being pregnant just made me cry more!

Atticus pushes my long beach curls to the side that I spent about an hour on. For no reason might I add because it's now frizzy from the hurroundus humid weather.

Of course Diamante and Carlo have us sitting directly under the beaming hot June sun. Me and Atticus weren't given the luxury of the shade much like Carlo's side of the family. Actually come to think of it, no one in our family was given the luxury of shade.

Diamante and Carlo are sharing their first dance, while a couple of park benches surround them. Not a lot of people are here. Shocker.

The park benches are decorated as good as it gets I suppose. With little daisies in a vase as the centerpiece and white table cloths. It's nice. It's perfect for Diamante and Carlo. At the end of the day, that's all that matters.

The good news is, I'm finally wearing my favorite *Pamella Roland* dress. I figured what better place to wear it than a wedding. It's absolutely the most fab dress I've ever seen! What else would you want with it's marabou pink ostrich feathers all throughout.

Although it's short and straightneck, the dress is heavy and making me sweat even more than I should be. And trust me, B.O at your sister's wedding is the last thing you want.

So I've been obsessively spritzing myself with my *Marc Jacobs* perfume I always put in my bag.

But... the downside to that is I'm attracting more bugs to our table then I would have liked. (Hey, it's not my fault the bee's think I smell good! It's better than smelling bad.)

Atticus rolls the sleeves up to his button up black dress shirt. He looks so handsome. As always.

He has on black slacks and pointed toe, leather dress shoes. He's wearing a tiny chain hanging from his pants and the necklace I bought for him.

"Do you think your sister could use a band at her wedding?" Atticus asks with a playful smirk.

"Maybe you should bring out your guitar." I begin to giggle. "How are they dancing without music?"

"I don't know…" Atticus chuckles. "the voices in both their frickin heads are singing to them." We both begin to laugh.

Sometimes I still can't believe I'm with Atticus. Sometimes I don't know what I did to even deserve him. I never met anyone with a kinder heart, someone who is more passionate about what they do.

With the new promotion, with Diamante getting married and being pregnant, and being in a relationship with Atticus I know everything is changing. And that scares me. But also, it's all good things and I know I'll be ok.

Atticus has been getting a lot of gigs as well. A lot of people know him from our article in *DuVull*. He actually has a gig down in Atlantic City next weekend with the band. (I still have to figure out what I'm going to wear!)

Atticus is already an absolute star in my book. He's my star. He's already extraordinary and brilliant. But one day he's going to do something extraordinary and brilliant.

He has the world in the palm of his hands.

When I tell him that he looks at me, puts his hands on either side of my face and says he's already looking at his world.

I spot Uncle Duncan and dad tying some balloons to trees and congratulation signs as well. Probably attempting to make the wedding at least a bit more festive.

"A little to the right." Aunt Eva says to them, caring less, eating a granola bar.

"No, to the left!" Argues my mom.

"Uncle Duncan, you're gonna fall off the ladder…" begins Tiff.

"Oh my god, Uncle Duncan's going to fall off the ladder…" Helen repeats, on the phone with Lottie.

"Why are we even hanging up this sign? It's not like Diamante and Carlo care!" Aunt Eva retorts. Carlo's family is just glaring at mine like we're crazy. I mean, at least we're not boring stick-in-the-muds.

"I'm going to help your dad and uncle." Atticus gets up.

"Alright, I'll be there in a sec." He pecks me on the lips and he's off.

I grab my phone and fan and shove them in my purse. I spot Diamante's positive pregnancy test I shoved in there as well. God, I need to find a good place to hide it. I'm obviously not throwing it out.

If I was her I would of course want to keep it. I promised I'd keep it safe for her.

Just then though I realize that Atticus has forgotten his phone on the table. As I'm about to pick it up and put it in my purse it begins to ding like crazy.

I squint my eyes and pick it up, shielding my eyes from the sun so I could see it better. The texts just kept coming in a second ago. I hope everything is ok. Is it Finn?

But no. The caller ID reads JD. JD? Who's JD? What is this, *Heathers?*

JD- 'SORRY THIS IS LATE, I WAS IN A MEETING. I'M AWARE YOU'RE AT POPPY'S SISTERS WEDDING. WATCH OVER HER WILL YA? I TRUST YOU'LL MAKE SURE NO ONES BEING A JACKASS TO HER. ANYWAY, TEXT ME WHEN YOU GET HOME FROM THE WEDDING. I THINK IT'S TIME TO MEET UP IN PERSON.'

What? Who the hell is this? What is going on?

I look up to see Atticus occupied with dad and Uncle Duncan, Helen yelling at all three of them to 'just stop before they hurt themselves.'

I bite my lip, reading the text over again. Who has every right to know? Who is this person?

I was never one to go on my significant other's phone. I never did it with Liam and I won't do it with Atticus. Snooping gets you nowhere.

But...there seems to be more to this text than meets the eye.

I open his phone and find a whole bunch of texts from this JD person, dating back to just a couple of weeks ago.

It's a girl. Great. Just great. Is he cheating on me? I feel tears begin to form in my eyes from the thought.

But no. That's not what it seems to be. Especially from the last text I read. She seems to know me, care about me.

I read back from texts a couple of weeks ago.

ATTICUS- ' I'VE GOT QUESTIONS I WANT ANSWERED. YOU KNOW THAT.'

JD- 'I KNOW WE HAVE THINGS TO DISCUSS, THINGS TO TALK ABOUT. IT NEEDS TO BE DONE IN PERSON THOUGH. ME, YOU, AND YOUR FATHER...'

Could this be a long lost relative? That's what it sounds like...

It can't be his mom, can it? Surely he would tell me if she got in touch with him, right?

As I read back, I'm seeing that she got in touch with him just a couple of weeks ago. There are not a lot of texts. There are probably more calls exchanged. She keeps begging that he meet up with her but he keeps declining.

The tone of this person sounds so familiar...

ATTICUS- 'IF YOU SAY ANYTHING TO POPPY, YOU'LL HAVE NO CHANCE AT A RELATIONSHIP WITH ME. I SWEAR.'

JD- 'ATTICUS, SHE NEEDS TO KNOW. SHE'S GOING TO FIND OUT EITHER WAY, I'M EXTREMELY CLOSE TO HER. YOU KNOW AND I KNOW THAT POPPY ISN'T DUMB AND IF YOU DON'T TELL HER THIS SOON, SHE'S GOING TO MISINTERPRET IT AND YOU'RE GOING TO BE SORRY, AND YOU'RE GOING TO LOSE HER.'

My stomach tuns and I'm pretty sure im going to throw up those stupid vegan meatballs I had at cocktail hour. Why is he going to lose me? What am I going to misinterpret? Who is this woman, and why does she claim to be close to me?

ATTICUS- 'SHUT THE HELL UP. DON'T YOU DARE BRING HER INTO THIS, JANE.'

Jane... JD.

Is it... no... That's a silly thought...

Well actually... is it?

It can't be...*Jane*. As in my Jane. As in Jane DuVull...

Surely it can't, because this person sounds like...Well, It sounds as if he's talking to his mother.

And then it feels as if the world stops and I get dizzy. I feel this intense heat wave hit my cheeks and it almost stings with this numbness of realization. I feel my palms get sweaty as his phone still sits in my hands and I could practically feel all the color drain out of my face.

My heart drops to my heels when a clear image of Jane suddenly pops into my head. And at that moment I realize, her and Atticus have the same exact eyes.

CPSIA information can be obtained
at www.ICGtesting.com
Printed in the USA
LVHW041218180322
713736LV00001B/17

9 781665 532945